G000097363

Sandra Dennis

SHADES OF
TIME

First published in Great Britain 2015
Copyright © Sandra Dennis, 2015

www.sandradenniswrites.wix.com/sandra-dennis

ISBN No. 978-1-84914-833-7

Brooch illustration on cover design: Sarah Elizabeth Butler
Copyright © Sarah Elizabeth Butler, 2015
www.sebutler.co.uk

Photography for cover design Trevor Hart

For my husband, Paul; my daughter, Isolda; my family and friends: for believing in me and encouraging my dream.

In memory of my father: Keith Ernest John Cowell, 1929–2002, for teaching me determination and perseverance.

Prologue

Disturbed...

I observe them in their peculiar costumes, their strange weapons uncovering my refuge; I feel anticipation and fear simultaneously. I watch them uncover my bones and gradually discard the earth that has been my sanctuary for all these centuries. I wonder what they will make of me...what they will surmise. Will they ever know that I was a young woman, with hopes and dreams; a strong-minded woman that had far to go but was cheated of my destiny? Perhaps they won't ever discover the facts which could never be fully written amongst the remnants of my tomb.

Beside me, my treasures: brooches, glass beads...part of my secret...my family thought I would need them for the next life...I am not there yet. I have been unable to move on; until I've had my revenge, ensured the truth is known...I cannot rest...

Chapter One

Megan's mobile rang...she glanced at the number calling, sighed heavily and cut it dead. No, she wasn't ready for that conversation...he had *promised* not to call her, but then he wasn't very good at keeping his promises.

On her solitary walk, Megan was acutely aware of the wildlife and scenery around her; its beauty forced itself upon her, like a stunning woman who gains everyone's attention with effortless precision when she enters a room.

A watery sun struggled to cast its weak rays onto the surrounding countryside; the wild-birds' cries sounded sharp through the silence of the early afternoon and various forms of fauna appeared now and then through the mist like eerie shadows of troubled souls who could not pass from this world to the next.

The unwelcome ringing of her phone again startled her; he certainly was persistent. Taking the phone out of her pocket, she turned it onto silent.

Although the countryside brought some solace, Megan was grateful there was nobody about. Having awoken early that morning and sobbed her way through her first coffee, she'd decided to go back to bed with her grief. When sleep evaded her, Megan decided that she needed to get out in the fresh air to try to steer off the feeling of despair that threatened to engulf her. She shivered amongst the hoar frost, which clung to the branches of the trees like white lichen spreading its fungus - a cold hearted poison. The blood-red berries of a hawthorn tree showed up a stark contrast.

Megan smiled at her spaniel, who, a short distance off, snorted, inhaling delicious scents and enjoying the six-mile loop that they had walked together. The countryside around her was quiet as she neared her gran's cottage, just the odd car in the distance could be heard making its way into the nearby town and she began to feel a little brighter, having stomped her way through the miles of countryside which surrounded this small town in the Cotswolds, beside the River Thames. She was almost back to the cottage now; perhaps she would manage the other half of the sandwich she'd tried to eat at lunchtime, and definitely a cup of tea.

"Bartie, come on, boy!"

The dog looked up at her with his brown, sorrowful eyes as they continued along the riverbank. After a short while, through the mist, Megan could just see the unusual outline of the Roundhouse. It loomed large and mysterious (but familiar to her) in the distance – its singular tall tower rising like a shadow in the mist; built from the local stone in 1790. A light was on in Megan's gran's cottage, which stood next to the Roundhouse on the banks of the river, warm and welcoming, but she knew that nobody was home.

Five minutes later, unlocking the door with the large iron key, she made Bartie wait until she had hauled off her boots before grabbing his collar and drying his paws with the towel hung from a nail just inside the porch. Bartie's claws clipped on the stone floor as he hurried through the dark hall to the kitchen, where Megan could hear him lapping up his water. She hung her coat on the peg beside her gran's long wax coat, her hand brushing against the stiff, weathered surface and swallowed the growing lump in her throat.

In the kitchen, the light was still on as she'd left it, not wanting to come back to a gloomy house, even though darkness would not arrive until about five-thirty. The day was dull and so made the house seem shadowy. Cup of tea in hand, she noticed the local paper that she'd discarded onto the kitchen table and sat down to take a look, a good distraction from her thoughts. As she turned the pages, her heart skipped a beat. She glanced over the classified section, and lifted up the pages so she could take a closer look at the advert that had caught her eye:

Oxford University Professor is looking for archaeologists to join him on a local dig. If interested, please contact Sasha's Recruitment Agency on... a local number was given.

It couldn't possibly be that easy, she was not that fortunate – not with everything else that had happened recently. She got up and walked through to the hall, checking the fire hadn't gone out and picked up the telephone. It was now mid-afternoon; she hoped somebody would still be at the office.

"Sasha's Recruitment Agency," trilled a young voice at the other end of the line.

"Good afternoon. I was wondering if you could give me more details about one of your adverts...the one about the local archaeological dig."

"I'm sorry, I think that vacancy might possibly have been filled, Sasha's dealing with that one herself..."

Megan's heart sank. How silly... "May I speak with Sasha?"

"She's out of the office until tomorrow; I'll get her to phone you in the morning...if it's still available."

"Yes, thank you." Megan gave the girl her details and telephone number then rang off. *That's that then*, she thought miserably.

As she hung up she noticed that she'd had another missed call from Tom on her mobile – he was unrelenting...she would not be returning his call.

Later that evening, Megan reclined on the comfy, saggy old sofa that her gran had had for many years; the sofa where she had read to her, as a child, each evening before bedtime; snuggled up against her gran's warm and reassuring presence. She had opened a bottle of red wine hoping that a couple of glasses might help her sleep, and was reading a novel in front of the roaring fire. After a while, the wine started to take effect and her eyes grew heavy. She dog-eared the page and placed it on the coffee table in front of the sofa, then got up to turn on the TV to watch the news headlines.

As she moved, Bartie, who was sitting up against her on the sofa, his warmth comforting, gave a wide yawn. He watched her move, then jumped down and went to the kitchen to have a drink; his loud slurping could be heard in the distant room. A few moments later she heard Bartie's claws on the stone floor come down the hallway, but he stopped and she heard him give a low growl. Frowning, she entered the hall. She saw that he had stopped at the bottom of the stairs, his hackles were raised, and as he looked up the stairs he gave another low, throaty growl.

Bartie looked at her and then back at the stairs, hackles still raised.

"What is it, Bartie?"

Walking cautiously towards the stairs, she switched on the light that lit the stairwell – she could only see the bottom half before the stairs turned the sharp corner that took you up into the top part of the house.

Nothing.

Bartie growled again. Megan frowned. A sharp, cool breeze drifted past them...it felt as if a window had been left open upstairs and the wind had found its way down through the house...an unwelcome intruder. Megan took a deep breath and climbed the stairs, Bartie keeping to her heels. The family photos that hung on the walls either side of the stairs reassured her as she climbed them; she had never once felt afraid in her gran's house – until now. She turned the corner and took the last few steps up onto the landing; she knew that the guest bedroom windows were certainly not open, but she was unsure about the bathroom. She had opened the windows to dry out the condensation that ran each morning down the single glazed panes and onto the windowsill – had she closed them? Megan walked into the bathroom, it felt cold but the windows were shut, as was the one in her room. Where was the cold coming from? It was a bitter, damp cold, which smelled of wet earth.

Megan shuddered.

Pull yourself together, she told herself harshly walking back out onto the landing where Bartie seemed to relax once more and his tail began to wag. As suddenly as it had appeared, the coldness vanished. Perhaps it had been from the loft hatch, she thought, as she craned her neck and looked at the ceiling above her head – there seemed to be no further explanation for it. Megan shrugged, but felt a little unnerved and returned downstairs to the kitchen where she made herself a cup of tea. Passing the kitchen table she noticed she had two missed calls on her mobile; the signal at the house was sporadic. She looked at the number. So, Tom had left a message this time. Reluctantly, she dialled the answer phone and listened anxiously as the message was delivered to her in waves as the signal came and went.

Darling, I know I promised not to call but I need to speak to you, phone my office not my mobile, of course. Ok, I hope you're all right? Where are you anyway? Karen wouldn't tell me.

Sitting on the sofa, watching the orange and yellow flames in the wood burner, she tried hard to think of something else, but his face kept popping into her mind…when would it stop, this incessant longing? She still wanted him, she knew that, but she was not prepared to be with him any longer – she'd had enough of the promises, the hurt, the anxiety and living on her nerves. The time had come to forget completely – but would he let her?

With tears in her eyes, sighing, she pushed herself out of the sofa and decided to go upstairs to bed. She shut the dampers on the stove and called to Bartie, who followed her up the stairs and jumped onto the bed. He turned round and round at the foot of the bed until he had found his sleeping position, then he placed his head on his paws and watched as Megan prepared herself for bed and climbed in amongst the sheets and blankets. *Sheets and blankets are much warmer,* her gran had always insisted. Waiting for sleep to take her, Megan thought of the archaeological dig and hoped that the position was still vacant – if not, perhaps she could volunteer for a bit? The possibility of getting back in the field again filled her with excitement – to feel the soil between her fingers, searching and discovering the secret past of the place in which her gran had grown up, and that she too held close to her heart. Suddenly the flood gates opened as she thought of her gran, old, frail and riddled with cancer in the hospice bed where Megan had held her hand and witnessed her take her last breath.

'All will be well,' she'd told Megan, and had ever so lightly squeezed Megan's hand and whispered the words of the famous poem by Henry Scott-Holland – her pale, wrinkled mouth curving into a gentle smile as she slipped into unconsciousness and, a few hours later, into death.

Would all be well? Megan wondered through her tears. Strange how the words of her gran's favourite poem had been comforting then and at the funeral where Megan, tears rolling down her face, had read the poem aloud at her gran's request. How would anything be well again without her gran, her rock to run to when things went wrong? Bartie, who sensed her every mood, snuggled closer to his mistress and started snoring gently. Neither human nor beast sensed the other presence in the room, a presence that was watching them silently from the shadows; watching and waiting.

***

An icy breeze seeped through the cracks in the wooden-slatted walls of the hut, winding its way amongst the few people huddled together over the wooden cot where the body remained motionless. The fire, slightly raised in the middle of the wooden floor, had been kept burning strongly throughout the night – it gave little warmth now to the king's closest men; his sons, Wilheard and Wulfric, and the one woman whose presence was permitted, Lindi. All had kept an overnight vigil. A few lamps were scattered about the hut, casting peculiar shadows about them, endeavouring to keep the light of hope amongst them and the darkness at bay; praying to their gods in order to keep the malevolent Death from triumphing.

Now, as dawn was breaking, the shallow breathing of their king ceased; the slight rise and fall of his chest, that had kept all hope alive during the night, stopped and with it the suffering.

Wulfric and Wilheard stared at each other over the body of their dead father. Wulfric's dark head of hair was a stark contrast to that of his father and half-brother's blonde locks. His eyes, although the same shape as his father and brother, were not the sky-blue of his closest kin; Wulfric's grey, hard stare showed no emotion. His brother watched as he pulled his woollen tunic and furs tighter round himself.

Wilheard glanced down at his father's dead shape beneath the wool blankets; his closed eyes gave the impression that he was sleeping peacefully. A hard lump formed in his throat and grew bigger and more painful as he tried to fight back the tears and ask the question that they were all hoping could be answered.

"My father was well yesterday morning, Ayken, so what is the cause of his sudden death?" Wilheard asked his father's aide.

"I fear Aelle, our king, was poisoned, Sire."

The whispers swept through the men like an incantation of doom; Lindi remained mute, knowing her place amongst them.

Wilheard stared disbelievingly at the aide. "How?"

Ayken peered around the room then anxiously back at Wilheard.

Instinctively, Wilheard ordered, "Clear the room – all except Wulfric, Lindi and Ayken must depart, do *not* breathe a word of our father's death to anyone, we will announce it later."

When the men had left the room, with heads bowed, Wilheard asked the question again.

"When death takes one like this, I believe it has to be poison, Sire," said Ayken, looking his new king in the eyes with a sad and fearful expression on his deeply creviced face.

Wilheard looked at Lindi, her blonde hair as unruly as ever, her ice-blue eyes wise and knowing for someone so young. Knowing she had permission now to speak she said, "Ayken is right, somebody has poisoned the king." The healer's young face was full of anguish and grief. "I did not want to alarm you last night when I was unsure, but his symptoms point to this and the remedies I have tried have all failed. I am sorry, Wilheard, Wulfric, sorry that I have failed to save your father." Lindi bowed her head.

Wilheard's blood ran cold. "But *who* would want our father dead?"

Ayken looked at Wulfric's bent head. "There are some that might see they would benefit."

Wilheard's head shot up and he stared straight at Ayken. The older man nodded slowly, sadly and walked out of the hut. Lindi followed.

Once alone, Wulfric stared at his brother. "Who would want to *kill* our father?"

Wilheard glared at his brother. "How would *I* know? Our father was a good man, a strong king; perhaps *you* have some idea?"

Wulfric ignored his brother's accusing tone and shook his head. "I can't think of anyone that would wish our father harm. However...there are some that might see that *you* are to benefit, Wilheard. After all, you are to take his place..."

Wilheard stared hard at his younger brother with suspicion, "I don't think that is what Ayken was saying...he didn't mean that *I* would benefit, that is the ancient law, but there are *others* too."

Wulfric read the suspicion in his eyes, but again wouldn't be drawn in. "I will leave you to grieve, brother, however, we must avenge our father's murder…"

"Of course we will; I will make certain that the guilty man will pay for this with his life." He watched as Wulfric strode out of the door, which creaked loudly, then sank to his knees and took hold of his father's limp, cold hand. His father's strength had been immense, it was heralded throughout Britannia; Wilheard had admired him, had watched and learned from his father…his king.

"I promise that I will capture whoever did this to you, father, and they *will* pay." Wilheard said his prayers to the gods and as he rose from his position he noticed that Ayken had returned and was standing in the doorway.

"Sorry, Sire, I did not mean to startle you, but I felt I *had* to warn you. I have known you since the day you were born – your father thinks…thought…the world of you, and knew he could leave his kingdom in safe hands when the time came. However, I think you must be vigilant, Wilheard…if somebody wants this kingdom, then your life and that of your future queen could also be in danger."

"You mean somebody could want both Mildryth and I dead too?"

Ayken nodded.

Wilheard stared at Ayken. "We must take steps to ensure Mildryth is kept safe."

"And you of course, Wilheard; I will arrange to have more soldiers on guard and trained…just in case."

"Do you think invasion is likely, Ayken?"

Ayken shrugged. "I do not know. Your father had no concerns over that – we seem to be in a time of peace, thank the gods. I think…" He paused.

"Tell me, Ayken."

"I think perhaps we need to look closer…"

"One of our own?"

Ayken nodded. "I wouldn't like to say who though, not without some proof."

Wilheard sighed deeply. "Organise more guards and have some more watching over Mildryth especially."

Ayken bowed and left the room.

Wilheard felt himself grow cold. Why now? Why would anyone wish the family harm? Had they not always been fair, generous and loyal to their people? Wilheard looked down at his father's body. He looked so vulnerable. He had never seen his father look weak or defenceless – he had always seemed invincible; a powerful and respected king with a strong mind and will, who loved his people, but especially his family. He was seen as an impervious force in Britannia and the lands to the north, not to be reckoned with. Wilheard felt his grief rise up in him with an unwelcome vigour. He had loved and respected his father more than anyone else he had known. What would they all do now? He knew the answer was that he himself would become king; but how could he ever keep pace with his father, Aelle's rule; how would he ever earn the same respect of his people?

Aelle had been born in the lands to the north. The family had come to Britannia to fight the defending Christians; their Pagan beliefs unwelcome and superstition ran rife amongst the Romano-Britons. The Christians spreading rumours about the Saxons, that their beliefs were all about witchcraft and evil spirits....sorcery and the devil. He had been a respected and feared king, now Wilheard would have to take over this rule and he was afraid he would fail.

Wilheard thought back to his tense conversation with Wulfric. Did Ayken really think that *Wulfric* could have had something to do with his father's death? Was that what he was inferring? Just because Aelle was dead, that did not put Wulfric any closer to being king, unless...Wilheard shook himself, no...but Wulfric had called him brother – it was the first time he had done so for fifteen years – was it just a coincidence? Was he trying to be an ally, or was the familiar name just used to soften him, or trick him into thinking that Wulfric truly wanted their kinship to be on friendly terms.

Later, Wilheard called his father's most trusted men to a meeting in the Great Hall. Until now the only people who knew of his father's death were the family and his personal attendants. However, Wilheard was sure that news of his father's death would have been leaked, nothing this big could be kept a secret for long in such a tight community. He waited, sitting in his father's large, ornately carved chair at one end of the hall, a place he had often wanted to sit in as a small child, pretending to be king. He need pretend no longer – it was now his rightful place, however odd that felt. The walls were lined with long wooden benches, the shutters were closed against the sometimes fierce elements outside and a fire roared in the centre of the hall, the smoke weaving its way up and through the blackened thatch at the top.

When the men entered through the carved doorway of the Great Hall, he could tell that some of them knew of his father's death already by their grave faces. When he officially announced that Aelle was dead and that it was possible he had been murdered, their faces became twisted with anger and grief. Wilheard looked at the men standing around him, and one by one they sank down onto their knees to acknowledge Wilheard as their new king. Twenty of his father's most revered soldiers; he was almost certain that he could trust each and every one of them – almost...

A great anger threatened to overwhelm him. When he spoke, his voice was harsh. "It is vital that we find my father's killer. I demand that all of our trustworthy men are put to this task immediately." His face was flushed; spittle flew out of his mouth. "It's conceivable it is someone we know – we must be vigilant and I am asking you all to watch and protect me, your king, and especially Mildryth too!"

The men roared in agreement, nodding their heads and shaking their fists.

"Leave it to us, Wilheard. Aelle's vengeance will be ours!" bellowed one of the soldiers.

"We must search for the killer – ask everyone who had any contact with my father yesterday, or his food, to come and see me. I will question them all myself..."

"I will go and find the cook," said Ayken.

"I will find whoever poured the wine at dinner last night," said another soldier.

Wilheard was pleased with their obvious desire to discover their king's traitor.

"There will be only one outcome for my father's murderer!"

The men left the Great Hall, the search for vengeance in their hearts and minds.

Left alone, Wilheard retreated to his chamber, where he sat and thought of his father and of the new responsibility placed on his young shoulders. He had been guided and taught all his life in readiness for his role as king, but now that it was upon him he wasn't sure he felt ready for this great task that his father had always seemed to make look so easy – although Wilheard knew it hadn't been.

***

Mildryth was with her father when Ayken arrived and told her she must go with him to Wilheard. She rushed to him immediately, embracing him, not speaking whilst he sobbed in her arms; holding him tightly, caressing his long, blonde locks. She waited patiently for his tears to subside enough for him to speak.

"Somebody has killed my father."

"I know. Ayken told me, I am so sorry, Wilheard and so...shocked! I can feel your pain, my love."

11

"I understand more fully now, how you must have felt when your mother died just a few months ago."

A tear escaped down Mildryth's cheek. She cursed it, having promised to stay strong for him; he needed her to be strong now, just as he had been for her when her mother had died.

"We must postpone our union," stated Mildryth.

Wilheard pulled away from her suddenly, a determined look in his eyes, mixed with pain and grief. "We will not, it will still take place in three moons time. I won't let whoever has done this think that they can damage our lives even further...we must remain united. Our union will show how united we are, and that my father's death will be avenged and...and...who knows, maybe an heir will be born?"

Mildryth watched as a small smile curved the corners of Wilheard's mouth, just for a moment. Their eyes held each other's and Mildryth knew that he was right. Their marriage must go ahead as a sign of strength and union between them and perhaps a future heir would unite their people even further.

Chapter Two

The telephone woke Megan from a deep sleep. Coming to and noticing the light outside the bedroom window, she knew she had slept later than usual. She ran down the stairs, pulling on her bath robe and trying not to fall over Bartie, who pushed past her on the stairs in his eagerness to go outside – his first port of call each morning. Megan thought she would hear the dialling tone as she placed the receiver to her ear; sure she had missed whoever it was calling.

"Hello?"

"Is that Megan?" asked a well-spoken young woman at the other end of the phone.

"Yes."

"This is Sasha Peters, from Sasha's Recruitment Agency. My secretary said you phoned about the archaeological dig position advertised in the local paper."

Megan was now wide awake. "That's right...she thought it might have been taken though."

Sasha sighed. "Well, it was, but unfortunately the person who was going to do the job has decided a better job has come along for them, even though they were supposed to start in a couple of days."

"Oh..." *What a shame!*

"It's my uncle who is the professor in charge of the dig; he really wanted somebody local that he could rely on, which is why he asked me to look for somebody rather than asking an agency in Oxford. I feel like I've let him down, and he is not happy, I can tell you. Are you able to come in this morning and see me? The thing is, he really wants somebody to start next week – do you have any experience in this type of thing?" Sasha sounded rushed.

Megan smiled. "Plenty – I'll email you an up-to-date CV straight away. What time shall I come in?"

"Eleven?"

"That's fine, I'll see you then," she replied, without actually having a clue what the time was, and hoping she had enough time to email and print off a CV and get herself ready.

Megan hung up with a grin on her face. Her heart was racing as she went to the back door to let Bartie out and glanced up at the kitchen clock. It was nine forty-five. Thankfully the agency was in the town centre, which if she drove would take her about five minutes, then there was the problem of parking – but there was always one of the residential roads around St Lawrence's Church if the market square was full. She flicked the kettle on and made some toast while her laptop whirred away setting itself up; attaching it to the printer,

13

she set it to print her CV. She had recently updated it when her last contract came to an end, so it was just a case of reading it through quickly before sending it to Sasha as promised and printing off a copy.

Megan glimpsed Bartie out of the bathroom window as she undressed ready for her shower. He woofed loudly from the garden; he was doing his usual rounds of the boundaries, chasing off any birds or ducks that dared come into his territory from the hedgerow or the river. Her heart warmed slightly, he really was a lovely dog, she was so glad she had him for company right now.

After her shower, Megan dressed rapidly, noticing that her suit was rather creased – however, there wasn't time to do anything about it.

Megan let Bartie into the kitchen and he lay down by the range where it was warm. "I've got an interview, so you will have to stay here this morning," she told him. He looked up with his chocolate-coloured eyes. She grabbed the CV off the printer and downed a second coffee as she read through the pages. She was quite proud of her achievements and knew she had all the qualifications; if anything, she was over qualified, but at the moment she wanted to be back out in the field…getting her hands dirty, discovering what secrets the earth possessed. How excited her gran would have been to know that her grand-daughter would be involved in searching for the history of her lifelong home town and determining its secrets, hidden for centuries. These thoughts made Megan even more excited and determined that she was the best person for the job. She needed something to get her teeth into, to help her forget about the sorrow of the past few weeks; something that would give her more purpose to each day. She had her gran's cottage and its renovation to do – but she didn't feel ready for too many changes just yet; the comfort of her gran's things and familiar surroundings was just what she needed right now. As always, her gran was there, her rock, again, but now in a slightly different way…

Megan found a parking space in the market square, which was fairly unusual for the time of day, and walked the few hundred yards to the recruitment agency. The golden stone building was in the centre of the town on the High Street – housed in an old bank, which for years now had been many different businesses, from estate agents to solicitors' offices. She opened the door and stepped into a modern, open-plan office with three desks which held computers and telephones. A young girl of about 20, smiled at her as she entered, standing up from her black leather seat and approaching her, hand outstretched.

"Megan?" she asked.

"Yes," she replied, shaking the woman's hand firmly.

"Please take a seat, Sasha won't be a minute, she just popped out to the Post Office, she obviously didn't foresee how long it might take this morning. I expect she's got caught up in the gossip!" The girl laughed lightly. "Can I make you a coffee?" she asked.

"No, thank you. I've just had one."

"Water, then? And, please, take a seat by the window.'

Megan nodded. "Thank you."

The girl disappeared and came back a few moments later with a bottle of mineral water and a glass placed neatly on a napkin on a small black tray. Megan sat and looked around the office: there were a few paintings and photographs on the walls and many files lined the shelves, it was all very neatly kept. Sasha was organised.

After about five minutes, the door opened and a young woman, in her early thirties – about the same age as herself, she thought – stepped through it in a suit and smart high heeled boots. She was slim and very attractive. She sighed and smiled, "Megan? Sorry, I thought it would be quick in the Post Office, but there was a long queue and some people are such gossips...putting the world to rights, complaining about everything and everyone...The ladies are always helpful though." She walked towards Megan, hand outstretched. Megan stood up and smiled as they shook hands - she immediately warmed to Sasha, the young woman was attractive, with friendly eyes and a warm smile.

"Please, come through to my office," she said, nodding towards a closed door. Megan followed her into a small and extremely disorganised office – *I think I was wrong with the first impression*, thought Megan to herself, stifling a giggle.

Sasha sat down and gestured for Megan to do the same in a chair opposite hers.

"As I mentioned earlier, my uncle, Professor David Peters, is about to start a dig here in the town and he is looking for somebody local, somebody who will actually care about the dig rather than just looking for bones and history, somebody who perhaps has some local knowledge too. You did say you were local?"

"My great-gran and gran were born in the town and spent their whole lives here. I spent a lot of my childhood with her, after my father died. My mother was glad to get rid of me during holidays so she could... well you don't need to know about that...' *Why was she rambling?* 'What you do need to know is that I'm now living in my gran's house – she died recently – and I would love to get involved in the dig."

15

"I am sorry…about your gran, I mean. I've had a quick glance over your CV and you are certainly qualified – but I wonder if perhaps you are a little over qualified…*Doctor* Shearer?"

"I'm not really looking for anything more at the moment; I've had many years of sitting behind a desk and giving lectures, not getting my hands dirty enough. I really want to get outdoors again and discover what secrets lie beneath the soil, especially as I love this place so much, and know how much it meant to my gran…" She stopped, realising how passionate she sounded – it was probably way over the top.

Sasha looked thoughtful for a moment. "Hmmm. Well, if it were entirely up to me, I think you'd be perfect…but I had better just run it past Uncle David. I tell you what, if you pop over to the tea room and order us some coffee (I'll have white with one please) I'll phone him, then come and join you – we can discuss it further. I already emailed him your CV, so hopefully he's had a chance to look at it."

"Sure." Megan felt she was given no choice, but a coffee would be good and even if Sasha brought bad news, she could perhaps have a good natter with her – would be good to have some female company of a similar age.

Sasha smiled. "See you in about ten minutes."

Megan left the office with a tinge of excitement; really hoping that Professor Peters would take her on despite her being over qualified. She walked into the tea room. It was quite a non-descript place from the outside, a little tatty looking, but when you entered, you were greeted with a large glass counter full of delicious home-made cakes, and as you walked through to the back it became apparent that this was a very old building, with bare Cotswold stone walls and a welcoming open fire.

Megan took a table next to the fire and removed her coat. There were only two other tables taken, even though it was near lunchtime, and an elderly couple smiled at her as she took her seat. Almost immediately a young man approached her.

"Can I get you something?" he asked politely.

"Two coffees, white, please." There were sugar sachets already on the table.

He scribbled it down on his notebook and hurried out the back to the kitchen. Megan picked up the menu. If she didn't get the job she could always have chocolate cake for lunch and drown her sorrows in sugar.

She didn't have to wait too long. A few minutes later, the door opened and Sasha entered, looking round to locate Megan. She headed towards her at the same time as the waiter arrived at the table with their coffees. Sasha removed her coat and sat opposite Megan.

"Glad you picked the table by the fire, I'm freezing!" She rubbed her hands together. Sasha took a sachet of sugar and tipped it into her coffee, and taking a sip, she sighed deeply.

Come on, what did he say? Megan thought to herself.

"I've spoken to David, he's looked at your CV and he is really keen. A little anxious that you're so qualified but he would like to meet you." Sasha took another sip of her steaming coffee. "It's a little unorthodox, but I wondered if you were free this evening? That way I can cook dinner for you both while you talk about the job, see if you're both satisfied. He is ridiculously busy at the moment so I suggested this to him, I hope you don't mind?"

"Not at all," replied Megan, thinking it would be nice to get out for an evening.

"So where do you live, in the town?"

"Have you heard of the Roundhouse?"

"Oh my God, you live *there*? *That* was your gran's house?"

Megan nodded, pleased that she had impressed Sasha on a personal level, not just professional. "Well, the cottage next to it. I don't actually live in the Roundhouse; at the moment it's used for storage."

"It is such a beautiful spot and *so mysterious* – I walk my dog round that way quite often, along by the river."

"I do too – I have a mad spaniel called Bartie; what's yours?"

She threw her head back as she laughed. "Me too! She's a black and white Springer called Jess, she's nuts too – although she has calmed down slightly; now she's five!"

"Oh God, do I have to wait another two years? Bartie's only three and he is so full of energy!"

"Why don't you bring him along this evening? If you come about six we could walk them together before dinner. David is coming over about eight; I hope that isn't too late?"

"I'd like that, thanks – so would Bartie, I'm sure."

"Excellent. Well, I'd better go – I'll see you about six." Sasha grinned, finishing her coffee quickly with one final gulp.

"Where do I come?"

"Oh yes," Sasha laughed again, she was a real tonic for lifting one's spirits. "I live at number two Blossom Way, just off Blandford Street – do you know where that is?"

It was Megan's turn to laugh. "I know it really well…my gran's friend Vi lived there when I was little!"

"What, at number two? Wow – what a small world." Sasha frowned. "Sorry, must dash, awfully busy – see you later then."

As Megan watched Sasha leave the tea room, she felt a sense of excitement…it had been a long time since she felt things were going her way and Sasha was like a breath of fresh air. She immediately felt comfortable in her presence, as if she was already a very old established friend.

When she returned home Megan checked the answer phone for messages; there was one from her mother:

"Hello darling, I thought I would give you a call make sure you weren't moping around the place (She's a fine one to talk, thought Megan) *Thought I might pay you a visit next weekend, can't make this one I'm afraid, we could go shopping or for dinner or something – anyway give me call this evening, before seven as Gerald is taking me out for dinner at eight and one must look one's best for a date. Ciao for now."*

Megan had no idea who Gerald was and didn't really care – as for phoning her mother…she wouldn't…probably. She made herself a cheese and salad sandwich and a glass of apple juice, then took an excitable Bartie out for a walk.

Arriving back at the house an hour later, she felt refreshed and excited about the forthcoming evening. She had some time to kill between now and then, so she decided to go through a few of her gran's things. She didn't want to throw everything out and burn it like her mother suggested – *get rid of the junk; burn it; make the place your own, you will feel a lot better about it* – more proof that her mother barely knew her. It was raining hard again and she felt she needed to keep busy. She thought about phoning her mother, but decided against it as she started to dial the number – she really didn't feel like making small talk, and besides, she hadn't thought of an excuse yet to stop her mother visiting at the weekend. She couldn't face her at the moment.

Megan sat on her gran's large iron-framed bed and opened the carved wooden jewellery box that sat on the mantelpiece in her gran's bedroom. The familiar twinkling of its music roused old memories of childhood visits. Her gran had played it to her on the nights that shortly followed her father's death. Megan had never really forgiven her own mother for what felt like a rejection when she needed her the most. Bundled onto the train at Paddington, picked up from Swindon by Gran, then driven the 18 miles from there to the Roundhouse,

Megan had felt alienated from her family and home. The first journey she'd made after her father's death, she'd had to pretend she was asleep all the way in the first-class carriage for two reasons: one, she was terrified, being only nine years old and travelling alone for the first time and, two, to hide the tears from the elderly lady who shared her carriage.

The music box stopped, which brought Megan back to the present. She looked down into the tangled treasure of her gran's jewellery – a web of pearls, silver, gold – nothing overly valuable, but it had been hers for use as a source of amusement as a child. Fingering the treasure, she caught a glimpse of a key at the bottom of the box; it had not been there in the past, she was sure of it. She fished it out and gazed at it upon the palm of her hand. What was the key for? It was certainly too small for a door. It must open a box, or desk. Her eyes moved around the antique furnished bedroom, finally resting upon her dressing table, where a small drawer below the mirror caught her attention. There was a keyhole about the right size. Curious, Megan moved across the bare floorboards to the dressing table and slipped the key into the lock; she turned the key gently – effortlessly, it turned and a small click ensured that discovery was moments away.

Megan pulled the drawer gently open and inside she found a diary – 'Diary of 1979' – the year Megan was seven. The year her grandparents had divorced, or rather her gran had finally had enough and left her boarish husband whom she'd later told Megan 'made her life hell.' She was 50 at the time and had fallen in love with another man! '*Scandalous*' at that time, her gran had told her. Megan wondered if she had taken this man as a lover, and what had happened to him if she had? Although a gran, she was young – and young at heart, with still a lot of living to do, even though her grandfather didn't feel the same way.

Were divorce or affairs just as scandalous today, she wondered briefly before pushing the thoughts purposely to the back of her mind and opening the diary. She hesitated before reading – should she really be looking at this at all? How would her gran feel about it? Megan finally convinced herself that she probably wouldn't mind, after all, she had always been more open and honest than anyone else she'd known. Randomly, Megan picked a page and started to read:

May 2nd 1979

It happened again today. I was walking towards the river when I caught it looking at me. It was just sitting on its hind legs watching me – it was as if everything else around us didn't exist, had shrunk away

19

into another world. Its large, long ears and enormous back feet made me instantly aware that this was no rabbit. It twitched its nose and flicked its ears before running as fast as it could away from me.

I had heard my gran talk about hares and how they were associated with ancient beliefs of magic and witchcraft (I had been terrified of them as a child because of this) but today I felt no fear as I watched it bound away from me, I felt sad; bereft. More curiously though, I saw the woman again shortly afterwards. She was standing on the other side of the river, quite some way away, so I couldn't distinguish any features. However, when she turned round I could see her long, blonde hair and that she was dressed in some type of Kaftan. She glanced in my direction and held my gaze, even at this distance I could see her shoulders were slightly stooped as if the day held sorrow for her. I smiled but she turned and walked away. That is the third time within as many months that I've seen her, I'm certain it is the same woman. It is always shortly following my sightings of the hare. How strange it all seems.

Megan frowned and wondered why the woman seemed to be staring at her gran...she felt a small shiver run through her, not able to establish why. She continued to read...

No wonder Robert doesn't understand me even at my age I don't always understand myself; he doesn't even care anymore – perhaps he never did. Frank, on the other hand, he understands me perfectly...he is sensitive to my needs both physically and spiritually. It's almost like I have known him all my life. When we met by the river yesterday I knew I was falling in love with him. The way he laid me down among the grass, his hands caressing me, wanting me...

Megan shut the book with a bang, her heart racing and cheeks burning. A lover? Her gran *had* taken him as a lover! That must be why she and her grandfather had finally parted company. What had happened to Frank? He'd understood her *'physically and... spiritually'*. Megan remembered now how her gran always spoke of her spirituality and had actually joked quite often about how she was a witch – a *white* one of course, that did *good* deeds – unless of course somebody crossed her! Megan's own mother had said it was ridiculous and proved that her mother was slightly insane and always had been. Megan would always stick up for her gran, which particularly annoyed her mother. She hurriedly put the diary back into the drawer and placed the key back in the jewellery box – she felt embarrassed, as though she had intruded too far into her gran's secrets.

Had her gran truly believed that she was a witch? Was there really such a thing? History books, ancient and modern day cults certainly believed that there was...Megan smiled; she had always taken it really lightly, with a pinch of salt. Yes, she'd had a black cat, but she'd also had a tabby one too. Yes, she had fairly Pagan beliefs and, *and* there had been that time when her boyfriend, Timothy, came to stay at the Roundhouse cottage – could it have been coincidence?

Megan had been young, 18, and besotted. Timothy had sworn to Megan's gran, and to her, that he was so much in love that he planned to marry her once he had graduated from Oxford and taken on his father's estate in Gloucestershire. How she had dreamed of that white wedding. How naïve she had been. Six weeks later, Timothy was no longer in love with her! He had been told by his parents that he 'must concentrate on his studies and forget girls for a while'. It didn't help that a mutual friend told her that he'd been seen snogging Harriet Barton at another friend's 18th birthday party. Heartbroken and feeling like her world had come to an end, Megan caught the train and stayed with her gran, who baked her cookies and gave her hot chocolate and affection. To help with the pain, her gran had 'cast a spell' on Timothy to help Megan start the fight against the rejection she felt. Another six weeks later, she heard that Timothy had been rejected from Oxford, due to bad exam results, and dumped by Miss Barton! Was that coincidence or had the spell worked? Some things could never be explained for sure, she thought with a smile.

The clock in the hall struck five-thirty; if she was to be at Sasha's for six, she had better get ready. Opening her bedroom window, she hung out of the open casement to see whether it was still raining or not. The outside light was on by the front porch where Bartie sat waiting for her – poor dog! She had forgotten that she'd let him out earlier. It was windy, but dry. Deciding on jeans and her cream cashmere jumper – smart/casual – and a change of jeans in case it rained hard on their walk together, she changed her clothes with a new sense of excitement returning. She put on a small amount of make-up and a quick squirt of scent and ran down the stairs.

She arrived in darkness, at Sasha's, at five minutes past six – she'd decided to drive to the centre of town; she could always walk home later if she had had a few glasses of wine and collect the car in the morning. Megan, with Bartie pulling at his lead, walked down the cul-de-sac and found the little lane that led to a row of six very old cottages. Each pair stood together like old friends, familiar and private. She found number two, immediately recognising the front stable door from her childhood visits to her gran's friend, Vi. Raising her hand, she knocked; instantly from within a loud barking started. Bartie returned his own greeting, wagging his tail hard and sniffing at the bottom of the door.

Sasha opened the door, already in bright yellow 'Hunter' wellies and waterproof coat, hat and scarf. "Thought we could go straight out with the dogs, if that's ok?" She held a torch and a lead in her left hand.

The dogs bounded around each other, sniffing, barking and generally saying an enthusiastic hello, almost knocking Megan off her feet.

"Jess, get down!" laughed Sasha.

"I think that's a great idea, perhaps it will tire them out!" Megan giggled her reply. "They are mad!"

"That's what I love about spaniel."

"Oh, I bought wine and chocolates for you…." She handed Sasha the gifts and waited while she put them on a table inside the front door.

"Cool, thanks. I thought we could walk them over the cow field. It's not far, but they can run around the field while we take a leisurely stroll. I have a chicken in the oven…my God, you're not vegetarian, I didn't even think!"

"No, I'm a carnivore through and through!"

"Thank goodness. The cow field is this way." Megan followed Sasha, torches shining brightly, down another small pathway which led through some houses and then into a field. "This is what I call the cow field although there are rarely cows in it nowadays; it will take us past where the dig is going to be – thought you might like to see where you will be working, not that you'll see much now as it is quite dark."

"*Might* be working…" Megan corrected.

"Oh, I think David will give you the job, I think he just wants to meet you in person so that he can suss you out."

"Great." Megan raised her eyebrows in alarm.

"Don't you worry, Uncle David seems a bit of a monster when you first meet him, but he's a big softie really."

"Good, I think." Megan began to feel a little nervous about the meeting, she had mostly been excited by the prospect, but now as the time drew nearer she began to feel more anxious. What if he didn't like her…it didn't usually bother her too much if people didn't warm to her…but somehow this did matter, it mattered very much.

"So how long have you lived here?" Megan asked.

"About five years now. I moved here to open the recruitment agency. I was going through a nasty divorce...needed a change of direction. My divorce settlement was quite good and so I opened up my own agency...my ex owned the one where I worked in Oxford, still does...he slept with his secretary – sounds pretty cliché but that was what happened."

Megan was surprised and pleased about her openness. But when Sasha asked her whether she had anyone special in her life at the moment, she didn't feel she could be quite so open.

"Not at the moment. There was someone, until recently, but it's over – for the best really. Do *you* have somebody new?" She wanted to direct the conversation away from herself again – she didn't want to go into all that just now, that could wait for another time.

Megan could hear the dogs barking in the distance, but couldn't see either of them in the darkness of the field. An owl hooted close by.

"I have a new boyfriend, Brad. I say new, we met about six months ago. He lives in Burford. We see each other a few times a week and on Sundays mostly. I don't want it to get too serious too soon. I want us to have fun and I like my independence, being able to do my own thing as well."

"He's not coming this evening?"

"No, he and Uncle David don't get on that well. David is like a father to me; I never knew my father, he was killed in a riding accident when my mother was pregnant with me. David, my father's brother, has always looked out for me."

"That's good of him."

"Yes, it is." Sasha slowed down and stopped. "This is where the dig is going to take place." She shone the torch at an area around the edge of the cow field. "It doesn't look much, but apparently the farmer found quite a lot of Roman artefacts when ploughing, and now a local developer wants to build some houses for the local elderly residents, therefore, they need to have archaeological investigations done too."

"The sites never look like much when they're first discovered – that's part of what I love about the mystery of archaeology. It fascinates me that something that looks like nothing was ever there can be hiding some amazing secrets and can tell us about our ancestors."

"Well, I find it quite interesting, but I was never any good at History at school – I could never remember all those damned dates!" She laughed loudly. "We'd better head back before I cremate the chicken and have to feed it to the dogs!"

Back at Sasha's cottage, Megan sat on the sofa and drank her wine whilst Sasha finished off the dinner preparations. The cottage was small, built of Cotswold stone, and not much different from when she visited it as a child. The only major differences were the small kitchen extension that had been built onto the back of the house, making what used to be the kitchen, a dining room. On her visit to the bathroom (which was now inside the house, not the small brick shed at the end of the garden) she had noticed that one of the bedrooms had been altered so that a bathroom could be installed. The walls, where the stone was not bare, had been whitewashed and photographs of the local area and wildlife were hung around the walls. There were a few of foreign countries too.

"Who's the photographer? Someone you know?"

"Oh yes, Brad...he's a photographer – I have to say I think he's brilliant, don't you?"

"Yes, I do." Megan said honestly, gazing at the selection of photos on the wall in the lounge. Many of them were landscape and of wildlife; one in particular caught her eye. It was of a barn owl, cream wings outstretched, swooping across a field of corn at twilight.

"That's my favourite." Sasha had come in from the kitchen holding a glass of red wine and the bottle which she poured into Megan's glass. "Brad took that one especially for me, he sat for hours waiting for the perfect shot, he says..."

"Do you like owls then?"

"Yes, I think they are really beautiful. I have this funny notion, or so Brad calls it, that each person has an affinity, a special bond with some type of animal or bird. Almost another part of their spirit...weird, I know but..."

Megan was reminded of the hare in her gran's diary. "Not overly strange. I've heard similar theories before, think of witches and how they were believed to shape shift..."

She was interrupted by a knock at the door.

"That'll be David."

Megan felt her stomach do a flip. She sat up straighter on the sofa and placed her glass of wine upon the coffee table in front of her. She watched as Sasha opened the door, greeted her uncle and took two more bottles of wine from him as he entered the lounge. The dogs started barking from the kitchen at the back of the house.

"Jess, be quiet! It's just David."

A tall man, with greying hair and dark-rimmed spectacles, entered the lounge. He smiled at Megan as she stood and held out his hand. "Pleased to meet you, Meg. Thank you for coming over this evening, I do hope I haven't put you out?" He was very smartly dressed and although he had a beard, it was neatly trimmed and suited his dark, but ageing complexion.

"Good to meet you too," she replied.

"David, glass of wine...need I ask?" said Sasha, smiling. "You two get chatting while I finish dinner...I'll be in the kitchen."

David sat on the chair by the fire and took a sip of his wine. "So, you fancy getting your hands dirty again, I hear?"

"Definitely, it's a while since I worked on an actual dig – you've seen my CV?"

"Yes. Sasha emailed it over to me this morning so I could take a look. You are rather over-qualified..."

"Perhaps, but I do need a change. I've had enough of giving lectures for a while; don't get me wrong I loved my job, but I feel I need to get out in the fresh air and discover something exciting."

"Well, we hope there is something exciting to discover on the site." There was a pause and then he added, "I understand you know an old friend of mine, Dr Tom Howard? He highly recommends you."

Megan felt her stomach flip and felt herself blush. "That's good of him." *Shit, did that mean he knew where she was? If he knew she would be working in this area, the first place he would look would be her gran's house...*Megan had to force her concentration back onto David, as she realised he had continued talking.

"...I need somebody reliable, I've been let down badly and I don't take kindly to it – tell me about some of the digs you've worked on previously."

Megan began to tell him about some of the work she had done in the past. He nodded and smiled, listening intently. He was friendly enough, but she could tell already that he would have very high expectations of his staff.

When she had told him most of the important things she'd worked on, he interrupted her "...I want to start the dig next week, Tuesday to be precise; I have a previous engagement I can't change on Monday. Are you able to start then, if we needed you too?"

"Yes, I'm living locally now, this is my new home. Are there many others who will be working on the team?"

"There are a few. The main ones would be Dr Finlay Edwards; he will oversee the dig while I'm not there. I don't intend to be there all the time you see, and there will be times when neither of us will be there because of giving lectures and of course marking papers – this is why I need somebody I can really rely on. If I needed you to, would you be prepared to take charge if neither of us were able to be there?

25

The others are mostly PhD students and need a lot of guidance and encouragement, you know the score."

"If it was necessary, of course. I do want to take a bit of a back seat and enjoy the nitty gritty part of the job, but I'm willing to take more of a lead at times if it's needed."

"Fantastic." He grinned widely and took a large mouthful of wine, seeming to relax as if he had it sorted.

Did that mean she had the job?

"Dinner's ready!" called Sasha from the kitchen.

"Let's eat, I'm famished," said David, rising from his seat and wandering through to the dining room.

Megan followed him through into the small dining room. The table had been set and there were three bottles of wine on the table, and the flowers that Megan had bought Sasha in the middle – scattered about the surface were nightlights in coloured glass holders, which gave a welcoming glow around the room.

As they sat down to eat, Sasha asked, "Well…did you get the job?"

Megan was unsure what to say and hesitated.

"Of course she got the job," David said, taking a big mouthful of chicken.

"Excellent. Here's to the dig." Sasha raised her glass for a toast.

Megan began to feel more relaxed now she knew she had a job to go with her new home. It wasn't the high position she was used to, however, it was just what she wanted right now; something she loved doing but without the stress of the top end of the career line.

"So your specialism is mainly Roman, then?" David asked her.

She nodded. "I've worked on some medieval sites too, but I'm always eager to learn about a new period of history – although I believe the dig we're about to start is Roman?"

"Yes, that's what the early studies have indicated."

"Great. I wonder what we'll find."

"I might have to come and have a look one day," said Sasha. "See what treasures you've dug up."

Megan felt a flicker of excitement run through her – this was just what she needed. It had all come at the right time.

"I can't tell you how excited I am to be joining your team," Megan smiled.

"I think it will be good to have you on board. I can't believe I was so wrong about the other candidate…he let me down at the last minute, imbecile. Mind you, if he hadn't we wouldn't have found you!"

"Some people don't always understand the organisation and time it takes to set up a dig...and to find the right people."

"You're right. Some people are just thoughtless idiots!"

Sasha and Megan's eyes met across the table, Sasha raised her eyebrows and a hint of a smile played at the corners of her mouth.

"Roast chicken is lovely, Sasha, thank you," said Megan.

"There's lemon tart for pudding."

"My favourite!" exclaimed David, raising his glass to his niece. "Now, Meg, tell me how you know Tom?"

"Oh...I...em, we...we worked together at Kent University for a number of years..."

"Good man, Tom...but I could tell you a story or two about when we were at university together!"

"David..." interrupted Sasha and winking at Megan. "Before I forget, can I ask you about that other contract...?"

"Oh, yes...of course."

Megan took a deep breath and sipped her wine as the two discussed the contract; David had taken her completely off guard, she must be more prepared next time, in case David happened to mention Tom again.

When the clock struck midnight, Megan stood up to leave. "I really should get back, thank you so much for a lovely evening, Sasha and good to meet you, David."

"I'll walk you back," said David, getting up out of the armchair.

"No, I'll be fine. It's almost a mile away. I've got Bartie, for company."

"I insist – the fresh air will help with the forthcoming hangover."

Megan shrugged. "If you're sure, I really don't mind going alone."

"Shall we walk the dogs Saturday afternoon?" suggested Sasha. "If you're free?"

"Sure. Let's meet at the end of the Roundhouse lane at two o'clock," replied Megan, and then followed David out the door.

David and Megan walked down the little path and out towards the main road and the river.

"If you don't mind, we may as well walk down by the river, that way Bartie can go off the lead and have a good run."

"Great. I love walking at night, there aren't many people around – not that I mind people that much – just sometimes it's a good way of switching off."

"I know what you mean."

They walked together, with the two dogs, along the river bank with quick strides, the frost crunching loudly beneath their feet; the

27

moon was full and low in the sky. Its glow cast a mysterious bright light across the landscape; the trees and bushes were silhouettes against the dark blue sky, and the river ran silver between the fields where cows stood or quietly slept – swans and ducks moved silently on the river.

It was a few minutes before David spoke again. "You've said that you worked most recently at Kent University in Canterbury, did you enjoy your position there?"

"I loved it, and it was a fabulous faculty to work for. However, with the government cut backs they had to let some of us go and I was only on a temporary contract, so I was the easy target. Fortunately, if you can call it that, it coincided with my gran's illness and death, so in a way it was good timing – I had some time to spend with her before she passed away and then to organise everything afterwards."

"Maternal or paternal?"

"It was my mother's mother, and Mum is pretty useless when it comes to things like that, they weren't close, sadly." The reminder of the possibility of her mother descending on her next Saturday morning filled her with dread – now perhaps, she had an excuse?

"We didn't get to finish our conversation about Tom..."

There was no avoiding the conversation now, but perhaps she could take more control of the situation this time. "Of course, you said you knew him at University?"

"Oh, Tom and I go way back...went to Oxford together...don't see much of him these days though...both really busy I guess, but I did see him at a conference last week and spoke to him on the phone earlier today about a dig he's working on in Kent, near Maidstone. Roman actually...his speciality! That's when I found out he knew you – funny coincidence, I thought."

Megan was desperate to ask what he had said about her, but on the other hand didn't want to know...surely he wouldn't have bragged about their relationship...their affair. God, she hoped not. Why was it only now, after all this time, that she could see the ridiculousness of it, when previously it had seemed such a good idea...had felt so right...even though, in hindsight, it was beginning to look more and more wrong. When David didn't say any more about him, she figured that Tom hadn't said anything, either that or David was too polite to mention it. She felt herself cringe.

"Yes, funny coincidence...but I guess it is a rather small field of professionals...Anyway, I will be fine from here. There's the cottage, just over that bridge amongst the trees."

David glanced to where she pointed, nodded and shook her hand. "I'll see you Tuesday."

"Thank you for walking me home."

"My pleasure," he said, and then walked away from her back towards the town.

Bartie cleared the stile that led over the footbridge and tore off towards the cottage at high speed, leaving Megan to walk the last part on her own. The silhouette of the Roundhouse and the willow trees that surrounded it seemed slightly eerie tonight, everything was so still and quiet. Megan continued along the path towards the private drive that took you to the cottage, this meant walking over another bridge; one wide enough for cars to pass over.

Approaching the cottage, something in the bright moonlight caught her attention in the willow trees on the opposite bank of the river and made her glance up. She felt her mouth go dry – there across the silvery water, stood at the edge of the tree-line, was the silhouette of a man. Perhaps it was David just checking she had got home ok, she tried to rationalise, although that was the wrong direction and this man was much taller and broader than David. She quickened her step, calling to Bartie, so that the man knew she had a dog with her. Bartie did not reappear and when she looked back over to the spot where she had seen the man, he was gone. Maybe it was somebody else out walking their dog she thought, as she let herself and Bartie in through the front door, but she double-locked the door behind her and switched the light on quickly, trying to stabilise her rapidly beating heart.

The shadow hadn't gone...it had slipped among the darkness of the willow trees, closer to the bank of the river – all the time watching the cottage and its occupants closely.

Chapter Three

A pale yellow sun was setting on the horizon as Aelle's body was engulfed in the fire of the funeral pyre; a murmuring of prayers went out to the gods. On everyone's lips was the wish for the king's murderer to be found and brought to justice.

Mildryth slid her hand inside her sister's arm that hung loosely at her side. "I am so glad you came, Sunniva," she whispered to her older sister. "It helps having you close. Mildryth had missed her sister when she had moved to lands to the west after her union with Treddian.

"I am glad to be here, it is awful to see Wilheard so grieved. We were all so close as children *and* we feel his pain, having lost Mother ourselves so recently."

The two women stood together with their father, one of Aelle's most honoured aides, watching as the dark smoke trailed skywards, taking their most highly revered king's spirit to the next life. The sun sank slowly to start with, then with more speed...leaving the countryside in a grey darkness.

Wilheard and Wulfric knelt near to the dying embers of the pyre, as the other mourners began to disperse, leaving only the closest kin.

"Is your union still to take place?" asked Sunniva, gently as they walked slowly towards the Great Hall.

"Yes, in three moons time. Wilheard is insistent that we carry it through, says Aelle would have wanted us to be joined and happy; he even mentioned an heir..." Mildryth said with a hint of excitement, but felt it inappropriate at such at time.

Sunniva smiled and stroked her own stomach. "Yes, I hope that you are blessed with children too; our mother was so wonderful, she would be very happy to know that we too were mothers, and could teach our own children in the ways that she taught us." A tear escaped from Sunniva's eye and slipped slowly down her face. Mildryth pulled her sister closer into her embrace.

***

"I know you think me just a bastard, Wilheard, but he was my father too!" whispered Wulfric angrily, as he walked beside his brother back to the Great Hall, where a feast was to be held in honour and celebration of the life of the king.

"That is not true, Wulfric. I have always accepted you as my brother..."

"Then why can I not be your number one soldier?"

31

"It is not your place, Wulfric. Aart is my number one, you are my brother!"

Wulfric growled in his throat.

Wilheard continued. "Your place is at my side too, but in a different way..."

"I want to have more say in what goes on now..."

"The king would not have wished that...I am happy to listen to your advice, Wulfric, but my word is law!"

"Damn the law!"

"Then you damn me too, brother."

"Forgive me...I am angry. Our father's death brings to mind that my mother is gone too and that she was never accepted by my father..."

Wilheard stopped and looked Wulfric in the eye. "Wulfric, your mother used magic to gain the love of our father, he may have lain with her, but Aelle was never truly hers...he belonged to my mother. Magic should never have been used. I understand your innocence in all this, which is why I have always called you brother...I just wish you could do the same."

Wilheard thumped him on the back in a friendly manner then walked purposefully towards the Great Hall, where his people awaited him.

***

Wulfric thought that two full moons since his father's funeral would have been enough time to leave his plans aside, but his impatience, and the forthcoming union, now had him taking long strides across the village to Lindi's hut. Smoke ascended through the reed roof of the healer's home adding to the mistiness of the grey, dull day. As Wulfric had walked along the banks of the river earlier that morning he had noticed that it was frozen at the edges – the weather did not help his disposition. The odd bird, mostly black crows, strutted around looking for carrion, cawing sulkily at their fate. The sheep in the fields grazed, heads down, miserable-looking beasts but a commodity that the community could not do without. Trees were stripped bare of leaves and a white frost clung to the branches; Wulfric barely felt the cold in his bones due to the heat of his mood.

The villagers were going about their usual business: outside the weaver's huts women were dying the wool, while young girls wound the wool ready to be used for weaving; children were playing with a gaming board with wooden pieces, and scrawny chickens pecked around the hard ground in search of any dropped grain or small insects. The low cloud kept the home fires' smoke amongst the village, the stench choking and making eyes water; men were returning from a successful early morning hunt with a wild boar hung on a pole between them.

Arriving at his destination, Wulfric flung the door open, making it bang as he did so, and stared around the dimly lit space before him.

"Good morning, Wulfric," said Lindi without looking up; when she did, her ice-blue eyes were sparkling even though the room was only lit by oil lamps and the fire in the middle of the room. The room was quite large and rectangular, wooden slatted walls were covered in pots and pans; more stoneware storage pots lined the shelves – she hurried about these, replacing their stoppers. Above her, hanging from the ceiling, a collection of vegetation was drying, herbs and other plants that were vital to her art; the scent in the room was acrid. A large pot hung above the fire to which she was adding some more ingredients; it certainly wasn't dinner that she was preparing.

"You have to help me, Lindi," said Wulfric, his brow creased and eyes full of anger.

"Mildryth?" she asked.

His frown deepened.

"You have to be *patient*, Wulfric," she continued, softly.

"*Enough* of being patient; if I continue to do nothing she will marry Wilheard at the next full moon!"

"Like I said before, it's in the stars that she *will* be yours!"

"How can you be so sure?"

Lindi stirred the pot again and added something else – she muttered something under her breath before turning back to Wulfric; she looked at his handsome face, his eyes were a pale grey and his strong jaw and straight nose were framed by thick black curls.

"You don't trust me?"

"I trust no-one."

She sighed. "Wulfric, how can you ask me to help, if you don't trust me? You have asked me to make this potion, so you have to trust me somewhat."

"Well…why does it have to take this long? It has been weeks."

"These things take time. It takes time for the potion to blend ready for use; use it too early and things could backfire upon you…and for the worse, mark my words." She walked towards him and took his hand in hers.

Wulfric had no idea how old Lindi was, her beauty belied the years she had been amongst the villagers.

"Have you really thought this through?" Lindi urged.

"Of course I have," he said gruffly.

"I don't want you to regret this..."

"It's the only way!"

Lindi's hand was warm and soft, the circular motion of her caress seemed to soothe him. He relaxed a little. She smiled at him and held his gaze, her bright eyes danced merrily in the firelight; Wulfric felt a slight draw to her, as always; he had known her so many years that she was like a big sister to him, but sometimes, when she was this close he felt that there was an invisible tug, a physical want that began to rise in him. He shook his head and broke the gaze...it was probably the potency of the potion over the fire that was going to his head. Lindi snatched her hand away suddenly and before she could hide it from him, an irritated look crossed her face.

"What's wrong?" he asked.

She remained silent, busying herself. He frowned after her as she crossed to the other side of the room, knocking a couple of pots to the floor and not bothering to pick them up again.

"Your potion will be ready by the end of the week," she snapped, dismissively.

"Lindi..."

"I have work I must do..."

He left the hut feeling confused – he felt he had offended her and had no idea how he had done so; he certainly didn't want to upset her – not just because of what he feared she could do to him, but also because he needed her on his side. He needed her help to achieve his ambitions; some were already in progress. If the gods decided that he was not to be king, then they would need to have their forecast changed by magic and Lindi was the best witch for miles around. He knew too that she held him in high regard, but was there more to it than that? They had known each other since they were children, she saw him as just a brother, didn't she? He straightened his shoulders – he had more important things to be anxious about, and did not need any distractions.

He stepped out on to the main path and looked out across the village; the day was set to stay damp and misty. The villagers were all at work, including many children who played with small tools, made as toys but in reality as preparation for their future as working individuals. Wulfric walked back across the muddy tracks towards his own home – one of the huts within the compound of the Great Hall. The vast wooden structure stood majestically and imposingly above the rest of the village. The sound of the metal workers; the harsh repetitive clanging held close to the village by the low mist that hung heavily over the community. Wulfric entered the hall and went in search of his brother, his king, he thought bitterly.

Wilheard looked up at his brother as he entered the hall. It was already full of Wilheard's men.

"You're late!"

"Apologies."

"We have been discussing our father's murder, or do you not care enough to make the effort to be on time!"

"Have we made any progress in the search?" Wulfric asked calmly, sitting down on the long bench that was beneath the window; a cold draught filtered through from outside.

Ayken shook his head. "No."

"It seems everyone we ask knows nothing; somebody must know *something*! We must keep searching and asking...I will not give up until the bastard is found!"

"Are there any others that can help?" asked Ayken.

"Wulfric, what about Lindi? Could you ask her to see if she can look into the fire, or water or whatever she sees her thoughts in...you two spend a lot of time together...I want you to ask her."

"Of course, Wilheard," agreed Wulfric, not meeting his brother's eye. "I'll do anything to find our father's murderer."

***

Inside the hut, Lindi's mood had changed. She had awoken that morning knowing that Wulfric's potion was ready; however she had hoped that by stalling things somehow it might change the course of things to come. Having tried now for weeks to seduce Wulfric, she wanted him as much as he wanted Mildryth; but she would *not* use magic for this to happen, it was against the rules of her craft. She wanted Wulfric to want her for herself, they had always been very close growing up; thought she perhaps had a chance, but not with Mildryth around it seemed. She knew the secrets of how to keep herself young; could use the same potion that she had made for Wulfric to win the heart of Mildryth, on him – that way he *would* fall in love with her.

Her mother's words filtered into her mind, "*You must never break the oldest and most sacred rule. Never use a potion to make someone love you...if you do the penalty for those with the gift, is worse than death; the loss of power and an existence devoid of magic.*"

Lindi cursed, she had made the potion many times for others, but to make one for herself...

Many times she'd thought that surely Wulfric didn't really love Mildryth, it must only be because Wilheard was in love with her.

Anything, it seemed that Wilheard had, or wanted, Wulfric *had* to have. The two men, both handsome in their own differing ways; Wilheard was handsome, strong; intelligent and thought of as the only future king. Wulfric, on the other hand, was the bastard son of Aelle, this made Wulfric the subservient brother; something he did not take kindly to. Lindi shrugged there were still ten days until the full moon when Mildryth and Wilheard were to be married, the quicker they were joined the more likely it was that she might be able to have Wulfric to herself.

A long while later there was a small knock at the door of her hut – it seemed timid and uncertain…Mildryth…she called for her to enter.

"How did you know it was me? You *always* know it is me…you truly are a great sorceress!"

Lindi laughed. "Thank you, but it is because you always use the same knock, so I have come to know it well…so, not much magic is needed."

Mildryth smiled. She had always felt a little in awe of the slightly older woman with striking looks, whom she had known all her life, had been childhood friends too. Mildryth's parents insisted that she saw nobody else when she felt unwell – Lindi was the best healer and was respected by the king's household and friends. Only the servants and less important villagers went to see Godric who they believed was an aging wizard and not to be trusted – his power was nothing compared to Lindi's, or so it was believed.

"I was told you wanted to see me?" she said, hesitantly.

"Yes, come and sit down, I have something for you."

Mildryth sat on a wooden trestle bench close to the fire, wondering what Lindi wanted her to have; she watched as Lindi walked purposely over to her workbench, whose surface was smothered in pots, phials and plants of all shapes and sizes.

Lindi turned back to face Mildryth with a look of concern upon her face. "Sorry, Mildryth, I am not sure how to tell you this without scaring you, it's just I…I am worried that there are dark forces working against you."

"You mean the same dark forces that took Aelle from us?"

"I am not sure, but…here, this is for you." Lindi handed her something wrapped in a woollen cloth. "I think perhaps you should wear this…I may be overreacting, but it may help to protect you…"

"A talisman, it is that serious?" She took the parcel from Lindi, unwrapped it. Inside there was a beautiful square-headed brooch, large, bronze and intricately carved with animal symbols. She turned it over and over in her hands admiring the craftsmanship of the

36

geometrically carved patterns, wondering why Lindi thought she might be in danger.

"Enough for me to be concerned, I think that maybe there are people who might wish you harm."

"Poison me, too? I have been given a taster..."

"Possibly, magic may be used too..."

"I have been getting some awful headaches..."

"Then we must be vigilant. Mildryth, you are my friend, I will do all I can to protect you."

"But, why would anyone want to hurt me?"

"Mildryth, when you marry Wilheard you will become queen – there is always somebody who would wish the queen harm! You are young, perhaps naïve in these things...here, put this on, wear it as much as you can – it will help protect you." Lindi took the brooch and placed it on Mildryth's long cloak, muttering a few words under her breath as she did so.

A shiver ran through Mildryth. Thank goodness she could trust Lindi to help protect her; she knew Lindi would always shield Wilheard's family from evil forces, either human or otherwise. Thank the gods they had her power on their side.

When Mildryth left Lindi's hut, the sorcerer sat heavily down on the wooden seat by the fire, exhausted. It had been a busy day and her energy had been used for many purposes. With Wulfric's potion ready and Mildryth's enchanted brooch in place, things would now be easier to manipulate – they would both soon be fully under her control.

***

Wulfric was passing the Great Hall when he noticed Mildryth walking towards him; she didn't see him as she had her head down and was fingering a bronze brooch on her cloak. He looked at her soft, beautiful features and felt the passion rise within him; although she was promised to his brother he wanted her, each time he saw her he didn't know how he stopped himself from making advances and damn the consequences.

"Good morning, Mildryth," he nodded to her and smiled.

"Good morning, Wulfric."

"Where are you going?"

She looked at him with sadness in her green eyes. "I am going to my mother's grave."

"I'm sorry...Swanhilde was a wonderful and graceful woman."

"Thank you for your kind words, Wulfric. You know what it is like to lose a mother, and you lost yours when you were so young – I am sorry for that too. There seems to be so much death – perhaps the gods are unhappy with us? That's why I am so thankful we have the wedding to look forward to; Wilheard's aides suggested putting the marriage on hold after the death of your father, but he won't hear of it – he believes his...your...father would have wanted us to go ahead – Wilheard says the people need a queen as soon as possible and perhaps an heir."

Wulfric nodded slowly, trying to contain his growing anger, his eyes never leaving hers. "Would you prefer to be left alone to attend your mother's grave, or can I walk with you?"

Mildryth looked at Wulfric. He was a very handsome man, not in the same way as his brother, but beautiful in a wild, mysterious sense and those grey eyes...just like a wolf's...

"You could walk with me a little way if you wish." She did not want to alienate him; there were enough arguments and hatred between the brothers, if only she could help them reconcile their differences. If only they could be friends, surely that was not beyond hope and it would be so much better for the people of the kingdom.

Wulfric offered her his arm and she looped hers through his, after all, he was soon to become her brother too. They walked towards the burial ground where their family and friends were buried.

"You will come to the wedding, won't you?" she asked.

"I don't suppose Wilheard will invite me."

"*I* am inviting you."

Wulfric grunted.

"I wish you two could be friends, real friends...Wilheard is eager for you to be one of his aides...with the two of you as allies you could reign this kingdom successfully and powerfully."

"I'm afraid I don't agree with you, Mildryth. Wilheard just sees me as a threat...he doesn't want us to rule together. He wants the power all to himself."

"Wulfric, the kingship is rightfully his." she said gently, turning to look him in the eye. "But I am sure, if I spoke to him..."

He turned from her sharply. "I do not want your sympathy, Mildryth; the king was my father too...even though he never really wanted to acknowledge me in the same way. My poor mother was just used and cast aside like a whore; I can never forgive him for that. I have almost as much right as Wilheard to be king, just because my mother was not of your kind doesn't mean she was any worse than some of yours."

Mildryth took his hand in hers. "I did not mean to offend you or your mother; that was not my intention. I would just like to see you and Wilheard both as friends and the brothers that you are."

"I can't see how that is possible...Wilheard doesn't respect me."

"Do you respect him?"

Wulfric looked into her gentle green eyes. She was right, he didn't respect Wilheard, how could he? He had always made him feel inferior, just as his father had done – always questioning whether Aelle was actually his father and if he was, was it only magic that had made him love his mother Beomia, as was suggested by many? Wulfric tensed, he was becoming angry again and didn't want Mildryth to see this. She had to believe that he *was* trying to make amends with his brother. He put his hand out and stroked her cheek – they were near the burial ground now and so out of sight from the village.

"Dear Mildryth, if only everyone was as kind and forgiving as you are...I will leave you with your mother now – she was very proud of you, you know that, don't you?"

Mildryth felt the tears spring to her eyes as she watched him leave. She watched his strong figure walk across the fields back towards the village and could not help but sympathise with him. So many people saw the bad in him, but although she knew he was not perfect, he was a victim of circumstance to a degree. He had always been kind to her, ever since they were children, but as she watched him grow to become a man, she had seen the hatred within him also develop. If she was kind to him now, it might work in Wilheard's favour. She remembered the feeling of his touch upon her skin, it had made her start; she was shocked to discover that his stroke had felt like a caress and had awoken a strange, unknown feeling within her. That could not be possible – she was in love with Wilheard, was going to marry him within a matter of days, she did not feel that way about Wulfric. She knew of how a man's touch could make you feel lustful – had heard other women speak of it, but it did not mean you were in love with them. It was just nature's way and the gods testing you. She sighed, things were so complicated now; everything had been so much simpler as a child.

Oh mother, if only you were here to guide me...how am I to be queen of the people? I have no knowledge...I don't feel ready to rule. Mildryth sighed and looked at her mother's grave. *"I know...the gods require it of me, therefore I should abide, but it does not stop me from feeling terrified.*

Something moved in her peripheral vision, she turned towards it. A large hare stood there, staring at her from near her mother's

39

grave...it flicked its lengthy ears then fled across the fields towards the river and out of sight.

Chapter Four

Although the night following her dinner with Sasha and David had turned wet and stormy in the early hours, Saturday dawned bright, but cold; a north-east wind blew round the side of the cottage when Megan went out to get more logs for the fire, making her shiver. She looked over towards the trees where she could have sworn somebody had been watching her the previous night. There were quite a few things making her nervous at the moment, she tried to understand why. Perhaps she was a little emotionally unstable after the death of her gran and the break up with Tom? The things she had held most dear for a long time had slipped away from her, one by choice – although it still didn't make it any easier – and the other she'd had no control over. That must be it, her nerves and emotions were stretched to their limits, and her mind was working overtime, leaving her feeling very unsettled.

There was a busy day ahead of her; she wanted to clear some of the garden this morning (it having been neglected for the past two years as her gran had deteriorated), then she was meeting Sasha for a dog walk at two o'clock, but the late afternoon and evening were hers; she wanted to snuggle up in front of the fire, eat pizza, drink wine and read her book. She felt she needed to relax and stop her mind from whirring, forget about everything for a few hours and lose herself in a good book, away from the harshness of reality.

Carrying a heavy load of logs in from the garden, she heard the phone ring in the hallway. Quickly, she went into the lounge and dropped them into the basket on the hearth, and reached the phone just as it stopped. She cursed, and had turned to walk away from the phone when it rang again.

"Hello?"

"Hello, darling, it's Mummy. How are you? I have been so worried; you didn't return my call the other night."

"Hello Mum, sorry, I've been really busy. How are you?"

"Oh, I'm *fine*, busy as ever, don't have a moment to stop and think these days…"

Megan let her mother prattle on for a few moments making all the right noises in the right places; all the while thinking that the only thing that kept her mother busy was shopping, lunches and men. She tried not to be so uncharitable where her mother was concerned, but they were so different and she was often surprised that they could be so closely related. Megan always felt she was so much more like her gran; they'd had so much in common, whereas her own mother…

"Are you still there, darling?"

"Oh, sorry, Mum…em, Bartie was pawing at the bottom of the stairs and distracted me for a moment."

"I was saying about me coming to visit next weekend; that is still alright isn't it?"

Megan was lost for words. "Em…Can I let you know at the beginning of the week…the thing is…I have a new job…"

"A new job, what *already*?"

"Yes, I'm working on a local dig – it was a last minute thing, I saw it advertised locally and went for it – I got it."

"Are you directing it then?"

"No. No… I decided that I wanted to get back to getting my hands dirty."

The silence was loaded with disappointment. Megan waited.

"But, but darling *really,* you are so much better than that…are you sure you're okay?"

"Mum, I am fine. I need a job…"

"If it's the money…"

"No, I have plenty, I need to be occupied and this is what I really enjoy."

"Well, I really do think I should come down. We could go to Oxford shopping…or to the theatre…"

"I'll phone you Tuesday, see how the job's going – they may want to work into the weekend…"

Her mother sighed heavily. "Okay, if you're sure. But phone me if you need me…or money; or anything…promise me."

"I promise…I am a big girl now, you know?"

"Yes, darling I know, but even big girls need their mothers some time."

"I'll speak to you Tuesday then."

"Yes, ok…bye…oh, Megan. Are you still there?"

"Yes…"

"I almost forgot. An old friend of yours phoned here…said he was a colleague from the University of Kent…I told him where you were…ever so charming, very well spoken – are you and he…"

"No Mum, we're not!" She tried to stay calm so her mother wouldn't notice her anger. "And…thanks for telling him, I'm sure he'll be in touch. Bye Mum."

She hung up. Her heart, which had sunk heavily throughout the conversation, had now started beating rapidly in her chest. Why the hell did her mother tell him where she was, and how *dare* he phone her mother and be so sneaky! *Jesus*, what if he turned up on her doorstep – why wouldn't he leave it alone? He obviously hadn't had the balls to ask David where she was when he had spoken to him, so he had cunningly got in touch with her mother! Surely he must have guessed she was in Gloucestershire when David had told him that she was going to be involved in the dig. So why involve her mother?

Bastard.

Bartie had sensed her change of mood and was climbing up her thighs trying to comfort her. He looked at her with concerned eyes and then started to lick her hands. She smiled at him and ruffled his ears; she squatted down and hugged him tightly.

"Come on, Bartie, let's go out in the garden," she said despondently. The day she had been looking forward to had suddenly been tinged with concern, and her heart felt heavy again. "Come on, boy, I mustn't let him affect me this way anymore."

Megan spent the rest of the morning in the garden, tidying the borders and cutting back some of the shrubs and weeds that had crept ever so silently, but deliberately, across the garden – choking the flowers, ensuring they would become dead and lifeless. During the final months of her gran's illness, she had hired a gardener to come and help out, but he, like so many others in these parts, was just 'passing through' in his narrow boat and was no longer available. Now though, Megan was pleased with the distraction, she enjoyed pulling up the weeds and cutting back the overgrown plants, it felt very satisfying, therapeutic even.

The River Thames that ran past the cottage and Roundhouse was high against the riverbanks and flowed quickly, carrying on its murky waters bits of branches and a few pieces of rubbish after the heavy rain and wind of the previous night. The sun shone now on the sandy stone of the cottage, giving it that golden glow that the Cotswolds are famous for. She felt extremely fortunate that her gran had left the cottage to her; she had to admit it was not a totally unexpected inheritance but you could never be sure about these things. Her mother had feigned her pleasure saying that she didn't need, or in fact want, her mother's house – why would anybody want to live out in the sticks when she had London and all its excitement on her doorstep? She knew how much Megan loved the place and was genuinely pleased that her mother had wanted it to go to her own daughter…she could sell it and buy a lovely place in the City near to her – London had so much more of what Megan needed…

Megan, on the other hand, had always loved her gran's house, which was about a mile from the town centre, full of character and mystery, it felt like home, unlike the house in which her mother lived in Wimbledon. It stood on the banks where two rivers met, liable to flooding after very heavy rain; insurance a nightmare nowadays, but

43

her gran had lived there pretty much all her adult life and had loved it as much as Megan did now.

The Thames meandered through the Cotswold fields and dipped in and out of the counties of Gloucestershire, Oxfordshire and Wiltshire – the three counties could be visited on a four-mile circular walk. Megan remembered, as a child, the town children and those from further afield who had come and jumped off rope swings, hung from the weeping willows, into the cool waters of the river during the summer months – shrieking and laughing as they swung high and then dropped to the water below. The wooden footbridge, near to her Gran's cottage, was a firm favourite of teenagers who had just left school after their exams. Further up the river, near the town centre, lads, men and some women dared each other to jump off the stone bridge into the water below – shouting out to warn of the boats and canoes on the river beneath them. The invasion of their river made the locals a little uneasy; they didn't mind sharing the waters but grew a little tired of them not taking their rubbish home after picnics and barbecues on the river bank.

Megan slowly became aware of Bartie whining, and this distracted her from her thoughts. She looked up and into his chocolate brown eyes that held their sorrowful expression; a pleading expression, if she had read it correctly.

"Ok, ok – must be almost time to meet Sasha." She glanced at her watch and was surprised to see how fast the morning had gone. She was due to meet Sasha at the end of the lane to the town at two; she was going to have to hurry.

Bartie wagged his tail and whimpered.

Taking off her gloves and placing all the tools in the wheelbarrow, ready for returning to her task when they got back, Megan grabbed her light waterproof coat from the nail on the lean-to adjoining the shed and slung it round her shoulders. She walked up to the house, picked up her purse and mobile and locked the doors, before grasping Bartie's lead, just in case she needed it, and walking across the low bridge that took them to the track down to the main road. The cottage stood about three quarters of a mile from the main road. You either took the public footpath along the Thames Path along the river bank towards the town centre, or you could drive up the uneven, muddy track from the main road out of the town. The closest neighbours were at least quarter of a mile away which had perfectly suited her gran, who could be a bit reclusive by nature.

Bartie trotted along ahead of her, stopping now and then to sniff the breeze or a patch of grass where something had left an interesting scent. The sun shone down warmly upon Megan and she found herself thinking she should have left her waterproof at home, but some of the clouds were dark and threatening. She looked across at the river where swans and ducks floated aimlessly upon the rippling waters, bobbing up and down but graceful and serene. In the middle of the field a movement caught her eye – at first she thought it might be a duck, but this was too quick to be a duck – a hare! She stood and watched as it bounded across the field away from the river; she glanced at Bartie hoping he wouldn't take chase – not that he would catch it but it might terrify the poor creature. As if it felt her watching it, it stopped dead in its tracks and looked in her direction – it stared at her as still as a stone.

Then all of a sudden it was gone.

Megan smiled to herself, feeling privileged at seeing such a secretive wild animal. She called to Bartie to follow and continued down the track, her boots crunching on the pathetic attempt of gravel to stop tyres and boots sinking into the mud of which the track was made. A couple of ducks flew up out of the stream and startled her gaining Bartie's interest and making him bark loudly. A little way off she heard another bark; probably a dog out for an afternoon walk too – quite often she would meet familiar faces along the track; sometimes complete strangers – perhaps it was Sasha and Jess.

Ahead of her she could just see, above the treetops, a thin vapour of smoke curling its way upwards and then being swept away on the breeze. She frowned; there shouldn't be anyone lighting a bonfire in this area. She quickened her step, concerned it might be teenagers lighting fires in the fields by the river; perhaps it was somebody having a barbecue, albeit a little early in the season? As they were about to turn the corner, Bartie stopped in his tracks as a collie dog ventured towards him, hackles slightly raised. Bartie gave the collie a good sniff and as the collie started to wag its tail, Bartie did too. They did a sort of ritual dance around each other, determining their status. Megan expected somebody to walk round the corner towards her but nobody came. She could still see the smoke above the budding trees and guessed the dog belonged to whoever it was that had the fire. She walked on round the corner, calling to Bartie as she went. Beneath the trees, tucked away into the corner by the side of the lane was a traveller's caravan; its rounded roof snug against the high hedge and low branches of the trees. A small, sturdy-looking black and white pony was flicking its tail while chewing on the grass of the verge – it was tied to a young tree. The caravan's little chimney was the culprit for the smouldering and made the surrounding air smell of wood smoke. Megan glanced up at the doorway, which stood open, and she

45

could hear somebody moving around inside; a kettle started to sing, there was a small crashing sound followed by a man's voice cursing.

She was about to walk on by when a man appeared at the doorway and started shouting in an Irish accent, "Angus, Angus, where the feck are yer now...oh...." He nodded at Megan. "Jus' looking for me dog, but I see he's makin' friends."

The man didn't smile, and he seemed quite put out that she was standing there looking at his caravan. He didn't give any explanation of what he was doing there on private land – not hers admittedly, but her neighbour's; she wondered if Mr Garrett knew he was there – she very much doubted it. He had obviously only just arrived as he hadn't been there two days ago. The man looked at her with wide grey eyes. He was handsome in a rugged sort of way; dark hair and thick stubble at his chin. Megan felt a shiver run through her – he disturbed her, made her feel unsettled; she felt the need to fill the silence.

"Yes, Bartie likes to make friends - he's ok with other dogs.'

"Yeah, so is Angus."

The silence continued, the man obviously did not want to make conversation but he continued to stare at her, taking her in. Hurriedly, she said goodbye; beginning to feel a little flustered, she called to Bartie and continued on her walk.

What a strange man; not overly friendly, but certainly handsome. If she remembered anything about the travellers that came each summer during her childhood, he was probably used to having a lot of people telling him to move on and probably suspected her of doing the same; although the land was not hers at that point of the track. As a child, she had naïvely thought that the travellers had a romantic way of life, moving from place to place; seeing the world in a gentle unrushed way. However, the reality was probably very different; being chased off land that didn't belong to them, upsetting local people and being accused of many things.

It was odd because he seemed familiar, something about his face, perhaps his eyes? Megan remembered that the travellers often stayed in and around the town when she was a child, perhaps he had been one of them? She had witnessed them arrive, sometimes in a convoy with their brightly coloured vans pulled by horses with dogs trotting behind, unleashed. They would often set up camp in the farmers' fields and have their horses tethered nearby; the dogs, some chickens and their barefoot children running around and swimming in the river. Locally, they would offer to do odd jobs or sell their wares – one woman in particular used to have a sign outside her caravan offering to read palms, or tarot cards. Megan remembered her gran going to see her once or twice. The first time she had come away really happy and agreeing that the woman knew what she was talking about, however, on her second visit she came away angry and a little afraid, telling Megan never to have her cards read by a tarot reader; they hadn't got a clue what was going to happen in the future, nobody did.

Megan remembered that day clearly now, it having slipped from her memory for years. It had been a bright and sunny day and they had needed to go into the town for some provisions. As they had come out of the back door of the house, they could see the brightly coloured vans in the distance; they were pulled up next to the river in a semi-circular shape facing the water. Horses were grazing and the children were splashing about in the river on rafts that they had made from old bits of wood and barrels possibly from local farms.

"Oh, they're back again!" cried her gran, excitedly.

"Let's go to the town along the river, that way we can be a little nosey." Her gran had winked and smiled, unusually for the first time that morning, before striding off towards the footpath. It seemed to Megan that her gran always had so much energy and she almost had to run to keep up with her.

As they had neared the traveller site, the voices of the children in the river had carried themselves towards them on the light breeze. Their excited shouts and squeals, the splashes from the water all made it seem to Megan a very exciting and thrilling way to live. There didn't seem to be many adults around the campsite, the few that were there were either chopping wood, or were sitting on the steps of their caravans. Outside one of the caravans was a board with 'Madam Gizelle's Palm reading & Tarot' painted with bright, purple lettering.

"Oooh, "Megan heard her gran say. "Will you be all right out here for five minutes, while I go in? Don't stray too far though."

Megan had been unsure, but her gran had seemed so happy and excited about it that she hadn't the heart, or courage, to say no. She wanted her gran to think that she was brave and was growing up now that she was eight. It had been good to see her gran smiling again.

Earlier that morning she had been in a really bad mood, when Megan had gone downstairs for breakfast, which was very unlike her. Oddly, Megan had heard raised voices from the back garden while she had been reading her book in bed. She had looked at her clock – 7.00, breakfast was at 7.30, so she decided to read for a while longer. Hearing her gran speaking to somebody in the garden, she had gone to the window to see who she was talking to at such an early hour. She could see her gran under one of the willow trees; she was talking to somebody, a man, but Megan couldn't see his face as the willow branches and leaves were hiding it from view. Her gran was shouting at him (was he the gardener? Did her gran even have a gardener?)

47

Megan couldn't hear what she was saying but she was obviously upset. The man shouted something back at her, and as her gran reached out to touch him he knocked her hands away and stormed off. She watched in horror as her gran sank to her knees and started to cry. Megan didn't know what to do; she wanted to rush out into the garden and put her arms around her gran and tell her everything would be ok, but something stopped her. She felt torn between rushing down the stairs to her, or jumping back in bed and pretending not to have seen anything. She chose the latter, feeling that her gran would not have wanted her to have seen the argument, and certainly not her tears.

Megan had watched the children and dogs swimming about in the river and wished she could join them – they seemed so adventurous and carefree – they weren't at all bothered by her watching them. Suddenly, a small boy appeared at her side – he was wearing nothing but some scruffy-looking shorts and was saturated, water dripped off his dark hair – he grinned at her. 'You can join us if yer like."

"Thank you, but my gran will only be five minutes or so."

"Ok, perhaps another time." The boy ran back to the others and launched himself back into the river, making a loud splash as he hit the water; screams of other children carried on the air.

Megan had to admit that it looked very tempting and she was about to change her mind when her gran appeared on the steps of Madam Gizelle's caravan. Megan noticed her smile had faded again and that her black mood had obviously returned.

"Are you all right, Gran?" she asked.

Her gran looked at her, her face set in a fierce expression. "Bloody travellers, they don't know what they're talking about – don't ever have your cards read – it's all a load of codswallop!"

Megan didn't dare ask what had happened – it was just like this morning, she felt she would be overstepping the mark if she asked any further questions. She figured her gran would tell her if she wanted her to know.

"Shall we have an ice cream, Gran?" she asked brightly, trying to get her to cheer up and be herself again.

"Sure, why not?" she replied, with a tight smile.

All of a sudden, Megan was brought out of her thoughts by Bartie, who barked and ran off at high speed away from her. She called out to him sternly but he took no notice. She started to run after him as he was heading for the main road, which was always busy. As she turned the corner she saw Bartie and Jess jumping all over each other; Sasha was calling to her spaniel too, trying to get her to come –

both dogs ignored their owners completely and took off across one of the fields to the side of the track, running rings around each other. Sasha waved to Megan and strode quickly towards her, laughing.

"I'm so glad it's not just my dog that is completely insane and does nothing I tell her."

"I don't know what you mean, my dog always behaves perfectly well until yours is around," Megan replied with a straight face, but immediately started laughing too.

The two women fell into step side by side and walked across the field in the direction of where the dogs had run off to.

"So, are you looking forward to your new job?" asked Sasha.

"Yes. I'm so glad I saw the advert – thank you."

"What are you thanking me for? You're the one with the qualifications."

"I know, but it was a well-needed piece of good luck."

Sasha looked at Megan. "You miss your gran?"

Megan nodded. She felt the tears welling up in her eyes and embarrassingly one escaped down her cheek.

"Oh, God! I am sorry, how insensitive of me!" exclaimed Sasha, placing her hand on Megan's forearm.

"It's okay. I get a bit like this at times. I hadn't realised I was still feeling quite so raw about it all; it takes me by surprise sometimes!"

"I'm truly sorry, I didn't mean to pry!"

"Really, please don't worry. I'm a bit out of sorts right now…"

"Life can be a bit like that at times, especially when you're grieving. Don't be so hard on yourself."

"Yes, but I'm even imagining strange things happening at my gran's house. There was *never* a time before now that I felt even the slightest bit of unease at the cottage."

"What, do you think that your gran is haunting the place?"

"No, no not her…I don't even know if it is haunting as such…"

"Do you believe in ghosts?"

"I'm not sure, I don't think so – but then I've never had any experiences like what has happened recently." Megan went on to tell Sasha about the strange cold that had permeated the air at the cottage and the damp smell of earth that went with it. She even went as far as to tell her about the figure she had seen in the trees, watching the cottage when David had walked her home the other evening.

"Blimey, sounds like it's straight out of a ghost story! I'm not sure I'd want to return to the cottage, not by myself anyway."

"So *you* believe in ghosts then?"

Sasha looked thoughtful for a moment. "To be honest, I'm not sure about ghosts in the Halloween sense, but I do think that there could be unsettled spirits in this world."

"Really?"

"Yes. I know David would laugh at me – he thinks that as soon as the person is dead it's just future archaeology; nothing remains except what the earth has preserved. I think there must be more to it than that. I'm not really sure what though."

Megan continued. "I've never really thought about it seriously before, never had a reason to really think about ghosts or spirits – but the things that have been happening at the cottage are a little odd." She looked at Sasha and shrugged her shoulders.

"Like you say, it could be that you are in a highly sensitive state at the moment, but to see and feel things must be a little unnerving. Are you scared to stay there?"

"Not really. Bartie usually starts acting rather oddly and warns me if there is anything unusual happening but I'm sure there must be a rational explanation…"

Sasha stopped in her tracks and stared at Megan, wide-eyed. "Bartie is also sensing things? Jesus, I'm not sure I'd be brave enough to stay there on my own!"

Megan stopped too. "Now you're making me *more* nervous. I've sort of been taking it with a pinch of salt…"

Sasha laughed. "You're probably right, I'm sure it's probably all coincidental, like you say, you're in a sensitive, emotional state at the moment. As for the cold air and earthy smell, old cottages are draughty and often damp, especially when it's so close to the river."

"So, you won't accept a dinner invitation then; unless, of course, I ask the ghosts to vacate for the evening?"

"What, are you kidding? I'd love to come over, I've always loved that cottage and the Roundhouse – will you show me that too? I'm certainly not going to let a few ghosts ruin my opportunity of taking a look around such an intriguing place!"

Megan thought about her plans of pizza and a quiet evening in front of the fire with her book, and suddenly relished the idea of Sasha's company. "What are you up to tonight, you could come over if you like; we could get a takeaway?"

"Sorry, I am going out with Brad tonight, but what about we meet up next week for a drink at the pub? How about Friday? You can tell me how your first week has been at work, then we can organise another evening for me to come over."

Megan tried hard to hide her disappointment. "Sure, that's a good idea!"

"I'll text you Friday afternoon and we can see what time suits us both."

Sasha and Megan parted company at the bridge back to the town, and Megan headed home, trying hard not to feel disappointed. After all, this morning she had been really looking forward to a quiet evening, but now she suddenly felt very alone – perhaps it had been all that talk about ghosts. She liked to have her own space, but occasionally, recently, she had felt a bitter loneliness; especially on the weekends…this was when she missed Tom too. She couldn't believe she was thinking about him now, it was during these lonely moments that she felt her strength of will waver – what if he *did* turn up? Would she send him away? She *had* to, she had to stay stronger this time, there must be no more turning back to him, ever!

As she had promised herself, Megan ate some pizza, then went to have a long soak in a candlelit bath, pamper herself and have a warming glass of red wine and read Oscar Wilde's *A Picture of Dorian Grey*. Bartie lay along the foot of the bath and snored gently, as she lay among the jasmine-scented bubbles, lost in the sinister world of *Dorian Grey*. After a while, having refilled the bath with hot water a few times, the water began to run cold. She must have a new boiler and heating system installed before next winter, she thought to herself, and decided to get out before she felt chilled. She dried herself off and slipped on her bathrobe.

Entering the bedroom, she discovered that Bartie had not taken up his usual position at the bottom of her bed – he must be downstairs. She was putting on her thick, not-to-be-seen-by-any-man pyjamas, when she heard Bartie whimpering. She quickly slipped on her top and pulled the robe around her shoulders and went to the top of the stairs, listening. Yes, he was whimpering, he must want to go out; he did this sometimes when he had an upset stomach or had been too busy sniffing around to actually go the last time he'd been outside. She descended the stairs and found him standing by the front door.

"Sorry, boy, want to go out?"

Megan opened the front door, expecting Bartie to fly outside as he always did, but instead he cowered away from the cold blast of air that came through the door, then turned and ran into the lounge with his tail between his legs. This astounded Megan, Bartie never recoiled from anything; he was brave and fearless, or perhaps just plain stupid in the face of danger usually, so she couldn't understand what was wrong.

Hurriedly, with slightly shaking hands, she managed to lock the front door again before going into the lounge, where she found Bartie curled up on the sofa, looking at her with his hangdog expression. Megan frowned and went to make a fuss of him. She stroked his head and spoke softly to him, and after a few moments his tail began to wag again.

"What was all that about, Bartholomew, boy? Are you not feeling well?"

Sometimes he was a bit subdued when he had eaten something that was a bit off, an old bone or something a bit more disgusting that he'd discovered and devoured without her knowing.

"If you're going to be sick, my boy, make sure you *do* go out – I don't want to have to clear it up, thank you."

Megan went to the kitchen and poured herself another glass of wine. She checked the back door was locked and then wandered into the lounge. Bartie was snuggled next to the wood burner now and seemed more peaceful. Feeling sleepy and unable to read more without falling asleep, but not quite ready to go to bed, Megan sat on the sofa and flicked through the TV channels until she found a film to watch.

She must have dozed off, because she found herself waking up to a completely different film and Bartie snuggled up next to her on the sofa. She yawned and stretched, then called to Bartie. She made her way to the back door to let Bartie out then the two of them went upstairs to bed.

The light of the moon lay across the floor and her bed; it was almost as bright as day, although her clock told her it was half past two in the morning. She went over to the window to pull the curtains, as she found it difficult to get to sleep when there was too much light. Looking out across the river, to where the willow trees stood like silhouetted sentinels against the sky, she started when she saw the same dark figure that she had seen the previous night. She screwed her eyes shut and opened them again trying to get a clearer look, but the shadow had gone. With her heart beating fast inside her chest, she quickly pulled the curtains across the window and turned to look at Bartie who was watching her closely. He whimpered.

What the hell's going on? I must be going mad, I am sure *there was somebody there again amongst the trees...*But as she climbed into bed, she wondered if she hadn't imagined it tonight – after all she was half asleep and was probably sub-consciously thinking about the figure from last night, which of course had to be somebody out for a late night dog walk. That had to be the explanation...the other one was too chilling to comprehend.

Chapter Five

Wulfric sighed heavily. The question was *how* was he going to get Mildryth to drink the potion? What if, after all this, the potion didn't work? Lindi had assured him it would – it wouldn't fail. He thought about what he was about to do, he wanted Mildryth, had always been in love with her, but had always known that she was in love with his brother. The way she looked upon Wilheard with those magical, beautiful, green eyes; the love and desire that was so apparent to everyone – why couldn't she look at him that way? She looked at him with sympathy, pity even – he did not want her *pity* – he wanted her mind, spirit...*body*; he must have her before he went insane with desire. The potion was the only way. His more rational side told him that to be truly his, he must win her over naturally, without the help of sorcery – after all, was that not what his father had accused his mother of, tricking him into thinking he loved her? He picked up the small phial of liquid and put it into his pocket. There had to be an opportunity, and soon. The new moon was only a week away now and Wilheard and Mildryth were to be married upon the last day of the current moon when it was full and at its most powerful, fertile time – a good time for a marriage and subsequent heirs.

Wulfric knew she often went to her mother's grave, but over the past few days he'd been unable to locate her there. Today, as he approached the site, he was beginning to think he'd never find her alone again, that he'd missed his chance! So, he almost ran towards her when he saw her there, but managed to hold himself back. She was standing beside where her mother had been buried; he observed her for a while before he approached, which was when he noticed she was crying and whispering, her soft voice carrying towards him on the cold, gentle breeze. He coughed quietly, hoping not to startle her. She jumped nonetheless.

"Wulfric, you startled me. What...what are you doing here?"

"I have come to pay my respects to my father. I am sorry that I scared you and to have disturbed your own grieving."

Mildryth quickly wiped away the tears from her cheeks and felt herself flush red.

"It is nothing to be ashamed of, Mildryth, you have lost your mother, probably your dearest friend."

"Thank you, Wulfric." She smiled at him, but then the smile faded and she overbalanced; she cried out as she fell towards the ground. Wulfric was there in an instant and caught her; his strong arms wrapped tightly around her.

"Mildryth, what's the matter?"

"I'm sorry, I just felt really unsteady. I've had a bad headache for the past few days. It must be to do with that."

Wulfric saw his opportunity, took off his cloak, lay it upon the grass and then sitting down beside her pulled the potion from his belt. He took the bottle stopper out and handed it to her.

"Perhaps this will help…I…I take it for bad headaches…I quite often get them. Lindi made it up for me…it works every time."

"Lindi made it? It must be good." Mildryth took the phial from him and drank the potion.

"Hopefully that will make it better," said Wulfric, smiling at her gently.

Lindi had warned him it would not have an immediate effect, it would probably take a short while to get into her system; he would have to act quickly enough though when it did.

"I think perhaps you should rest a while," he suggested.

They sat in silence a while, listening to the noises around them; there were birds singing close by and the sound of the wind. In the distance they could hear the sheep bleating. Other than that the place was quiet as often the burial place seemed to be; a place of resting and peace for their ancestors who had already passed on to the next life.

"I am feeling a little better, thank you." Mildryth smiled at him as she started to stand up. He helped her to her feet. "Thank you for your help, Wulfric. I have an offering for Eostre and wish to go to her temple near the river."

"I will come with you."

"No, I will be fine."

"I insist. What if you have another fall?"

She hesitated then replied, "If you are sure I am not keeping you?"

He shook his head – he couldn't believe how easy it had been…now he just had to be patient a little while longer; the passion was rising more quickly than ever before but he had to stay calm – he hoped she didn't notice the quickening of his breath.

Mildryth walked beside Wulfric and listened to him while he spoke of a boy who had been imprisoned for stealing some bread from a local house, a stranger who had come into their village in search of food and shelter. The punishments were harsh, especially to outsiders. The headache was subsiding and Mildryth was beginning to feel much more relaxed as she listened to Wulfric's story. He still had his arm around her for support and it felt comforting.

They arrived at the point where the rivers merged; a sacred place to the villagers. Mildryth had brought along a suitable offering – she hoped that it might bring her a child soon after her marriage to

Wilheard. She longed to hold a baby in her arms and let it suckle at her breast; she knew it felt more urgent now that she had lost her own mother – she wanted her own family to love and nurture.

"I'll walk on a bit further; give you some time alone – I'll come back in a while – sit and wait for me here, I'll leave my cloak for you to sit on. I don't want you having another fall on the way home and nobody finding you," Wulfric stated.

Mildryth nodded and gave him a weak smile, then turned from him and walked closer to the edge of the river bank. She threw her offering of flowers and greenery into the fast-flowing water and watched as they floated downstream; whispering her offering of prayers to Eostre. After, she sat on Wulfric's cloak and watched the flora and fauna disappear into the rapid, muddy waters further down river, hoping that Eostre would hear her prayers.

She sat quietly, pondering her union with Wilheard – she loved him without doubt; he had always been a kind and gentle man to her, he would make a fantastic husband and father, was already a fine king. She hoped that there would be no more fighting for kingdoms in the near future and that their own kingdom would remain peaceful. Her head began to swim again; it was if she had drunk a lot of wine and was beginning to feel a little drowsy. Wulfric's soft footsteps approached, she turned and looked at him. He smiled as he sat beside her, his grey, wolf-like eyes glittering with some emotion she couldn't quite capture – he too had lost his father...he was clearly moved by this.

Mildryth shivered.

"Are you cold?" he asked.

She nodded.

Wulfric put his arm around her shoulders, as he did so she drew closer to him. "I don't want to go back to the village yet," she said sadly. "I love the peace and quiet here by the river, besides, I'm not sure I can walk yet."

"Is your head still painful?" he asked looking at her.

"It feels as though it is full of sheep's wool." She smiled up at him, trying to make light of the sudden heaviness she felt.

Pulling her even closer to him, he left his arm around her shoulders, it felt good: warm, comforting; she started to become more aware of his physical presence and closeness. Wulfric's breathing seemed slightly irregular – perhaps he had walked quickly – but what she noticed most of all was his scent. She had never been aware of it before; it was musty, but not in an unpleasant way and definitely masculine. Surprisingly, she felt an odd stirring in the depths of her stomach and moved slightly away from him, glancing at the profile of his face, his long straight nose and full lips.

Wulfric turned then and looked at her, it was shocking to see the raw, direct passion in his eyes; she took a sharp intake of breath at his own obvious desire. He leant towards her and suddenly pinned her to the ground; she was stunned and had no control over her body. He kissed her fully on the lips, his tongue probing gently, but firmly and passionately against her own soft mouth. She felt disorientated as Wulfric began running his hands over her torso finding her breasts and then groping beneath her garments to find her soft, young flesh. She shuddered. It felt intense, not loving and gentle as when Wilheard held her in his arms but an animal-like desire.

Mildryth's trembling continued as he ran his hands over her skin; she felt she was drowning in his desire...she looked up at Wulfric's face and saw the mixture of pleasure and pain as he climaxed crying out her name; she felt the strength and solidness of his muscles beneath his clothes. Her own climax took her by surprise and shocked her to her core...it was as it she had lost all control of herself!

Wulfric held her closely, both of them breathing hard and fast; he whispered her name again and again finally looking her in the eyes and saying, "Whatever happens now, Mildryth, know that I will always and have always loved you." As he watched her eyes grow heavy he wondered at their passion, she *must* have true feelings for him, surely this was not only the working of magic? A small, sly smile crossed his lips as he thought about their lovemaking, what if his seed was now beginning to work its way deeper into Mildryth – what if...what if she was to have *his* child? What would that mean for him...if nobody ever knew...perhaps their child would reign, after all? But how could he bear his brother bringing up his own offspring; he could never allow that to happen – if, if a child was to be born out of this union then something must be done to prevent Wilheard thinking that he had a right to the child, as he thought he had a right to everything else in his life!

As they lay in each other's arms, Mildryth drifting off to sleep against Wulfric's large frame, neither of them saw or felt the presence watching them from close by...neither of them knew what those eyes witnessed or what consequences would follow.

***

A little way off, hidden behind some trees, was Gifre, an aide of Wulfric. He had seen Wulfric and Mildryth walk away from the burial site and towards the river in an embrace. It had seemed odd that they were walking together in the opposite direction to the village, arms around each other. What could they be doing? Why were they going to the river together, towards Eostre's temple? As he watched them now, he was stunned and enraged at their actions. Wulfric and Mildryth were quite oblivious to anything else around them. Mildryth had her arms and legs wrapped around Wulfric's strong body – the whore; they were lost in each other and in that moment Gifre felt that it was not the only thing that would be lost.

**

Megan walked back towards the Roundhouse, she and Bartie had almost completed their circular route of five miles. A number of narrow boats were moored up along the river; most of them she recognised as local and a few regular weekenders. It was a nice weekend now, cold but bright and this quite often got more people out on the river. A couple of young lads were racing their canoes down river, scattering ducks and swans as they went. The sound of the church bells could be heard chiming, being carried on the wind across the fields and river, calling the congregation to worship. A few other people were out exercising their dogs; another Sunday morning ritual.

As she got nearer to the boats, she noticed that one of the narrow boats was one she had not seen before; it was of simple navy and gold décor and was more tasteful than some of the ones that were moored occasionally along the riverbank of the Thames. Smoke was coming from the navy blue barge's small chimney and a duck sat up on top proudly, as if it was the captain of a very large ship – this made her smile.

A young man's head popped up from the doorway, he was dressed in running shorts and a long-sleeved top that stretched tightly across his muscular chest and well-toned arms. She noticed he was rather red in the face as he turned to face her and caught her staring, she tried quickly to turn away but he had obviously seen her, he smiled.

"Morning," he called, brightly.

Bartie barked at him.

"Morning," replied Megan, embarrassed at being caught eyeing him up. 'Beautiful isn't it?"

"Yes. Spring seems to be on its way at last."

Bartie ran towards the boat and jumped aboard before Megan could stop him. "Bartie, **heel**!" she called, but he was already jumping all over the man – something he didn't usually do. "I'm so sorry," she called, and started to run towards them.

The man was laughing and petting Bartie, and didn't seem in the least bit bothered. Megan walked alongside the boat and called again to the dog, who continued to ignore her.

"He's friendly," said the man, laughing.

"Not usually *this* friendly." Megan looked more closely at the man; he didn't seem quite so young close up, about mid-thirties she thought, with amazing bright blue eyes which were full of the laughter that played on his full lips; again Megan had to look away quickly and stop herself from imagining kissing those lips…

"Perhaps he can smell the bacon I'm cooking for breakfast. Come aboard."

"That would be it, yes – he is a bit of a scrounger. Good job you're not cooking sausages, you'd never get rid of him." Megan climbed aboard the boat and grabbed hold of Bartie's brown leather collar; she slipped his lead into the catch and pulled him to her side. "Again, I apologise – he can be so embarrassing sometimes."

The man laughed a wide smile. "Wait a moment, don't go." He slipped below deck and resurfaced a few moments later with a piece of cooked bacon. "Can he have it?"

"I don't think he deserves it…" Megan started.

"Oh, all dogs deserve a bit of bacon now and then," he said feeding the bacon to Bartie, who wolfed it down in seconds. "Besides, I have far too much just for me. If I eat the whole pack, I'll have to go for another run later on today, and I was so looking forward to a quiet afternoon."

Megan laughed. "But if Bartie eats it I'll have to take him for another walk…but he gets two good walks a day anyway."

"There then, he needs the bacon to keep his energy levels up."

She laughed. "Thank you. Again, I apologise for my mad mutt."

"No worries – have a good day!" The man gave Bartie a huge fuss and Megan a lovely smile, then turned away from them as Megan jumped off the boat and made her way back along the riverbank. He was definitely a new face around here; she couldn't help but wonder if there had been a similarly good looking woman below deck – although he had said he couldn't eat all the bacon *himself*. She wondered if she walked back that way later whether or not she might bump into him again…*behave*, she scolded herself with a smile.

After her conversation with the man she felt lifted and was still smiling to herself about the recent episode when her mobile rang. She didn't recognise the landline number. Frowning, she answered the call.

"Hello?"

"Megan; it's Tom."

Her smile faded and her heart sank. "Tom, what do you want?"

"To talk."

"I have nothing to say to you."

"*Please*, Megan, I miss you..."

"Tom, I don't want to hear it, you promised...you said you wouldn't contact me..."

"I can't help it, I *am* trying."

"I'm sorry Tom, *try harder*, I don't want to speak to you, I'm hanging up..."

"No, please...hear me out..."

"Where's Sophia?"

"At her sister's for a few days...look, I know where you are...a colleague of mine...completely coincidental...and your mum..."

"Goodbye, Tom." She hung up, she couldn't listen to any more, didn't want to hear what he had to say, not this time. She was not going to relent again...this time it was well and truly over. She didn't care who had told him where she was, either her mother or David, she was just so angry that Tom had called her after all the promises he had made her – she should have known he wouldn't keep them. Her phone rang again, same number. She switched off her phone and put it into her pocket. Her happy mood had been damaged, damaged again by Tom – well, not anymore. Nervously she thought about what he'd just said about knowing where she was...shit, how could she ever get over him if he wouldn't leave her alone? There was only one thing for it...if he came, she would send him away; send him away like she should have done right from the beginning.

Megan was not far from her gran's house...home...so she let Bartie off his lead and watched him as he shot off like a rocket, straight for the bridge and the Roundhouse.

When she arrived back at the house, Bartie was having a good sniff around the garden to see which creatures had trespassed on his territory whilst he had been gone. Taking off her boots, she went through into the kitchen. The smell of the bacon had made her hungry, she had no bacon but she did have eggs – poached eggs on toast would be a good brunch, she decided, good comfort food. From the kitchen window she could see the dog scratching at the dirt beside the stone potting shed. The bulbs were just beginning to push their spurs of greenery out through the soil. She didn't want him to disturb the flowers, as she needed the brightness and cheer that they would bring her in the coming weeks. She called out to him; he totally ignored her, continuing his task. The pile of dirt was growing. She slipped on her wellington boots and went to join him. What was he digging for so intently...must be an old bone he had buried there perhaps on a previous visit. As she approached he stopped digging and looked up at her – he whined.

"What have you got there?" she asked.

He pawed at the ground. She looked down into the hole he had dug and saw something just protruding out of the dark, damp earth. It was made of some type of metal, but was beginning to corrode at the edges. Bending down, she moved the damp earth carefully, as she would do on a dig, away from the item, which was still fairly well covered. As it became free from the soil, Megan could see that it was some kind of brooch, it had a large square head, but much was concealed because of the remaining mud. It was certainly ancient. As she delicately brushed away some of the earth, she knew she had found something important.

Taking it indoors, Megan washed it very carefully under the tap: a geometric pattern started to emerge; she was astounded at its wonderfully preserved condition. A little thrill ran through her, she would have to show it to someone more in the know as it certainly didn't look Roman. Tom's expertise sprung to mind, he would have been the first person she would have asked in the past, but now he was the last person she wanted to contact. Maybe David could take a look at it, although Megan felt a little reluctant to show it to anyone; she didn't really want any archaeologists invading her gran's garden and digging around in search for other clues of what might lie beneath. It was too soon for this. She would give herself time.

Wrapping it delicately in tissue, she took it upstairs and put it in the top drawer of her gran's dressing table along with the diary.

Heading back down the stairs, unwelcome thoughts of Tom forced their way into her mind; the short conversation with him earlier had left her feeling unsettled again. To keep her mind off of him, it would be good to do something practical – perhaps she should start looking through the stuff in the attic? She made herself a cup of tea and headed up into the roof of the house; it was a job that needed doing, going though her gran's stuff, it might as well be now.

Later that evening she turned on the TV and slipped 'Gone with the Wind' into the machine, she had watched it many times with her gran, as it had been one of her favourites, but hadn't seen it for years now. The wine was still beautifully smooth, even after having been opened for 24 hours, and she settled into the sofa and opened the box of chocolates that she had found in the cupboard, bought last week, but forgotten about until now. Just what she needed...

Megan was deeply engrossed in the film (Bartie, huddled up close to her on the sofa snoring gently) when she heard a car approaching the house. She glanced at the clock...eight forty-five, who on earth would be coming down the lane at this time on a Sunday night? Bartie must have either heard the car or felt the change in Megan's relaxed state because his head popped up from his paws and then he jumped off the sofa and trotted towards the front door, a low growl in his throat. Megan followed.

"Who is it, boy?" she asked, peering out of the window next to the front door without putting on the light.

The estate car that pulled up outside on the drive was not one she recognised. The security light on the house came on and Bartie began to bark loudly as the driver got out of the car and started to walk towards the front door – she immediately recognised the tall, confident frame, the thick, wavy hair...she felt sick...what should she do? She wanted to turn and run upstairs and hide, she wanted Bartie to stop barking so she could make out that she was not at home, but he would know that she was there...

Feeling like a guilty child, she slipped down behind the front door and waited for the knock. Bartie was now whimpering excitedly, perhaps sensing who it was on the other side of the door. The knock jarred her every nerve. She waited for what felt like an appropriate amount of time and then stood, took a deep breath and opened the door.

"Tom."

"Megan, I was worried about you...I had to come," he leaned towards her and kissed her on the cheek. Not waiting for an invitation, he walked straight past her and into the dark hallway. Bartie jumped all over him...*traitor*, thought Megan to herself.

"Why is the house so dark? I was beginning to think you weren't home."

"I was trying to have a quiet evening with a film – Tom, what are you doing here? You promised you wouldn't contact me, you keep phoning and now a visit, on a Sunday evening – what's going on?"

Tom started to take off his coat, at this point Megan felt like she was losing control of the situation. He started to speak, "When I spoke to your mother the other day, she sounded like she was worried about you..."

"My mother is always worried about me, you know that!"

"I just wanted to check for myself that you were ok and perhaps have a chat. You must be lonely out here without your gran."

Megan felt she must regain control of the conversation. "No, Tom. Look, you can see for yourself I am fine and I don't want to *chat*, I'm sick of chatting! I want you to leave, *now*."

"Please, just half an hour. I've driven a long way."

"I didn't ask you to come, Tom, you're being unfair. You promised you would give me some space."

Speechless, she watched as he hung up his coat, walked through to the lounge and started pouring himself a glass of scotch from her gran's drinks table. He walked over to the coffee table and took out his mobile and keys from his pocket and placed them on top. Bartie was now up on the sofa again, watching Tom suspiciously from the corner of his eye.

"I suppose Sophia's still at her sister's?" she said, coldly.

Tom downed the scotch in one. "Yes...you see..." He turned to face her and took hold of her hands, which she realised with shame, were shaking slightly. "Sophia and I are separating."

"*What?*" she cried pulling her hands free of his. "After all this time, why?"

"I want to be with you, Meg." He smiled at her, his eyes softly watching her, waiting for her to say something.

Megan was dumbstruck. For five years she had waited to hear these words, these words that meant he was free to be hers at last. She had met Tom at the University of Kent, had fallen for him straight away, but had known he was married and so tried to keep her feelings hidden and their relationship on a professional level. However, as time had gone on, it became clear that he too felt more for her than perhaps a colleague should. On a faculty night out, after spending most of their night in their favourite pub in Canterbury with their colleagues, he had offered to walk her home – this was not unusual as they lived only a few streets apart, but this particular night, she sensed his mood was different.

Arriving at her house, he'd asked if he could come in and use the bathroom – he'd seemed a little awkward and embarrassed at having to ask, or so she thought at the time. Once inside and having been upstairs, he had walked into her kitchen, where she had just put the kettle on to boil, and stood looking at her.

"Coffee?" she'd asked, her heart in her throat.

"No, I'd better head off." He paused, watching her face carefully. "Oh, go on then."

Thrilled, she had pulled another mug out of the cupboard and put it on the side. As she went to take hold of the coffee pot he grabbed hold of her hand.

"Meg, wait..."

Turning round, she looked up at him, her heart quickened in her chest and she waited, breathless.

"I don't think I need to tell you how I feel about you...I have tried..."

Megan looked at him and felt her will weaken completely – she gave into his arms and they pulled each other close. This was where it had all begun – an emotional roller coaster ride of five years. She had wanted him to be hers all along, he kept promising that when the time was right, he would leave his wife, but there had always been excuses...

There had been previous splits, when Megan felt she could no longer take the deceit, the heartbreak or the thoughts of him with Sophia – she had no rights, she knew this, but she just couldn't keep away, loved him so much.

But now?

What now?

Here he was, telling her that he was now a free man...free to be hers.

Tom pulled her towards him. "Meg, don't you see, we can be together now – you could come back to Canterbury with me, Sophia and I are selling the house, we could sell this place and find something beautiful for us both back in Kent, perhaps by the coast; it's just what we wanted." He kissed her then and again she felt her resolve begin to weaken as it always did with Tom.

He was hers finally, hers and not Sophia's.

He pulled away gently, stroking her face, smiling; his face happy and relaxed.

"This is terrible timing but you must excuse me for minute, I need to use the bathroom; it's been a long drive. Don't go away."

"First door on the left, at the top of the stairs." She smiled at the irony and sat on the sofa to await his return. He had been gone only a few moments when his mobile vibrated on the coffee table in front of her. The interruption brought her out of her thoughts and she stared at it, feelings of suspicion rising in her. Instinctively she reached forward and looked at the screen.

It was a text message from Sophia. Megan felt herself grow rigid, she glanced back at the door to the hall and then back at the mobile. Tom had not yet flushed the toilet, she had a few moments...with shaking hands, she pressed the button to read the text, just couldn't help it:

> *Tried the house ur not home,*
> *phone me when u get this msg*
> *still miss u babe, be back in a few days*
> *ghastly hotel. keep the bed warm for me*
> *xxx*

Megan felt sick. How *stupid* she was, how could she have believed him *again*? What was she *thinking*? She didn't need him anymore, why didn't she just tell him that? She had a home (did she even want to move back to Kent?); had a new job too! The toilet flushed upstairs and hurriedly she replaced the phone on the coffee table as Tom descended the stairs; jumping up and away from the table she scowled at him. A large frown crossed his brow.

"I want you to *leave*, *now*, Tom."

"But I thought…"

"Yes, Tom, you did…but I have my own thoughts too. I have a lovely home here, a new job to start next week and I am beginning a new life…*without you*!" She pushed his belongings into his hands and went to the hall to get his coat off the peg.

"Goodbye, Tom…do not get in touch again; I will not respond to ANY of your calls or texts…"

"But Megan, please…"

"Goodbye…" she pushed him determinedly towards the door.

He looked at her and shook his head. "It could have been really good…"

"Yes, past tense *could* have…but you were never really mine to have, I should have known that!"

"I'm…"

"Save it!"

"Megan…"

"Tom, just piss off will you and leave me alone!" Traitorous tears started streaming down her face.

"I can't leave you like this!" he cried, his voice full of genuine anguish.

Giving him one last shove out of the door, she closed it quickly. She watched him turn and walk across the driveway to his car. He turned and took one last look at the house before climbing into the driver's seat and speeding away up the track towards the main road.

Megan, sobbing, walked slowly into the lounge and sat heavily down on the sofa. Bartie was there immediately, climbing onto her and sitting while her tears soaked into his soft, fluffy coat. "I've done the right thing, Bartie," she gulped. "I know I have, but it still hurts."

During the night, Megan awoke with a start. Bartie was sitting on the foot of her bed, a deep growl in his throat. She sat up and fumbled to switch on the bedside lamp, trying hard to focus her eyes in the same direction as where he was staring. She could hear and see nothing out of the ordinary, and wondered to start with if it was a mouse in the eaves of the house – a regular occurrence and one that sent Bartie mad with excitement – but this was more of a warning growl, not one of enthusiasm. Had Tom returned? She hoped not.

Bartie growled again and jumped off the bed, running onto the landing and then down the stairs. He was certainly acting strangely and Megan felt the fear start creeping through her. She heard him whimpering at the bottom of the stairs, probably by the front door. Grabbing her robe from the chair by the bed, she wrapped it around herself and went down the stairs quickly, thinking now he only wanted to go out.

What *was* unusual was that Bartie rarely went out of the front door, preferring to sniff around the back garden and do his business there. She switched on the outside light and opened the front door; a cold wind blew past her and Bartie went out like a bullet, barking as he went as if there was something to be chased. It was probably a badger or fox that had had the audacity to venture onto *his* territory. She closed the door with a little force, due to the strong wind that had obviously blown in that night since she had gone to bed. Feeling wide awake now, as she often did when awoken in the middle of the night, she decided to get herself a glass of water from the kitchen before she let Bartie back in.

Entering the kitchen, she left the light off, hoping that if the house remained as dark as possible she would fall back to sleep easily once back in bed; the light from the hallway was enough for her to see her way around. She let the tap run for a few moments so the water would be nice and cold; as she let the water run over her fingers, she looked up at the window and saw a reflection in the glass.

"Shit!" she cried, staggering backwards in terror...the glass she was holding slipped out of her hands and smashed in the stone sink. The woman, who stared back, was younger and had long, blonde hair unlike her own dark – the young woman, barely out of her teens, looked terrified almost to the point of insanity. Megan turned and glanced behind her then looked back at the window, still expecting to see the other face, but now only her own stared back at her in shock.

A knife-like fear coursed through her. Her heart thumped in her chest and she began to tremble all over. Megan moved further away from the window and bumped into a chair making her cry out again in fright. She stared and stared at the window, unable to look away, disbelief flooding through her.

"What...the...hell?" she breathed, sitting down on the chair to support her legs which had turned to jelly.

Who was that young woman? She knew for sure she hadn't imagined it. Her thoughts suddenly turned to Bartie he was still out there...still out there with...

Hurriedly, unable to make herself open the back door in case there was somebody out there, she made her way to the front door to let Bartie in. A few feet from the front door she stopped dead; there were small lumps of wet mud on the stone floor inside the door and on the door mat, as if they had fallen from somebody's boots. Tom certainly hadn't had mud on his shoes when he had come into the house, she would have made him take them off. Where had that come from? Had Bartie let himself in – had she left the door slightly ajar? She was sure she had shut it tightly because of the wind. Bartie must have come into the house, but where was he, why had he not come into the kitchen to find her?

"Bartie?" she called. There was no response from within the house – so he wasn't inside then. Trembling, she pulled the door open – another cold blast of air; this time filled with the scent of freshly disturbed earth.

"Bartie – come!" she commanded, her breath quick in her chest.

No response at all.

Her mouth went dry.

"Bartie, come *now*!" she shouted loudly against the cold, wild wind. She could hear the sounds of the night; the gusts amongst the willows by the river made them creak and groan.

"Bartie!"

A vixen cried eerily above the wind and she slammed the door shut and locked it quickly... Bartie could fend for himself.

She walked quickly back to the kitchen, this time turning on the light and not looking towards the window at all. She kept her head bent as she picked up the pieces of glass from the sink, trying hard not to cut herself as her hands were trembling so much. She had just put the final shards into the newspaper, which she was wrapping them in when there was a scratching at the back door. She tried to think that it was Bartie trying to get in, but her thoughts had turned slightly irrational now and she swung round, grabbed the iron frying pan from the Aga and quickly opened the door, pan raised ready for self-protection. A blast of cold wind, followed by the scent of damp earth and then: Bartie – wagging his tail ferociously and panting as if he had out-chased the wind, a slight insane look on his face, with the whites of his eyes exposed.

"Oh my *God,* Bartie – what the hell are you *doing*?" she shouted at him angrily, slamming the door, locking it securely and then hugging him nonetheless. "You scared the shit out of me!"

Bartie licked her face, his warm tongue slobbery but welcoming, almost knocking her off her feet as she was bent down to his level. He panted and she could feel his heart beating rapidly in his chest.

Megan filled herself another glass of water, still not daring to look up at the window. The wind outside continued to howl round the house, a real gale which did nothing for Megan's heart rate. She climbed the stairs again deciding to sweep the mud from the floor in the morning. Bartie was at her heels all the way up to the landing area, here he stopped, his tail as still as a pointer's who has spotted its prey, staring without blinking – straight at her bedroom door. A chill ran through her again and she looked towards the room. The light from the lamp gave a warm glow but she could see nothing from where she stood – just the smell of damp, again. Megan fought with herself, trying to be brave but feeling quite terrified inside; she took a deep breath and stomped loudly into her bedroom, singing at the top of her voice. Bartie looked confused and followed her, tail between his legs.

Inside the room it was as if nothing had been disturbed, everything seemed to be in its place – except...except...why was there mud on the floor here too? It *must* have been Bartie, he must have pushed his way in through the front door and up the stairs looking for her when she was in the kitchen; finding she was not there he probably went back outside and the door must have slammed shut in the wind behind him on his way out. But why had she not heard the door slam, and how could it with the wind in that direction? She shook her head. What the hell was going on? Glancing at her iPod docking station across the room, she hurried over and turned the music onto loud, she then turned to put the glass of water on the dressing table. She took the key from the jewellery box and unlocked the little drawer – the diary and brooch were safe. Ensuring that the drawer was tightly shut and locked before replacing the key in the wooden box, she climbed into bed. She lay there listening to Bartie's gentle snores from the foot of her bed and the music, which she had now turned down a little, for what seemed like ages. She couldn't quite believe what had happened. Had it perhaps been a trick of the light behind her that made it seem as if her own reflection was not her at all? Megan shivered and buried her head under the sheets and blankets of the bed, willing for sleep to come.

Chapter Six

Mildryth awoke with another headache. Where was she? What time of the day was it? Glancing around her, she tried to focus on what there was to see: the river was to her right, a small copse of trees to her left. She moved her head a bit more and the pain shot through it sharply. She realized she was by Eostre's temple and slowly began to remember her morning's activities, she had been to see the weaver to see if her new cloak had been ready to collect – it hadn't. She had then decided to visit her mother's grave and then go onto make an offering to Eostre, which explained why she was at the meeting of the two rivers. Mildryth couldn't remember the walk from her mother's grave to the river: had she passed out? Slept? She felt as if she had lost part of her day somewhere along the way – it must be to do with the headaches she kept having – perhaps she should go and see Lindi, she would give her a cure. Lindi's name sparked something in her thoughts, but it was so fleeting that she could not capture it before it fled her consciousness.

Mildryth thought back to the reason she had come to Eostre; she so wanted a child to follow quickly after her marriage to Wilheard – she needed a child to care for and love, a daughter perhaps to teach the ways of the world to, or a son – a miniature version of Wilheard who one day would become king like his father and grandfathers' before him. Something caught her eye not far from her and the copse of trees; a flicker of brown – a hare! A very good omen for fertility...perhaps Eostre had heard her prayers after all?

Mildryth went to stand and again felt faint and a little nauseous; the sick feeling was new, she hadn't had this before – she had to see Lindi, she would go on her way back through the village. Lindi would know what to do.

As she walked away from the river bank towards the village, she failed to notice the sun glinting on the brooch, half-hidden among the grasses, the talisman that Lindi had given her for protection.

Mildryth called out Lindi's name as she entered her hut; she was standing next to the fire stirring something in a large pot.

"Mildryth, back again so soon?"

Lindi barely glanced up at Mildryth as she entered. Was she unwelcome, or perhaps she had interrupted something?

"I had hoped you might be able to give me something for the pain I have in my head. I keep having headaches and feeling unsteady on my feet, I think I may have even passed out."

69

Lindi didn't speak for a few moments…the atmosphere seemed strained, normally the two women spoke easily to each other, but Mildryth felt that she *had* disturbed her.

"Is this a bad time, shall I come back?"

"No, no – sorry, things are not going as I had hoped they would today, that is all." Lindi still avoided her eyes.

"Anything I can do to help?"

Lindi shook her head. "How long have you had these headaches?"

"Since not long after mother died, but they seem to have got worse in the past few days."

"It could be to do with the grief you feel – you have lost two of the dearest people in your life." Lindi started picking up a few herbs and started mixing them together in a stone pot. "Mind you, you also have the forthcoming union to think about. Do you have much to do?"

"I am not that much involved in the organizing of the banquets or ceremony, but I have my robes and jewellery being made as we speak."

"How is the handsome Wilheard; have the brothers called a truce?"

The atmosphere seemed to clear a little; perhaps she'd imagined Lindi's coldness towards her. "Sadly not, I think Wilheard would like his brother to be one of his aides but he doesn't trust him enough to give him any main responsibilities."

Lindi shook her head. "Such a shame. If they were to work together they would make a formidable force, perhaps then have the strength and courage of their father."

"Hmmm. I try to stay out of it now – I have tried speaking to them, but both are stubborn."

"Have you seen Wulfric recently?"

"No …no, not for a few days." Although the mention of his name brought back fleeting thoughts that had eluded her earlier. "Why?"

"Is he coming to the marriage ceremony?"

"He's been invited…whether he'll come or not, I don't know."

"Mildryth, sit down," said Lindi pointing at a stool by the fire. "I want to try something."

Mildryth sat; Lindi placed her hands on her head. She felt the heat of Lindi's healing hands gently massaging her head either side of her skull – it felt good and she began to feel the tension melt away.

Suddenly, Lindi sharply pulled her hands away from Mildryth's hair. "Where's the brooch I gave you?"

Mildryth frowned. "It was there earlier." She glanced down at her cloak for the brooch; she had worn it every day without fail since Lindi had given it to her. She was certain she had put it on that morning. "I must have lost it, this morning…I'm really sorry, Lindi."

"How could you be so careless?"

Mildryth frowned at her viciousness. "I…I didn't mean to lose it, Lindi…I will pay you for it."

"That's not the point, it was there for your protection, Mildryth…how can I protect you from danger if you don't care about it yourself?"

"I do care…ouch!" A pain shot through her head again and Mildryth held her head in both hands, rubbing at the temples.

The anger in Lindi's face subsided and she became once again concerned. "Come here." Lindi gently pulled her head into her hands again and started to massage Mildryth's temples.

Mildryth felt the pain begin to recede, her thoughts started to relay the day to her bit by bit – Wilheard would be wondering where she was, she would tell him she had been to see Eostre and had made an offering; she would watch his face light up with excitement at the dreams she had of having his child; watch his eyes fill with tears of joy…his lovely blue eyes – but the eyes she was seeing were not blue, were not Wilheard's, they were grey like the eyes of a wolf….the eyes were close and watching her, full of desire and passion….she started and jumped up off the stool…crying aloud.

"What is it?" asked Lindi.

"I, um….sorry, it's just that I was having a…some thoughts…it doesn't make sense!"

"What thoughts?" Lindi was watching her closely.

"I, I'm not sure…" Why did her head feel so muddled, her thoughts jumbled and in disarray? She couldn't explain it to Lindi, had a sensation of shame, but had no idea why; guilt…why should she be feeling guilty? The sensation started to pass.

"Head still hurt?" Lindi asked her as she walked over to her shelf of phials and scooped something onto a spoon.

"Yes," she nodded, sighing.

"Take this." Lindi handed her a paste on the spoon.

Mildryth took it, its bitter taste was foul and she hoped it was worth it, hoped it would work. "That's revolting."

"But it's good and has long-lasting effects."

"Oh Lindi, I am so sorry about the brooch, I feel so bad about losing it and it was so special. I can't think what happened to it…it must have fallen off when I was walking along the river this morning."

71

"I will give you another one for protection...but it will take some time and may not be as powerful as the original. In the meantime, come and see me if you need more of that medicine."

"Lindi, you are so kind, thank you." Mildryth stood and embraced Lindi, she was surprised to feel that she was hard and cold like stone, but she returned the embrace.

Later, Mildryth retraced her steps back to the river and Eostre's temple – she had to try to find the brooch. Not only did she feel guilty about losing something that was clearly valuable, but it had been made especially for her own protection and with Aelle's murderer not yet captured, she could be very much in danger herself! She wandered slowly around the site of the temple and the nearby grasses, but she could not find the brooch. She then walked back to the burial ground. The brooch seemed to have completely vanished. Mildryth decided she must continue to search for it another day.

***

Back in her hut, Lindi seethed; angry and bitter – she knew that Wulfric had obviously lain with Mildryth and her memory was hazy because of the potion and the brooch – although now she had lost it, stupid girl! The memory of that afternoon with Wulfric would resurface at some point – what would Mildryth do then? Would she remember the passion with lust or loathing – would she seek Wulfric out for more? She hoped that now Wulfric had taken her he would be satisfied – perhaps now Lindi could start to woo him for herself. Another amulet would help with this – keep Mildryth's memories at bay, although a second one would not be as powerful as the first. It was not, as she had told Mildryth, a form of protection for her, more of a way to manipulate her. All the time Mildryth wore the brooch, she would be easy for Lindi to control – she must hurry in getting the other one ready. At long last, perhaps Wulfric would be hers – she had waited long enough.

***

Downhearted at not being able to recover the brooch, Mildryth walked back to the hall to find Wilheard; her head still feeling strange. Her thoughts seemed disjointed and her head was still a little muddled. She thought back to when Lindi had been massaging her head, those eyes...they were not Wilheard's. Why were those eyes looking at her with so much longing? Why did it seem so vivid, like a recent memory, rather than a dream? It must have been a dream while she had been sleeping by the river, after she had made her offering; perhaps she had lost the brooch there too? How could she be so irresponsible with something so precious? Lindi was clearly furious with her and she couldn't blame her – and what if the new brooch was not so strong in its protection – what then?

Wilheard was sitting in his chamber with two of his aides; he dismissed them both, then welcomed her warmly. "Where have you been, my love?" he asked, taking her in his embrace. It felt warm and protective, she felt herself physically relax even though her head was still pounding; she hoped the remedy would take effect soon. She smiled up at him and he kissed her forehead.

"I have been to make an offering to Eostre."

"Eostre? The goddess of fertility?" His eyes lit up.

"Yes – I want to give you a baby, Wilheard – wouldn't it be wonderful if I gave you a son, or daughter, conceived on our wedding night?"

"It would be the best gift that any man could wish for. The gods will surely bless us; there is the full moon on the night of our union too!" He kissed her gently on the mouth, the usual warmth and familiarity washed over her, but something didn't feel right, something was missing, felt strange, but she couldn't fathom what. She looked up into his eyes.

"Your colour is very pale, are you sick?"

"I still keep having headaches. I went to see Lindi and she has given me something to help, she is also going to give me something else."

Wilheard looked at her curiously. She hadn't told him about the brooch, didn't want to worry him further. She explained now, about the one she'd lost too.

"I'm going to see her tomorrow and she's going to give me another talisman, she is concerned that there are dark forces working against us, and she wants me to wear it for protection."

"Anything to keep you safe." He held her close. "I will ensure that no harm comes to you, I promise. She thinks that the headaches are related to someone trying to hurt you?"

"Possibly, she thinks that perhaps another sorceress or darker power is trying to reach me, cause me pain, or worse. Although I think it may be because of the forthcoming union."

"You are worried about being my wife?" He pushed her away gently, so he could see her face, look into her eyes.

"No, no – it's the responsibility of being queen perhaps that is concerning me."

73

"But you will make a wonderful queen and I will be your king, to help guide and protect you. You are a strong and intelligent woman, Mildryth; many women would not have the courage and strength that you have to call upon to do your duties as queen."

"Thank you." She smiled up at Wilheard's handsome face, then embraced him, holding him hard against herself.

"I want you to rest before dinner, go and have a sleep." He touched her cheek tenderly.

"I am not tired."

"Then at least lie down and rest...please?" he insisted.

She nodded and bade him farewell.

On returning to her home, she found her father and brother out. Hamia was making bread and Mildryth went to her bedchamber where she lay down on her bed amongst the animal skins. She closed her eyes and rubbed her temples, trying to ease the pain in her head, but was not sleepy, or tired, more heavy and her mind unclear. She had felt this way for most of the day, as if she was still half asleep; still in a dream world where things didn't seem to have the same clarity as in the daylight hours when one was wide awake. Her eyes felt heavy, as did her limbs but she did not feel particularly drowsy. She thought back to the river and her offering to Eostre. Wilheard had been as excited as she had hoped he would be, and of course there had been the hare – another good omen. She wondered what it would be really like to hold her own baby in her arms; friends and her sister, Sunniva, had babies which she had held, but it must feel different if it was your own. She had heard some horrific tales about giving birth too, that she wished she hadn't, and a close cousin of hers had died last year in childbirth, just two years older than she was herself. She shivered; she must ensure she kept the gods happy.

***

The following morning, Megan awoke with a splitting headache and tired, gritty eyes. She took a shower, trying to enliven herself. Once dressed, she went downstairs and, after letting Bartie into the garden, sat at the old scrubbed wooden table, pondering on the events of the previous evening, a strong, steaming coffee in hand. Firstly, there had been Tom, she had almost, *almost* relented, given in to him again. She vowed once more not to let him back into her life, but this time she had reached the precipice, there was no going back now, as she had said to him last night, she had a lovely home; a new job to look forward to; she had the opportunity to start her life anew and she was going to grab this firmly with both hands. He was history, in the past, there was to be no looking back anymore.

Then, there were the strange night events, she wondered now if she had imagined or dreamt them. She stood and went towards the dustbin, yes, there was the newspaper with the broken glass inside...she then went out into the hall, carrying her warm cup of coffee with her...no, no mud on the floor...strange – she didn't remember clearing it up. Finally, she went back to the kitchen, slipped on her boots and coat and went outside. The wind had died down and the sky was bright blue, the sun shining brightly with a promise of spring days to come; the wind had brought down small branches and twigs from the trees which were scattered about the garden. Bartie came bounding towards her, tail wagging; she patted him on the head and walked towards the kitchen window. If there had been somebody standing at the window last night perhaps there would be footprints beneath it. She looked down at the soft soil where some daffodils were sprouting up through the earth – no footprints – no damage to the plants. Maybe she had imagined the face at the window, or perhaps because it was quite dark in the kitchen it had been her own reflection, after all. The lack of light may have made her own hair seem lighter somehow, but had she really looked that terrified and concerned? In the light of the day she didn't feel as afraid as she had last night, she had rationalised some of the events and now wanted to forget about them.

Back inside the house she telephoned Sasha.

"Hi, I wondered if you fancied meeting for lunch?" she asked Sasha, already noting, by the noise, the hands-free sound of her mobile in the car.

"Hello, Megan. I'm sorry, I'm in Bristol all day at a boring conference," she replied.

"Oh, not to worry, another..." But the phone went dead, obviously another black spot for mobile reception. At this point, Megan decided to go into the town and buy some groceries and much-needed supplies, she really had to keep busy to stop herself from thinking too much.

A while later, arriving back at the cottage, she made herself a cheese sandwich; collected Bartie and strode out of the house towards the bridge that would take her across the canal and off the little island, formed by the joining of two rivers, where her gran's cottage and the Roundhouse stood. It was still bitterly cold, but the sun was shining. She felt like taking a slightly different route today and headed upstream towards the next village, which was about a mile away – it could barely be called a village really, because it was pretty much deserted – except for a few close inhabitants: the manor house; a farm; the vicarage; two farmhand cottages and a minute church.

Megan's mood did not alter much as she walked along the riverbank; it was good to be outside and the sunshine was lovely, nevertheless, with all the recent events and the strange happenings at her gran's cottage, she felt low. Loneliness weighed down on her and she wished that Sasha had been around...perhaps she could have opened up and told her about Tom; talked about the face at the window. Unfortunately, this would probably have Sasha running in the opposite direction, away from the mad woman who'd moved into the area!

A terrible abyss now replaced her gran; she missed her dreadfully! The cottage, although it still felt as welcoming as it always did, was missing something, not just her gran, but its spirit; it was as if it too were in mourning – perhaps that was why there had been that sense of bitter cold in the house last night? As for the woman at the window...purposely she moved her thoughts away from the memories of the previous night...she just couldn't comprehend them, and for now, did not have the energy to try too hard to do so.

As she approached the squat, ancient church across the field, which was waterlogged from recent rain, she frowned up at the blackening sky. Although cold, it had been bright sunshine when she had left home, with alluring blue skies scattered with white clouds. However, just upon the horizon, the sky ahead of her was bruised black and purple as if a storm was approaching. She tightened her scarf around her neck to keep the chilled wind from seeping into her warm neck and back, she hated to be cold; loved the spring, but hated not being suitably dressed when the weather turned bad.

Her gran said the church had always been locked...hadn't been a service there in years, decades...even as a young and curious child she had always found the heavy oak door locked against her, an unwelcoming pile of old stones and graves.

Bartie, filthy and drenched from the river – his spaniel curls enviously like nothing she could ever create with her own dark hair – was enjoying the walk. Today, though, he hardly left her side, deciding instead to patter along just ahead or behind her with the occasional paddle in the river.

Megan's coat was not waterproof. She wished she had put on her gran's wax coat. She had thought of doing so, as she'd pulled on her own when leaving the house, but had decided against it. She had considered that it might comfort her and then decided it was perhaps a little too weird. As she approached the church she could see the twin bells and wondered when had been the last time they had rung. It seemed an odd place to have a church, the middle of nowhere – the only other dwellings seemed deserted, perhaps everyone was at work? The church's ancient stonework drew her closer, as did the gravestones and tombs, so few...but people who had once lived nearby with families and friends nonetheless.

She called Bartie to heel, as he'd now wandered off a little way ahead; feeling that his walking all over the graves was somehow disrespectful. She read some of the graves' inscriptions; one in particular touched her...a young woman of twenty-five had died in November....to be followed only eleven weeks later by her child. A young mother dying in childbirth...followed only weeks by that same child...Megan imagined a young man...stricken with grief at his tragic loss. *Life can be so cruel*, she thought to herself. Even in that time, when infant mortality and death in childbirth were much more the norm, it would still have been tragic and unbearable for those whom it affected.

The rain started then, all of a sudden; it had gone almost as dark as night and the rain came down in sheets. She ran to the porch door and pushed it gently, expecting it to be shut fast against her – it moved...ever so slightly...she pushed again, harder this time, it opened. She felt like a guilty intruder, she wasn't religious, but she did need shelter: surely God wouldn't mind? Bartie followed her in; a light bulb (energy efficient, she was surprised to see) sprang slowly into life, giving off a dull, yellow glow. The smell of ancient, damp stone infused her nostrils – oddly bringing back to her the same scent as in the cottage. Bartie also found this scent exciting, his nose immediately sniffed the crumbling stone beneath them. As her eyes became accustomed to the light she saw a notice:

PLEASE COME AND BROWSE ROUND OUR ANCIENT CHURCH. Minimum donation £1. Churches Renovation Trust

Unfortunately, Megan didn't have any money on her, but she promised to bring it another day. To her delight, when she pushed it hard, the inner door opened too, and allowed her to enter. The interior took her breath away. Its antiquity, simplicity and sense of peace enveloped her completely. She sighed deeply; this was truly a sacred place, not just in its Christianity she felt but long, long before that new religion had found its way to British shores. Her eyes feasted on the faded frescoes, nothing like the intricate ones she had seen in her travels to Italy, but amazing all the same. Mostly text and some symbols had once brightly adorned these walls; faded remnants of these were still obvious. To her left and right, all round the tiny church, were boxed pews, some larger than others, probably depicting the past of larger boxes for the gentry; small for the peasants. The church's congregation could never have been large. The wooden arches and rails were modestly carved with flowers. Megan wondered who had carved them, how long had it taken, was he well paid, or did he do it for his love of God? The small pulpit and font made her smile, thinking that the church was just a miniscule replica of the many other enormous churches and cathedrals she had visited on her travels abroad and in Britain.

As she approached the altar with its simple wooden cross she had a sudden urge to pray. This feeling astonished her, she shook her head physically at the ridiculousness of it; she never prayed, not to this Christian God...or any particular god...she had her beliefs, but they would surely be more commonly known as Pagan by some. Nevertheless, she felt the urge to kneel at this ancient altar; she didn't put her hands together, feeling as if that was taking it a step too far – perhaps it was the recent events; the peace and quiet of the church, or some other, unseen force that made her fall slowly to her knees. She bent her head and found herself asking for peace for her gran, hoping that she was happy. She then found herself asking for some inner peace for herself...something to take away the anguish.

From the porch Bartie growled...

Megan was instantly alert; was somebody coming? She stood, looking up at the window above her, and as she did, she saw a face pass by outside. Bartie's hackles rose and the deep guttural growl made Megan's own neck hair rise...the door opened from the porch into the church and a man stood there, shaking off the rain. His hood was up and he looked soaked; just another person taking shelter from the rain? No, she recognised the shape and, more so, the dog that he had at his heels.

The traveller.

Taking down his hood, he smiled at her. "Did I make yer jump? I was just takin' shelter."

She tentatively returned his smile, but her body grew tense.

"Sorry, am I interrupting your prayers?" he asked.

She laughed and shook her head. "I came in for shelter too."

"Ah, I see. I'm not a man of God either, do yer think he would mind?" he asked, raising his eyes heavenward.

"Hopefully not, rather unchristian of him if he did..."

The man smiled and came towards her.

Megan looked at his grey eyes, as they lit with his smile, and again felt the familiarity of them.

"Didn't I see yer somewhere before?" he asked.

"Our dogs were making friends near your caravan..."

"Oh yes, so they were."

"I was thinking that you looked familiar too, but not from the other day...were you around here as a child? It's just I remember the caravans arriving in convoy when I was young – wondered if you might have been amongst them."

"I did, most summers in fact, with me family...they don't come so much now – just a few of us, only me this year, I think. We're not welcome, but I love this place. It draws me back year on year. It's a special place, don't yer fink?"

"I do, I love this place, always have done..."

He glanced out of the door. "It's eased a bit; I'll be off...be seein' yer." He nodded at her and as quickly as he had arrived, he turned and left.

Megan was unsure of him, he seemed friendly enough, was really good-looking too in a rugged sort of way, but somehow he made her uneasy; funny how you can just hit it off immediately with some people, such as Sasha and then others you were more wary of – instinct she told herself, it must be to do with instinct.

Looking out of the church door she could see that it was only raining very lightly now – she was in no great rush though, she would wait a while longer and sit and enjoy the peace and quiet; that was until Bartie got bored and started to whine, wanting to go out into the fields – he didn't care that it was raining.

After a while, she walked back across the fields towards home. It was strange, but lovely, that her gran's home was now her home. A place which had been a second home to her all her life was now hers. She looked at the Cotswold stone cottage in the distance, its stone walls grey in the dull daylight. On brighter days the stone shone golden in the sunlight, giving the cottage a more welcoming glow.

Megan thought again of her gran's diary and wondered if perhaps she should read some more of it that afternoon. She was curious to find out what her gran had been like as a younger woman, what her private thoughts had been; was it wrong to want to do this? *Surely* her gran would have got rid of them had she been worried about her finding them after she'd gone.

Later on, sitting on her bed, Bartie at her feet, Megan opened her gran's diary once more.

The diary was not filled in daily but sporadically throughout the year. Megan wondered why the diary was locked away in the dressing table drawer – perhaps her gran had it locked away from prying eyes...the sense of intrusion returned...or could it possibly be that her gran had *wanted* her to find it.

May 10th 1979

I met with Frank again today. I think Robert is beginning to suspect something is wrong. The more time I spend with Frank the more I realise he's a kindred spirit; we have so little in common in some respects but so much in others. I told him about the hare and how each time I see it, shortly afterwards I see the woman.

Megan read on:

May 21st 1979

The woman appeared again today, she seems afraid and desperate – I cannot fathom who she is but she keeps appearing in the garden and on the banks of the river.

My thoughts are constantly filled with Frank, it's almost as if he has possessed my mind. Whatever I'm doing, he fills my thoughts, dreams – I am in love with him.

May 23rd 1979

Robert caught us talking together today by the river, he is angry. He hasn't challenged me about it, but says I should not talk to vermin. He is so narrow-minded, just because these travellers are different to us.

June 1st 1979

I dreamt of the woman last night – she is now invading my sleep. This time she led me near to the river. I do not understand what it is she requires of me – did something happen at the river, did somebody she know drown? I feel my life and emotions are getting out of control – something will give soon, I fear.

Megan realised she was holding her breath. Her gran was going through emotional turmoil just as she was now, was this relevant to whoever the woman was that kept appearing? How on earth was she influencing her gran's dreams...it didn't make any sense. A thought crept slowly into Megan's mind, the woman, the one her gran had seen...could she be the same one she'd seen herself, last night at the window – but that was decades ago. Did that really mean she was a ghost?

Megan read on, eager to find out more about the woman.

June 15th 1979

Horror of horrors! Robert caught me kissing Frank. He must have followed me down the track towards the town. I had told him I was going to the Post Office, which was true…however, he walked straight past Frank and I as if we didn't even know each other. I went straight home, promising Frank I would find him later and let him know I was all right. Robert was gone most of the day; I've no idea where – he told me he was 'out walking'. He has called me all the names under the sun – some perhaps justified, but he doesn't see how he is at all to blame as well – all the years I've been a good, devoted wife, whereas his bullying nature and unaffectionate ways have driven us apart.

June 18th 1979

We are getting divorced.

June 19th 1979

Robert has moved out. I am so sad that it has come to this…even though I love Frank, Robert is the father of our daughter. We were happy once – what will people say? Do I really care?

Megan could feel the anguish coming in waves off the pages of her gran's diary. Poor Gran – she knew herself what it was like to love the wrong person. Frustratingly there were no more entries in the diary – it was as if she had stopped writing when Robert and her gran had parted…unless there were more diaries in the attic yet undiscovered? Disappointingly, the woman hadn't had another mention.

Chapter Seven

Tuesday morning, the first day of her new job, dawned bright and sunny. Megan knew the wind would be cold, how it whipped across the valley, so she dressed warmly. She was very excited and ever so slightly apprehensive due to having to meet a whole new team. How well would they all work together? What would the students be like, know-it-all lazy good for nothings, or hopefully, keen to learn and eager to get stuck in? She wondered what Dr Edwards would be like too, he would be the one she would be working most closely with; she would be taking her orders from him in the absence of David. Hopefully he would be reasonably laid-back and not too intense like some of her colleagues in the past.

Megan had received an email from David the previous day; they were all meeting at eight-thirty at the pub by the river in order to have a 'hearty breakfast' on their first day and discuss their plan of action.

Megan walked into the pub at eight o'clock, expecting and hoping to be the first to arrive. She walked to the bar and told the barman she was with the archaeological dig team, then asked if she could have a coffee while she waited for the others.

"Ah, there's another of your chaps over there already." He pointed towards a table, where a man sat, by the fire at the far side of the room; although it was early, the fire had been lit and was roaring away nicely in the grate. "Take a seat and I'll bring your coffee over to you."

"Oh..em...thank you." She hesitated, so she wasn't the first to arrive then? She wondered who she would find at the table, she didn't know anyone...unless it was David of course. As she took a closer look at the seated man, she was astonished to see it was the same guy from the barge whom Bartie had mugged for his bacon the previous morning.

"Are you sure he's with the dig?" she asked.

"Sure, said exactly the same thing you did when he came in." The man walked off into the kitchen leaving Megan staring at the man at the table...unsure of what to say to him and feeling her cheeks grow warm as she remembered Bartie's antics the day before. She sighed, took a deep breath and walked over to the table.

"Hi," she said.

The man looked up, then smiled; surprise evident in his eyes. "It's the lady with the mad spaniel!"

Megan felt herself go red. "The very one...em...the man at the bar said you're with the archaeological dig that starts today – is that right?"

"Depends, are you press?" A slight smile curved at the corners of his mouth.

"No, as a matter of fact, I'm working on it too. Professor David Peters employed me just a few days ago...somebody let him down last minute and I'm the replacement."

"Then you must be, Megan," he said, extending his hand and standing up, smiling again. I had no idea when I met you yesterday! What a small world we live in. I'm Dr Finlay Edwards, assistant director to the dig."

"Oh," she laughed nervously holding out her hand and shaking his, he had a firm, confident grip. "That was a great first impression then?"

He laughed loudly, his blue eyes twinkling. "It's fine...I love dogs, we had spaniels when we were children, in fact my mother and father still have one, he is about fifteen and deaf, but still has the occasional mad moment. Please...sit down. Have you ordered?"

She nodded and took a seat.

"Great. The others should all start to arrive soon."

"Do you know them well?"

"Some. The student volunteers I don't know so well, although I do lecture some of them."

"Yes, I won't miss that for a while."

"David tells me that you are rather over-qualified for the job, but you'd like to get your hands dirty again?"

"Yes." Megan smiled but didn't want to elaborate.

He didn't press her and subtly changed the subject; she was surprised at his perceptiveness.

"You didn't bring Bartie with you this morning then?"

"No, I thought he might be a bit too excitable for the first morning; I might bring him out certain days – a nearby neighbour has said she would walk him for me this morning; I don't think she knows what she's let herself in for."

There was a moment of silence but it was not uncomfortable or awkward. The barman arrived with her coffee and Megan, enjoying the strong aroma, took a tentative sip of the steaming liquid.

"Do you live on the barge permanently?" she asked.

"I do, it is my home...for now..."

"Is it not totally miserable during the winter – the cold and damp?"

"Not at all, in fact that can sometimes be the best time. It is so much quieter on the river than in the summer and with the log burning stove and central heating it is very cosy in the winter. Have you never been on a barge?"

84

"No. It's something I have talked about doing, perhaps having a week on the Broads or somewhere but never got round to it – you know what it is like...."

"I think lots of people have great intentions of doing things they want to, but other things tend to get in the way...with me it's always work, although I do try to do the things I really want to do."

Voices permeated the quiet bar from the doorway; three young people had arrived and were looking around the room anxiously. They looked enquiringly at Megan and Fin's table. One of them, a very attractive young female, smiled at him and started walking towards their table.

"Dr Edwards, we're not late, are we?" she asked, plonking herself in the seat next to him.

"No, Bella you're bang on time...Megan, this is Bella, Stuart and Oscar, our PhD volunteers."

"Guys this is Dr Megan Shearer; she is helping out with the dig – she is highly qualified and you can go to her for advice. However, she *is* going to want to get her hands dirty too so don't pester her too much if David or I are around."

Bella gave Megan an odd look. Bella was in her early twenties, fairly attractive and obviously out to get her hands on her lecturer – Megan felt that immediately.

"Cool," she said and then started to talk to Fin, turning her back on Megan, quite rudely she thought. Megan turned and started to talk to Oscar and Stuart; she asked them about their experience and current studies. A few moments later another group of voices entered the pub, followed by a group of slightly older people and headed by David.

"The cavalry have arrived," said Oscar.

"Excellent, perhaps we can get started," said Fin. "I'm really enthusiastic about this site," he directed this comment at Megan. "I'm not sure we'll find much, but I have a good feeling about it, it's about time we found an important site – it's been a while."

Introductions were made and Megan tried hard to remember the peoples' names and what they meant for the dig. Eager chatter surrounded her as she drank her coffee, she felt very much on the outside of things – she knew no-one particularly well and the group seemed to gel very well together. David was obviously very much admired by his colleagues and students alike; he was clearly in his element. Likewise, Fin was animatedly joining in the conversations. She took a deep breath...she knew from experience that it was only the first day and that soon enough she would feel very much part of the same team.

After a while David clapped his hands together and everyone fell silent. "Right guys, we need to make a start before we blow the budget completely on tea, coffee and bacon butties."

Everyone laughed except Bella who scowled at him beneath heavily layered eyelashes. Megan wondered if she was always this brooding.

David continued. "I want everyone on site and ready to start at ten this morning and nine o'clock from tomorrow. We will meet here every morning at eight o'clock for a team meeting for plans for the day – please try to be on time!"

They all filed slowly out of the pub, continuing their conversations, eager to start, but not so eager to go out in to the cold morning.

"Are you walking down to the site or driving?" Fin asked her as they walked across the car park.

"I'm walking – sorry I can't offer you a lift…"

"You can both come with me if you like," said Oscar. "If you don't mind an old banger."

"Not at all," replied Fin.

They got into Oscar's 'old banger' which turned out to be a very old Morris Minor. "Belonged to my gran, bless her – thought she was doing me a favour by letting me have her car rather than buying one; haven't told her that it's cost Dad more to repair than it would have been to buy a newer, second-hand one."

Fin laughed. "I had an old banger for years too – an old VW Beetle – but I bought it myself – it was great fun but cost me so much money!"

"An old Morris is not really a good car for pulling the girls, but I have become strangely attached to her." He said stroking her steering wheel and grinning mischievously.

"I suppose it depends on the type of girl you're trying to pull," Fin turned to Megan and winked. His smile was so devastatingly handsome; no wonder Bella had the hots for him.

They drove round the narrow country lanes at the back of the town to where the site was. It had been arranged by the local farmer that the dig workers could park in his yard a little way away from the site as it would have been too dangerous to park at the side of the road; they were far too narrow and winding.

Fin explained to Oscar and Megan that the site was going to be developed for local housing for the elderly and local authority needs, but before they could do that the site had to be investigated due to it being a Scheduled Ancient Monument. English Heritage had been consulted and it was agreed that the council had to fund the

86

archaeological dig to investigate the site. Early investigations had pointed to the fact that this was no ordinary green field site that they wanted to develop. Aerial photographs of the site showed dark shadows which may have been Roman buildings and a Roman Cursus. It was also believed that they might find some prehistoric material.

The investigations and exploration of the site made a slow start – the geophys guys had found some interesting results, different shapes of things hidden beneath the field. Annoyingly, the JCBs that had been organised had let them down, so they promised to arrive first thing in the morning – some misunderstanding in the admin department which David was furious about.

At lunchtime, they met back at the pub for sandwiches and cakes. They discussed the morning's finds but no more really came to light than they already knew; a very disappointing beginning for them all.

During lunch Megan received a text from Sasha inviting her for a drink at the Oak; saying she was curious to discover how her first day had gone.

Megan was pleased and replied that she would meet her at 5.30pm – Bartie was being walked by a neighbour about 3pm, so he would be fine.

"Bit of a disappointing start," said Fin. "I had hoped we'd have some trenches dug by now."

"Bloody contractors," grumbled David, taking a large bite from his sandwich.

"At least they've agreed to start earlier in the morning, so by this time tomorrow we should have made a better start," said Megan brightly, trying to lift the bad mood that had descended upon the two men.

"I think I might head back to Oxford after lunch, mark some essays. You ok to stay on here and help with geophysics, Fin...you too Megan?"

"Sure," said Megan.

"Of course," said Fin.

Later that afternoon, Megan noticed the woman as soon as she stepped into the pub; one couldn't fail to miss her. She had dead-straight blonde hair to her waist, which she almost definitely coloured due to the whiteness of it. She flung her head back in laughter, the hair followed like a shadow as did the eyes of a few men; all captivated by her. As she turned to face Megan she noticed the crystal blue eyes above a large, straight nose and a bust many women would pay thousands of pounds for...perhaps she had? However, Bartie's hackles rose as the woman let out another laugh and looked straight at Megan, a look Megan felt said, "*What are you doing in* my *pub?*" Not a particularly pretty woman, but one who openly flirted with the men, making them imagine they stood a chance with her.

Megan headed to the bar where she ordered a white wine. She felt the continuous stare of the blonde follow her...*what* was her problem, did she want to be the only female in the pub; perhaps ensuring the chance of somebody taking her home for the night? Well, she was welcome to them all, Megan wasn't interested in men right now! The lad behind the bar smiled at her warmly handing her a glass of white wine which had condensation around the bulb of the glass, making her thirst all the more for the well-earned cool drink.

It was busy in the pub with many locals and a few tourists having a meal. She recognised a few faces, especially the one tucked away in the corner, sitting alone, scowling at the men that crowded around the blonde; at his feet, with a sad expression, sat his dog.

The traveller again.

Megan was surprised at how many times he had been in the same vicinity as she had been the past few days. It must just be coincidence. Although...suddenly springing to mind, was the man's figure amongst the trees, in the darkness, the other night! He looked up and his grey eyes fell upon her, held her gaze. She felt the same familiarity that she had previously felt, but her cheeks started to redden, was it fear or attraction? She didn't know; she headed quickly to the window seat at the opposite side of the room.

Settling down on the window seat she could still just see down the road towards the river where a few people were heading for an evening walk; it was far too early in the year for any swimming or jumping off the bridge to be done. Now, the sun was about to disappear beyond the horizon and darkness gathered in the distance. Her gran had told her how they used to have a diving competition next to the bridge with a diving board a few feet off the ground – she was sure the river was not deep enough now! She took a long, slow taste of her wine, enjoying the cold, dry liquid slide down her parched throat to her stomach. Now, Bartie, with his long brown ears spread over his front paws, sat at her feet. Megan had been overjoyed when Mrs Clark had brought him along to the site to meet her at the end of the day (Megan thought it was probably Mrs Clark being curious about what was going on).

Megan returned to her book, *The Picture of Dorian Grey* while she waited for Sasha to arrive. It was a book she had read many years ago while at university and in recent years there had been a film made of it – as always though she had thought that the film did not do the book justice; she had argued about this with Tom and had then found a copy, her copy, at her gran's and decided to re-read it, just to make sure she had been right. She had to believe she did some things right where he was concerned. She had been thrilled, so far, to realise that her feelings towards the book had remained the same. Occasionally, having read a book, years before, and then reading it again her perspective of it had changed, sometimes dramatically; mostly dependent on her own life experiences.

The door opening interrupted her thoughts; a man walked in, she had been expecting Sasha now for the past ten minutes...she must have been held up. Just then her phone vibrated on the table, a text:

> *Sorry, Megan. Been to see client,*
> *car broken down. Brad to the rescue.*
> *See you another day. Sorry again!*

Megan felt the disappointment much more sharply than she had realised she might, she really was ultra-sensitive at the moment – ah well; she would have her drink and then walk home for some dinner and perhaps make the phone call to her mother she had been avoiding.

After a while, the atmosphere of the pub began to sink into the background: peoples' voices and laughter; the smell of food being cooked – Bartie's light snores; so when a shadow fell across her, it took her a moment to realise somebody was standing next to her. It was Bartie's slight growl that caught her attention and she looked up and into the familiar grey eyes of the traveller.

"Can I buy yer a drink?" he asked. "Yer glass seems to be empty, we can't have that!"

She faltered. If she refused it would seem very rude and her glass was empty so she could not use that as an excuse. "I...er...well, yes, thank you. White wine, dry...please."

Watching him walk to the bar, his broad shoulders (apparent even beneath the thick, wool sweater he was wearing) and confident air, she felt that same feeling of unease. What was it about him? Was it attraction – it certainly felt like it, but her intuition screamed that she should be wary of him. She did not need or *want* another man right now, but the physical attraction was fierce.

He returned with a glass of wine for her and a pint of beer, for himself. As he sat opposite her, he eyed her closely – it felt like he was searching for something within her eyes. She turned away with the pretence that Bartie needed her attention and adjusted his collar.

"You live round here then, I keep bumpin' into yer."

"I do now…I spent a lot of time here as a child. My gran owned the Roundhouse and cottage by the Thames."

"Owned. Past tense."

"Er, yes, she died fairly recently and I, fortunately, inherited it."
Damn, should she really have told him where she lived?

"You believe in Fortune then, not God, although yer used his house for refuge?"

Megan frowned. "Yes, more Fate than God…but I also think it's about choices we make…the paths we take."

"My gran could tell your fortune if you like," he stated, matter of fact. "Actually so could Bridget…" He nodded towards the blonde. As if hearing her name, she stared across the room at him – her expression unreadable.

"You know her?"

He nodded, but did not elaborate.

"I don't think I want my future read. My gran had hers done a few times, perhaps even by your gran if she used to come here in the Seventies…although if I did have mine read I suppose it might stop me from making stupid mistakes."

He laughed. "You've made some then?"

"Hasn't everyone?" She smiled at his more friendly air.

His eyes held hers for a moment. His eyes were grey, but stark, the feeling of unease returned. She realised that she didn't even know his name; to break the silence she asked him.

"Kai," he told her.

"Megan," she replied, taking his offered hand in hers, but almost immediately snatched it away, the electrical current was severe; he let go of her hand casually, too casually, as though he had perhaps felt something too, but was trying to hide it - she couldn't be sure.

"Mr Garrett hasn't thrown you off his land yet then?"

He smiled and his eyes sparkled mischievously.

"What is it?"

"I thought the land was yours…."

"Oh, so you thought you might butter me up by buying me a drink?"

He didn't reply, but carried on smiling.

"Old Garrett obviously hasn't spotted you yet, but he will when he's next down the lane that way – he quite often goes out to the main road via the other route."

"Thanks for the warning."

"Hey, Kai, who's your friend?" The blonde was standing over them, glaring with ice-blue eyes at the pair of them.

"Bridge, this is Megan."

"You're a new face here, Megan," she stated accusingly.

"Not really," she replied.

"I'm....Kai and I have been really close friends for years...I could tell you a thing or two about him." She winked at Megan and gave Kai an extremely curious glance.

Megan felt that she was trying to set up some type of female comradeship between them against Kai, but her instincts again told her to be cautious of the woman too. Kai seemed completely oblivious and Megan did not feel that she wanted to encourage conversation with this woman who had glared at her since she had entered the pub – as if sensing this, Bridget flounced away in an ungraceful manner.

Kai's mood shifted. "She finks she knows everything about me, but she don't."

Megan sipped her wine and nodded. "I know somebody like that."

Kai raised his eyebrows. He then downed his drink quickly and stood up. Megan assumed that he was about to leave, realising that he had made a mistake in offering her a drink...she wasn't the landowner after all...she didn't need to be softened up.

"Thank you for the drink," she said.

"You're welcome...I'm walking back to me van; are yer going that way...or are yer staying awhile?"

She looked at her drink, which she had almost finished too...the wine had started to go to her head...perhaps she should leave it at that and walk home...but did she want to go with Kai? He was rather odd – friendly one minute, distant the next. As if to answer for her, Bartie got up and wagged his tail; in an instant Angus, who had been asleep by the bar, trotted over to them. The dogs greeted each other happily.

"I guess that answers that, Bartie seems ready to go, probably wants his tea," she laughed.

He smiled at that and his grey eyes lit up, making his face more handsome and personality warmer. She relaxed a little at that moment but it didn't last due to the look and laughter she heard as they left the pub together. The laughter was not altogether humorous and not in the least bit friendly – she didn't dare look at Bridget, knowing those ice-cold eyes would be boring straight into her.

Kai and Megan walked down the main street, out of the town, towards the surrounding countryside and the lane that would take them towards the Roundhouse and Kai's van. They strolled along together in the twilight with dogs on leads, due to the traffic along the main road. When they reached the lane to the Roundhouse the dogs were given a free rein, and they sped off at high speed, barking and chasing each other.

91

"I remember some travellers coming here when I was a child they used to stay in the fields by the river. I used to love watching them run and swim in the Thames...I always wanted to join them."

"What stopped you?"

"Childish fear."

"Of what?" he frowned and looked her straight in the eye.

She faltered. "Of...of intruding, they seemed to be so happy, so free. I felt that they were so different to me. "

"We're free to a point...however it ain't just about runnin' and swimmin'. Sometimes we 'ave to do a lot of runnin', usually away from someone we've upset. It can be real 'ard on the road, 'specially in winter. Imagine the coldest, bleakest nights when yer tucked up in yer 'ouse, we are in vans; not that I'd want the tie of an 'ouse – I like to roam, be free...please meself. They can be warm, but that cold seeps into yer bones during the early hours and it takes a long time to get warm again. Not so bad if you 'ave someone with yer to keep yer warm, but I'm alone, now...and prefer it that way."

Was he warning her off? It was the first inkling that she'd had of him not showing an interest in her, perhaps he had only been trying to butter her up as he had thought it was *her* land he was on. When they reached his van she bade a casual goodbye without breaking stride, not wanting to encourage him in anyway despite the conflicting evidence. She could feel the intensity of his gaze following her until she turned the corner, not daring to look back.

Megan was confused and bewildered by the two travellers; she assumed that Bridget was one too, perhaps wrongly? Looking back on the strange events since leaving work that day, Megan realised how much Bridget had unnerved and upset her. *What* was her problem? She had never met the woman before, never said anything to upset her and yet the feeling of animosity she had perceived from her was acute.

Megan could only put it down to jealousy – perhaps Bridget and Kai had been in a relationship in the past (there certainly was some history between them) and it had ended, or Bridget didn't like him talking to other women; maybe it was a case of unrequited love – she shrugged and called to Bartie as she made her way up the path to the cottage...she had enough to worry about already without playing games with some immature woman. She decided she would have some dinner and then phone her mother as she had promised, then perhaps she would call Sasha and rearrange a drink, or invite her for dinner one evening this week. She needed some light-hearted company.

Chapter Eight

Gifre poured himself a large horn of wine and sat down heavily next to the fire in the Great Hall. The hall was dark, lit only by the large central fire and a few lamps. The smoke was making a few cough, even Gifre's eyes were streaming due to the smoky atmosphere around him. It was full of people eating and drinking, a daily routine where some of the higher status people and servants (in case they were needed to serve) gathered each evening after sundown. Soon the bard would start his story; then Gifre could sink further into his private thoughts on what he had witnessed earlier that day. Having slipped away from the temple, by the river, he walked a different and longer way back to the village, avoiding the burial ground and the Great Hall at the south end of the village, trying not to bump into any of Wulfric's other servants in case they asked him where their master could be. He was so shocked and furious he needed time to calm down before he spoke to anyone. He had spent the day hunting, until evening, so nobody would ask him what was wrong, because clearly something was and he knew he would not be able to hide this from his comrades.

Sitting by the fire, he was still reeling from the disbelief of what he had seen. He couldn't believe that Mildryth, who seemed so pure and innocent, so in love with their king, could be such a traitor. He could believe it of his master though, Wulfric, he had seen the way he watched his brother's bride-to-be with lust and wanting in his eyes. He had thought that Mildryth was besotted with Wilheard, that they had been together for years; friends first and then the announcement of their marriage had surprised no-one. So, the little whore was no better than a commoner! She did not deserve to be queen.

What should he do now? The information could easily be used to his advantage...but perhaps he should bide his time? If he blackmailed Wulfric into keeping his secret, he could be a richer man. Alternatively, he could run to the king and tell him everything; perhaps make his way up the ladder in his king's esteem. He would have to ensure that his life was not in danger; he needed some way of being sure that he would not be murdered – this was very dangerous information; he needed some security and this is what might take the time. He poured himself another large horn of wine and settled back to listen to the bard's tales of adventure, while he deliberated the predicament he found himself, unwillingly, in.

***

The ringing tone of her mother's phone rang on and on. Megan was about to hang up, thinking her mother wasn't at home, when she heard the phone click and her mother's breathless voice answer. "Hello."

"Mum. It's Megan."

"Darling, hello!" she said still sounding breathless, but obviously pleased to hear her daughter's voice.

"Are you all right, Mum?"

"Yes, sorry, I was just bringing in the shopping bags – had a hoot of a day with Amanda…do you remember her?"

"Em, no, can't say that I do." This didn't surprise Megan as she didn't really know her mother's many friends, or rather, acquaintances; she wouldn't really call them true friends, stab you in the back as soon as look at you, most of them.

"Well, how are you? How's the new job?" asked her mother.

"It was great, a bit slow going as we were waiting most of the day for the preliminary reports; the digging hasn't begun yet as the JCB drivers let us down, but hopefully they will be there bright and early in the morning."

"Oh. Well hopefully you will dig up something exciting. Are the team behaving?"

"Mum, I told you…I am not directing this dig, I am just enjoying it. It's what I need right now."

"Yes dear, of course. How are you getting on in Mummy's old cottage? Not too lonely?"

Megan guessed she was fishing about Tom, but she wasn't going to discuss him.

Her mother continued. "Have you sorted through much of Mummy's things? You need to de-clutter and put your own stamp on it; I could suggest an interior designer for you…"

"No thanks Mum. I'm going through things slowly and at my own pace. I miss Gran and I'm not ready to get rid of all her things yet."

The silence at the other end spoke volumes.

Megan changed the subject. "Do you remember Gran ever saying anything about odd things happening here at the cottage?"

"Odd? What do you mean?"

"Just that, strange happenings…"

Her mother spluttered at the other end. "Of course not, don't be so ridiculous." Then she hesitated. "Although…"

"Although, what?"

"Em…well, it's probably nothing, but I do remember Mummy saying something about a woman that she kept seeing near the house one summer. It really unnerved her – she said she couldn't be sure if

94

the woman was real or a ghost! But, really darling…I think Mummy was probably imagining things, she was going through a difficult time with Daddy. Are you *sure* you're okay? I am worried about you…are odd things happening to you?"

"No, not really, it was just something happened the other night, but I think I must have been dreaming." She didn't want to elaborate on what she'd seen and she certainly didn't want her mum to think she thought she'd seen a ghost! She couldn't be sure herself.

"Yes, I'm sure you must have been. Oh blast…"

"What is it?"

"The *weekend*, I completely forgot…Meggie, I am so sorry, I have just remembered, I *can't* come for the weekend, Amanda reminded me today that we are all having lunch in Covent Garden on Saturday to celebrate her becoming a gran, poor thing! I can't let her down…can you forgive me?"

Megan tried hard to hide the relief. "Oh, don't worry, we can do it another time, besides…I will probably be working," she said, hating herself for lying, but on the other hand, hating her mother for putting her friends before her, again.

"I'll call you next week, Sweetie, and we'll talk about another date."

Immediately after her phone conversation with her mother, Megan phoned Sasha. It was nearly nine o'clock and she hoped it wasn't too late, or she was disturbing her dinner.

"Hi, it's Megan."

"I'm sorry about earlier, the bloody car broke down and I hadn't realised my breakdown cover had expired! So poor Brad had to come out and tow me home. Did you wait long?"

"No. I got your text about twenty minutes after I arrived at the pub, but I sat and enjoyed my book and a cool glass of wine…"

"Sounds lovely, might have to see if I've a bottle in the fridge!"

Megan went on to tell her about Kai buying her a drink and how Bridget had been giving her evil stares all evening.

"Oh, yes, I know who Bridget is."

"You do?"

"Yes, not the most pleasant of women, on the surface she seems all smiles, but underneath she is pretty nasty piece of work. You don't really want to go and upset her though. She moved here about two years ago; she's from a travelling family that always came here when she was a child, she moved in with a local guy, it lasted about six months and then they broke up, funnily enough, he moved on and she stayed."

"Do you know Kai, also?"

95

"Not by name, but I might recognise him as one of the travellers that comes here regularly in the summer months."

"He's certainly an odd one...really unnerves me one minute, then is quite friendly the next."

"Hmmm, trust your instincts there if I was you!"

"I think perhaps I should," she agreed.

The next day, Megan arrived at the pub early. The students were all there and so was David, but there was no sign of Fin; she wondered at her disappointment, but tried not to let it show.

"If you're wondering about Dr Edwards, he has a lecture to take this morning, he will be here about eleven," said Bella smiling, knowingly.

"Thank you, Bella, but you don't need to keep me informed of Dr Edwards' whereabouts," she stated, walking off towards David. *What a little madam.*

When they arrived at the site, the JCB drivers were there with their diggers as if they had been waiting all day for them. David told them where he wanted them to take the topsoil off and dig the first of the trenches. The work had begun at last.

Later that morning, Fin strode across the windy field towards where Megan was digging. She had been given a section of the Cursus to investigate. So far she had found little of interest and was beginning to get cold. Fin held out a steaming mug of coffee for her, the scent of it carried on the wind smelled delicious, and she hoped he had put sugar in it.

"Morning!" He was his usual chirpy self.

"Hi Fin!" She smiled and climbed out of the trench. "Thank you so much, I was beginning to lose feeling in my fingers."

"Yes, it's a bitter one this morning. How's it going?"

"Slowly...not much here I'm afraid."

"How about you?"

"I've only just arrived...biscuit?"

She took a chocolate digestive and bit into it, it crumbled into pieces, but she welcomed its sweet taste after the bitterness of the coffee.

"You take sugar in coffee, don't you?"

He really was quite observant. "Yes." She nodded.

"Here have another biscuit, to make up for the lack of it in your coffee. I'll try to remember in future." He smiled at her, his bright, blue eyes holding her gaze for a moment, then suddenly looking off in the direction of the other workers as they heard a shout. They both turned to see Bella running towards them waving excitedly.

"Fin, Megan, David wants you, seems Oscar's found something really interesting." Her eyes were wide with excitement.

"Already?" Fin raised his eyebrows at her.

The three of them walked quickly over to a trench where Oscar and David were kneeling down, gently scraping away the dark earth.

"What've you got?" asked Megan.

"Saxon, I'm pretty sure of it!" replied David, without looking up from the trench where he was watching Oscar's every move with scrutiny.

"Fantastic!" said Fin.

"Wow," said Megan. "Not exactly what we were expecting..."

"No, not at all but look..."

David stood up and they all looked into the trench where Oscar had been digging since first thing that morning. About a foot below the topsoil Megan could see a dark, cylindrical pot, partially smothered in earth emerging from the soil.

"A cremation pot?" asked Megan.

"Almost certainly," said Fin. "May I?"

David stepped aside and Oscar came out of the trench to allow Fin to crouch down and look at it more closely.

"Your area of expertise, Fin," said Bella excitedly.

"Hmmm," he said, as he began to scrape away more of the soil.

After quite some time, the whole of the top of the pot could be seen. As Fin brushed away the earth a simple pattern of lines was just made visible.

"Definitely Saxon." He stated. "What a pleasant surprise. I wonder if there are any more. Bella, can you go and get the photographer?"

Megan knelt down next to the trench to take a closer look. Shards of what looked like burnt bone were mixed up in the soil. She wondered what else the pot may hold; what secrets it might reveal. She knew a little about the Saxon era, but Fin was obviously the expert. What she did know was that in comparison with other periods of history, very little was known about the Saxons, because of their techniques and the way they lived; most of their belongings and buildings were made of materials that disintegrated over time – leaving very few clues about themselves. There were few written documents too, them preferring to tell tales verbally to each other. One of the most insightful things into their history was a work of fiction called, 'Beowulf', Megan had read one version written by Seamus Heaney; this could not be taken fully as fact, but at least it did give some details of the early Saxons along with their homes and beliefs.

"Well…what a surprise," said David, sitting on his haunches next to Megan and Fin. "We certainly weren't expecting Saxon."

"This is great!" cried Fin, his face alight with enthusiasm, he jumped out of the trench and looked round the field. "We must get some more trenches dug – I want to see if there are any more cremation pots." He strode off towards the JCB drivers and geophysics guys to discuss where more trenches could be opened up.

"That's made Fin's day," said David, smiling at Megan.

"But not yours, you would have preferred Roman?"

David laughed. "I suppose, but there could quite possibly be both. I was just hoping for something huge in the Roman field, but hey, Saxon is great too, in fact less work for me, but more for Fin. However, I hope he won't be disappointed."

"How come?" Megan looked over at Fin who was talking to some workers, waving his arms around and really full of enthusiasm to get things moving.

David hesitated slightly before he continued. "If this is just a one-off grave, or a small cemetery then there won't be much here. However, if he finds a large cemetery that means there would have been a large settlement nearby too – he could have a really large job on his hands if that's the case, and if we can get the funding of course!"

"That would be amazing," cried Megan.

"Yes. You'd still want to continue with the Saxons…"

"Of course, it will be great to cover a period I've not had much experience of yet. Add it to my repertoire…"

Megan watched as Bella approached Fin and slapped him on the back, she laughed along with him and hung off his every word as they walked back towards the hole where the cremation pot was being photographed.

"This is excellent," said Fin, brightly. "I've asked the guys to dig more trenches over there and there," he pointed in two directions fairly close by. "Then we can get the graduates in and search for more finds."

The day continued to be successful for finds. By five o'clock they had found four more cremation pots excavated carefully from the clay. A couple were broken, but two were pretty much complete.

"I think we're going to have to call it a day, the light is disappearing fast now," said Fin, a big sigh escaping his lips. "Anyone fancy a drink? I'm going to stop at the pub on my way back to the barge. I feel the need for a celebratory beer."

It seemed everyone was busy, except Bella and Oscar. Megan said she would join them a bit later if they were still there, she needed to go home and walk Bartie; she would meet them at the pub when she'd collected him. Everyone started to disperse; an air of excitement and anticipation amongst them.

Megan walked home full of excitement; she still loved being an archaeologist, discovering things that had been hidden under the surface for years; veiled and forgotten until perhaps (only perhaps) they were rediscovered one day by curious hands or accidental unearthing like Bartie had…

The brooch!

Megan was surprised that the piece of jewellery that Bartie had dug up in the garden of the cottage, the intricate design, had slipped her mind. Perhaps she should show it to David, or perhaps Fin? Either of them may know the origin of the piece. She would fetch it when she got home and take it with her to the pub, see what Fin could tell her about it, as long as he didn't expect her to let him dig up the garden!

As she walked up the driveway to the cottage, Megan saw Bartie pop his head and paws up on the windowsill; his floppy ears pricked forwards in a questioning way - she felt guilty at having left him for so long on his own, although Mrs Clark had been in to see and walk him about lunchtime.

Megan called his name and he disappeared from view. She turned the key in the cottage door and opened it. Immediately she was bundled by Bartie, wagging his whole back end as well as his short tail.

"Bartie, it's *so* good to see you, boy," she said, giving him a lot of fuss.

Bartie soon disappeared into the garden to do his business and have a good sniff round. Megan took the opportunity to slip off her boots and go upstairs to the bathroom. As she ascended the stairs there was a distinct smell of cold, damp again – the air cool too. *I must get a builder in to take a look under the stairs, see if there is any rising damp,* she thought to herself.

She passed by her bedroom door and saw, again, that there was mud on the floor by her gran's dressing table. Bartie must have come upstairs during the day after Mrs Clark had taken him out for a walk earlier. Walking in to the bedroom and taking the key out of the music box on the mantle-piece she strode over to the dressing table and opened the little drawer. As she pulled out the brooch an icy wind blew past her and she was sure she heard a whisper upon it…but when she turned, there was nobody there.

Megan quickly went to the bathroom, then she fled downstairs grabbing her mobile and purse; slamming the door behind her she whistled to Bartie and stomped down the driveway back towards the river and the warmth of the pub, her heart pounding in her chest. She felt sure she'd heard somebody speak to her, but that was impossible.

As she walked along the riverbank, in the twilight, Bartie ran rings around her, telling her that he hadn't had a walk that day and that Mrs Clark had *not* let him out or made a fuss of him. Megan always marvelled at his endless energy and search for adventure on every walk. The sky above them was charcoal grey, streaked with deep purple; the odd star was beginning to twinkle and the temperature began to plummet – there was definitely going to be a frost tonight. However, with the promise of spring in the air some days now, Megan found she didn't mind that much. Nevertheless, it would be cold for the team first thing in the morning, but with the exciting finds of today that would drive them on.

The Oak, in town, was quite busy when she entered and she was not surprised to see Bridget glaring at her; it was almost as if she knew she was about to walk through the door. Megan smiled at her and walked through to the back where she hoped Fin and the others would be. Thankfully, they were all smiles to see her, even Bella.

Fin stood up immediately and asked, "What can I get you?" He bendt down and made a fuss of Bartie, who instantly rolled onto his back so that Fin could stroke his belly.

Megan said she would like a glass of red wine, feeling the need of a nice warming, heavier drink than a cool white today. Fin left them and went to the bar.

"What a lovely dog," said Oscar getting off his stool and making a fuss of Bartie.

Bella quite clearly didn't like the attention being taken away from her and said coldly, "I am allergic to dogs, so keep him away from me!"

"Sorry, Bella, I will keep him round this side of the table," replied Megan. "I don't want Bartie to be the cause of a red nose and watering eyes..."

Bella's phone beeped. She picked it up and frowned "Damn. Sorry, I have to go," she said, standing up and pulling on her coat.

"Do you need a lift, or are you going to catch the bus?" asked Oscar.

"Well, if you're going back to Oxford now...I don't mind waiting for a bus..."

"It's not a problem...I was only staying for another few minutes anyway."

Megan watched as Oscar hurriedly downed his pint, before grabbing his coat and following Bella to the front bar. He had seemed quite keen to give her a lift.

Megan felt slightly alarmed at the fact it would just be her and Fin. What if he had been just about to leave, and now felt he had to stay on because she had only just arrived? He returned a moment later with a bottle of red wine and two glasses.

"Just us, then..." he said. "The kids have had to go back."

Kids. So he saw Bella as a kid?

"Sorry, were you about to leave too?"

"Me? No, I am bedding down here for a couple of hours...thought I might grab one of their delicious pies in a bit." He poured them both a generous amount of wine and sat back in his chair. The fire in the grate was lively and warm; it cast an orange glow on his face. His blue eyes were full of excitement.

"What an incredible piece of luck," he smiled at her. "I'm thrilled that the site is Saxon as well...I don't know...I somehow had a feeling that this was going to be a good dig..." he laughed.

"Well, not everything can be explained in life..."

"Oh? Sounds like you've had some experience."

"I mean..." She thought quickly. "There are things that happen, things we can't explain or sometimes understand."

"No, you're right, still, can't wait to see what other things we might dig up!"

"Oh, that reminds me..." Megan put her hand into her pocket and pulled out the brooch. She carefully unfolded the tissue and laid it on the table in front of Fin. "Bartie dug this up...I wondered if you knew what period it might be from?"

"Wow," said Fin looking at the brooch on the table in front of him. He pulled it a little closer to him and looked at the intricate patterning on the square head. "It's Saxon! I'm sure of it. Look at the shape and style of patterns...see the animal depictions? This must have belonged to someone of wealth and importance."

He looked up at Megan, his eyes lit even more. "Where did you, sorry *Bartie*, find this?"

"You promise you won't tell anyone? I don't necessarily think the person would want her garden dug up..."

"In your *garden*?" he said, incredulously.

"Yes."

"Where is your house, near the site we're excavating?"

She shook her head. "No, it's at least a mile away, but doesn't mean it couldn't have been lost when somebody was walking in that area..."

"Possibly. If somebody dropped it while walking it could just be a one off, however, if there are more items buried there then it's possible that there might have been a village there. Burial grounds were usually within half a mile or so of their village."

"I would've thought it unusual to have a main village where I live it's in the middle of nowhere. It's on a small island where the River Thames and River Coln merge...and now the canal is there too, but wouldn't have been during Saxon times, of course."

"Ah, that could explain it...rivers were often sacred places to the Saxons, a place they may have worshipped. Perhaps somebody gave it as an offering to the gods, or perhaps it just came loose and fell off a cloak while the person was walking."

"Well, I don't want diggers trudging across my garden at the moment...I think my gran would turn in her grave!"

"Your gran...she died recently?"

Megan sighed. "Yes, a few months back...I inherited the cottage from her...I've only just moved here from Kent, I'm not sure I could cope with that right now."

"I'm sure it wouldn't be necessary anyway...maybe...when you're feeling strong enough, I could come and just take a look – not dig anything up – just to see what I think about the site."

Megan gave him a half smile and nodded. She could deal with Fin just taking a walk around, but to disturb anything at the moment just wouldn't feel proper. She wondered if she'd done the right thing in telling him; he did seem to respect her grief though, for now.

Bridget arrived at the table with two menus. She flashed a wide, flirtatious smile at Fin, who smiled in return.

"Hello, Megan," she said turning to face her, her smile dipping slightly and her eyes glistening ice-blue and cold.

"Evening," said Megan.

"I'll have the pie," said Fin. "How about you, Megan?"

"Yes, I'll have the same, please."

"I'll bring them over when they're ready," replied Bridget, her voice bright, but eyes still cold.

"You two know each other?" Fin asked.

"No, not really...I came in last night to meet a friend and she was in here."

"Tell me to mind my own business, but there seemed to be a bit of atmosphere between you..."

"So, it's not my imagination then. I don't know why, but she seems to hate me. Perhaps it was because her ex-boyfriend was talking to me. That's the only reason I can think of. Mind you, she makes me go cold, bizarre I know, I don't usually judge people that quickly, but she seems to dislike me considerably." Megan shrugged.

"Well it must be a bit of a problem, not yours, can't imagine you upsetting anyone..."

"Thank you, I am sure I've had my moments!" Megan was enjoying Fin's company and the discussion soon turned back to the Saxons; he was clearly very well read and definitely an expert in his field. She was learning so much from him already. He had had written some books on the subject; two of which he wrote down the titles of and recommended Megan to read in order to broaden her knowledge of the Saxons.

During their conversation, a young girl brought them their dinner, the aroma was delicious, Megan hadn't realised how hungry she'd been.

They were halfway through their second glass of wine, having almost polished off their pie and mash, when a dog appeared from the other bar, a collie; on closer inspection Megan realised that it was Angus. Bartie let out a low growl, but wagged his tail.

"Hello, boy," said Fin, bending down to stroke him. The dog growled quietly and Fin quickly withdrew his hand. "Shouldn't assume they're all friendly like Bartie, I suppose."

"It's Angus," said Megan considering how to tell Fin about Kai. "He belongs to a traveller, called Kai, who is camped out on my neighbour's property."

"Ah, really, dark-haired guy, eyes like a wolf?"

She nodded.

"Seen him a couple of times walking the dog along the river – seems awfully, shall we say, brooding?"

Megan smiled and glanced at the doorway; if Angus was here, then Kai must be too. "Yes, you could say that about him, couldn't you? He's Bridget's ex-boyfriend."

"The unfriendly barmaid?"

Megan nodded.

"Strange couple, but oddly suited," laughed Fin.

Megan laughed too.

"Angus...Angus...come 'ere, boy." Kai appeared in the doorway. He looked at Megan, nodded, shot an indistinguishable look at Fin, and then disappeared back into the other bar, followed closely by Angus, his tail between his legs.

"Friendly couple too." Fin winked at her and they both laughed again.

It was ten o'clock when Megan decided she must get home and get to bed, the wine had gone to her head and she was feeling tired and sleepy. She knew the walk home would clear her head, it was a cold night. Bartie would enjoy his extra walk too.

"Where is your cottage, shall I walk you back?" Fin asked.

"It's along the river towards Cricklade, not Oxford, but we will walk past your barge...I can walk on alone from there, it's not much further."

The two of them walked through the front bar and called out *'thank you'*. There was no sign of Kai and Angus, but Bridget was there, again surrounded by local men of all ages, hanging off her every word, she didn't reply, or even look up.

Outside it was beginning to freeze; there was a near full-moon and once away from the street lights, towards the river, the natural light was illuminating enough for there to be no need for torches. They walked in silence for a bit. Bartie pulled at his lead, impatient to be free to run madly around the darkened fields.

Fin stopped and stared up at the stars which were bright in the dark, indigo sky. "It's amazing to imagine that people, strangers who we'll never know or meet, have trodden these paths before us, hundreds if not thousands of years ago, leaving tiny clues about who they were for us to discover, having no notion that future generations, would be treading them as well. We live our lives very differently, but in the same places where they had set down roots."

"I find it fascinating. I'm sure that's why I got into archaeology in the first place, that and my gran's love of history, her traipsing me round historical landmarks here and in Wiltshire. I remember the first time she showed me Avebury stone circle, it had me mesmerised from the start – I couldn't help but wonder why on earth anyone would want to put giant rocks in a circle...but it got me wondering and that started my curiosity and it has never been satiated since."

They continued to walk along the river. The moon reflected its face into the silver waters of the Thames; a few sleepy ducks were being carried along on the current. It was very quiet until an owl screeched quite close by, making Megan jump.

"My great-grandfather was involved in the 'tomb-raiders' of the early nineteen hundreds in Egypt. My grandfather was a historian and used to tell me stories of his and his father's adventures. My own father wasn't in the slightest bit interested in history, he was...sorry, is an actor." Fin laughed lightly.

"Wow," said Megan.

"Not really, he's never been that successful, but he loves what he does and it just about pays the bills. My great-grandfather became rather wealthy you see, although I wouldn't say I agree with the morality of the treasure hunting and selling, so my father has inherited quite well; but hasn't really added that much to the family fortune. Their house in Oxford is far too big for them and I have mentioned that I think they should sell and buy somewhere smaller in a few years, but they are reluctant at the moment."

They arrived at Fin's barge. Megan was just wondering if Fin would invite her in when he said, "Goodnight then – you *will* be all right, walking back on your own? Sorry, you probably do it all the time…"

"I'll be fine, thank you," she said, looking round for Bartie. She couldn't see him to start with so called his name and whistled, within moments he appeared at her heels snorting excitedly in the damp grass at her feet.

Fin climbed aboard his barge as she walked away towards the cottage. It was easily a third of a mile further up the river and on the other side. It wouldn't take her long, but she found she had enjoyed his company and didn't relish the thought of entering her gran's cottage which would now be dark and cold. She realised there would be no time to light a fire now – the old electric blanket would have to suffice tonight.

Megan was approaching the footbridge that curved up and over the breadth of the river like a crescent moon, when she stopped in her tracks, Bartie was stood still staring up at the bridge, his tail as still as a pointer's. She could just make out in the moonlight that his hackles were raised. Her eyes followed his: on the bridge – stood in the centre – was a figure. Megan tried to adjust her focus and capture the image of whoever it was. She felt a chill run through her body. Was it the same man that had seemed to have been watching the cottage from the trees the other night? No…the figure was smaller, more slender…it was a woman. This would normally have brought some comfort to Megan – somehow women seemed less threatening than men when you were alone in a deserted place – however, seeing the woman's figure turn slightly towards her in the moonlight, she could see that the woman had long, blonde hair which looked golden in the lunar light. The woman turned and looked in her direction, but appeared to stare right through her. It was too dark and the moon was behind her so that the female's features could not be seen, but her stance suggested she was in some anguish. Suddenly, she raised both arms above her head…then the moonlight faded behind dark clouds and Megan could no longer distinguish her in the darkness of the night. A cold wind blew hard along the river bank; Megan could hear it in the branches of the trees, heard a strange, foreign whisper upon it. She looked down at Bartie who was very still, hackles raised.

A moment later the clouds dispersed and the moon shone again, flooding the night with silver light once more – the woman on the bridge had vanished. Had she jumped? There had been no sound of anyone jumping into the river – had she walked away? If so, was she coming this way, or walking in the opposite direction? Megan guessed she must have walked away from her; there was no sign of anyone in the near distance.

Bartie's tail began to wag again and he trotted up towards the bridge. He jumped over the stile and onto the wooden boards, happily running across the bridge ahead of her. If Bartie was happy to go over, then she would have to be too.

As she walked across the bridge quickly, almost running, her footfalls quite distinct around her, she looked down the track the other side of the river, the track that took you away from the cottage and back towards town – there was no sign of anyone now. With her hand shaking uncontrollably, she managed to slide the key into the lock. Megan called to Bartie and went over the threshold into the hallway of the cottage. It wasn't until the door was locked behind her that she realised how shaken she felt. Megan left her boots on the newspaper in the hall and went through to the kitchen. She took a tin of dog food out of the fridge, Bartie's tail was wagging hard and he groaned at her to hurry up. She put it in his bowl and stood watching him wolf it down hardly chewing it at all. As Bartie licked the empty bowl around the stone floor, Megan felt herself relax slightly. It was about ten-thirty, there were always people out walking by the river, it seemed to attract walkers, with or without a dog – furthermore, it was part of the Thames path. There was nothing sinister about the woman she was just becoming more paranoid. However, she couldn't fathom why these people were making her feel anxious...her nerves seemed to be shot to pieces.

Megan made herself a cup of tea and decided to go straight to bed where it would be warm, it was too late to light the fire now and she didn't fancy going in to the sitting room in the cold. Bartie followed her up the stairs; she turned on the electric blanket as soon as she entered the bedroom before walking back along the landing to the bathroom. Bartie followed her again and plonked himself outside the door while she cleaned her teeth.

Megan was halfway through putting her pyjamas on when her phoned signalled a text message, there were only sporadic places at the cottage where she could get enough signal for them or calls to get through:

Did you mean for me to keep the brooch?
I will get it cleaned up for you.
I am in Uni tomorrow, will be at dig about noon.
See you then, Fin

She replied:

Yes, that would be great, thanks.
See you tomorrow.
Megan

She had thought they'd already discussed this earlier in the evening. Perhaps Fin had forgotten (they'd had quite a lot of wine) or maybe...maybe he was checking she had got home safely? The thought brought her a feeling of warmth.

As Megan slid between the cold covers of her bed, thoughts kept intruding into her mind; she couldn't help but imagine that the woman on the bridge was somehow related to the one she had seen looking through her kitchen window in the early hours of the morning. What could this woman possibly want with her? Was it the same woman who her gran had seen? Did she need help or was she just a mad woman who lurked around these parts, or (and this concept only penetrated her thoughts as she was on the periphery of sleep) was she searching for something or someone?

Chapter Nine

Wulric's eyes were full of passion and longing, he stared at her from across the market place, didn't seem to care that she was with Wilheard and they were surrounded by many of their friends. They were walking towards him, his eyes didn't leave hers; they were locked together. Unable to move her gaze away from his, she wondered why he had started to smile, his wolf-like eyes shining brightly as she drew nearer and nearer. Suddenly, he took her in his arms and in front of everyone he kissed her full on the mouth. Instead of struggling away from him, she found that the other people started to melt away into the background and it was just them, them and their passion...

Mildryth awoke with a start; sweat covered her whole body as if she had a fever. She tried hard to focus on what the dream had been about – determined that it wouldn't elude her. The images started flooding back uncontrollably and amongst them other, more disturbing images and feelings that she wasn't sure belonged to the dream. Her head was spinning, fleeting illusions that fluttered like moths swept through her consciousness, seemingly real and then impossible...Sitting up in bed she threw back the covers; the first light of dawn was sneaking through the gaps in the wood around the windows and walls. She walked across the herb strewn floor, the rosemary and lavender quite potent first thing in the morning; splashed cold water from the bowl onto her face and then cupped her hands so she could drink too. Her head was splitting, she *must* find Lindi – perhaps she could make some sense of all this...give her another potion to get rid of the pain.

Mildryth walked quickly and quietly through the village that wasn't yet awake. However, Lindi was outside the door to her hut, the look of surprise on her face told Mildryth that for once she had not been expecting her. Lindi tried to cover this up with a wide smile, her ice-blue eyes still giving away the slight suspicion that she obviously had at Mildryth's dawn visit.

"Good morning," she said, brightly.

"Lindi, you have to help me..." she cried, the anguish in her voice quite clear.

The healer frowned. "You had better come in."

Mildryth followed Lindi into her hut. The acrid smell that normally permeated the air was not so strong this morning, perhaps it was because Lindi had not started with her remedies yet. The fire was bright though as if it had only been lit a short while ago; a pot of boiling water hung over it.

"Sit down and tell me what ails you, dear Mildryth." Lindi looked at her closely.

Mildryth sat on the wooden bench next to the fire and Lindi sat adjacent.

"I don't know..." she hesitated. *Should she really be telling anyone this?* "It's just that..."

Lindi placed her hand over Mildryth's. "It's all right you can tell me anything you know that. We've known each other our whole lives."

"I don't know what is real and what isn't though."

Lindi's stare seemed to turn harder, a shadow crossed the ice-blue of her eyes. She didn't say anything further, just sat and waited for Mildryth to continue as if she knew she would without her coercing her.

"I had some strange dreams last night, but when I awoke this morning some of the images were more like memories than dream. I can't comprehend why this would be – I don't see how..." she faltered again, the memories and dreams were still filtering into her mind.

Lindi got up from the bench and went to her shelves. She got down a jar and spooned some dried herbs into a goblet; she then poured boiling water onto it and handed it to Mildryth. "Drink this."

Mildryth took the steaming liquid and held it in her hands, waiting for it to cool down enough to drink.

"Tell me what you remember."

"It's awful, Lindi, I'm not sure if I can..." She felt herself blush.

"Take your time."

They sat in silence for a few minutes then Mildryth began to cry, gently at first and then huge great gulps, sobbing in Lindi's arms as if the grief and guilt she felt would never cease. Lindi held her closely and stroked her hair like a mother would a child, soothing her and trying to calm her, but all the while a soft smile played on her lips.

After some time Mildryth calmed enough to drink the bitter drink that Lindi had given her, between short breaths she started to tell Lindi what she remembered.

"It was so strange, Lindi. I was walking through the market with Wilheard and some of our friends...Wulfric was watching me, not us, just me, from across the way...the next thing is that he and I are kissing passionately."

"What happened?"

Mildryth sighed, her tears abating. "I woke up at that point...but I then remembered...at least, I think I remembered...about the other day. I knew that I had lost part of my day when I came to see you

110

about the headaches, but I couldn't fathom what had happened...Oh Lindi, this is just too awful!"

"You must tell me if you want me to help you." Lindi took Mildryth's hands in hers and stroked them gently.

Mildryth cleared her throat and looked away from Lindi's eyes that were watching her intently. "Down by the river, I-I have this dream...or perhaps, I hope that it was a dream...Wulfric and I...we – I think we lay together! Lindi, oh gods, what am I going to do? I am marrying Wilheard in two days – I can't marry him if I have lain with his brother! And, why can't I remember – what is happening to me? Do you think it's because I lost the brooch? You can't protect me...is somebody using dark forces to play with my mind?" Tears cascaded down her cheeks once more.

Lindi let go of Mildryth's hands and took her chin in her fingers. They were icy cold; she forced Mildryth to look at her.

"This is what you must do. You must go ahead with the wedding as planned. Obviously, this was just a dream...these headaches you've been having and what with the grief of your mother's death, the death of our dear king and the forthcoming wedding have all got too much for you...unless somebody *is* interfering with your mind! Mildryth the idea that you and Wulfric had sex is ridiculous, more than that – can't you see the impossibility of it? This is the work of a powerful force, I am sure of it. I have the new brooch, but it is not quite ready yet, I need a few more hours."

Mildryth looked into Lindi's eyes. Yes, she could see the ludicrousness of this notion, but *why* did she feel that this was no dream and that it was more of a reality? When she awoke that morning she could still feel the touch of Wulfric's hands on her body; that had felt real enough and, more worryingly so, her body had responded to his touch.

"Are you *sure* you think it was part of the dream?" she asked.

"Of course. Listen, you love Wilheard, don't you?"

She nodded.

"Well, then why would you have lain with his brother? It was most likely one of those elusive dreams that one has and then is reminded about by another – that is exactly what has happened here, Mildryth, I am sure of it. You must marry Wilheard as planned and put this ridiculous concept out of your head. I will give you a potion that will help calm your nerves and hopefully you will get a good, dreamless, night's sleep tonight. I will endeavour to bring you the new brooch as a matter of urgency."

111

"You're right. I think I just panicked slightly at the realistic nature of the dream and felt guilty as I am marrying Wilheard – the man I love."

"Who is helping you dress for the ceremony?"

"Hamia."

"The servant girl?"

"Yes...although, I do wish my mother was here...and my sister, Sunniva, will not arrive until past the middle of the day."

"Would you like me to come and help you in the morning?"

"Lindi, that's a lovely idea, thank you." Mildryth embraced Lindi briefly, but was again surprised by the coldness of her.

"Today you must rest completely, you do not need to do anything, the servants and Wilheard's aides will do all the work. You *must* rest."

"I will try."

Mildryth left Lindi's hut and walked back towards home. The villagers' fires were all being lit, smoke was whirling up through the roof-tops and the sun was getting higher in the sky. A few voices could be heard coming from the sleepy huts and the animals were awake too. The day promised to be bright, dry and warm. Mildryth began to feel a bit better after speaking with Lindi; she must have seemed completely mad, but her friend was non-judgemental as always. Smiling to herself, she looked towards the Great Hall: just ahead of her there was a man looking directly at her...Wulfric. He started to walk towards her – her heart skipped a beat and she felt her mouth go dry.

"Morning, Mildryth," he said, with no emotion whatever, but his grey eyes smouldered just as in the dream; she felt a shiver run down her spine.

She nodded at him. "Wulfric."

"I'm glad I have seen you, I wanted to say that I am going to put all our differences aside for you and come to the wedding – despite everything I wouldn't want anyone to think that I wished ill of you both."

"Thank you, Wulfric; that is good of you. Wilheard will be pleased...now if you'll excuse me..." She needed to get away from him; those uncertain feelings were in danger of possessing her. He seemed to take the hint and stepped out of her way, although she could feel his eyes on her the whole time she walked back towards the sanctity of her home.

It was believed to be a bad omen if the woman should see her husband within a week before the ceremony, but she longed to run to Wilheard and have him hold her and reassure her as he always did.

112

Her excitement about the forthcoming ceremony had somehow been marred by her dreams. Lindi had to be right though, of course they were *only* dreams, the idea of her and Wulfric was preposterous.

***

Meanwhile, back in her hut, Lindi was calling on the spirits to ensure the brooch, she was to give to Mildryth, was as powerful as it could be. As it was after the magic had been used on her, there was no guarantee that it would work as well as the first. Besides, Mildryth must be a very strong-minded woman if the drugs were not keeping those memories at bay. At all costs, Mildryth must believe that it had all been a dream, thank the gods she didn't go running to Wilheard and blurt it all out to him, being the naïve young woman she was – she would probably hope that Wilheard would forgive her and marry her anyway – *foolish girl.*

Once Wilheard and Mildryth were married it would give her, Lindi, more of a chance to concentrate on wooing Wulfric herself. She had not seen him since the morning she had given him the potion…he was avoiding her, she knew…he was ashamed of his behaviour in one sense, but as she had feared, instead of satisfying his yearning for Mildryth it had strengthened his craving for his brother's wife. A future for the two of them was impossible, but now he had tasted more of his desire he was cruelly in want of more than he would ever have again. Lindi knew that Wulfric believed if *he* was the future king then Mildryth would have agreed to marry him instead of Wilheard, Lindi knew differently…

***

Not far from the village, amongst the trees of the wooded hillside, Gifre was out hunting with some other of Wulfric's men. They had killed deer and boar that morning in readiness for the wedding feast – this was to be their master's gift to the king and queen. Gifre was still undecided about what he should do. It had been days since he had witnessed the treason and he still feared for his own safety; if he told either the king or Wulfric, especially Wulfric, could he successfully bribe him? Would he pay him to keep quiet or would he just behead him and bury him in these woods, or worse, just let the wild animals eat his corpse? He shuddered. The image of his own corpse being scavenged on by birds and beasts sent his blood cold. It wasn't worth the risk…he would tell no-one, he decided. He would remain loyal to his master and let the king sort out his own problems; he would be no part of it. Strangely, making this decision made him feel a lot lighter and later that day found him whistling away to himself, finally looking forward to the feasting and drinking of the forthcoming marriage – after all, it would be a fine celebration with plenty of wine and meat to be had.

***

Wulfric sat by the river and pondered over his brief meeting that morning with Mildryth. The earthy water was fast flowing after heavy rain the previous day, but it made the colours of the flora vibrant against the now bright blue sky. The sun was warm on his face and it helped to warm his chilled spirits. Although genuinely pleased at his acceptance of the invitation to the wedding, it seemed Mildryth couldn't get away from him quickly enough. Had she remembered what had happened? Lindi had made it clear it was a possibility he might have to face, unlikely, but possible. If she had remembered then how did she feel? Did she find that she had feelings for him, after all, as he had hoped? Or, unthinkably, did she detest him and, worse, would she tell Wilheard? He hadn't considered that...

A wave of nausea swept over him. Why did he have to fight for everything in his life, when his brother was given everything and anything he could wish for? Why did *he* have to be born the bastard?

Taking a deep breath, he threw the stick he'd had in his hands into the river and watched it float down stream, swept away by a current. The stick bobbed and sank as it went and he felt, he realised, that his life was out of control too; somehow he must regain control of his life again. It was clear that Mildryth was going to marry his brother and that he would have no say in the matter; if he tried to intervene in any other way now, it would be at the detriment of his life – Wilheard would kill, or have him killed, he was sure of it. Laying back into the damp grass he stared up at the few white and grey clouds in the blue sky, he had to accept that Mildryth could never be his – as much as he loved her, he had to let her go...

***

Wilheard was pacing his chamber, impatient at having to wait to see Mildryth again. He needed something to help pass the time so he had sent his servant to get his best friend and some wine. In the meantime, he felt that as he was the king surely he could send for her too, wasn't he allowed to bend the rules? However, instinct told him that Mildryth would believe that it was a bad omen for them to see each other. He

114

thought about their forthcoming wedding and, of course, the consummation of their love. For years he had waited and wanted Mildryth, but had had to find comfort in other women's arms until now. In a few nights he would be able to take her in his arms and make her truly his; for now and always. He loved her gentle and generous nature, but knew she had a strong and intelligent mind, which was why she would make a great queen. His brow creased as he thought of her pale face when he had kissed her goodbye two days ago. He was concerned about the headaches she kept having and the dizziness.

Was Lindi right and were there dark forces working against her too, just as they had his father? He became irritated at this thought and frustrated that they still hadn't been able to find his father's killer, perhaps never would – all trails had run to nothing. They were certain now that it had been poison, *somebody* had to have administered it, but who and why? His mind turned to his brother again as it often did when he was thinking who would benefit from Aelle's death; but why would Wulfric kill their father when he knew that it would be him, Wilheard, who was to inherit the title? Unless...unless he was next. *Was* Wulfric working against him still? Was it him that was working against Mildryth? Wilheard knew that Wulfric had always had a soft spot for his future bride, ever since they were children, so why would he want to make her ill? No...no, not Wulfric then, but who? And why hadn't his men been able to find Aelle's murderer, somebody, somewhere must know something!

***

Lindi tapped gently on the door of Mildryth's hut. It stood very close to the Great Hall as did all the most important peoples' huts in their village. Mildryth's father called for her to enter and as she did so, he said, "Great, some company for my girl, I just have to go out for a while, I have some errands to run for Wilheard, I won't be back late." He kissed Mildryth on the head and then left the two women alone.

Lindi noticed the wine and bread untouched on the table. "Not eaten yet?"

Mildryth shook her head. "No, join me if you like, there is plenty here." She smiled at Lindi.

"You look better," she stated.

"I feel much better. It seems ridiculous now that I came to you so early this morning in such a panic. Of course I had been dreaming, and now, as the day has passed, the images have receded." She laughed.

"I am glad you are feeling calmer about it. You were in a bit of an emotional state this morning, believing that you'd lain with Wulfric!"

Mildryth blushed and looked down at her feet.

"Come, show me your jewellery for the ceremony and I will try and think of how we can add this brooch amongst it; I don't think it will look out of place with the rest." The brooch was identical to the one she'd lost, made of gilt bronze and had a square head; images of animals were intricately carved upon it; the brooch must have been worth a lot and again Mildryth wondered why Lindi would have had such expensive items of jewellery. We must still be vigilant after all, the headaches are still happening so frequently; I must protect you, especially for the ceremony."

Mildryth nodded. "You pour the wine and I'll get the jewellery." Mildryth disappeared into a small cordoned off area at the end of the hut which was draped in brightly coloured woven hangings, her bedchamber.

While Mildryth was out of sight, as quickly as she could, Lindi slipped some powders into the horn from which Mildryth would drink her wine and poured the wine on top of it. *That will make her sleep tonight and dream of nothing.* She couldn't risk Mildryth waking up again in the morning in a panic and calling off the ceremony.

Mildryth returned with the jewellery that she was to wear. "Some of these are gifts from Aelle; before he died he commissioned them especially for me."

"That's a beautiful amber bead necklace," said Lindi, gesticulating to the beads that shone golden in the lamplight.

Mildryth sighed. "This, my father gave it to me, just before you arrived. He told me that it belonged to my mother and she asked him to give it to me on the day of my marriage to Wilheard; knowing she would not be able to be here." A single tear ran down her cheek.

Lindi looked at the jewels and said, "You have some beautiful and very expensive pieces of jewellery; suitable for your new status as queen – I do hope we will still be friends once you are married."

"Of course we shall," replied Mildryth, taking a bite of bread followed by a mouthful of the wine.

"Your new brooch will keep you safe against the dark forces that I can feel surround you..."

"You can *feel* them?" said Mildryth, aghast.

Lindi nodded. "They are getting stronger. You *must* take care of this one..."

"I did try to find the other one, Lindi, I searched and searched. I am scared that this new one, as you said, might not be as

116

strong...perhaps it would be better if I could find the other one...I can't imagine where it could have gone. I remember putting it on that morning, visiting my mother's grave and the temple of Eostre, but I have spent many hours trying to find it in those locations; I cannot. I'm sorry!"

Lindi patted Mildryth on the hand. "Try not to fear, I will do my best to ensure it is as powerful as possible." she said.

The two women ate and drank until Lindi suggested that Mildryth should get some sleep. Mildryth didn't protest, she was extremely tired and felt very sleepy. Mildryth's father was still not back, but the servant girl had come in a while ago and Lindi insisted that she stay with Mildryth until her father returned.

***

Once Lindi had left, Mildryth went to her sleeping chamber and stood looking out at the night sky. The moon was almost full...in two nights it would be full and this would mean that there was more of a chance for Mildryth to conceive on her wedding night – an heir! Her stomach turned over; her excitement and anticipation was continuing to grow; she had not been allowed into the Great Hall all day where the banquet and celebrations would be held – there was no place for her amongst the preparations.

Staring up at the moon and stars she questioned again her own thoughts and fears from her recurrent dreams. The moon was silvery and bright – its shadows discernible amongst its hoary light; the stars were sparkling brightly against the deep blue sky as if in celebration of the coming union and the moon's full cycle. If she *had* lain with Wulfric then to marry Wilheard would be seen as treason and she would be slaughtered and thrown to the wolves. Again she realised the stupidity of these thoughts, nevertheless, as she lay down in her bed and closed her heavy, tired eyes, Wulfric's grey, wolf-like eyes, held that same longing, passionate gaze they had held that morning as he had spoken to her. However, as she tried to make sense of this, sleep engulfed her and she fell into an obscure and dreamless sleep.

Chapter Ten

Fin wasn't sure what had awoken him. He felt groggy, perhaps from the wine he'd had in the pub or the fact that he'd been woken from a deep sleep. He lay in his bed and looked into the darkness, listening intently to see if there was any noise, such as the wind, that had awoken him. He heard a vixen cry then, long and eerie into the darkness...a sound that always unnerved him slightly. He wasn't afraid of foxes, not in the slightest, but that sound, that high pitched cry made shivers run down his spine. It felt unusually cold in the room around him; the stove must have died right down, or worse, gone out. That would mean having to relight it in the morning before going to work, otherwise it would be cold in the boat when he got home later in the day. He sat up and reached for his robe. Wrapping it around himself, he went through to the lounge area to investigate the stove...it was very low, but still a few embers glowed within. He reached under the stove to pull out a couple of logs and some kindling to get the fire going again. Placing the logs into the stove, he watched as the fire rekindled and the flames began to engulf the well seasoned wood.

Now he was up, he felt wide awake; a warm drink would help make him feel sleepy again. He sauntered into the kitchen area and opened the fridge to take out the milk. As the light from the open fridge fell across the floor, he noticed some clumps of mud on the floor running from the doorway to the lounge area. He frowned. How on earth had the mud come in from outside? He always took his boots off and stowed them in the little cupboard by the door – it saved on domestic chores! Fin turned the overhead light on and stared, bewildered, at the earth scattered across the floor...it was wet and sticky, dark, and the odour of it filled the room.

He went quickly to the door to check that it was still locked and secure; it was. He frowned again and turned his attention back to the rest of the boat...everything seemed to be in place.

He racked his brains for a few moments. Maybe...just maybe, it had been Bartie...of course he must have snuck on board, to see if there were any morsels of bacon still to be had, when he had been chatting to Megan at his doorway, leaving clumps of mud inside. *Thanks, Bartie*, he thought to himself.

Fin made his hot drink and then went back to bed, thank goodness he had put Megan's brooch in the drawer next to his bed. It could be quite valuable and he didn't want anyone stealing it before he had had a chance to have it cleaned and valued. He slipped back beneath the duvet and shut his eyes; he was just dropping back to sleep when the vixen cried again, once more sending a chill right through him.

*****

The morning of the ceremony, Lindi was up and about early in readiness to help Mildryth in her preparations. Hot water had been boiled up and her garments hung, like spirits of those that had already passed to the next life, around the hut. The ceremony was to take place at sunset; the festivities to continue well into the night beneath the light of a full moon.

Mildryth felt anxious and excited, she had been waiting for this day for years, ever since Wilheard first kissed her on his fourteenth birthday on a hunting trip in the west of the Kingdom. They had been walking along the river, on a warm spring day, when he had suddenly, nervously taken her hand and pulled her towards him; he had embraced her gently and then kissed her passionately. He had then told her that one day she would be his queen, he had stuck true to his word ever since that day.

Now that day had come.

Mildryth was going to be his queen and her children would be kings and queens too. What an honour. However, sometimes it also felt like an enormous burden; how could she help rule the people? Would they respect her? What of Wilheard's mother, would she be keen to step aside and let a younger woman take her place? Bertrade had always been kind to Mildryth, especially since her own mother had died. However, Bertrade was a formidable woman and had been a strong queen at the side of Aelle. Could Mildryth ever be that woman? She feared not. Yes, she was strong, but knew she was young and perhaps naïve. Her popularity amongst the people of their community was evident, but what she feared was that she was not as powerful, or would be as well liked, as the previous queen.

Mildryth was just washing when Lindi appeared in the doorway: she blushed, aware of her nakedness – she hadn't heard her come in. Lindi openly stared at her body and smiled.

"You really are a beautiful woman, no wonder the men all love you," she said, with an edge to her tone that Mildryth did not miss, but couldn't fathom.

Mildryth covered herself up slowly to try and conceal her embarrassment. "What do you mean, men? I am only aware of Wilheard's affection for me…"

"Yes, of course, but others definitely admire you too. Here let me help you with your gown." Lindi held the red garment out for

120

Mildryth to step into. She helped her slip it up over her shoulders and tie it around her waist with the golden braid. As she did so, she stopped for a moment with her hands lightly on Mildryth's stomach.

Mildryth moved away from her, looking her in the eyes, she had noticed a quick flicker of an expression she couldn't read on Lindi's face. "What is it?" she asked.

"I think that your womb is ripe..." she faltered a moment. "I think another king, or queen will soon be amongst us."

"Oh Lindi! Do you really? That is what I want most in the world...to give Wilheard a son, or daughter, I know he wouldn't really mind." A dark shadow crossed Lindi's face, but it was gone so quickly that Mildryth wondered if she'd imagined it.

"I am certain you will bear a child within the next nine moons!"

Mildryth's heart skipped in her chest, she was so excited about bearing a child for Wilheard; to cradle her own child within her arms. She could imagine it now, Wilheard, herself and their child snuggled up amongst the furs on their bed, warm and close as she had done with her parents as a very small child; it was moments like that she treasured now in her memories of her mother and the childhood she had so taken for granted.

"Have you eaten this morning?" Lindi asked her.

"Not yet, I was too anxious..."

"Hamia," Lindi addressed the servant girl who was sitting by the fire in the next chamber, mending a hole that had appeared in the cloak that Mildryth was to wear over her gown for the ceremony. "Go and get your mistress some bread, cheese and wine."

Hamia nodded and left them alone.

"How is your head this morning – did you have any further dreams last night?" Lindi asked.

Mildryth blushed and shook her head. "No, I had almost forgotten about it all since last night. I have been so busy this morning that it had faded into the background, until now you've just mentioned it. I slept soundly last night. Today it seems even more preposterous that I ever thought it could possibly have happened in reality." She laughed nervously.

"Perhaps the potion I gave you helped, although perhaps the evil ones who are plotting against you decided to leave you alone last night..."

"But what of today?"

"Let me worry about that...here, get dressed..." Lindi held out the ceremony cloak towards Mildryth.

A shiver of fear and excitement ran through Mildryth's body as she pulled the cloak around her. Lindi stood back to take a look at her future queen; Mildryth stood before her in a gown of reddish orange; woven especially for her by the best weavers in the village – only the very best cloth was fit for their queen.

Lindi smiled at Mildryth. "The final touch..." she said, pinning the square-headed bronze brooch onto her cloak to secure it at the shoulder. "This will keep you safe. Don't lose this one...I cannot ensure that a third brooch would have any protective powers at all...this, like I said, is not as powerful as the first, but it should still give you some protection."

Mildryth took her hands in hers. "Thank you, Lindi."

A noise in the doorway startled them both. They turned towards the door where a woman stood, smiling warmly at Mildryth; a child on her hip.

"Sunniva, sister, dearest!" exclaimed Mildryth exuberantly, rushing towards her and embracing both her and the child who chuckled warmly.

"Mildryth, my baby sister, on her union day!" Sunniva returned the embrace. "You look beautiful!"

"Sunniva, how lovely to see you again after all this time," said Lindi.

"Lindi," said Sunniva. "I hope you are helping Mildryth?"

"She has been very kind," replied Mildryth.

The two other women embraced, friends from childhood, but Sunniva soon dismissed Lindi, asking for time alone with her sister.

"Lindi looked at little put out!" said Mildryth, once Lindi had left the hut.

"She'll understand. I want to talk to my little sister before she goes to the marriage bed..." said Sunniva, winking at Mildryth mischievously.

A woman came and took Sunniva's son from her arms and out of the hut, so that the two of them could speak freely.

"Are you anxious?" asked Sunniva.

Mildryth laughed. "A little..."

"About the consummation?"

Mildryth shrugged.

"Mother would have wanted me to have this conversation with you, Mildryth, she would have been sad that she could not have done this herself..."

The two young women looked at each other sadly, both seeing aspects of Swanhilde in each other's features.

"I so want to give Wilheard a child..."

"You will, there's nothing to be afraid of, Wilheard loves you and would do nothing to hurt you."

Mildryth smiled as she thought about her embraces with Wilheard, how he was always gentle and affectionate. A thought probed at the edge of her conscious, a more passionate embrace, strong arms...she sighed deeply.

"What's wrong?" asked Sunniva, her face full of concern.

"It's, it's just...oh it's nothing, really."

"There's no need to be afraid, I promise."

"I am not afraid of Wilheard; it's more the threat to both of us, the dark forces that seem to be against us..."

"Dark forces?"

"Lindi is convinced there are evil forces that are trying to harm us all; after Aelle's death she fears that Wilheard could be next and even me. She has given me this amulet to help protect me..."

"It's beautiful...she has given it to you for protection?"

Mildryth nodded. "Why do you look so concerned?"

"I don't know; I realise that you and Lindi are closer than I ever was, but I am not sure...I've never really trusted her..."

"Really?"

Sunniva shrugged. "It's just I remember her as a child, she could be quite spiteful at times, but you never seemed to realise."

Mildryth shook her head. "Lindi has never given me any reason to dislike her; she has always been a good friend!"

"Of course, I am sorry if I offended you." Sunniva embraced her sister once more. "Come on let us have some wine...."

Later that day, with the sun setting across the lavender sky and casting flames of red and yellow across the surrounding countryside, the river ran golden brown into the distance, like a liquid path of gold ready for a new queen to walk upon. The trees seemed to bow slightly in the light wind as Mildryth walked with her father towards the temple, a clearing in the woods where the two rivers met, and her future husband and king. Wilheard walked towards her, smiling, and embraced her in front of the crowds of their people who were mirroring the trees with their bowing heads. Mildryth could feel the sense of celebration in the air and knew, without doubt, that she was embarking on a magnificent journey of love and respect; not just that of her husband, but that of the people too.

***

Wulfric, close by at the edge of the crowd, watched as the two of them embraced and knew, at that moment, all was lost to him. He would never be king; he would never be able to hold Mildryth in his arms

123

again, not even with the use of magic. A part of him now despised himself for having sunk so low as to use magic in forcing her to lay with him; it had been delightful, like nothing he had ever felt with the other women he had lain with over the years. Now, having tasted what it could be like, he felt more desperate for her to be his. Was there a small glimmer of hope still? Had Lindi been right in saying that she might remember their union in time; what if she found she liked those memories...what if she actually came looking for his love again? As he watched his brother and his new bride kiss passionately to seal their union he felt that small flicker fade away to nothing.

***

As the sun sank into the horizon and darkness descended, the feasting began. The new king and queen were seated at the head of the table, which was laid out at one end of the Great Hall; a low roar of laughter and conversation filled the hall to the great wooden rafters above them. Mildryth's father sat the other side of his daughter; Sunniva the other side of him, smiling at her sister. A feast of wild boar, deer, bread and wine was being consumed by the guests, all that was, except one.

Lindi could see that Wulfric was sitting, with yet another horn of wine, and a plate full of meat (untouched) to one side of the hall; his face as ashen as the dust around the central fire.

"If you don't stop staring at her, somebody will notice."

"Lindi..." he started.

"Don't despair so Wulfric – you had your chance – took it – but I did warn you it might make you want her more," she whispered closely in his ear.

Wulfric's eyes darted around his present company, a couple of soldiers, and glared at Lindi.

"Come on, let's go somewhere we can talk," she suggested, taking his hand in hers and leading him further down the hall away from the main feasting table and the crowds. Wulfric staggered slightly and she realised he was drunk, but he came readily enough; probably relieved to have a distraction. They sat closely together at the other end of the red, glowing fire, nearer the back of the Great Hall; it was warm and much darker than near the table where the new king and queen remained eating, drinking and laughing. Wulfric took a long, deep swallow of his wine and threw the horn to the floor – gesticulating to a servant to bring him more.

"You knew this was going to happen," said Lindi, sitting closer to him and taking his hand in hers.

124

He grunted and looked up at her with a fire of anger in his eyes. "I'm sure she must have *some* feeling for me...the way she responded to my loving was magnificent...she seemed..."

"Yes, Wulfric, *she seemed*..." she said gently. "She only 'seemed' because of the magic; I warned you that it could make your yearning for her worse – you have to forget her now."

"Yes, but I didn't realise how much more I could possibly want her!"

Lindi gently stroked his face and looked deeply into his eyes. "You have to accept this and move on...I am happy to help you do that...come on, let's go for a walk, it's a beautiful, clear night and I could do with some fresh air away from this smoky atmosphere." Taking him by the hand, she helped him to his feet. He got up, reluctantly, but followed her lead, despite still looking miserable. She led him outside and away from the Great Hall, across the village. Nearly everyone was at the wedding feast either as a guest or working; there were a few night watchmen on patrol as there was every night. The full moon was bright and there was hardly a cloud in the sky; the stars flickered in the deep, blue-black sky and the hoot of an owl was heard in the distance. Lindi shuddered.

Lindi led Wulfric to her hut. She sat him on the rugs and furs by the fire whilst she busied herself pouring them some more wine. The fire was burning low now; Lindi put some more wood on it and it leapt back to life within moments. She saw Wulfric as he watched the flames surging with newly found life, creating light and shadows around her hut. Shadows loomed large and strange. Wulfric looked uneasy, but Lindi imagined that the vast quantities of wine he had drunk that day had taken hold and his senses were numbed – all of them except his inner turmoil, which seemed to be in a heightened state.

Lindi came and sat herself down beside him. "I thought it would be better for you to be away from there now, just in case."

"Just in case of what?" he demanded.

"You've had a lot of wine; I see and feel your anger, Wulfric. If you had said anything, anything at all that could have endangered yourself; I couldn't have borne it."

"What do you mean?" he stared at her, the anger still evident in his grey eyes.

"Just that."

They drank their wine in silence, the flames of the fire still kept high by Lindi's constant supply of wood. The darkness and warmth of the hut was comforting and soon Wulfric began to lose a little of his aggression; soothed also by Lindi's soft breathing and close proximity. Despite the warmth of the fire, Lindi shivered, she'd had an unusually deep-rooted sense of foreboding all day; she had put it down to the undercurrents of the forthcoming wedding and her involvement in this love triangle that seemed never-ending. Wulfric had noticed her shiver and picked up one of the furs to wrap around her shoulders; as he did so, Lindi shifted slightly and caught his hand in hers. She brought it up to her face and kissed it ever so gently, she waited for him to pull away, when he didn't she kissed it again, this time teasing her tongue ever so gently between the fingers. Hardly daring to, she lifted her eyes and looked at his face, his eyes were closed and he seemed relaxed. Continuing to caress his hand, enjoying the strong scent of him as she kissed her way around his hand and then up to his wrist. The skin on his hand was rough but the wrist was soft and smooth, she could feel the beating of his heart, rapid in his wrist.

Suddenly, he pulled away.

Lindi began to retreat; it was too soon…she should have waited, listened to her instincts…

However, Wulfric, growled deeply in his throat and grabbed her towards him; he held her hard against him then pinned her down amongst the furs, his touch urgent and thrilling; his kisses deep and wanting. *At last*, she thought, as she became lost…falling, drowning in the deep, dark caverns of passion.

Some time later, having satisfied their desire, they lay naked and entwined among the furs by the fire, which was now low again in the hearth. Lindi watched Wulfric's sleeping figure; his face was peaceful at last and his arms were tightly wrapped around her as though he never wanted to let her go. She smiled to herself and let out a long, deep sigh. Finally, she had her wish, all these years of wanting, and waiting, for the right moment; the right time for them to be together. Things would be very different now, she would no longer be alone all the time – who knows he may even have given her a child – if it had been the wish of the gods! Her heart felt light, she snuggled closer into his arms and kissed his strong, muscular chest.

He groaned, sleepily. "Mildryth…" he whispered.

Instantly Lindi's heart froze, she pulled away from him and sat up, fury filling every tissue of her being – she pulled her gown back over her shoulders and was about to start thumping him when she heard a spine-chilling scream from outside…

Chapter Eleven

While the lovers had been caught up in their passion, the night of festivities wore on; with music and dancing by the majority, whereas a few, who had drunk too much wine, were falling asleep where they sat around the hall. All of a sudden, an agitated murmur arose amongst the guests. It wasn't until people started to leave the Great Hall that Mildryth and Wilheard noticed something peculiar was going on. They watched in surprise as the guests started to leave by the enormous great doors at the south end of the hall.

"Where are they all going?" Mildryth asked, looking at Wilheard, whose smiling face was now taking on a more serious expression, and one of concern, she noticed.

"I don't know. Whatever it is it has got them rather unsettled..." Wilheard replied. He called to one of his aides to go and find out what was going on.

Without warning, an unearthly scream was heard from outside and they looked at each other in alarm.

"Are we under attack?" Mildryth asked, jumping from her seat.

"I don't know..." replied Wilheard, now also on his feet.

The aide returned to Wilheard's side. "If it please you Sire, I think you should come and see what it is that our people are witnessing." He hung his head as the king took Mildryth's hand and walked down the hall to a side door through which they stepped, away from the mass at the end of the south entrance.

Outside, it was uncannily dark for the night of a full moon – the clouds must have come in since earlier in the evening when the sky had been clear. At first they could see nothing amiss and wondered why the people, guests and now servants too, had amassed at the end of the Great Hall. Moreover, they wondered at the cries of a few women who stood not far away from them – they were not cries of joy and celebration as they had been earlier that evening, but those of woe and foreboding.

"Wilheard....what is..." Mildryth faltered as her new husband pointed upwards to the sky above them; it was no cloud that had covered the moon, but a strange black shadow, a very bad omen...and one that did not bode well for a couple married on such a night.

Mildryth gasped and started to tremble. She felt Wilheard's arms wrap themselves protectively around her. "Do not worry, my love, I am sure it is nothing to be concerned about."

"But Wilheard, it is not a good sign. It means the gods are displeased! Do you think that they are unhappy at our union?"

Wilheard took Mildryth's chin in his hands and pulled her to face him. "It does not mean that they are unhappy with us, it might be something else..."

"But you know what they say..."

Sunniva and her father appeared at her Mildryth's side, hearing the end of the conversation. "You must not worry, Mildryth. I am certain this is nothing to do with your union with Wilheard; it has been written in the runes for many years now, there would have been another sign before now if they weren't happy about it," said Sunniva.

"Your sister is right," her father agreed.

However, even with the reassurances of her family, Mildryth felt a shiver of unease creep over her; in the wine-induced state of her mind, she felt the sudden flutter of a memory...but again it evaded her full senses.

***

The thrilling atmosphere of the wedding feast was over. The musicians had stopped playing; the guests lost their appetites and most had even stopped drinking – the mood was awash with hopelessness and gloom. People walked in a dejected manner back to their homes, or just lay down and slept on the floor of the Great Hall. It was as if nobody dared speak of the bad omen...nobody, or rather very few, would have any idea of what misfortune it could bring their way.

Very few, that was, except Gifre.

Gifre in his drunken state found terror rising within him; he had kept this secret to himself and now everyone in his community would suffer. He should have told somebody what he'd seen, the gods were angry that the marriage had gone ahead – she was not fit to be queen, that woman...that whore...she should not have married Wilheard if she had wanted his brother! Perhaps she thought it was all right to bed one brother whilst marrying the other just so she could be queen!

***

Meanwhile, Lindi, on hearing the scream, had left a deeply sleeping Wulfric and the warmth of her hut to go out into the cool, dark night. She saw the moon shadowed in darkness by a black sphere; knew immediately that her sense of foreboding that day had not been unfounded. The gods were angry for the very reason of the events that had taken place in the past days. Why had she become involved? What had possessed her to even think that she had the right to use magic to change the course of events for her own gain? She knew it was sacrilegious. She had started off by thinking she was helping Wulfric in perhaps realising that Mildryth would never be his. If he knew that the only way for her to love him was to use magic then he would surely know that she would never be his. But had she done this for his sake, or for her own selfish needs? She had been in love with Wulfric for years, but had had to stand by and watch both the brothers fall for the beautiful Mildryth – why hadn't one of them, especially Wulfric, reciprocated her love? But now she had committed misconduct towards her art for the sake of herself, the gods would not only punish her, but those that were close to her too – the shadowing of the moon was a sure sign that things were about to change, and not for the better.

***

Later, as Wilheard held Mildryth close to him, he wondered at the shadow across the moon – what had displeased the gods? Why on their wedding night did it have to happen? He could see how much it had unsettled the guests, but most importantly, Mildryth. What did this mean for them? Were they doomed as a man and wife, king and queen, or was it something bigger…something that would affect their whole community? They had already lost one king, one ruler…

The bed was strewn with herbs and flowers in celebration of their marriage; thoughts of the eclipse faded as Wilheard embraced Mildryth with more fervour. The intensity of the embrace was not as he had imagined it to be on their wedding night – the passion was there, but it was masked beneath a much stronger feeling of trepidation. There were no misgivings on his account as to whether or not they *should* have joined as man and wife, just an uneasy feeling that the gods were not happy about the union.

Voicing his concerns aloud, he stated, "I cannot think why the gods would be displeased at our union."

"Nor I," replied Mildryth, frowning and moving closer into his arms.

Wilheard looked down into his new bride's eyes and smiled gently. "Come then, let us not think upon it further…I have waited many, many years for you to become my own and although I do fear what the omen may mean, at this moment I have you in my arms as my wife and I intend to take that consternation from your brow and replace it with smiles again."

Mildryth smiled up at her husband and responded to his gentle kisses.

129

The fire in the room was roaring and warm, having been made up by Wilheard's aide before they retired. Wilheard's gentle kisses became more urgent as he held her tighter to his strong, hard chest. Mildryth reacted with an urgency of her own...not so much passion, but the need to forget things, the need for Wilheard to make everything all right again. His kisses moved away from her lips to the soft, smooth skin of her neck, she shivered with pleasure and held him closer to her. Wilheard picked her up off her feet and carried her over to the bed where he lay her down and began to undress her. When she was naked before him, he looked down upon her, his eyes caressing every part of her body; the desire in his eyes grew. Removing his own clothing he lay down beside her and pulled the biggest fur over them to keep them both warm.

Wilheard caressed her body, taking care to ensure she was finding it as pleasurable as he was and when he felt she was ready, he entered her and smiled as she called out his name.

Afterwards, entwined in each other's arms, Wilheard had a minute seed of doubt plant itself inside his mind...it had nothing to do with what the gods thought, he knew he had loved Mildryth his whole life and this had grown in maturity as they had moved into adolescence...what worried him, *ever so slightly*, was that he had bedded virgins before...had it not been her first time? Surely Mildryth was a virgin, had been with no other man? It must mean that she was just relaxed with him, having known him so many years and being comfortable with him. He glanced down at the furs on the bed – no blood...

Within that moment, his conscience turned on him.

Wilheard glanced at his wife's beautiful, serene face that was aglow from their lovemaking and the heat of the furs and fire and resented the thoughts he was having. He would surely have known if she had ever had another man, or perhaps it had been a boy...a quick mistake made as a young and naïve maiden. No, no, not her. However, that minute seed (which had so innocently planted itself within his mind) now began to germinate.

***

Outside the Great Hall, the sky became brighter as the night gave way to dawn. The first fingers of sunlight came creeping over the horizon, red and orange, casting a fiery glow across the ashen sky. As the cock crowed only a few stirred in their beds; most still in a heavy drink-induced sleep. The new king and queen slept on, Mildryth snuggled

130

up against her husband's back, an arm encasing his torso in a possessive style of embrace.

Further down in the village, Lindi's hut was empty. Small wisps of serpent-like smoke trails climbed heavily from the dying embers of the fire. Having woken in the night, despite the amount he had drunk, Wulfric crept quietly out of the hut, leaving Lindi sleeping. He understood now that she loved him, which was why she would always do *anything* to help him; the feelings were not reciprocated. His head felt like it was splitting and it hurt to walk upright, but he had to leave, had to get away before morning.

As he walked towards his own hut, near the Great Hall, where he knew his brother and Mildryth would be together, he felt a pain inside so sharp that he knew it wasn't just Lindi he had to get away from. He had to leave his home; his brother's kingdom. He could not bear to watch his brother and the woman he loved rule together, be together – and worse still – what if they were to have a child? He would have to watch that grow too; be even more removed from his rightful place to the throne.

A thought entered his head, slithered there without warning: struck. He could kill them both, now...or he could kill Wilheard...and take Mildryth for himself? Would they ever discover that it was him – the way nobody had discovered or proved that he'd had his father murdered?

Walking through the village he noticed the smokeless chimneys of the huts; all still too drunk, or asleep, to rise and light the fires. A few had not even made it home to bed, sleeping instead where they had fallen, at the side of the track, in their attempt to make it home. Wulfric ran his hands through his hair as he entered his hut. He collected a few necessary belongings, including some jewellery his mother had given him before she died – the rest having been buried with her – and with one last look around the hut he walked out of the door and away from his childhood home. He wasn't welcome, he wasn't needed. Wulfric could not live amongst his brother's people anymore; would not bear witness to Mildryth's love for him either.

Wulfric made his way slowly to where the horses were kept and untied his horse; speaking quietly and reassuringly to her as he walked her out into the golden morning. As he walked with his horse away from the village towards the river, which he would follow until he found a place in which he could start a new life, he took one look back at the Great Hall – the smoke had started climbing from the chimneys now – people were stirring. He quickened his pace and didn't look back.

131

Lindi had heard Wulfric leave the hut and had pretended that she was asleep to see if he was going to wake her or just leave – she had feared the latter. Precise in her thinking, she opened her eyes a crack and observed his back disappear from the hut without even a backward glance in her direction. With acute pain she remembered how she had given herself fully and willingly to him that previous night and how he had cried out Mildryth's name within his passion. Despite her power and foresight, she had underestimated the depth of his feelings for Mildryth; it really was love, not just lust he felt for her. Lindi had lain awake all night listening to his breathing, his agitated dreams and felt herself grow colder towards him and Mildryth. She had loved him for many years, stood back and watched his love grow for Mildryth, as had Wilheard's. The bitterness now tasted foul. Lindi felt sick, she had always been a strong and forthright woman, but something about Wulfric made her weak; weak in a way she did not like. Now, he had betrayed her!

Discreetly, and at a distance, she followed him back to his hut, witnessing the same unusual quiet and empty feel of the village compared to a usual dawn. She noticed Wulfric's stance and frowned…he entered his hut as if he had set his mind on something. She watched and waited, from her hiding place behind the animal pen of the hut opposite his, to see if anything else should occur, however, she was staggered when she saw him re-appear shortly afterwards with what could only be a departure parcel. Subtly she trailed after him watching, with distress, as he took his horse from the stable and walked away from the village only stopping once, not to look towards her hut, but towards the Great Hall, that was the centre of all things; now the centre of her growing loathing.

***

Inside their bed-chamber the new king and queen were rousing – Mildryth had been awake for a few minutes watching the form of her sleeping husband; the rise and fall of his bare chest which was broad and toned – she felt the passion rise within her again. She wasn't sure how many times they had joined as one before they fell into an exhausted sleep. Wilheard seemed to have a small smile upon his face as he slept and she hoped that it was due to her. A few moments later, he opened his eyes and looked into hers, the smile spreading into a wide grin. He grabbed her and pushed his lips onto hers and she felt the rising passion almost overtake her; she responded with delight and gasped as he entered her once again.

Later, they lay in each other's arms, warm and satisfied. All servants had been ordered not to disturb them, but now Wilheard was feeling his appetite again and Mildryth laughed as his stomach grumbled loudly.

"I must call for some food and drink, the jugs are empty," he said, climbing out of bed and wrapping an animal skin around his naked body.

"I am certainly thirsty," said Mildryth, sitting up and pulling the furs up around her body to keep off the chill of the room. "Can we have the fire made up again too?"

"Of course, my queen," he smiled at her and shouted for his guard outside the door. Wilheard gave his orders and returned to the bed.

"Happy?" he asked.

Mildryth nodded, but Wilheard noticed a small frown cross her brow.

"What is it?"

"The moon, the eclipse…"

"I told you not to worry about it. All will be well; don't let it spoil our first day as king and queen."

"Of course not," she replied and pulled him close.

"It will be expected of us to surface at some point and walk among our people," stated Wilheard.

"Yes. I know that is part of our duty today, but can we just have a bit more time, just the two of us?"

Wilheard pulled her close and lay down next to her. There was a knock at the door.

"Enter…"

A servant entered with a jug of wine and a platter full of bread, cheese and apples. He placed them on a low table at the foot of the bed, bowed and left quickly – seemingly embarrassed by the intimacy.

***

At noon, Ayken arrived to wish them both well, but Mildryth soon realised it was the guise for something else…she sat by the fire, trying to hear what was said, in hushed voices, between the two men in the adjoining room. Although difficult, she could just discern what was being said:

"What do you make of it, Ayken?" asked Wilheard.

"The shadow across the moon was foretold by a couple, including Godric, but not Lindi! I have been unable to locate her at the moment, but they tell me she never mentioned it."

"That is unusual for her as she is usually very accurate in her foretelling of things to come."

"Yes, she is..." Ayken hesitated.

"What is it, Ayken?"

"Lindi did not foresee the coming death of the king either..."

"No, but nobody did...perhaps because it was poison..."

"I don't know, Sire. Things are definitely at odds at the moment...I will ask Lindi, and perhaps Godric to do a reading again...see what they can see."

"Hmm, Godric is a bit of an old wizard; I think I would trust Lindi's word over his, even after this moon shade...we can all get things wrong at times..."

"I will go and see if I can find her."

***

In the afternoon, Wilheard and Mildryth, with a troupe of guards, walked out amongst the village. Men, women and children came out of their huts and workshops to bow and greet their new queen. Although they were friendly and clearly excited, there was a slight reserve among them. Mildryth feared it was because of the eclipse the previous evening – they were a superstitious community and would be wondering why the gods may have caused the eclipse on the night of such an important union. What had upset them so?

Mildryth pushed these thoughts to the back of her mind so that she could concentrate on her new role as queen. Lots of children ran up to her with handfuls of early wildflowers and greenery from the riverbank and woodland nearby. She smiled warmly at them and then remembered what Lindi had predicted about her having a baby within the next nine moons. She felt her stomach turn over with excitement – how wonderful that would be. How marvellous for Wilheard to have an heir of his own; a rightful one, not one that coveted it from a distance. Subconsciously she placed her hand upon her stomach.

As they re-entered the Great Hall, the closer family members and special guests from the wedding were present, standing in line to greet the new king and queen. Sunniva gave her a knowing smile and Mildryth blushed and nodded; a smile upon her lips too. Another, smaller banquet had been laid on and the villagers and servants (except those that were working in the Great Hall that evening) were absent, going back to their homes and work in their usual manner. The celebrations now were just for the royal household and their guests.

Wilheard and Mildryth embraced them in turn; it wasn't until they reached the end of the line and Mildryth embraced Lindi that she noticed the absence of Wulfric. Lindi's embrace was brief and she barely smiled at Mildryth, her blue eyes sparkled like ice that hung down in spears from the roof of the Great Hall in the winter sunshine; there was no warmth of any sun about Lindi today. Mildryth frowned at her questioningly. Lindi avoided her gaze. Mildryth had noticed the previous evening during the marriage banquet that Lindi had led a very inebriated Wulfric to the further end of the hall – had he been that bad that he was still sleeping it off somewhere?

As they took their seats at the table, Wilheard searched the faces around him.

"Where's my brother?" he asked.

Lots of heads were shaking, looking slightly troubled – would this be seen as an insult to the king? Wulfric had been at the wedding and had been seen to raise his drink to celebrate the union, so where was he now?

"Lindi, may know..." suggested Mildryth.

"Lindi? Bring Lindi to me..." he ordered the servant that was pouring his wine.

Lindi was brought before Wilheard; she bowed slightly then looked Wilheard in the eye.

"Where is my brother, Wulfric?" he demanded, he seemed to be becoming more agitated.

"I can't be certain, Sire, but..." she said steadily.

"But?"

"I think he may have left...I saw him riding out early this morning, he seemed to have his belongings with him..."

"Gifre? Where's Gifre...bring him to me, immediately." He commanded his voice full of anger. "How dare my brother insult me!"

Mildryth put her hand over Wilheard's to try to reassure and calm him, but he had the look of murder in his eyes.

***

Gifre was at home with his family when the guards came to the door of his hut; it was small and ramshackle; his under-fed pig in a stall attached to the side of the main hut. He was alarmed when he knew his presence had been requested by Wilheard, and almost fled. He managed, with difficulty, to steady his nerves and ask why he was being summoned.

"We can't tell you that," he was told by the guards.

As they walked up towards the Great Hall, Gifre wondered if he had been discovered.

Gifre could see the king's displeasure on his face as he approached the long table; he felt the bile rise in his throat. As he stood before Wilheard, he bowed, scared to look him in the eye, but knowing he had to, otherwise Wilheard would know something was wrong.

Surprisingly, Wilheard spoke calmly to him. "Have you seen, Wulfric, Gifre?"

"By the gods, I have not, not at all this day, Sire. I went this morning to see what he required of me, but I couldn't find him. Nobody, nobody, Sire, has seen him. I just went about my usual business waiting for him to return. I thought, Sire…" Gifre hesitated slightly. "I thought perhaps he was sleeping off the wine somewhere…"

"Thank you, Gifre, you may return to your home – if you do see Wulfric, please tell him I wish to have his presence."

Gifre felt relief flood through him as he backed away from the king and made his way out of the Great Hall; he had been certain he and his observations had been discovered. He wished he'd never seen what he'd seen – feared it would be the death of him…still could be.

***

Wilheard turned to Mildryth. "Where can he have gone?"

"I don't know, Wilheard. It seems an odd time to leave…the morning after our marriage." Mildryth felt an odd tug at her conscience, a picture of Wulfric's grey eyes, sad and longing…the image disappeared almost as soon as it started to form in her mind, as though she couldn't quite capture her own thoughts again.

"Perhaps it was something to do with the moon…I know he is quite superstitious at times. However, it feels as if he has turned his back on us now we're married. Lindi…well, she seemed a little uneasy just now too, perhaps she knows something. Would she confide in you? Talk to her tomorrow, will you? See what you can discover."

"Of course, Wilheard. She did seem a little strange, didn't she? Although, you know she can be at times…" She would ask Lindi tomorrow, but she feared that Lindi would not confide in her – she seemed to confide in nobody.

The following morning dawned bright and cold. Frost clung to every part of the natural world, sparkling brightly like tiny stars in the galaxy. Mildryth felt light and joyful; she'd had a wonderful night with Wilheard and was relishing the thoughts of that as she approached Lindi's hut. She became suddenly aware of shouting and banging within the hut – as though somebody was throwing things around inside.

She called out loudly as she approached the door. Everything went quiet.

"Lindi, Lindi…it's Mildryth."

Lindi opened the door of her hut, she looked dishevelled and her eyes looked as though she'd been crying.

"Mildryth…" She didn't seem to know what to say.

"Is something the matter?"

Lindi shrugged and stepped back into the hut. Mildryth was not sure whether she should follow or not, she hesitated, then stood tall and entered.

Ordinarily Mildryth would have expected Lindi to follow the conventions of having the queen visit her, however, they had been friends since childhood and clearly something was wrong!

As her eyes adjusted to the darkness, inside the hut, Mildryth could see that there were some broken pots on the floor; the fire was low and the pot above the fire that was usually bubbling away was quiet, empty.

"Lindi, what's wrong?"

Lindi looked at Mildryth coldly, her blue eyes dark and lifeless.

"Is there something I can do to help?"

"No, nobody can help, it's nothing…" She sat herself down onto a seat beside the fire, her body was slouched, her face hard.

Mildryth looked at Lindi who sat as silent as mist. It probably wasn't the best time to ask about Wulfric, but she had given her word to Wilheard that she would find out what she could. Taking some wood from the pile near the fire, she threw some of it onto the dying embers – slowly the flames started to lick the rough edges of the wood; stealing around their prey, ready to devour and destroy…to make ashes of something that was once strong and seemingly invincible.

Lindi lifted her head slightly and looked at Mildryth. "I am sorry…my queen." She dipped her head in a subservient manner, as if suddenly remembering what she should be doing.

Mildryth spoke softly. "Tell me why you are so angry…"

Lindi shook her head. "You've come to ask me about Wulfric, where he is?"

Mildryth smiled and nodded, she always felt rather naïve in the presence of Lindi, her power and knowledge were remarkable.

137

Mildryth wished sometimes she had a very tiny part of her knowledge, her astuteness.

"I do not know where Wulfric has gone."

"But you know he has left the village?"

"Yes. I was awake early yesterday morning and I saw him go to the stables and take his horse. He had his belongings with him, like he was going away…"

"I wonder what has made him leave. I thought he and Wilheard were more amicable now, he came to the wedding, I thought it was a peace-offering."

"Perhaps it has made the gap widen…he sees Wilheard with all the power *and* the beautiful queen. Perhaps he will return when he has got used to the idea."

"He has known all his life that Wilheard was the rightful heir…he shouldn't still be angry with him…it's not Wilheard's fault, it's *his destiny*!" Mildryth felt her anger rise. Wulfric had no right to feel an injustice had been caused to him.

"Do you think it could have had anything to do with the darkness of the moon? The shadow…"

Lindi shook her head slowly, "I am sorry I cannot help you further…I really *do not* know where he might have gone, or why." She was quiet for a few moments, then added, "How are your headaches, your dreams?"

Mildryth fingered the brooch on her cloak and replied: "My head has been mostly better and the dreams, so far have been fine…in fact I don't think I've dreamt the past two nights…"

"Too busy with your new husband, no doubt?"

Mildryth smiled and pretended to look shocked. "I suppose it may have something to do with that, I feel more relaxed and happy than I have for a while, although I was upset and afraid by the moon's darkness. At first I thought the gods were angry with Wilheard and I, but he says I shouldn't worry and that it wasn't anything to do with our marriage – that had been in the stars for a very long time; they would have shown their displeasure much earlier, many years ago."

"He's probably right."

The two women were quiet. Mildryth knew she would get no further information about Wulfric from Lindi, she was afraid of what Wilheard would say, but if Lindi didn't know where he was then there was nothing more she could do.

"If anything comes to you about Wulfric, please let me know. Wilheard is very angry, he thinks that Wulfric is against him; he sees it as an insult."

"By the gods, if I see or hear anything, you will be the first to know," replied Lindi.

***

Lindi watched as Mildryth walked out of the door, she was not lying about not knowing where Wulfric had gone; she wished she did know – that way she may be able to find him, get him to come home or at least persuade him that *she* was the better woman for him. She was free, she had powers that mixed with his malevolence could become a powerful force, why could he not see this?

She stood up and paced the floor of her hut. She had to follow him and find him – they were meant to be together, she was sure of it. All she had to do was to convince him that now Mildryth was married, *she* was the woman for him. The gods could not always be right...her mother had been mistaken – sometimes the gods got things wrong. Lindi gazed into the fire and muttered an incantation into the dancing flames...gradually pictures began to form.

Chapter Twelve

Megan's alarm woke her. It was just beginning to get light outside, the birds chirruping in the trees around the river and house, their song was cheerful as though they knew that spring was just around the corner.

Walking to work, she was pleased she didn't *have* to walk along the river to the dig; although the sun was shining and the sky was blue with a few white clouds ahead of her, she didn't relish the idea of crossing the bridge again after last night; the golden haired woman had unnerved her further. She had also left a sorry-looking Bartie at home and felt rather lonely without him. However, she couldn't help her thoughts cascading into the depths of the unusual happenings of the past few days. Firstly, the woman at the window; this was followed shortly afterwards by the woman on the bridge, were they the same person? They looked *very* similar. What of the male figure watching her in the trees too? She shivered. On top of that there was the strange damp, coldness in the cottage and the wet earth that she had found on the floor...her mind could not make sense of these things, but put together it was like something sinister was happening.

She walked more quickly towards the area of the dig, away from the river, but could not get rid of the sense of foreboding and fear that weighed heavily upon her. The recounts in her gran's diary about the woman enhanced that feeling too. Her rational side told her the events were all just a series of coincidence, but her rational side seemed to be diminishing.

She jumped as her mobile signalled a text message. It was Sasha – good, someone sensible to ground her...

> *Hiya. Fancy inviting me over*
> *this evening for that glass of wine?*
> *Sasha x*

She replied:

> *That would be great! Come over for 7.30*
> *& I'll cook us supper. x*

Having made plans for the evening, Megan felt a little less anxious about going home. She hated the fact that she had started feeling worried about going home – all the time her gran was there it had never felt at all strange, just Gran's cottage, comfortable, welcoming and warm.

Megan walked up the lane towards the main road where she would cross over and make her way up past the 'modern' cemetery and through the field to the Saxon burial ground. It wasn't until she had walked past the spot, she realised that Kai's caravan had not been parked in its usual spot – he'd gone!

No caravan, no dog, no horse and certainly no Kai.

She was slightly surprised, as it was only eight-thirty and she knew he had been there yesterday; he'd been in the pub last night. Maybe Garrett had moved him on, or maybe he had got itchy feet and fancied a change? She couldn't decide if she felt disheartened at his leaving or relief…

Arriving at the dig, she found that neither David nor Fin were there…she knew Fin had said he would be in around noon, but there was no sign of David either. Bella approached her with a cup of coffee and a Danish pastry. Megan was surprised at her kindness.

"Morning," said Bella. "It's just us at the moment and Oscar."

Megan nodded and took the offered coffee and Danish. She looked over the site to where the JCB driver was digging another trench further over. Oscar stood watching, a steaming drink in his hand.

"Oscar's keen, very dedicated," Megan announced more to herself than Bella.

"A bit like an eager puppy," said Bella, looking over at him.

"He's nice though," stated Megan.

"Sure. He's a bit young for me though!" replied Bella with a smile.

"Oh?"

"Yes, I prefer them a bit more mature…like Fin," Bella gave her a strange look and walked off.

Megan stood staring after her. *Well that leaves me in no doubt,* she laughed to herself at being put well and truly in her place. *I wonder if Fin's aware of this attraction*, she pondered.

During the day, the team discovered more cremation pots and surprisingly lots of burials too, showing that the site was used for their dead for many centuries. Both early, pagan, and later Christian burials were uncovered. The pagan graves were orientated from North East-South West, whereas the Christian burials were North-West to South-East. The sun shone, but the wind was cold. Megan felt her fingers go numb and remembered how, as a student, she would feel miserable and wonder if she was heading down the correct career path; hating the poor weather, but then it fading into insignificance as an important discovery was unearthed.

Later that day when Megan arrived home, she opened the front door, expecting Bartie to come flying out to greet her in his usual manner. When he didn't appear, she called to him, but still he did not come. Alarmed, Megan quickly took her boots off and rushed into the house, calling his name and whistling. Maybe Mrs Clark had come later today and was still out for a walk? She had almost convinced herself of this when she heard a whimper from upstairs. Sprinting up the stairs she stopped on the landing.

"Bartie, Bartie – where are you, boy?"

Another whimper came from behind her bedroom door. The door, as usual, was shut; Megan tried to keep the doors upstairs shut when Bartie was at home alone, to head off any chewing of socks or anything else that took his fancy. He must have shut himself in her bedroom, but what was he doing up here? She walked across the landing, the uneven floorboards creaking under her feet, and lifted the latch. Bartie shot out at high speed and fled down the stairs without even saying 'hello' to her. She took a step further into the room and looked about. She gasped. The room was in disarray. The bed covers were disorderly; the chest of drawers open and clothes were hanging out; the wicker chair was on its side and there was mud all over the carpet.

"Bartie!" she shouted and ran down the stairs after him.

He sat looking forlornly at her by the back door, head down; ears forward. She walked past him, glaring, and opened the back door. He ran out quickly, his tail between his legs then shot off down the garden out of sight.

Megan shut the door, switched on the kettle then went back upstairs to assess the damage. What could have happened in her bedroom – Bartie certainly couldn't have caused all that dirt - his paws didn't seem particularly filthy? On entering the room again, she felt the chill this time, smelt the scent of wet, cold earth…she shivered. She thought back to Bartie's behaviour as he had shot down the stairs…it wasn't that he was feeling ashamed of himself it was that he was afraid…but afraid of what?

Boldly, she took a deep breath and started to attend the chaos. There had to be some rational explanation regarding all this. It certainly appeared like somebody was searching for something…but what and who? What was most disconcerting was that there was never any sign of any break in; almost seemed like an 'inside job'. This was happening too often; perhaps she should call the police, but tell them **what** exactly? It '*seemed*' like someone was breaking in and leaving the place dirty, but '*no officer, nothing has been taken*'. It all seemed too incredulous to speak aloud; what could they possibly do? It was not like they would put 24 hour surveillance on the cottage on the off chance that somebody might break in and leave the place in a mess.

Having tidied up and vacuumed the floor, Megan returned downstairs. She called Bartie from the garden. He reluctantly ventured over from the flower border where he was sitting and came towards the back door, his tail still between his legs.

Megan bent down and stroked his soft head. She spoke to him gently and he looked up at her with apologetic eyes. "It's all right, boy," she said calmly. "Sorry, I shouted…I thought it was you had made the mess…now…now I don't know *what* to think."

For the next couple of hours, Megan busied herself with attending to her emails and then on preparing dinner for herself and Sasha. She wondered if she should tell Sasha more of what was happening; about the 'visitor', and the woman she had seen on the bridge the previous evening. She didn't know Sasha very well and didn't want her to think she was a bit weird, or *completely* insane. However, she did feel she needed to speak to somebody - her mother had already made her feel foolish, even though she had admitted to gran having talked about seeing a strange woman – *could* it be the same woman? It all sounded too absurd and Megan was beginning to feel weary from the turmoil of her thoughts. She put some music on the iPod and danced round the kitchen, whilst she let the smooth sounds of the jazz drift over her. She laughed as Bartie looked at her as if she was completely nuts, but at least his tail had started to wag again.

Megan was singing along to some music, that she had download fairly recently in order to keep her spirits up after her gran's death, when she heard Bartie's warning bark that Sasha was arriving. Opening the front door, she could see Sasha, with Jess galloping ahead, approaching; a bottle of wine in hand. She looked up and smiled as the two dogs greeted each other, darting off round the back of the house.

"What a beautiful cottage," said Sasha. "I've never seen it from this side before, only from the banks of the river, it's gorgeous."

"Thank you. My gran loved the fact that it was quite secluded and frankly so do I."

"It has a friendly feel to the place, despite what you've said," stated Sasha as she followed Megan into the kitchen.

"That's why it's so strange…it has always been a wonderfully tranquil and warm home, until now. I don't understand why it's changed."

"Is that Duran Duran?" Sasha said, looking towards the iPod and smiling at Megan.

"Em. Yes...I em..."

"It's great...takes me right back!" Sasha started to sing along, Megan joining in whilst she poured them both wine.

"I've made paella, I hope that's ok?"

"Smells divine," replied Sasha, pulling out a chair from the table and sitting herself on it.

Megan put the steaming dish in the centre of the table and handed Sasha the serving spoon, while she helped herself to a chunk of crusty bread from the wooden board next to it.

"So, tell me about Brad's exhibition then..." asked Megan.

Sasha, her eyes bright with excitement, told Megan about Brad's forthcoming exhibition and how they hoped it would be really successful for him, he worked really hard.

When they had finished their dinner, Megan suggested they look at the Roundhouse before it got completely dark, and then she would show Megan round the cottage too. Megan picked the key for the Roundhouse door off the hook on the mantle, above the range, where it had hung forever. It was heavy and slightly rusty, a little like the key to the cottage.

Stepping out of the house into the dusk, the dogs shooting off across the garden, Megan and Sasha walked on the soft, muddy ground towards the circular construction.

"I've often wondered what the Roundhouse was used for, as I've walked these paths with Jess a lot," said Sasha. "I could have put it in a search engine, I guess, but never really got round to it – I suppose I like to romanticise about it a bit..."

"I'm not sure there's much about it that's romantic; it was built in 1790, it was to do with the canal...the lock keeper would have had accommodation on the first and upper floor, and the lower floor would have housed the horses or donkeys."

"Fascinating..." replied Sasha. "There's so much history on our doorstep and we know so little about it."

"That's why I love my job – we get an insight into the past."

Together, they walked up the stone steps to the entrance and Megan placed the key in the lock. It was stiff and the door heavy to shift, but finally they managed to get it open and Megan switched the light on. It only gave a pathetic glow but there was enough light to see that it was not really that impressive as it stood at the moment. It smelled of damp and rotting; there were a lot of dark stains on the walls and ceiling above them; the building barely looked safe to stand in. There were a lot of old implements, some unrecognisable, stacked up against the walls.

"I won't take you up onto the first floor, it's not safe," said Megan.

"What are you going to do with the place?"

"I have thought about making it into a holiday let…but it's too soon for me to make any decisions yet," Megan trailed off, swallowing the lump in her throat.

Perceptively, Sasha moved away and stepped back outside the Roundhouse. "Any more wine in the house?" she asked.

"Sure, come on."

The two women were walking back towards the cottage when Bartie stopped and growled low in his throat. Jess stood stock still too, hackles raised…they were both watching the trees on the opposite bank. Sasha looked up and followed their gaze.

"There's someone over there," she whispered.

"Come on, let's get inside, it's getting cold – it's probably only a dog walker," she said hurriedly and stomped off towards the house.

Megan could feel Sasha watching her closely as she poured them each another glass of wine. The dark red liquid glided smoothly into the glasses. She handed one to Sasha, who was sitting on the sofa, then she flopped down into the cushions at the other end, taking a large gulp of smooth, oaky Malbec. The dogs were curled up close together in front of the wood burner, their snores almost in unison. The fire was warm and the roar of it comforting.

"Are you all right?" Sasha asked. "You couldn't get in from the garden quick enough just now…are you afraid of something?"

"That's very intuitive of you…" she smiled at her new friend.

"Are strange things still happening here?"

"Yes, occasionally, although it does seem to be becoming more frequent – take today for example…"

Megan conveyed the events from earlier when she had come home from work. Sasha's face turned from a smile, at the start, to a look of genuine concern.

"I think you should tell the police!" she stated at the end, sitting forward on the sofa and placing her glass on the coffee table.

"I did consider that too, but felt it was all too coincidental," she replied with a sigh.

"Megan, it sounds like somebody broke into the house…"

"I know, but although there was a real mess in the bedroom I couldn't see where anybody might have broken in. Also, I have the only key in existence to the cottage."

"Well that's something we must change for a start…you must let me have a spare…I can keep it at home, somewhere safe, then if you ever need it, I have a standby!"

"That would be sensible, yes, I'll do that."

"Why don't you show me round the cottage now…see if I can pick up any ideas as to what is going on."

"Sure, come this way."

The dogs lifted their sleepy heads to watch the two women leave the sitting room, but soon returned to their slumbering in front of the warm fire.

Megan led Sasha round her gran's cottage, starting with the ground floor. She explained to Sasha about the woman's face at the window in the kitchen the other night, at which she saw Sasha physically shiver. She didn't say anything at the time, but Megan sensed that she was scrutinising everything and would save all her observations until the tour was over. As they started to ascend the stairs, Sasha suddenly stopped a few stairs from the bottom.

"What's up?" asked Megan, a chill running through her.

"I *can* smell damp, I see what you mean…however, I do think that there could be a simple explanation for it; you should ask a builder to come and take a look, perhaps it's rising damp."

"You think it's just in the fabric of the building?"

Sasha nodded firmly.

They continued up the stairs to the bedrooms and bathroom – there was nothing out of place or extraordinary…this time.

Back in the lounge, Sasha poured them both more wine.

"I do think that some of this can be explained, however, it disturbs me that you keep seeing this woman. Have you seen her around the town, amongst other people?"

"No, always alone…"

"Hmmm."

"There's one thing I haven't told you…wait here."

Megan climbed the stairs once more and collected her gran's diary from the dressing table before returning to the sitting room and thrusting it in Sasha's hands at the point she had read previously…about the woman and the hare.

Sasha read the open page and then glanced up at Megan, another look of concern on her face. "This is really quite sinister."

"But you don't think I'm going mad, or that gran was too – perhaps I'm inheriting it from her?"

"I don't think that of either of you. Both of you sound like you're in a bit of emotional turmoil – she was going through an affair and a divorce and you've just split up with a lover too, you've also recently lost your gran, so it might be that your rational side is becoming a bit jaded. In spite of that though, there is the unquestionable fact that this woman seems to have some connection with you both, or perhaps the area?"

"What do you mean?"

"Well, this sounds awfully crazy, but what if she asked your gran for help and now she's asking you – I know it's over thirty years apart and sounds like some ridiculous ghost story when I say it out loud. What if she is looking for something and needs help in finding it?"

Megan sat down heavily in the armchair, her head in her hands. "This is just so bizarre, friends have told me of odd experiences that they've had; it just seems surreal now it is happening to *me*."

"Would it make you feel a bit better if I stayed tonight?" asked Sasha.

Megan looked up gratefully and nodded. "Thank you, the bed in the spare room is made up...." Megan smiled at her, grateful that she would have somebody else in the house overnight.

***

Mildryth felt the strong arms around her, wrapping her in a powerful and passionate embrace, felt soft lips upon hers, searching and probing, urging her to respond. Her senses were alive, her heart pounding in her chest; blood rushing in her ears...she opened her eyes and stared into the beautiful grey eyes that held so much longing...she felt a tugging at her consciousness – something didn't feel right. Grey. Why grey? Wilheard's eyes were blue...Wulfric's were...

Letting out a cry, she shot up in bed, immediately Wilheard was at her side, looking into her eyes with his clear, *blue* eyes...she felt disorientated and looked fiercely around the room.

"Mildryth, Mildryth, what is it? What's wrong?"

Mildryth looked back at Wilheard, then back round the room.

"It's all right, Mildryth...I am here...what is it?"

She took a deep breath and sighed loudly. "A dream...only a dream," she said, lightly.

"What happened?" Wilheard's face was full of concern.

"I...em...I'm not really sure..." she needed time to think, she couldn't tell Wilheard that her dream had been about his brother!

"It's all right, here have some wine," Wilheard spoke softly and poured her a drink.

148

Mildryth drank the wine and immediately felt slightly more relaxed. Her heartbeat slowed and she breathed more easily. She rubbed her fingers at her temples in a circular motion; her head throbbed and she shut her eyes and leaned against Wilheard's chest, finding comfort there.

"Are you still having the headaches?" he asked. "I had hoped that after our union you would feel more settled. Three full moons have passed since then and I am worried that you are still affected by these headaches.

She nodded.

"Has Lindi given you anything more to help you? I will send for her..."

Mildryth merely shrugged. She had no energy to argue and would welcome some relief from the headache that pounded in her mind. Wilheard laid her on the bed, covered her with the furs, then walked across the room and called for his servant.

When Mildryth awoke later her head felt clearer and she'd had no further dreams. There was no sign of Lindi, or Wilheard, so she decided to go out and get some fresh air. She got up and dressed, but in her rush she failed to notice the brooch still lying upon the stool, and went in search of Wilheard to see if he had managed to summon Lindi.

Outside the day was bright; the sun felt warm upon her, but there was a very cold, easterly wind. As Mildryth was walking towards the Great Hall she saw Wulfric's servant, Gifre, staring at her from a short distance away.

"Good morning, Gifre," She smiled at him.

He glared at her, not bowing as she passed by. She felt her smile drop and felt discomfort at his animosity. How dare he? Gifre should be more respectful...if he wasn't, it could be seen as treason and treason was punishable by death. She was the queen whether he liked it or not, Wulfric would never be king. Gifre may have his loyalties to Wulfric, but he should surely be more loyal to Wilheard, his king; especially as nobody had heard from Wulfric in months. Pulling herself up, she turned back towards him.

"Have you seen, Wilheard?" she asked.

"No, my *queen*, I have not...neither have I seen Wulfric - not for a long time – I would imagine it would have been *him* that you were searching for, rather than your husband."

"Why, have you *seen* Wulfric? I know that Wilheard is eager that his brother is found."

"As I'm sure you are too," Gifre almost spat his words at her.

Suddenly the air around Mildryth felt colder; her head began to spin and she again saw Wulfric's wolf-like eyes bearing into hers; she stumbled slightly and Gifre took her hand in his to stabilise her. However, the gesture was not friendly; the pressure of his hand on hers, as he squeezed her wrist, left his hard nails digging into her soft skin. She gasped. The blood was rushing in her ears and she heard, but could not quite fathom, the words that Gifre hissed at her next...

"I saw you, you whore...you traitor..."

"Gifre, how dare you speak to your queen in usch a way!"

"Queen? You don't have the right to call yourself a queen...what you have done is traitorous to our king and people!"

"What are you talking about?" Her head continued to feel light, her legs felt unsteady beneath her.

"You know very well what I am talking about, don't pretend you don't. I saw you...the two of you, entwined in each other's arms – together down by the river, moving together...you should have hidden yourselves more carefully..." Gifre stared hard in her eyes. "Call yourself our queen? I don't know what the two brothers see in you...you are a traitorous wench, not fit to be our queen – no wonder the gods are angry!"

Mildryth's head pounded again; the pain was searing through her brain like sharp claws behind her eyes. Her mind became a series of images and with each vision she saw those grey, wolf-like eyes, Wulfric's eyes – she felt his strong arms around her; felt his passion and urgency, and when she turned, Lindi was standing behind her, her face full of anger and hatred. Now, she knew the dreams had not been dreams after all, but a reality that she could not face...as Lindi reached for her, she collapsed into darkness and because of the fear and self-loathing she felt, she let it envelop her completely.

Mildryth was aware of the voices close by before she slowly opened her eyes. She could see in the candlelit room that there were two figures close together, speaking in hushed voices. While her eyes refocused, she could just make out the shape of one which was female, and the other's stature could only be Wilheard's. She felt a rising panic begin in her chest; she tried to sit and speak but vomited without warning onto the floor. The noise brought both Wilheard and Lindi to her side, Wilheard's face was full of concern – he didn't seem to be full of rage...had Lindi not told him what had happened, what Gifre had said? Lindi had heard every word.

Lindi spoke to Wilheard: "You need to go to my hut, she needs a potion to keep her calm – I must stay with her – go, Wilheard, now!" Lindi gave instructions of where Wilheard should find what she needed.

"I will be back, my love," said Wilheard, kissing Mildryth gently on the head before hurriedly, but reluctantly, leaving the room.

Lindi had taken control of the situation.

The waves of nausea passed as she watched Wilheard leave the room, on his errand; the king running an errand…everything seemed out of kilter.

"Lindi, what in the gods' names is happening? What have you told Wilheard, where is Gifre?"

"Leave Gifre to me…" she cried, glaring at Mildryth with a frosty countenance.

Mildryth faced Lindi. "So it's true, I did lay with Wulfric, it wasn't a dream – how did that happen? Why did I have no recollection of it?" Mildryth looked at Lindi and a sudden realisation dawned on her as she watched Lindi's eyes grow colder and fill with hatred and jealousy. "It was *you* – it's been you all along! You've used magic, magic *against* me…how *could* you Lindi, to what purpose, to what end? I thought you were my friend."

"I was…but they both wanted you…*always*. I have been in love with Wulfric for years, but he didn't give me a second glance, not when you were around. I thought that if I granted him his wish, he would find that he was just lusting after you…he had to realise that he wasn't *in love* with you…I still had a chance, if he was satiated with you then he might, just might, turn his affections and love to me once you were married to his brother."

"You used magic to get me to lay with Wulfric? Even though he hated the fact that magic was blamed for his father sleeping with his mother and how he was conceived? I don't understand! Why would he do that and *why* would you help him? You are both my dearest friends…"

"Touching, but of course you don't understand, you are so naïve, Mildryth. Everything in your life has been so easy, you were blessed by the gods from the moment you were born; everything has been handed to you. Well, you can't have everything, not Wulfric anyway – he is going to be mine."

Mildryth felt the anger and bitterness rise up in her. "So, are you going to use magic on him too, to force him to love you: you can't force people to love you, Lindi – yes, you can use magic, but unless the feelings are true and untainted then it can never be truly love. Wilheard loves me, unconditionally…Wulfric, well I don't know, it must be only lust – it is unrequited. If you want him, go and find him…see if he will have you! Once Wilheard hears about this, he will understand…he will forgive me and hunt you both down like the beasts you are…"

Lindi started to laugh, a low sinister laugh which became more of a cackle as she looked with venom at Mildryth. "Wilheard...you think you'll tell him...unconditional you say..." She laughed harder. "Don't you realise you *foolish* girl that if you, or anyone else, tells Wilheard then it will be you too that is put to death. What you've done is treason...you'll just have to hope that nobody tells him."

Mildryth felt the room spinning again as the realisation of what Lindi was saying suddenly dawned on her. Surely if Wilheard heard her version of the events; the magic and colluding of his brother and their friend, he would see that she was innocent in all of this, wouldn't he?

At that moment Wilheard rushed back into the room holding the phial that Lindi had sent him to find. One look at his concerned face sent Mildryth into a spiralling loss of control and she collapsed on to the floor.

Chapter Thirteen

Megan walked through the wet grass. The early morning was misty and cold – the damp seemed to seep right into her skin making her shiver. Bartie, nose to the ground as usual, was sniffing and snorting his way ahead of her. She was almost home; she could see the cottage clearly on the other side of the riverbank, the bridge was just a few feet away. She was about to cross the bridge when she suddenly realised that Bartie was nowhere to be seen, and worse than that, the blonde woman stood on the bank of the river. She was as still as a statue, staring ahead of her down river, but that did not stop Megan from hearing her desperate whisper...although she could not understand the words...but she could hear the desperation in her tone. As the woman turned her gaze slowly towards Megan, she seemed to disperse into the mist. Moments later, Megan gasped as a cold hand clasped her shoulder tightly, making her twist round precipitously and find herself under the scrutiny of a pair of grey eyes – eyes as cold as steel and filled with resentment. She tried to pull away but the grip of the hand held firm. She tried to shout...to run, but her legs would not move; they felt like lead weights.

Megan turned her head. The woman was now on her hands and knees, searching the ground, searching and crying as if her life depended on her finding what it was she had lost. The man's hold on Megan's shoulder was powerful and cruel.

Megan became aware of somebody calling her name in the distance; tried to look up the river to where the sound seemed to be coming from, but she felt disorientated. The woman continued to search, the man continued to stare, to hold onto her shoulder but suddenly, unexpectedly his grip seemed to loosen, the voice calling her name became louder, more urgent...

"Megan!"

Megan looked at the woman who was looking down at her from above; she couldn't quite figure who she was or what she was doing in her gran's sitting room. Slowly, it dawned on her that it was Sasha, her face full of concern...two dogs were now jumping on her as she realised that she was lying down on the sofa, having fallen asleep watching TV the night before, the fire in the stove now just a small, pathetic glow.

"Are you ok?" asked Sasha.

Megan struggled to sit up. "Yes...I'm fine..."

"You were shouting in your sleep, Bartie came upstairs to fetch me...he was clearly worried."

Megan ruffled his curly ears. The dream was slowly abating, but the images were still clear and disturbing.

"What time is it?"

"Nearly six a.m."

Megan frowned.

"Bit early, but fancy some coffee? You look like you could do with one," said Sasha.

Megan nodded. She felt she needed to ground herself into some reality – her head was still reeling from her dream.

"I'll put the kettle on," suggested Sasha, tightening the robe Megan had lent her and disappearing towards the kitchen; the dogs followed.

Megan sat up and rested her head in her hands. She couldn't believe that the woman was beginning to invade her dreams just like her gran had experienced. The woman had asked her gran for help...why hadn't her gran done anything? She would never turn her back on somebody that needed her help, it wasn't like her to do that. However, Megan did not know how she was supposed to help this woman either...what was it she was searching for: a person, a thing? She had seemed so desperately unhappy.

Megan found Sasha sat at the kitchen table. "I put the dogs in the garden," she said, placing two steaming mugs of coffee on the worn surface. Megan walked slowly across the tiled floor and sat heavily down in the chair opposite her friend. Sasha looked questioningly at her.

"I've just had the strangest dream..." Megan began and then realised she didn't know quite what to say. However, Sasha sat quietly, expectantly, so Megan continued.

"Who was the man?" she asked, when Megan was finished.

"I've no idea...although there was something familiar about him, but he seemed angry, bitter about something; his hold on my shoulder felt spiteful as though I had wronged him in some way and he wanted his revenge. I can't believe this is now penetrating my dreams, *what* is going on?"

"Have you thought about some counselling?" suggested Sasha, gently.

"So you *do* think I'm going crazy?" Megan sighed heavily.

"No, not at all, like I said before I think maybe you're suffering emotionally, you have been under immense pressure recently...losing your gran and moving here, being made redundant from your job. She hesitated for a moment. 'And...a broken relationship?"

"How did you guess?"

"Female intuition?" Sasha shrugged.

"Yes, you're right. It was a doomed relationship from the start though." Megan didn't really feel like talking about it, not even with Sasha who she felt so at ease with. No, she didn't want to discuss Tom, that was behind her, she was tired...tired of all the emotional stress – Sasha was right, she had a lot going on and it was no wonder she was having bad dreams and 'seeing things'.

"You go and have a shower and I'll get us some breakfast. I'm sure you'll feel much more refreshed once you've had a lovely warm shower." Sasha smiled at Megan and placed a reassuring hand on her arm as she walked behind her.

Megan lifted herself out of the chair and made her way up the stairs to the bathroom. A shower was just what she needed before a day outside in the cold. As the hot water helped her relax, she found herself looking forward to getting on with the dig and seeing Fin's friendly face.

***

Lindi sat staring into the flames; she had been trying for days, but to no avail, her chanting barely audible above the sounds of the crackling fire. This time it had to work, she stared hard into the flames; her concentration filled the air around her. To start with she saw only the orange flames dancing, their mesmerising moves licking around the blackened wood and white ash in the raised fire bed. Flames jumped and shifted shape as she watched them. A sleepy feeling was beginning to wash over her, when suddenly she saw something beginning to take shape...something large and dark: trees tall and thick; a river and a rock formation...a cave? There was another fire burning in the cave, which was probably why she could see this scene – it was like another mind, another vision.

Although unsure of the location, she was pretty certain in which direction it lay: south-west. She must travel south-west, that way she would find him. She would leave in a couple of days...follow the path; first she must prepare.

***

It was dark and still when Mildryth awoke. She heard the cockerel crow and noticed some dull, grey light seeping through the narrow gaps in the wooden walls of the hut; she could feel the cold breeze of the early morning and noticed the fire was very low, almost out. Wilheard's heavy breathing filtered through the air, his body still and turned away from her. She would make up the fire then return to his

155

side and move in close to him to keep warm; make love. She quietly rose from the bed and walked towards the fire, picking up some logs and smaller sticks; she placed them carefully on the fire. Standing up she turned, her head began to swim and without warning she vomited on to the floor. The noise woke Wilheard; he was beside her in an instant and helping her back to their bed.

"That's the third time you've been sick in as many mornings," he stated. "I am worried about you! I ought to call for Godric."

Mildryth smiled at him weakly. The time had come – she must tell him before he called in the elderly healer again. Godric was good and kind; she had convinced Wilheard to let her see him instead of Lindi, there had been tension between them for hours after Lindi had given her the potion. With careful manipulation Mildryth had persuaded Wilheard to keep Lindi at a distance, for a while at least.

"I think perhaps the potions she has been giving me are making me worse," she had said, through her tears. "I would just like you to keep her away from me for a few days until I've had a chance for her potions to cease having an effect on me – if it makes no difference, then I will see her again, I swear by the gods!"

Wilheard had agreed, reluctantly at first, but had seen his wife's distress and wanted to reassure her.

"Why are you smiling?" he asked, frowning. "Are you sure you don't want me to call Lindi back, you don't seem to be getting any better without her potions either – you are still being sick."

"I don't think you need to be worried about me being sick at the moment," she replied. "Wilheard, sit here, beside me." Mildryth patted the rough woollen blankets and held her hand out for his.

He sat on the soft furs, took her hand in his and waited for her to continue, his concerned eyes searching hers.

"I don't think it's a healer I need...I'm going to have a baby, our kingdom's heir," she stated, a smile spreading across her face.

Wilheard's bright blue eyes widened. In an instant he was holding her in his arms, then on their feet dancing round the hut. Mildryth's heart was in her mouth and she felt more happiness in that moment than she had ever felt - she was going to give Wilheard an heir. She had prayed to Eostre for a child, a family of their own and her prayers had been answered. Wilheard looked deep into her eyes and she saw then that he loved her more than anything in the world and that he was totally besotted with the idea of becoming a father.

**

The sky was a dull grey, threatening showers – the wind was moderate, easterly and cold. Megan felt it even though she was crouching down in the trench, gently scraping away the soil that had lain against the stones which were piled on top of each other. Gently she removed the stones one by one and placed them outside of the trench; carefully sketching and recording as she went – the photographer had already been over to take some photos of the stones.

Fin had asked her to study this particular trench that morning whilst he went to the university to drop off the brooch and pick up some papers he needed.

After lunch, having moved many of the stones away from the soil, Megan found she was uncovering some type of wooden structure – a grave? It had been mostly cremation pots until now, but she knew some burial sites had both. The trench lay from east to west and the structure seemed to continue along a south to north direction which indicated it could be a burial, not Christian but pagan, early Saxon. As she continued to scrape away the damp soil, she felt a chill run through her; she heard a voice carried on the breeze close by, not loud enough to hear what was said, but she turned anyway expecting to see one of the students – there was nobody there.

After a while, she had uncovered what she was certain was a grave, but the fact that there seemed to be a wooden coffin baffled her...surely the Saxons didn't use wooden coffins? She looked over to the trench where Fin, having returned from Oxford, and Bella were crouched, their heads close together, focussed on something in the ground – she felt silly at having to go and ask him.

The sky was darkening now, it seemed oppressive and close; the fact that the land was so flat around them seemed to emphasise the size of the sky above them. Its dark, grey clouds blackening on the horizon, threatening heavy rain – she hoped it would go around them, so the dig could continue.

Megan felt indecisive: should she go and get Fin, or continue with the trench herself? She thought it would be best to extend the trench in a north-east to south-west direction as that seemed to be the orientation of the coffin. No, she didn't feel confident enough to give the instruction, she would go and interrupt Fin and Bella – she was sure Fin would be interested in what she had discovered.

As she approached the trench, Bella looked up at her but didn't acknowledge her at all. It was only when she called Fin's name that he looked up from the trench and smiled.

"Hi," he said, stepping up and out of the trench. He stretched his arms above his head which resulted in his shirt riding up over his flat, hard stomach; she couldn't help but notice the dark, curly hair on his abdomen which led down beneath the waist of his jeans. Megan felt herself blush and suddenly lose her train of thought; she had to look away and straight at his eyes so she could focus on what she wanted to tell him.

"I…er…I think you might be interested in what I've found," she stated as calmly as she could, but feeling her body respond to his physique. She really must stop thinking about Fin in that way – he was her boss and she did not want a relationship right now, it was too soon after Tom. Unfortunately her body and mind seemed to have a different idea about that, and her body betrayed her.

"Show me," he said, walking towards the trench in which she was working. "Bella, stay here and make sure you accurately record everything you find."

She nodded, but looked irritated by his request.

As Megan and Fin walked together, side by side, across the field, Megan explained what she had found so far. Fin's pace quickened as he listened intently to what she was saying, clearly keen to see what was in the trench.

The first spots of rain began to fall as they reached the trench but Fin did not seem to notice. "Wow…amazing…look at this!" he said, his voice excited and eyes wide as he took in what he was seeing.

Megan showed him the sketches she had done of the stones which had hidden the wooden coffin beneath. He walked round the trench a couple of times, beaming and frowning in quick succession.

"It's pagan, early Saxon period. It's very rare to have a wooden coffin burial, most are just stones or cremation pots – it might indicate that it is an important burial!"

"Really?" Megan felt his enthusiasm filtering through to her; could she have just discovered something really significant?

"Certainly, we must extend the trench – see what else is down there."

Fin went to give instructions to have the trench made bigger, so they could uncover the rest of the wooden coffin carefully without any damage.

A while later, Fin and Megan were back in the trench, slowly and carefully revealing more of the wooden structure of the coffin. When they were about to remove the lid to find out what was inside, the wind picked up and the earlier drops of rain became more persistent.

"Blast this weather!" Fin shouted at the heavy sky.

As if in reply to his curse a huge gust of wind, filled with rain and hail arrived with vengeance upon them. Commands were distributed and followed in order for the grave to be protected until the storm had passed; it was vital all precautions were adhered to, so as to ensure the safety and preservation of the discovery and any artefacts.

After half an hour of heavy and relentless rain, having sheltered in the barn at the edge of the field where the tea and coffee resided, Fin reluctantly called it a day on the dig. The storm was obviously here to stay for the rest of the afternoon.

"We'll have to start again first thing in the morning," he said, despondently.

Some of the others did not seem as disappointed in having an early finish; they vanished quickly, all except the Find collators who were still logging earlier finds under cover of the barn.

"Just a suggestion, Megan, but I've got some more books back at the barge about the Saxon period if you'd like to come back and have a look?" Fin asked her as she was zipping up her wax coat and pulling her hood up over her head.

"Sure, thank you," she agreed, her curiosity now fully awake.

"I promise I won't just show you the ones that I have written." Fin smiled at her from beneath his hat, which was now dripping water down onto his face and nose from the brim. They fell into step side-by-side, and walked away from the dig towards the footpaths that would take them back to the river and Fin's barge. They talked about the grave they had found and Megan noticed again that Fin was rather frustrated at the weather and not being able to pursue their find. So, he did have a more passionate side to him, not always calm and cool about things.

They arrived at the barge extremely wet, and Megan felt quite chilled. She was glad to find that the barge was warm when they went aboard; the fire was low in the log burner, but Fin immediately added more fuel.

"Sit down," he said, indicating to a seat close to the fire. "I'll just go and hang the wet coats up." He took her coat and walked through to the other end of the barge.

Megan sat and looked around her. It was very tidy – she guessed you'd have to be quite tidy to live in such a small space. There were a couple of photos: one of a couple (arms round each other) laughing in the sunshine...his parents? The other was one of Fin finishing some type of race; perhaps a marathon or triathlon – *very energetic*, she thought to herself with a smile.

"Tea?" he called through from the galley kitchen.

"Yes, please."

A few minutes later he handed her a steaming mug of tea and sat down opposite her. "The fire's going well now."

"Yes, I'm feeling much warmer and a little less damp now."

The rain could still be heard pelting down on the roof of the barge; it was dark inside despite the lamps, which cast a warm glow around the lounge area.

He smiled at her, holding her gaze. "The brooch should be being cleaned now, as we speak. I took it in earlier today and they have promised me that we should have it back by the end of the week."

"Fantastic. Thank you for doing that, it will be good to learn more about the history of it too. I wonder if it's possible that it belonged to one of the people buried in the Saxon cemetery."

"Definitely possible..." Fin sighed. "I wish it wasn't raining so hard this afternoon, I really wanted to get on with the excavation, I think we're about to unearth something rather exciting."

"You said earlier that you think the burial might have been one of somebody important?"

Fin took a sip of his tea. "Yes. Most Saxon people when they died were either cremated or buried, but it was rare to have been buried in a coffin. Previous burials we have found (which are not very many) that have coffins or chambers seem to have a lot of wealthy grave goods buried with them; indicating that they were wealthy and possibly of high status, such as kings or queens."

"Wow. Imagine if we uncovered a tomb of a king!" said Megan.

"It would be great and I like your enthusiasm; I sometimes think I'm the only one who gets excited about the Saxons."

"I think I'm more enthusiastic because it's a new era of history for me, and of course Bartie digging up that brooch in my garden makes it all seem connected somehow." She realised she was saying far more than she had meant to about how she felt and stopped short, looking down at her mug of tea. She had always believed in being honest about one's feelings in the past, but after Tom she felt she had let too much be known and had been taken advantage of.

Fin always seemed to sense her change of mood and lightened the atmosphere by saying, "I think Bartie is a good archaeologist in the making!"

"Well, he's very good at digging!" Megan laughed. However, while they talked her mind started running away with questions; she knew Fin was an attractive man, but knew very little else about him. Was he married? There was no ring. Had he got a long-term girlfriend? There were no photos...Megan tried hard to concentrate as Fin showed her some of the books he'd written about the Saxon period, but was distracted by his closeness. She was impressed by his professional style and thoroughness of his research – she found that Fin was clearly proud of the work he had done.

Megan had immersed herself in his work, suddenly realising that an hour had passed by. Closing the book she got to her feet and said, "I really should go, Bartie hasn't had a walk since about one-thirty when Mrs Clark would have let him out."

Fin helped Megan on with her coat and she felt her heart beat faster as his arm brushed against her back – she couldn't fall for Fin, she was far too vulnerable; it would be a disaster to start another relationship now, especially with her boss! Why did she always fall for unsuitable men? She thought she ought to have learnt that lesson by now. He opened the door and stepped off the boat with her onto the riverbank; the river was murky and choppy because of the wind. The sky was still dark, but it had stopped raining and there was a hint of sunshine trying to break through in the distance.

"I'll see you in the morning," he said. "Bright and early, so we can get going!"

"Sure, I'll be there by eight-thirty," she called, as she walked away.

Approaching the house, she could see Bartie's face looking forlornly out of the window. He jumped up onto the back of the sofa and she could see his whole back end wagging with enthusiasm. The rain had stopped and it was much brighter, as it had been that morning; the wind was finally beginning to die down and the temperature had risen again in the sunshine that now peered out from behind the remaining clouds. She grabbed Bartie's lead and walked straight out of the house, knowing once she sat down she would be more reluctant to go out again later.

Bartie ran ahead, nose to the ground, making the ducks quack loudly in protestation of his interfering existence in their world. Megan felt lighter and happier than she had for days. Fin seemed to have that effect on her – but, she decided determinedly, that was not a good enough reason to let her thoughts run away on some impossible or unlikely fantasy about them being together! She forced herself to think about the cottage instead – wanting to keep it as homely as her gran had done; she wasn't ready to make enormous changes yet, however, she knew there was some modernising that needed to be done. She could also bring a few of her own belongings out of storage and perhaps put a small mark of her own upon it, gran wouldn't mind that.

Megan was so preoccupied with her thoughts, that when Bartie gave chase, barking madly at some creature, it took her a moment or two to realise he sounded more intense with his vocalised chase than usual. Looking up she watched as Bartie galloped past, paws thundering on the ground after the poor creature...a hare! It was large and fast, sprinting across the field away from the dog. Usually Bartie would only chase birds and apart from one unfortunate pigeon, had never caught anything. However, it seemed he was fully intent on catching this hare.

"Bartie! Bartie, come!" Megan shouted at him as loudly as she could, she mustn't allow him to catch the poor thing, weren't they an endangered species? Bartie was oblivious to her calls and she started to chase him, calling after him. Suddenly, the hare stopped and turned to face the dog, Megan thought that that was it – the hare would be dead in seconds. Instead, the hare stood still as a stone and Bartie stopped dead in his tracks too, just a few feet away. Suddenly, he sat and went down to a lying position – head on paws, watching the hare.

Megan stopped too, she couldn't believe her eyes – he was staring intently at the statuesque hare – the hare staring back, transfixed. Then all of a sudden the hare bolted, in a second it was out of sight into a hedge at the edge of the field. Bartie looked up at Megan incredulously and Megan stared back, hardly believing what had just happened.

It only took a moment for Bartie's attention to be caught by a whiff of something on the breeze and he was off again, nose to the ground. Megan stood still, feeling the cold creeping over her; she looked around. Would the woman appear again, just as she did in her gran's diary entries? She wasn't sure she wanted to see her, it was becoming increasingly creepy each time the woman appeared – who *was* she?

Megan waited for a few moments and when nothing happened she started along the riverbank again, keeping an eye on the countryside around her; it wasn't until she was really close to the cottage that something in the garden made her blood run cold. This time the woman was bent down, again as if she was looking for something; searching the ground beneath her feet as she had been in Megan's dream. Disbelieving, Megan walked towards her, but the woman walked away at quite a pace still searching amongst the grasses; her long dress was muddy at the hem and her blonde hair fell loosely around her shoulders. Megan couldn't see her face. However, she seemed frantic in her search; she hurried towards the trees by the river and disappeared amongst them. Megan followed and called out to her, but she was nowhere to be seen – she had gone, disappeared again.

Megan stood looking all around her, her heart racing in her chest...she jumped as her thoughts were interrupted by her mobile ringing in her pocket - Sasha!

"Brad's taking me to Florence, he wants to show me the Uffizi!" she cried, excitedly. "We're flying out in the morning; he's organised everything!"

"That's amazing!" Megan replied trying to steady her voice which felt like it was shaking. "You'll love it there, it's an incredible place!"

"Will you be ok?" Sasha asked, with genuine concern.

"Of course I will. If things get too weird I can always go to my mum's for a few days."

"You can still call me if you need to chat...anytime you know."

"I wouldn't dream of spoiling your trip with my nonsense."

"I don't believe it is nonsense. Promise me you'll call if you need someone to talk to."

Megan laughed. "All right, I promise. Have a fantastic few days."

Megan looked around her again; the countryside was flooded with warm sunshine again and the dark clouds had been replaced with white. The phone ringing and her conversation with Sasha had brought a sense of reality to the situation. She sighed heavily. Perhaps she should get away for a while? Rome...now there was a place she loved...but how could she leave now? She had just started her new job and it was obvious that it was a much bigger, more important site than they had first thought. No, she had to help out here...besides, she wanted to know if there was an important king buried in the grave she'd discovered that morning.

Megan wasn't sure what the time was when she first awoke, but she could hear Bartie whimpering downstairs; glancing over at the clock, she could see it was only 11.45pm – she had decided to have an early night, knowing she was going to be getting up really early the next morning. She was disorientated by the time being before midnight and it took her a few moments to get her head together. *Oh no, not again, Bartie, I wish you would actually go when I let you out before bedtime rather than sniffing everything in the garden.* She pulled herself up out of bed and walked out onto the landing: catching an odour...

Smoke...she could smell smoke!

"Shit," she said and rushed down the stairs – the hallway was full of thick, grey smoke and Bartie was scratching at the front door. Megan rushed to open the door and let Bartie out. What was happening, where was the fire? She opened the door to the living room and realised that it was full of smoke; the wood burner was belching out smoke into the room. She grabbed the cordless landline phone, dialling 999 as she shut all the doors and ran out of the house, Bartie now at her heels, a worried look on his face.

"There's already a fire engine on the way..."

Megan felt even more confused. Who had called the fire brigade?

"Megan..." shouted a voice behind her.

Megan turned towards the voice and saw Fin running towards her, Bartie jumping up and barking at him.

"Fin!" she cried. "Did you call the fire brigade?"

"Yes, I was walking along the river and saw flames coming from your chimney, I tried to call, but I guess you don't have much reception over here and I don't have your landline number!"

"Oh God, Fin, gran's cottage...what if it..."

"It'll be all right, Megan, it's probably just a chimney fire, the fire brigade will be here soon..."

"But what if it takes hold of the rest of the cottage before they get here? It will go up in flames in seconds, it's so old!"

Fin put an arm around her shoulder and gave her a squeeze, it felt comforting, but the sick feeling in her stomach was severe – what if the house burnt to the ground? She tried to bite back the tears, but they ran uncontrollably down her cheeks.

In the distance, the siren of the engine could be heard; each second that passed it was getting closer and closer, but it felt like it was not approaching quickly enough.

"I have to go back and get..." Megan tried to pull away from Fin, but he held her firmly.

"You're not going *anywhere*!"

Fin now had both his arms firmly around her; his presence was a slight comfort to her, as was Bartie, who sat upon her feet whimpering, knowing his mistress was distressed.

Within minutes the engine was there, and the firemen set to work immediately, orders being shouted to the men in protective gear and masks crawling all over the cottage...five minutes later, the fire was out and the officer walked over to where Megan and Fin stood.

"It's out now," he smiled warmly at Megan. "However, it's rather smoky in there still, and will need a good airing tomorrow – some of your fabrics might need cleaning or replacing, but no further damage, you were lucky. It's probably best you don't sleep there tonight – do you have somewhere else you can go?"

"You can sleep at mine..." said Fin immediately.

Megan nodded, too tired and emotional to protest. "Thank you," she said to the officer, who smiled, nodded and returned to the engine, which then trundled back down the farm track towards the main road.

Megan walked slowly towards the cottage, cautiously opened the door and stepped inside. Fin followed her.

Inside reeked of smoke: Megan felt her heart sink. Smoke particles could still be seen in the air and she wondered if she would ever get rid of the stench. Tears fell down her cheeks again and before she knew it she was slumped in a chair in the hallway sobbing great gulps of grief – she was unaware of Fin until he lifted her from the chair by her arms and held her close, letting her cry, not saying a word, but just holding her.

When the waves of sobs relented, she pulled herself away from Fin's arms, the embarrassment of her uncontrollable emotions filtering in. "Sorry," she whispered.

"Nothing to apologise for; completely understandable," he smiled at her although she found it hard to meet his eyes. "Get a couple of things together...if you can...I'll wait for you outside..." He gave her shoulder a squeeze and left her to it.

Megan went about gathering a few toiletries and some clothes, but everything stank of smoke; it was ingrained into every surface and fibre and she wept again as she descended the stairs.

Fin was waiting with Bartie outside the front door and they fell into step with each other as they walked down the path towards the bridge. From the opposite bank an owl screeched a warning cry, hidden among the weeping willows. Megan turned towards the noise, a dark, masculine figure moved into the shadows of the trees, now unseen.

"Did you see that?" she asked.

"What the owl? No..."

"No, there was a...a figure in the trees."

"Shit, no. Do you want me to go and take a look?"

"No, I'd rather you stayed if you don't mind?"

Fin gave her shoulders a squeeze then smiled at her. "Come on, let's get you back to the barge."

"Thank you, Fin...and thank you for calling the fire brigade, I dread to think what might have happened if you hadn't been out walking so late, or if Bartie hadn't woken me with his whining."

Walking along the riverbank, she glanced at the moonlight that lit up the trees on the opposite bank – there was no sign of the man now. A sudden thought crossed her mind. "Do you often go for late night strolls?"

He laughed lightly. "No, I'm not usually a walker, mainly a runner. Tonight I was fidgety because I'm itching to get to the dig in the morning; I knew I wouldn't sleep, so I thought I'd go out for a walk...I'm glad I did!"

Relief washed over her. "So am I." They reached the barge and climbed on board.

Within minutes, Fin had handed her a brandy, blankets and a pillow. He sat on the opposite bed watching her closely. Her hand shook as she put the glass of brandy to her lips; the soothing liquid slid welcomingly down her throat, a gleam of warmth following in its path.

"I don't want you to work tomorrow," he stated.

"What, and miss the unveiling of my trench?" she smiled. "Not a chance..."

"At least think about it, you've had a bit of a shock and I want you to see how you feel in the morning...promise?"

Reluctantly she nodded; the way she felt right now, she could sleep for a week, her nerves felt shredded. Bartie scratched at the door and she went to stand to let him out; she staggered slightly.

"I'll let him out," Fin said.

"He'll only need a moment or two."

Pulling the blankets up over her legs and arranging her pillow, Megan hoped she would sleep that night. It felt a little strange that she would be sleeping on Fin's barge, she didn't really know him that well and she was thankful that Bartie was there too. She didn't think that Fin was the type of man to take advantage, but you could never be sure...she lay back and felt her eyes grow really heavy, the smell of smoke still in her hair.

There was a whining from outside the door and Fin let Bartie back in; he left a trail of mud behind him. "Sorry about that..."

Fin smiled. "It's ok, I'm getting used to him leaving mud on the floor..." Megan was almost asleep... couldn't stay awake... the brandy was working its magic. As her eyes grew heavier, she was only partially aware of what Fin was saying... "Bartie left a whole pile of earth on the floor last time he was here..." and at that point she was not aware of its significance.

Chapter Fourteen

Gifre stepped purposefully out onto the path in front of Lindi, making her jump. She had been preoccupied with her thoughts, which always put a seer in jeopardy, as their concentration was lapse. She was furious at Wilheard for turning her away from Mildryth again that morning; he had said that Mildryth was resting and was not to be disturbed – she would be summonsed if needed. She had never been turned away from the royal family before, ever! What was Mildryth up to? Was she not afraid that Lindi could at any moment tell Wilheard everything? She couldn't though, not yet, there were still things that needed to be put in place *before* Wilheard was to know the truth about his beloved bride – the timing had to be impeccable.

"Gifre," said Lindi keeping her voice steady.

"You have to tell the king," Gifre sneered and spat on the floor at her feet.

"Tell the king what?"

Gifre grabbed hold of Lindi's arm. "That he has a traitor as a wife and will have a bastard as a child!"

Lindi snatched her arm away and glared sternly at Gifre. "I will do no such thing, and you will not either, not unless you want me to put a curse on *you*…"

Gifre took a step backwards shrinking away from the threat, but his eyes were glowering.

"I've told you to leave this to me; I will deal with it when the time is right."

"You will deal with it in your own way, for your own gain – you lot are all the same. I will keep my word, for now…"

"You will keep your word until I say so, Gifre, otherwise you might find you and your family suddenly get struck down by some incurable disease…"

Gifre watched in despair as Lindi stomped off towards her hut at the bottom of the village, just away from the other huts where she lived alone, alone except for her potions and poisons; all of which could cause as much harm as they could cure. He knew it would be to his peril if he tried to stand against her.

What of the king? He was innocent in all of this and he was, after all, their leader. Gifre felt a great loyalty to his king, had been a great admirer of Aelle too, even though he worked for Wulfric on a daily basis – he clenched his fists and headed towards the forest – perhaps a kill would make him feel better.

***

Megan was immediately aware of the aroma of coffee as she opened her eyes to the strange surroundings. She had been in a deep sleep, and it was a few moments before the events of the previous night became well-defined in her mind. A lump rose in her throat and she felt the tears spring to her eyes; she sat up and became conscious of the fact that rain was hammering on the roof of the barge. Bartie appeared and jumped up onto her lap, nuzzling into her, sensing her pain. A tear escaped and fell warm and wet down her cheek; she swiped it away when she heard light footsteps approaching.

"I told Bartie to tell me if you were awake, not to jump on you and wake you up," Fin smiled his warm, bright smile at her; he was clutching a mug of coffee and stood in lounge pants and a T-shirt.

She hugged Bartie and smiled.

"How are you feeling this morning?" Fin continued.

"Like I need a litre of coffee," she replied. "What time is it?"

"Nine o'clock."

"The dig!" she cried, leaping out of bed, then realising suddenly that she only had her very flimsy vest top on – where had the fleece gone? Oh, God, her nipples were erect; had he noticed?

Fin had discreetly wandered back to the kitchen with a yell of, "I'll get you that litre of coffee."

She grabbed her fleece that was laid neatly on the opposite bed, pulled it on over top of her near-nakedness, cringing slightly inside. She took a deep breath and followed him, hoping her face was not bright red and that her voice would not give away her embarrassment.

"You slept well."

"I did; thank you so much for letting me stay."

"You're welcome."

"What about the dig, the team?" she asked.

"The rain is torrential again."

"Yes, I can hear it."

"I've told everyone we'll meet there at twelve. It's supposed to be fine this afternoon – I can't risk this rain damaging anything in that grave. Also, it gives me a chance to help you this morning."

"You don't have to, I can manage."

Fin handed her a large mug of coffee. "I'd like to help, if you don't mind?"

"OK then, thanks. I'd appreciate it."

"Would you like to shower?"

She took a large gulp of coffee, nodded and headed through to the bathroom.

Having showered and vacated the bathroom so that Fin could take his shower, she walked through to the bedroom in which she had slept. She knew that Fin had removed her fleece before probably 'tucking her in'. It made her feel strangely warm and comforted, albeit a little embarrassed; he was a really kind and thoughtful man.

Megan picked up the clothes that she had grabbed from the chair in her bedroom the night before, and was reminded again of the chimney fire – her clothes smelled strongly of smoke. She felt the tears prick as the emotions of the previous evening racked through her. There was going to be so much to do, and she suddenly realised how grateful she was to have Fin's offer of help.

A while later, Megan, Fin and Bartie set off up the river path towards the cottage, the rain was still heavy, the sky dark. She couldn't imagine the rain easing by lunchtime, but knew in springtime it quite often did; dark ominous clouds gave way to a bright blue sky and white wispy clouds. Megan felt nauseous and was thankful for Fin's light-hearted chatter along the way. Bartie stayed close too, reluctant even to give chase to a duck that was sat right on the river bank just yards from his nose. The sick feeling in her stomach grew as she got closer to the cottage – what state was she going to find it in this morning?

Unlocking the door she peered round the doorway and inhaled. The stench of smoke was still very evident and she felt her heart sink – where on earth was she going to begin?

"I'll start by opening all the doors and windows...why don't you pull down the curtains and wash the ones you can and put the others in a bag for dry-cleaning," Fin suggested gently, but firmly.

She watched as Fin immediately took charge, walking through the house opening up the windows and doors – although the rain came in some of them, it was preferable to have the fresh air circulating throughout the house than the pungent smell of smoke.

Megan was in the dining room when she heard Fin call to her from the kitchen. She couldn't hear what he had said, so she walked through to find him. As she turned the corner she gasped.

"I think Bartie's made a bit of a mess..." Fin said, as she looked down at the floor, which was covered in lumps of mud.

"Has he just done that?" Megan asked.

"I don't know...I thought he was still outside, but the door is locked from the inside so I've no idea how he could have got in. He must have done it last night," Fin laughed. "I told you he likes to leave a trail of mud behind him!"

Megan wondered what he meant by this. "I'm not sure it's him," Megan faltered, warily looking up into Fin's eyes.

"It wasn't me..."

She laughed lightly. "No, no, not you but..."

169

"Come on, Megan, out with it."

Megan sighed. "This is going to sound ridiculous…"

Fin watched her, frowning.

Megan went on to tell Fin about the mud in the house previously, how it seemed to just appear, and that at first she had always blamed Bartie. However, it seemed unlikely to be him on occasions, impossible even.

Fin's brow creased. "That's strange, I had a lot of mud on the floor of the barge the other night when you'd left; I assumed it was Bartie then…but it did leave me feeling a little uneasy."

Megan shuddered.

"I'm sure there's a perfectly normal explanation," said Fin, decisively. "Why on earth would anyone keep coming inside, leaving a trail of mud, and then leaving without stealing anything…unless…"

"Unless...?" Megan was almost afraid to ask.

"Unless they can't find what they're looking for…so they keep coming back."

"Oh God, this just gets more and more weird…"

"What does?"

"I'll tell you, but you must promise not to lock me up in a lunatic asylum."

"I don't think they have those anymore." His eyes smiled kindly at her.

Megan went on to explain about the figure that watched the house, which seemed to be male – the woman at her window and on the bridge; the hare that appeared now and then and the mud on the floor; the break-ins at the house and her gran's diaries.

"You mean you haven't told the police?"

"No, I've talked to Sasha about it all, but it seemed a little too ridiculous to tell the police."

"I'm sorry, I disagree…I really think you should tell them. I think I might have to insist! It sounds like someone is either trying to scare you, or is after something in the house! Have you any ideas?"

Megan shook her head, feeling close to tears again. "What I don't understand is why you had lots of mud inside your barge too – perhaps that was Bartie, after all."

"I've no idea, but I really think you should at least report it to the police. Also, I'd feel more comfortable if you were to sleep at mine until the house is fresher and clean again. Then I'll help you fix some window locks and get the place a little more secure. Until then you can stay on the barge."

"Thank you, Fin, but I can stay in a local B&B for the rest of the week. Hopefully by then the place will be ready for me to move back into. I don't want to get under your feet."

"Think about it, it's up to you, but you're more than welcome to stay at the barge if you wish."

"Thanks Fin, that's really kind," Megan smiled.

They spent the next few hours with the windows open; the washing machine washing the fabrics that could be machine washed, while they bagged up others that had to be dry-cleaned. At midday, they locked up the house and walked back to the site in a lighter rain than they had seen for a few hours.

Finally, at just after one o'clock, the rain stopped and the sun started to shine brightly. At the dig, everyone had turned up at midday as Fin had said and watched as the sky turned brighter and the rain relented.

After a rather harrowing night and morning, Megan was eager to get started on the trench, focus on something more positive. She and Fin settled into the trench and started where they had left off the day before. Cautiously they scraped away the soil around the rest of the coffin; it was slow and their patience began to waiver, but their anticipation urged them on.

By three o'clock, they began to remove the wood that was on top of the grave, hidden beneath the stone. Just as they did so, Bartie – who'd come along as he couldn't be left in the smoky cottage or on the barge – started growling, a deep throaty growl.

"What's up with him?" asked Fin.

"I don't know...Bartie, be quiet or I'll have to put you in the barn."

Bartie's low growl continued, but as they slowly and carefully lifted the lid, he whimpered and became silent.

The burial was gradually, painstakingly revealed; its treasures slowly unearthed. Fingers gingerly, delicately, lifting items that had not seen the light of day for over a thousand years.

Then there were the bones.

Bones of a man or woman buried amongst their grave goods to be taken with them on their journey to another world, perhaps a more peaceful domain than the one they had left behind.

Megan wondered who the bones could belong to, who had lived in the same area as her so many generations previously. Who was he or she, and how had they lived? Why had they settled in this area – probably for the river and the fertile lands that surrounded the Thames; great for farming crops and sustaining cattle, necessities for Anglo-Saxon life.

As they unearthed more and more of the skeleton it soon became apparent that the bones were that of a woman.

Megan watched Fin as he became immersed in the discovery, absorbed in the hoard that revealed itself one fragment or piece at a time. Inside the grave, concealed beneath the soil, a skeleton could just be observed. The skull with its gaping mouth and eye sockets seemed as if its life had been cut off mid-scream – perhaps the death had been brutal? Megan reminded herself that skulls often looked like that when they were unearthed, as the upper and lower jaws become separated. Slowly and carefully, Fin and Megan scraped more of the soil away and further items were uncovered, revealing what this person's mourners would have seen: some amber beads lay across her chest, which would have been held in place with the two gilded saucer brooches at each shoulder; some blue glass beads, which may have held her hair in place, lay behind her skull; some spiral silver rings; a large ivory ring, which would have been a stiffener for a leather bag, and a bone comb. Most surprising of all was the massive square-headed brooch that lay just above her chest, which would probably have held her cloak together. It was exactly the same as the one Bartie had dug up in the garden at the cottage. Megan and Fin exchanged a look of disbelief. Megan felt a strange unease and a poignant sadness wash over her as they made this discovery and Bartie, too, sloped away from the grave, tail between his legs.

"It's exactly the same as the one Bartie found," said Megan, quietly, not wanting anyone else to hear.

"It's extremely unusual to find one brooch of this value, let alone two among what we might assume is the same settlement of people. The person wearing the one found in your garden could have lost it while walking in the local area, even though it's quite a way from the actual cemetery. It would be fascinating to discover where the actual village was in relation to the cemetery. I wouldn't imagine it was out towards the Roundhouse, but I might be wrong!" Fin shrugged.

"I wonder who she was...Do you think she might have been high status?"

"Most likely would be, looking at her wealthy grave goods here – possibly even a princess!"

"Wow...that would be amazing!"

"Maybe even a queen! I think we're looking at one of the most momentous sites in England here..." Fin smiled at Megan, his excitement was contagious, her heart seemed to stop; she had no control over her feelings, but she did have control over her actions, and she must not let Fin see that she was becoming extremely fond of him.

172

Over the course of the afternoon, the artefacts were taken carefully to the Finds conservator, who would oversee the transfer of the special items to be investigated further in the lab later on.

As everyone dispersed later that day, Megan found herself alone by the empty grave. She was waiting for Fin to finish his conversation with David so they could head off home...or rather to Fin's barge, her home for the next few nights at least. The sun was shining brightly and felt warm on her face; she watched Bartie in the distance eyeing up some crows. Suddenly, from the corner of her eye she spotted a hare, close by, sitting up on its hind legs watching her – again a whisper on the breeze and a sudden drop in temperature; her hearing was distorted as if she had water in her ears and the voice spoke again, more desperate this time...but again she failed to understand the words, they sounded foreign – who was talking to her, what were they saying?

A hand on her shoulder made her leap round – the rushing in her ears was clearing and she found Fin staring at her, a look of deep concern on his face.

"Did you see it?" she asked.

"See what?" he asked, touching her arm gently.

"The hare..."

"No, I've just been speaking to David, Bartie was chasing the crows and I saw you just standing, staring into space...you seemed to be talking to someone."

"No. I thought someone was talking to me, but...but it must have been you calling me."

Fin let his hand drop. "Come on, let's get back to the barge, you can have a shower before I treat you to a pub dinner; I have nothing in the fridge. Perhaps an early night will be in order too, after your ordeal last night."

Megan nodded and followed him away from the grave and back towards the river, all the time wondering about the voice in her head.

***

Lindi was waiting for the cover of darkness before she made her move; she had tried to busy herself all day to help pass the time. Her altercation with Gifre had unsettled her even more and she wanted to leave now, immediately, but knew how foolish that would be. She had gathered her belongings together, believing that the images in the fire had shown her the way to find Wulfric, and laid them on the wooden cot where she slept each night. She had then thrown the furs over the top of it in case anyone came to the hut and spied the things ready for

173

her departure. She had packed some clothes, blankets, food and potions; she might need them for her journey to where the sun rested each night.

It seemed to take forever to get dark that day, but eventually the sun started to seep into the landscape and dissolve in the sky amongst the distant hills. Heaping all her belongings into two manageable sacks, she quietly and stealthily left her hut, the home she'd known all her life, not knowing whether she'd ever return. The trees behind her hut provided good cover, and she left the sacks there whilst she walked slowly towards where the horses were kept. On her approach, she could see the night horseman's lamp was still lit. She approached quietly, in case he was sleeping. He was sitting among the straw stroking a young colt and talking to it softly; he jumped to his feet when he saw Lindi standing only a few yards from him.

"Sorry, M'am – I did not hear you approach."

Lindi could see his appreciative gaze, which wandered slowly across her face and body, resting on her breasts. "It's all right, lad. I've come to see the young colt, I'd heard it was beautiful and I may need a new horse in a year. I was passing, having been to see a sick man, and thought I would come now, on my way home," she lied easily, giving him a flirtatious smile.

"Pet her if you like," said the boy, standing aside.

"Here hold this: drink some if you wish, it's nice and sweet." Lindi handed him a bottle that contained a dark, red wine. She purposefully ensured her hand brushed softly against his as he took the bottle from her.

"Thank you." The boy clutched the bottle, letting his hand stay a moment on hers and then took a long drink then another sneaky one when he thought she wasn't looking.

"How old are you, lad?" Lindi asked, stroking the velvet nose of the young horse but holding the young man's gaze.

"Sixteen – a man now."

"I bet you've got all the village girls after you, handsome young man like yourself…" she laughed, capturing his gaze again with hers.

"A few…" he boasted, his eyes sparkling mischievously.

Walking towards him, she removed the bottle from his grasp and leant towards him. Just as her lips touched his, he stumbled to the floor in a deep, drug-induced sleep. She knew that he would remember nothing of this in the morning, and that would give her a few hours head start – if, and only if, they felt it necessary to send out a search for her. She knew Mildryth would be glad to see the back of her; if she was not around, then Mildryth might believe that she was safe in her treason. How naïve she was.

174

Lindi had slipped leather over-shoes on her horse, so that when she led it from the stables they wouldn't be heard; she just had to hope that nobody would see them either – the darkness could still have eyes. Her horse was quiet and let Lindi lead her easily down the back of the villagers' huts, away from the Great Hall and towards the trees where her belongings were hidden. She lifted the leather bags on to the saddle and climbed up into it herself.

With barely a backward glance, Lindi kicked the horse into a trot, then a canter as they left the village and the traitors far behind...possibly never to see them again, although she knew the conflict was far from over.

Lindi rode through the night and most of the next day, putting as much distance between herself and her home as she could, as quickly as possible. Aware that the horse would tire, she sometimes dismounted and walked by its side; stopping regularly at ponds and rivers so that it could drink and eat, and they could both rest.

The first night she found a copse of trees and lit a small fire; enough to cook a rabbit. In the dancing flames she could see where Wulfric was hiding; he hadn't moved from the place where she had seen him through the fire a few days earlier – for that she was thankful. Her heart skipped a beat as she thought of their bodies joined together, the night of the shadowed moon, but she felt its softness harden as she remembered whose name he had called out in his climax.

She was now past caring how he felt about Mildryth, or how he *thought* he felt about that pathetic woman who called herself a queen; now she had other plans. Plans that would bring them together to be more powerful than Wilheard and Mildryth could ever be. A combined union of command that could conquer the whole of Britannia and – if she was right about the subtle changes in her body – there would be an heir, a true heir, no bastard this time, to rule after their demise; a fierce and powerful ruler, whose name would be spoken about for centuries.

The following day dawned with a golden globe in the sky, which spread its rays through the low-lying mist that hung like a spectre over the river and marshland that Lindi had travelled. Today she was sure she would reach the caves, come face to face with Wulfric again and let him know of her plot against the king and queen. Soon they would be together, maybe not as lovers yet, but more than that too, much, much more.

As she approached the valley, where she would find the caves she'd seen in the fire, she felt a shiver of anticipation...there were so

175

many possibilities that could now occur and so much uncertainty. Would Wulfric be at all pleased to see her, had he thought about her since their night together? Was he still hankering after the queen, or had he now accepted that she would never be his? What if he didn't want to see her and sent her away, rejected her again – surely he wouldn't once he knew about his son, his heir...What if he rejected them both? Killed them – no, no he wouldn't do that, she was almost certain of that, almost...

A while later, Lindi found herself in the valley amongst the caves in the rocks. There was nobody about in this remote region. Previously, the caves would have housed the tribesmen of Britannia...centuries before Lindi's ancestors had invaded. Britannia had been ripe for attack, a small island with many resources and rich, fertile ground it had been conquered many, many times in the past. Had it all been in preparation for this time, this coming of a new king and queen...she felt empowered by her thoughts and lifted her head and smiled a secret smile.

Lindi travelled a little further on before she noticed the smoke. It was discreet, but could just be made out, seeping from the mouth of a cave above ground level. She stopped and listened: nearby there was a faint whinny of a horse. She grabbed at her horse's bridle and pulled it hard to try to stop it whinnying in reply.

He was close.

With her heart in her mouth she tied her horse to a nearby tree, just out of sight of the mouth of that particular cluster of caves and walked slowly towards the entrance. It was accessible only by a narrow path that wound its way up the rocky hill to the gaping mouth of stone that yawned out of the hillside. Her footfall was soft and she approached slowly, stealthily. Suddenly, her foot slipped and although she managed to right herself quickly, a fall of rocks tumbled down the rock face and landed with a thud below. She cursed silently. Seconds later she found herself with a strong arm around her shoulders and a blade at her throat; heavy breathing and the smell of smoke-filled garments filled her nostrils.

"Wulfric! Wulfric, it's me...you fool!" she cried.

He looked down at his captive and swore as he released her.

"What in the gods are you doing here? I nearly slit your throat, woman. Have you brought others?" He glanced below and around, keeping his dagger poised. "...Soldiers to arrest me?"

"No, Wulfric, it's just me...I believe we are now probably *both* wanted by the king. I am no threat to you...have you not realised that yet?"

Wulfric grunted.

"I had to come and see you…the king wants your head, he feels you have betrayed him by turning your back on him…I believe he thinks you are going to build an army against him."

"Ha!" cried Wulfric, his eyes flashing with rage.

"Wulfric, I – I…just needed, *wanted* to see you," she said tenderly, approaching him with her hands held out towards him.

He allowed her to take his hands in hers; she gently circled her thumbs over his palms and he groaned deep in his throat…then pulled her towards him forcibly, roughly holding onto the back of her head with his strong hand entangled in her long, blonde hair and kissing her deeply. Her body responded by pushing against his with wanting and desire. He picked her up easily and walked with her into the cave where he laid her on the furs next to the low burning fire. As he climaxed, she was thrilled that this time it was her name upon his lips…and it made her climax all the more intense.

Later, Lindi felt a peace and warmth in Wulfric's arms, but also a growing sense of empowerment. Their lovemaking had been intense, passionate: together they were amazing; together they were strong; together they could do anything.

Chapter Fifteen

"I'll let you shower first," Fin said, as he stepped aside and let Megan climb aboard the barge.

"Thank you. Fin, are you sure you don't mind me staying...I could quite easily go to a local B&B."

"You're welcome to stay...if by the weekend the cottage isn't ready to return to then we'll talk again...but for now, just relax and enjoy your time aboard."

He clearly didn't want to commit long-term, she thought as she stood under the shower, letting the warm water revive her, he was probably used to his own space. However, the narrow boat was small and only really suitable for one person, not another adult and a dog; she mustn't take it personally, he was being very kind. After all, he didn't have to offer for her to stay there, not if he didn't want her to.

At the pub, they settled at a table near to the fire. It was an old medieval building, dark and cold. Even though it hadn't been too cold outside, the warmth of the fire was welcoming beneath the black beams of the pub.

"It's becoming more and more obvious that the grave is that of somebody important," said Fin, taking a mouthful of his beer.

"Yes, some of her possessions are very valuable which means she was certainly of high status, possibly even a princess, or queen, I would guess."

"Wouldn't it be great if you could go back in time and see who she was, what it was like around here during the Saxon period? We can only interpret what we find."

"Well, we do have some idea of what it would have been like, but I think I still prefer our times, as fascinating as the Saxons are – to live in huts amongst the animals might not have been so pleasant – no offence Bartie!"

A while later, having finished their pudding, Megan sensed that somebody was watching her. She looked across the pub towards the door where Bridget was leaning, smoking and openly staring. Megan ignored her she hadn't been at the pub earlier when they had come in and Megan was thankful for that, but she was there now, watching her and Fin closely, making Megan feel very uncomfortable; was that her intention?

After a few minutes Bridget approached to clear the table.

"Haven't seen you for a while," she said. "Sorry to hear about your fire..."

Surprised, Megan said, "News always travels fast around here."

"Not much gets past me," she said. "This place is full of gossips…which is always good for a story or two to pass the time."

"It was very unpleasant for Megan," said Fin, with a hard edge to his voice.

"I'm sure." Bridget flashed a smile towards Fin and moved a little closer to him, pushing her large breasts out towards him.

Megan nearly laughed at Fin's uncomfortable expression.

"Not missing Kai, then?" Bridget asked.

"I haven't seen him in a while, if that's what you mean?"she replied, coolly.

"No, he's moved on for a bit," replied Bridget. "Might come by again soon, if you're interested?"

"Not particularly…"

"He was quite taken with you, I could tell."

Megan couldn't understand why she wanted to talk to her about Kai in front of Fin, was it to put Fin off? Or just to make things awkward between them? She really could not fathom this woman with her ice-cold, blue eyes. There was something inherently evil about her it seemed, or perhaps she just didn't like other people having any happiness.

"I think we're ready for the bill," said Fin, taking control of the situation again, clearly recognising Megan's discomfort.

Bridget walked away.

"Thanks," said Megan.

Fin didn't say anything, his expression unreadable. Had Bridget's jibes been successful in upsetting him? Why? They were just friends, he wasn't interested in her like that and had shown no signs of it. Moreover, if he was…was it such a good idea that they were sleeping under the same roof? Suddenly, Megan felt rather insecure, as if she was losing control of her own life. Bridget, like Tom, had a way about her that made Megan feel self-conscious, anxious somehow; the type of person who drained her of her positive energy, people she didn't need.

Fin was much quieter on the way back to the barge. He didn't mention Bridget or what she had said and Megan didn't feel like talking about it either, it had really unsettled her. Once back on the boat, Fin poured them both a glass of wine and then excused himself and went off to his own bedroom at the far end of the boat. It felt like a rejection, perhaps it would be better to go to a B&B after all; she didn't want to feel like an intruder, couldn't wait to get back home.

Megan slept fitfully that night and dreamed once again of the golden haired woman. This time she was walking around Megan's garden, at the cottage, but still searching for something and crying.

However, when Megan called out to her she turned, but her face belonged to Bridget and as Megan shouted out to her, she cackled in Megan's face, then vanished. When Megan looked down at the ground where the woman had stood, there in the grass, glinting in the sunlight, was the brooch...

She must have shouted in her sleep, because the next thing she knew was that Fin was kneeling down beside her bed, speaking to her softly. As she became more aware of what was happening, she smiled at him, feeling rather ridiculous.

"Bad dream?" he asked gently.

She nodded. "Sorry, I disturbed you."

"Want to talk about it?"

She shook her head, it didn't make any sense, as dreams often didn't ...it was just her thoughts and experiences of the day being processed by her mind as she slept.

He smiled at her; then left.

Alone in the darkness, with Bartie irritatingly washing himself at the end of her bed, she sighed and pulled the duvet over her head. Everything was becoming a bit too much: the dreams, the grief of her gran dying and her break up with Tom – it was no surprise she couldn't make sense of her dreams, her life itself was a bit of a nightmare right now. She tried to blank everything out of her mind and go back to sleep; tried focussing on Bartie's gentle snores now coming from down by her feet, but sleep eluded her. She lay awake for what seemed like hours, and when finally she started to drift off, she heard the plaintive cry of a vixen from across the valley.

***

Lindi woke with a start.

Something had woken her. She lay, still as stone, listening to the darkness around her: could hear the gentle crackling of the fire; Wulfric's loud snores beside her, from having drunk a lot of wine the previous evening.

There it was again. She could hear it, clearly this time, echoing across the hills and filling the night with its unnerving, deep-throated howl. It sounded quite close, but Lindi knew that the sound could be deceiving in these parts. Wolves had used these caves; the bones of dead animals which were scattered about the floors were evidence of this, evidence that these were killers, meat eaters and they probably didn't mind what that meat was, as long as it was fresh.

Wulfric moved and groaned in his sleep. Lindi placed her hand on his firm stomach, caressing him, wanting him. He turned over and

181

in a moment she was pinned beneath him, enjoying the look of passion on his face in the fire-lit cave where flames danced around the walls.

In Wulfric's arms she lay warm and happy. Would this be the right time to tell him? Not yet, she decided, she needed to be sure that Wulfric was finally all hers before she told him her news about the baby growing inside her.

"Has my brother sent men to find me?" Wulfric asked.

"He sent some soldiers the day you left…they thought you were shunning them, turning your back on your new king, your own blood. I waited a few more nights before I came in search of you, knowing that if they knew I was leaving, they might follow me too…"

"Why?"

"Mildryth now knows about the love potion we used."

"You *told* her?" Wulfric sat bolt upright and pushed Lindi away from him.

"She guessed. She lost the original amulet that was supposed to protect her against the memories of your coupling…I gave her another, but it wasn't as strong; the magic won't work so well unless it is the original enchanted item – she realised her dreams were no night visions but those of real experiences…"

"Then, she *hates* me!"

Lindi could see the pain in his face. "She hates *me*, but I'm sure she blames you too. Wulfric you must *forget* her now, you don't *need* your brother's wife…she is weak! You need a stronger woman at your side, to give you what you deserve…what you've waited your whole life for!"

His steel-grey eyes glinted in the firelight. "Pray, tell me what you think that is, Lindi, you seem to have it all worked out…"

"To be king," she replied, looking intently into his eyes with passion and admiration.

He grinned for moment, then sighed. "I admire your ambition, Lindi. However, they will come after us if Mildryth tells Wilheard of this he will put us to death! We will become nothing but fodder for the wolves."

"She won't tell him…she is too afraid; to start with she said she would, but I warned her that what she has done is treason; magic or not. I don't think she will tell him, especially with me out of the way. She will think she is safe in her little kingdom; they can go on playing their little game of king and queen, unsuspecting of anything until we invade…"

"Invade?"

Lindi nodded. "Wulfric, just imagine…"

He shook his head looking at her as if she were mad. "There are just two of us…"

"There are other men too, others that would follow you…"

"Me? I am the bastard of a dead king, *who* would follow *me* into battle against a legitimate king?"

"The men of Mercia." She reached out and touched his arm.

He pushed her away from him roughly. *"Foolish* woman. You are a witch and I shouldn't listen to you…"

"It could work, the men of Mercia, including their king…to start with."

"So you suggest killing the king of Mercia too, once we've got him on our side? Pray, when would this be…when he too is 'unsuspecting' I suppose, and then lead his men against my brother?" He stared at Lindi for a few moments and then Wulfric started to smile; he laughed aloud. Unexpectedly he took hold of her, still laughing, but now his eyes were shining brightly, full of mischief and excitement. "You are a mad woman!" he said laughingly, and precipitously took hold of her and threw her back onto the animal skins by the fire and penetrated her.

***

Feeling the need for fresh air, Mildryth was pulling her cloak around her shoulders when Wilheard entered; she immediately sensed that something was wrong.

"Has something happened?" she asked.

"I think that there is most certainly a conspiracy against me, or us, our family."

"What makes you think so?"

Wilheard walked towards her and held out his hands to hers, she took hold of them and was surprised to feel that they shook a little. "It seems that now Lindi has left the village too."

Mildryth couldn't hide her surprise. "Lindi? Why?"

"I don't know. First Wulfric and now Lindi; I don't trust them. I wonder if they have gone away together…I know that Lindi has always been in love with Wulfric…perhaps she *did* have some idea of where he went." Wilheard looked down into her eyes, his own blue eyes filled with concern. "Mildryth, did she tell you *anything* that made you think that they were together, before our marriage?"

Mildryth felt herself grow warm and awkward. "I don't think so…I know she has always been in love with him, but I don't think it was requited…"

"A bit like Wulfric and you, you mean?"

Mildryth's jaw dropped.

Wilheard laughed. "It's all right. I know my brother has always been in love with you...and that it is also *unrequited*!"

Mildryth smiled at his joke, although she had begun to feel her heart skipping inside her chest. He must never find out the truth about her and Wulfric, *never*, even though she was not to blame, it would still be treated as treason and worse than that...it would break his heart and she never wanted that to happen. She loved this man more than anything else and her betrayal, though faultless, made her shiver with fear. She didn't want him to feel rejected or to think that she didn't love him, when she did, so much.

"Mildryth, I want to ask you a question...I have not asked anyone this, not outright, although Ayken has hinted at it, I am sure..." he faltered.

"What is it? Wilheard, you can ask me anything you like." She watched as Wilheard struggled to ask her something, his jaw was tight with angst and he could hardly look her in the eye – gods, what if he *knew* about her and Wulfric? No, he couldn't possibly; something would have been said by now – surely?

"Do you think...do you think it's possible that Wulfric could have murdered my, our, father?"

Mildryth gasped and shook her head. "Surely not!"

"But, do you think it's *possible*?"

"Thinking back over the past few months, I would say it was unlikely, but yes, I suppose it is *possible*...he has always been jealous of you inheriting the throne...if he managed to get rid of your father, then perhaps he...Wilheard – he could have killed you too! He may still even try! You're right, it makes sense now." Mildryth's heart thumped against her chest and she felt fear creep up her spine like a dark shadow.

"I have not wanted to say these words aloud, but now I have, it seems more likely that they could be true...Wulfric is jealous of me and my place on the throne...perhaps he has gone away to...he must be stopped, I must send out another search party...he and Lindi must be found. They are a threat to us and to our future heir." Wilheard placed a hand on Lindi's slightly swollen belly. "I cannot let that happen! Stay here..."

"Wilheard..." she called, but he disappeared out of the bedchamber with a determined stride, and she heard him shouting for Ayken and his other soldiers.

Mildryth sat down on the wooden bench next to the fire and sighed. Things were getting worse, the whole village was in danger, but more than that – her baby was in danger! She gently placed her hands on her stomach and stroked the skin, there was a slight swelling and she imagined the little child growing within her, needing her protection and love just as much now as it would when it was born. She had been so excited about the fact she was going to have her own child to hold in her arms: to love; to guide; to teach and protect for as long as she lived. Now another darkness threatened to engulf their lives in addition to the deaths of their parents…the eclipse of the moon at their wedding feast had been a bad omen after all…this was just the beginning.

A few moments later, two soldiers entered. "M'am, we have been ordered to keep you within our sights," said a tall, broad man with a sword at his side. "We will be outside the door if you need us to escort you anywhere…but orders are that you do not go out alone!"

Mildryth realised with despondency that her freedom would never be the same again. However, she comprehended the seriousness of the threat to them all, and knew that Wilheard would defend his family and his community with his life; he would not allow Wulfric to become the ruler of his domain, never!

Nonetheless, at that moment, a dark and sinister thought weaved itself through to her innermost reason and wedged itself, piercing with a venomous misery any thoughts of happiness that remained – what if Wulfric's heir was already inside the guarded fortification of their small, but powerful community? What if Wulfric's child already grew within *her*? What if he had planted his seed in her that day he'd forced himself upon her? Perhaps it wasn't Wilheard's heir after all, but Wulfric's!

She cried aloud and placed her head into her hands bringing the soldiers darting from their sentry posts outside the door and catching her as she fell.

As they helped her onto the bed, the cold realisation of what she had done emerged and she felt herself shiver uncontrollably as the guards helped her to lie down and called for Wilheard to be sent for…*the queen was sick – what if she had been poisoned too, like Aelle?*

Mildryth heard all of this amongst the turmoil in her mind – what was she to do? She could never tell her husband of her union with Wulfric, use of magic or not, if she was carrying a traitor's child then they would both be sentenced to death…then there would be *no* protecting her unborn child.

***

185

When Megan awoke the next morning she immediately remembered the awkwardness between her and Fin the night before, the conversation at the pub with Bridget and the uneasiness in Fin afterwards. Megan now felt she must leave the barge and find herself a bed and breakfast; there were a few in the town, and as it was out of holiday season she should be able to find somewhere with vacancies. She dressed, then went out of her room to the galley kitchen where Fin stood next to a boiling kettle; instead of the rather subdued man from the night before, he smiled at her radiantly, clearly in high spirits again.

"Good morning. Coffee?"

"Morning, yes, please."

The awkwardness had vanished and Fin seemed on top form. Perhaps he had just been tired last night? However, Megan decided she would still talk to him about her moving out as soon as she got the chance.

Over their breakfast and coffee, Fin chatted away about what he wanted them to achieve with the dig that day. He was keen that they started to remove the skeleton of the woman, to have it recorded and then sent off to the university, for more thorough tests to be carried out. They would be able to date when the woman was buried and roughly how old she might have been. Look at her DNA.

Fin was so eager to get going after breakfast that there wasn't an opportunity to discuss Megan's decision about finding somewhere else to stay. Feeling that it was really not the time, she decided she would go back to the cottage that evening and see what condition she would find it in; hopefully if she spent a few hours there, she could open all the doors and windows to let the air through again. A few hours later when the team were removing the skeleton piece by piece, the sky clouded over and a storm again threatened the progress of the dig. The team worked as quickly and delicately as they could, but soon a large flash of lightening was preceded by a roll of thunder that seemed to roll across the valley and continue in the distance for some minutes.

"Not again..." cried Fin with frustration. "If I was superstitious, I'd think that the spirits of this place were in some way unhappy with us removing these bones!"

Megan thought she caught a slight nervous laugh at the end of his announcement, and wondered if he was slightly superstitious after all.

Later that day, when the sun was finally shining again, a woman approached the team with an indomitable step. She had a small terrier on a lead and Bartie woofed quietly as a warning of their advance. The lady, probably in her sixties, was wearing a large straw hat, a little on the large side for someone with small, delicate features such as herself; she was wearing a brightly coloured dress and thick cream cardigan, with green wellington boots.

Fin and Megan had been standing drinking their coffee, the storm had passed and they had managed to get all the bones segregated from the earth and recorded; they would soon be on their way to the university in Oxford and more research would commence, and along with it some more answers.

The woman smiled at them, she was carrying a jiffy-bag and seemed rather animated. "I'm awfully sorry to disturb you," she said smiling at Megan. "My name is Muriel Smythe and I thought I should bring this to show you – I have been following the progress of the dig, *fascinating*, from the local gossips really..." (She gave Megan a wink) "...but I was digging in my garden, just weeds, not bodies you understand..." The woman giggled at her own joke.

Get to the point... Megan thought impatiently.

"Well, sorry – should get to the point really, hubby's always telling me..." she sighed, pulling something out of the padded bag. "Here." She handed Megan and Fin what at first glance looked like stones, local rocks.

Fin turned the item over in his hands. "A Saxon loom weight."

"I think this one is a stone spindle whorl," uttered Megan with surprise, handling the stone item which Muriel had given her.

"You uncovered these in your garden?" asked Fin, his voice full of anticipation again.

The woman nodded. "I was digging up an old tree, helping the gardener actually, and we came across a pile of these things. I thought they looked like something to do with weaving...I remembered seeing something similar at Sutton Hoo many years ago. I immediately thought of you. My husband said I shouldn't really bother you lovely, busy people – but I thought *bother him,* I think these might be important. *Are* they?"

"They certainly could be...they are Saxon, the same period as this site...where do you live?" said Fin putting on all his charm.

"I live in Batsborne Manor, up near the recreation ground, been there for 25 years and never found anything else...yet, and thankfully no dead bodies!"

Fin laughed lightly. "No, the Saxons would have had their village a little way away from their burial grounds."

"Would they?" asked Muriel, clearly more than a little interested.

"Well, well…we could have just found where the village might have been!" Fin flashed the lady a smile, before asking, "Would you mind showing us where you found them?"

"Really, you'd like to take a look?" She seemed surprised and flattered that they might be in the least bit interested.

Megan knew, however, that if she was willing, this could lead to more exciting discoveries.

"If you come tomorrow…if that's not too soon…my husband will be out, he'll be playing golf. Then if you find something and need to do some more work, well, you just leave him to me…he will agree to having holes in the garden just for a while I am sure of it, positively sure."

Megan thought she didn't really sound that sure…but even they might be able to persuade him, if necessary.

"Tomorrow will be fine," said Fin, trying hard not to sound over enthusiastic. "Would 10am suit you?"

"Oh yes, that will be fine. I will ask Jinny to make us a nice cake." Then she turned and walked away, not only with a determined step, but with a little skip in it too.

"How exciting, what a character she is!" said Megan, keeping her voice low.

"Sure is," said Fin grinning broadly. "Now we have the major grave excavated, it might be that if there's time, and budget of course, that we have a second site to excavate. This really is turning out very well indeed."

The next morning at ten sharp, Megan and Fin arrived at Batsborne Manor; the house sat proudly, with an air of opulence, compared to the other houses along the quiet road that ran up to the main High Street. Megan was surprised to see that it was not far away from Sasha's cottage; they would have overlooked the manor if a modern house not been erected between them. They were greeted on the long gravel drive by the little terrier dog that they had seen with Mrs Smythe the previous day.

"Wow, look at the size of this place!" said Megan, as she gazed up at the three-storey manor house in front of them.

A large Georgian façade probably concealed a house from a much earlier period. The town still showed evidence of its medieval roots; small cottages used for the woollen industry, with roads and the river linking the trade routes to London and other large towns and cities. Wool would have been one of the major trading commodities of the Saxon period too, so the sheep that could be heard in a near-distant field would have been a part of this landscape for many, many generations.

Megan and Fin had not even reached the front door before Muriel was making her way towards them, her face full of smiles and an eagerness like that of a child.

"Good morning, my dears," she said kissing them both on each cheek like an old acquaintance. "Follow me, Fred's in the garden."

Fin and Megan exchanged an amused look and followed Muriel round the back of the mansion and into a walled garden to the rear. The garden was beautifully manicured and was an ocean of spring colour. A man, far too old and crooked to be an effective gardener stood with a shovel in his hand, drinking a glass of water and looking rather red in the face. He gave them a toothless smile as they approached. Megan was surprised to see how, closer up, he appeared much stronger and his muscles were defined and strong, despite his age.

"Mornin'," he said, tipping his cap at them.

"This is Fred, my gardener. Fred, these are the people from the archaeological dig. This is where we found those loom weights," she said pointing at a hole in a flower bed.

"Have you ever found anything else of interest?" Fin asked.

"I've dug up odd things over the 40 years I've been gardener 'ere," said Fred. "Didn't think much of it really, find lots of bits of pottery and ceramics, glass...never thought it were really important though."

"Did you keep any of the items?"

Fred glanced at Muriel shiftily. "I do 'ave a few bits in me shed. Like I said, don't think anything of value. You're welcome to take a look."

Muriel looked a little put out as Fred led them to the side of the house, where a stone shed stood with its door open wide. Fin and the two women followed Fred into the shed. It smelt of mown grass, oil and something else Megan couldn't identify. The shed was dimly lit by a single electric bulb; it was full of the tools and machinery needed to care for a large mature garden such as Batsborne Manor. Fred pointed at a large wooden table, which would probably at one point have been a kitchen table in the manor, towards the back of the shed. Fin and Megan made their way over to it, listening to Muriel's hushed voice as she reprimanded Fred for not telling her of the things he had found before now. On the table were numerous items that at first glance were just broken bits of ceramic, stones and rusty bits of metal. Fin started to pick through the pieces, gently and with great curiosity.

"Why didn't you show these to anyone?" asked Fin.

Fred shrugged and looked down at his shuffling feet. "I really didn't think anyone were interested, sorry Mrs S, I didn't mean no 'arm."

She sighed and smiled sympathetically at him. "It's ok, Fred."

"I call it my museum," he said, a little awkwardly but with a chuckle.

"Well, it looks like you might have found some very important finds in your museum, Fred," stated Fin, smiling at the old man.

"Do you think we need to do an excavation in the garden?" asked Muriel excitedly. "Hubby won't like it, but I'm sure he will come round…"

"I don't want to upset your husband, Mrs Smythe," replied Fin. "However, it would seem a shame not to dig a couple of trenches, see what lies beneath – it really could be quite important, especially if it is the site of the original Saxon village."

"Is that likely?" asked Muriel, her excitement visibly growing.

"You mustn't get too excited…we don't know anything for sure at the moment. When would be a good time to come and see your husband, Muriel?"

"Oh, well…I would probably need a couple of days to approach the subject, just so I can get him to think it was his idea…"

"Here, take my number and give me a call when you think it would be a good time," replied Fin.

Muriel took Fin's card. "Now, dears, you must come and have a cup of tea and some of Jinny's cake, always perfect her cakes. I am a lucky woman to have such a wonderful housekeeper and gardener."

After they had finished their tea and cake, Fin and Megan walked back towards the site of the burial ground.

"Do you really think that the site of the Saxon village could be at Batsborne Manor, or were you just being kind to Muriel?" asked Megan.

Fin grinned. "No, I really do think we could be on to something. Those bits and pieces Fred has found over the years are definitely indicative of Saxon workmanship which would have gone on in a village. I just hope that Muriel can persuade 'hubby' to let us dig a couple of small trenches."

"I think it's amazing how the gossip about the dig has spread, and now the locals are more aware of their own pre-history and keen to find out more."

"This does happen sometimes. Other times, as I'm sure you know, we face lots of closed doors and gates where people do not want their property or beautiful gardens disturbed."

"I suppose you could count me in on that too."

Fin frowned.

"The brooch; it was found in my gran's garden and I said I didn't really want you digging around; it's just a difficult time right now…" Megan was stunned to realise her eyes were filling with tears.

Fin looked at her with a concerned, but kind, look in his eyes. "It is fine, I told you when and *if* you were ready I could take a look."

Megan couldn't speak for fear of actually bursting into tears.

"Look, why don't you take the rest of the day and go and see how the cottage is doing. Perhaps it's smelling a lot better now…maybe you will be able to move back in by the weekend after all?"

"Are you sure?"

"Of course, I'll see you back at the barge for dinner at seven. I'll rustle something up for us; you just concentrate on the cottage for now. I think you, and it, need it."

"Thank you, Fin."

He nodded and she watched him walk away from her, eager to get back to work. Whereas she was more than happy to get to her gran's cottage, having failed the previous evening to get there due to the dig going on longer because of the earlier storm. Fin was kind to let her have a few hours to herself, either that or he was hoping the cottage would be ready so that she was no longer under his feet –he didn't really give her that impression, but perhaps he was just too polite and kind to say what he really thought?

Megan walked back down the overgrown track towards the cottage. She was about to turn the corner when a dog came running up to them and started jumping around wanting a game with Bartie – Angus!

"Hello boy," said Megan, patting him on the head. She looked up and just a little way ahead noticed Kai walking towards her – so, he was back? Bridget had been right. Her heart started thumping rapidly in her chest; she took a deep breath and tried hard to convince herself and him that she was confidently making her way back to the cottage and that all was fine.

"Hi," she called out as he approached her.

He looked more sullen than ever, but he smiled at her greeting and said, "Alright?" He stopped walking.

She wasn't sure whether or not to stop and talk to him and decided it would be dreadfully rude not to. "You've come back then?"

He nodded. "Yer missed me then?" A slight sparkle in his grey eyes unnerved her.

She laughed to try and cover up her awkwardness. "Bridget said you might..."

A dark shadow crept across his face. "She did, did she? Sorry to hear about the cottage and the fire."

"Thanks...I suppose it could have been worse! I'm on my way back there now to see if I can move back in yet. I've been staying with...with a friend, but I think I might be outstaying my welcome!"

He nodded watching her closely, "Oh dear...well, I'll catch yer soon."

"Goodbye."

She walked on, with Bartie at her heels, feeling slightly anxious at having bumped into him again. She turned the corner and spotted Kai's horse and caravan just inside a field, not that far from the cottage. It was tucked out of sight so Mr Garrett wouldn't see it there unless he walked down the track to the cottage, which would be very unlikely. Why was Kai back and why so hidden? Round the next bend she caught sight of the cottage among the weeping willows up on the riverbank; the Roundhouse stood proud and protective above the cottage which made Megan's heart pound for a different reason – home; her gran's cottage felt very much like home – it's where she belonged. Things did happen for a reason. Her break up with Tom, however painful, was at just the right time; her gran's death too – although she felt guilty for thinking this, but it did mean she had the chance to start a new life in Gloucestershire, but be independent. She walked quickly up the driveway and watched as Bartie took off round the garden, nose to the ground, his territory, his home too.

As she walked up to the back door she noticed immediately the soil spread about outside the threshold; someone had been here again! She tentatively unlocked the door and entered, calling out as she did so in case whoever had been there was still in the house. There was no response, only the sound of the wind in the willows outside, and the odd bark from Bartie from the garden. Who was so eager to keep coming to the house – what were they looking for? Nobody came this way much, the footpath led off to the other side of the river but somebody, *somebody* was definitely trying to either scare her, or take something from the house, something they knew, or thought they knew was there. Her thoughts jumped immediately to Kai; perhaps he had been here...he did look rather shifty when she bumped into him and he did know about the fire – how? She had assumed that Bridget had told him, but now she wasn't so sure...

Entering the house by the front door, the odour was more like the familiar damp than the smoke of a few days ago; she found this comforting, having previously found it rather sickening. Removing her shoes she walked across the flagstone hallway and into the sitting-room; everything seemed peaceful and there was no further soil in the house this time.

Bartie appeared in the doorway, tail wagging, pleased to be home again.

"Well boy, it looks like we can probably move back in again…it hardly smells of smoke at all!" Megan felt a huge weight lift off her shoulders, she hadn't realised how much she had missed the place and the familiarity of the cottage and her gran's things; hadn't appreciated how much comfort and security it had brought her.

She climbed the stairs to her bedroom and sat down heavily on the bed – she had all the bedding and curtains to put back in order around the cottage too, before she could move back in. Today was Wednesday, tomorrow evening she would move back here, back to the cottage and her sanctuary. Out of the corner of her eye she noticed that the built-in cupboard door was slightly ajar. She walked over to it and peered inside. She had been using this as her wardrobe and was concerned now that the smoke may have filtered into all her clothes; she took out a jumper and buried her nose into it, inhaling. There was a faint smell of smoke, but nothing heavy. Tomorrow she would get all the clothes out and hang them around the spare room with the window wide open, that should hopefully freshen them up a bit; the worse ones she would wash.

Sighing, she went to close the door, but something was blocking it. She opened it and looked at the floor, there was nothing there. She looked behind the hinges to check she hadn't left an item of clothing stuck in the gap, no…nothing there. Finally, she looked above her head, where the handle of a bag was preventing the door from closing. Reaching up, she took down a red leather handbag that had been one of her gran's. Megan remembered her using this bag when she was a child and it smelling of peppermints every time she opened it. A twinge of sadness crept over her.

Megan undid the clasp and peered inside. No smell of peppermints now, just a musty odour. However, there was another diary…

September 12th

I've buried it, damn thing! I hope it never resurfaces; it's brought me nothing but bad luck. Since I dug it up in the garden six months ago I have lost Frank and my marriage. I think it's cursed and I want nothing more to do with it – it's better off in the ground, just like I would be…

The last few words were smudged.

What had she buried, Megan wondered, and why would she think she would be better off dead? She must have been at a really low point in her life at that time as well. Megan couldn't bear the thought of her lovely, kind, happy gran feeling so despondent, wishing to die, it was so *unlike* her.

Megan flipped through the pages preceding the one she'd read and those that followed; two days earlier there was another entry:

I don't know what century it is from, but it looks pretty ancient. I've had it lying in the kitchen windowsill since I dug it up in the flower bed a few months ago. I realise now that perhaps it is this that has brought me all this bad luck...I can't help thinking that it's perhaps cursed. I'm sure it was once beautiful, its craftsmanship is like a piece of art – maybe I should give it to a museum, or perhaps just bury it where I found it! Perhaps a young lover gave this brooch to his loved one...ah well, I don't want to keep it, but I must decide what is best to do with it.

Megan felt her head spin...a *brooch*. Could it be? No, surely not...there wasn't a full description of the brooch that she could find, perhaps it was another one? There could have been a stash at one time, with a few pieces of jewellery, buried for safe-keeping, in their garden by somebody many years ago. People used to do that. But try as she might, Megan felt almost certain that the brooch her gran was talking about was the one that Bartie had dug up and was now at the University being preserved in readiness to be returned to her. If it was the same brooch, did she really want it back, especially if it was cursed? Perhaps she would do what her gran hadn't done and donate it to a museum.

She walked down to the kitchen and made herself a coffee – she would have to go into town and buy a few necessary items to restock the fridge and cupboards, also to collect the dry-cleaning if she was to re-hang the curtains the next day. Bartie was lying upside down with his paws in the air, by the back door snoring gently, content.

Megan's thoughts turned to Fin – how could she thank him for helping her out over the past few days? She could buy him something, but what? He didn't seem to have much in the way of possessions, but clearly liked it that way – after all, where would he put them? He seemed to like the simplicity of river living, furthermore he was a very private person and did not give much away about himself. Megan still didn't know if he had a girlfriend or not, there didn't seem to be any sign of one...but it was hard to tell. He did talk to people on the phone regularly, but didn't appear to go off out anywhere much after work; although she may have hindered his social life for the past few days…He was a hard one to read, for all his perceptiveness.

She decided she would cook him dinner Friday night at the cottage and buy him a bottle of whisky – the brand that she had seen him dipping into each evening before bed. That way she wouldn't be giving him anything he didn't need to clutter up his living space.

Megan immediately fished down an old recipe book of her gran's from the shelf above the Aga and started flicking through the pages for inspiration before she went shopping. She sipped her coffee and sat listening to the quiet snoring of Bartie and the songs of the birds in the garden – she smiled to herself as she realised that she felt happy for the first time in a long, long time – she was coming back to the cottage, she was coming home.

Fin was sitting on top of the barge in his shorts, reading a book in the early evening sun, when she arrived back. He glanced up then looked down at his bare chest, his face coloured ever so slightly, and he pulled his linen shirt on over his shoulders, leaving the buttons unfastened. Megan had to try hard not to stare. It wasn't the first time she had thought he was in rather good shape.

"You caught me sitting down," he said with a laugh. "I've just done a six-mile run and was having a cold beer whilst I cooked you dinner…I have showered by the way."

Megan smiled at him. Bartie, who had run up to Fin, was lapping up the last dregs of the beer in the bottom of Fin's glass.

"Bartie!" she cried.

"Better not have too much, boy, don't want you falling overboard, I think you've chased too many ducks on this river for them to rescue you!"

"He's a strong swimmer," said Megan.

"So am I, but not after a few pints! How's the cottage looking, much damage?" asked Fin, as they went below deck. He opened the fridge and poured Megan a glass of white wine.

"It's fine! It barely smells of smoke at all. I'm going to go home tomorrow, Fin; I'll be out from under your feet at last."

"That's a shame, I was kind of getting used to having Bartie around the place…" he smiled at his own joke but his eyes grew a little more serious. "It's been good to be able to help out."

"Thank you, Fin. I really appreciate your help and understanding. Having today to sort things out at the cottage has been really good for me. Oh…by way of a thank you, I'm going to cook you dinner on

Friday night, if you aren't already busy?" she asked, suddenly hoping that he wasn't, she hadn't even considered that.

"That would be grand, thanks. Now, I had better rescue our dinner – I've roasted a chicken and have a lovely fresh salad to go with it, I hope that's all right?"

"Perfect," she replied, taking a seat at the table and sipping her cold, dry wine. Megan realised for the second time that day that she was feeling much more content; it must be the fact that she would soon be back at the cottage so she could start the minor changes and the sorting through of her gran's possessions, that was making her now feel ready for subtle changes. A move forward at last.

Chapter Sixteen

"My soldiers tell me that you fell in the village. Are your headaches still bad?"

Mildryth sat on the wooden bench and looked up at Wilheard. "I am fine now," she said. Wilheard's face was full of concern and something else, anger? Why was he angry?

"Are you sure?" he asked, placing a hand gently on her shoulder.

She nodded and took his hand in hers, stood and embraced him, feeling comfort from his strong arms – everything would be all right, Wilheard would protect them. Now Lindi had left, it did make both her and Wulfric look like they were perhaps scheming together. Lindi really was jealous of her; she had tried and succeeded in breaking the spell of love Wulfric felt for her. She had been surprised that Wulfric had been so in love with her; had thought he just wanted her because Wilheard had her. The brothers had fought over everything all their lives, including her. Mildryth realised she was no different, other than that Wulfric's love for her was sincere, although unfortunately for him it was unrequited. However, she had given her body to him and the result could be growing inside her...how could she have let this happen? It was out of her control, she felt like screaming; how dare two of her closest childhood friends treat her this way? Poor Wilheard, he had no idea what had gone on recently, but now it seemed he was becoming more suspicious of his brothers disappearance and now that of Lindi too.

"I will be sending more soldiers to look for my brother; they are to send for me when and if they find him – I want him captured but kept alive...for now. There is to be a meeting of the guards this afternoon."

"What about Lindi?"

"She is to be arrested too."

Mildryth felt the fear encompass her again. What would they say? If they were found, they would turn everything against her; they would tell Wilheard that she was a part of all the treason. She had to find them first! She had to clear her name, before they ruined her reputation and family forever.

"I need to have some fresh air; I'd like to go for a walk around the village."

"You can't go alone," said Wilheard, firmly.

She shrugged. "All right, I will take the guards with me. I just feel like I'm suffocating in here. It's a beautiful day, I want to be outside."

Wilheard looked at his guards, they nodded.

They left the hut and walked outside into the sunshine. It was bright and warm, but didn't really make Mildryth feel any better inside. The guards walked on either side of her, the villagers greeted her with warm smiles. The people also noted the guards and their eyes were questioning – why was the queen being so closely guarded?

"Walk further off, I am safe with you nearby, you needn't to be so close!" she snapped at the guards. They looked uncertainly at each other, but took a few steps away to give their queen a little more liberty. Mildryth felt less like a prisoner with them walking at a small distance behind her, their hands at the ready to draw their swords if necessary; reassuring but intrusive all the same - despite the small space between them.

Wandering around the village, she could see the weavers busy at their work: the children winding the wool; the weavers threading the wool through the loom – the loom weights heavy at the base. The industrious villagers worked hard. Trade was important and was good presently, trade links in Britannia and further afield were vital to their community's upkeep and wealth.

As she walked past the metal-workers, the clunking of heavy metal and the acrid odour of smelted metal reached her senses. Although there had been peace in their community now for some years, there was always a threat of invasion from another kingdom or abroad, and now much closer to home. Her own family had come to Britannia and taken over the fertile lands, bringing with them their own religion despite the Roman ways already in place. She herself had been born in this very village and had only ever known peace. However, she wondered now what would happen with Wulfric; would he raise an army against his brother? She wasn't sure that he would, but with Lindi at his side, who knows what schemes they might come up with together...

She glanced across the fire and caught Gifre, Wulfric's servant, glaring at her; she frowned and quickened her pace, then stopped at a hut that sold leather goods, her back to where Gifre had been. The guards were now slightly more relaxed and were standing a good few feet behind her, laughing together, when she heard Gifre's voice in her ear.

"So, the queen is expecting an heir to our throne, is she?" he snarled. "Who is the father I wonder? Does he know; is he pleased?"

Mildryth felt a cold shiver run through her as she turned and held Gifre's eyes steadily with her own. "The king is delighted at the news."

"I am not so sure he would be if he discovered the truth about the bastard inside you," he whispered close to her ear.

"What in the gods are you talking about?" Mildryth began to shake.

"You know exactly what I am talking about," replied Gifre. "And with your witch no longer here to protect you, I wonder if somebody will tell the king the truth…"

"Is this man bothering you, my queen?" asked one of the guards, roughly pushing Gifre away from Mildryth's side.

"I was just congratulating the queen on her wonderful news," said Gifre, and with a grimace in Mildryth's direction, he walked away.

Mildryth felt the blood leave her face.

"Everything all right?"

She nodded. "I think it's time to go back."

Walking back to her hut, Mildryth felt sick. The guards were obviously worried about her, as they came and walked closer to her side again.

Back at the hall, Mildryth sat by the fire as she was served her food. She was told that Wilheard was busy with his soldiers, preparing for them to go in search of Wulfric and Lindi – he would not be back until later. She ate her bread and fruit without much of an appetite. What should she do? Everything was falling apart around her and she felt so helpless. If she told Wilheard the truth, would he believe her? Would he banish her and the child, or would he have her put to death, the baby too? Wilheard had a generous and kind nature, but he would never bring up his brother's child as his own, if indeed it was Wulfric's. Furthermore, would he be able to forgive her for lying with his brother, even though magic had been used – would that make any difference at all? She doubted it now as she sat in Wilheard's hall, his kingdom amongst their people – she would not be forgiven, or even believed.

Mildryth decided she had to leave, it was the only way.

She started to put together a plan of action whilst she ate slowly, chewing each mouthful without tasting the food in her mouth. She would leave tonight whilst Wilheard slept – she would give him a sleeping potion, just a little, to ensure he didn't wake when she slipped away. She would pay one of the horsemen handsomely to take her and protect her against harm. Piers would be best. But where would she start looking for Lindi and Wulfric? She had no idea, but she felt that they wouldn't be too far away, although they would be well hidden. The warmth of the fire made her feel sleepy, that mixed with the food and exercise she'd had that morning, her head lolled forward and she fell asleep. The guards covered her in a blanket and went to stand just outside the door.

Mildryth dreamt of a place, a dark cavernous place surrounded by many trees, with a gorge running through a valley. In her dream she was entering a large, damp cave, where she had seen the light of a fire dancing on the walls. Silently she advanced into the mouth of the cave and there, lying on the floor together, arms and legs entwined were Wulfric and Lindi. Mildryth gasped, and as she did so, Lindi looked up and stared at her, then started to laugh, a low, sinister cackle. Mildryth turned and ran...she ran back into her own consciousness and away from her dream as fast as she could.

She awoke by the fire, her heart thumping in her chest and sweat pouring down her back, although she was sweating and her skin felt like it was on fire, she felt as cold as ice. As her heart steadied and the sweat dried on her skin, she made her way to her bedchamber and lay down on the bed. She was trying to recapture her dream...the road...the forest...the...caves...she knew where she would find them, all she had to do now was to get her things together and wait for nightfall.

As quietly as she could, so as not to alert the guards that she was awake, she folded a few belongings into a roll and hid it beneath the blankets on the bed, on the side she slept so that Wilheard would not find it. In her bundle she had placed some jewels and gold to help buy her protection and food for her journey. She was about to pin the brooch that Lindi had given to her for protection to her gown, when she swallowed hard. She looked at the brooch, the intricate pattern and square head of it was beautiful and probably worth a lot of money. She hesitated, but only for a second, then discarded it into a pot – perhaps it was not for protection after all – perhaps it held some dark magic, if Lindi's recent actions were anything to go by...

If she was right about their whereabouts, then they would be on the road for about three days. She had to get to Wulfric and Lindi before the king's guards.

Later that evening, Wilheard arrived back at their bedchamber to find Mildryth alone with a jug of wine.

"We are sending soldiers out at first light, they are going to search all directions from here – north, south, east and west."

"What if they cannot be found?"

"We will find them, Mildryth, do not fear, and when we do we will question them both as to our father's death and why they feel it necessary to leave now that we are king and queen of this community – are they, in fact, going to raise an army against us? This is what Ayken fears will happen and I must confess that I think he may be right; I hope to the gods I am wrong!"

200

Mildryth poured him a horn of wine and put her arms around him as he drank thirstily. "You must be tired," she said stroking his back. "Come and lie down."

Wilheard smiled and kissed her gently on the forehead. "You're a good woman, Mildryth. I am exhausted," he said, walking over to the bed by the fire and lying down. Mildryth lay close to him and listened to his breathing as it became deeper and steadier; soon he fell into a slumber. She waited for a while for the drugs to take their full effect and then, kissing him on the cheek, rose from the bed to check that the guard outside the door was also asleep. He was.

Now was her chance.

Collecting the roll of her belongings together, she crept silently out into the darkness. Glancing back at his sleeping form, she felt a sense of loss and hopefulness at the same time. She wanted to make things right again, but she also wanted her revenge on Wulfric and Lindi for causing so much grief. Once they had confessed to everything, then she would ensure they paid the price for what they had done. She was not the weak queen that Lindi mistook her for, but a strong and powerful one, one that would not let them get away with it all. It wasn't always the most powerful person who could be the strongest aggressor; the meek could be resilient too.

**

Thursday brought torrential rain, so any field work was called off. Fin went up to Oxford to do some work in the faculty and suggested that Megan get some of the notes written up regarding the 'wealthy queen' as they had nicknamed the main burial on the site. Megan worked all morning on the barge at her computer and by two o'clock was at a stage where she could do no more until some of the finds had been cleaned up and restored. Taking Bartie's lead, she walked up into the town to collect her dry cleaned curtains and some groceries, then set out across the fields towards the cottage.

Megan was slightly apprehensive as she walked up to the cottage, wondering what she might find this time she came back. However, all seemed quiet and there was no evidence of any disturbances. Bartie ran into the garden and did his usual sniffing and exploring, chasing away some ducks and crows.

Megan spent the rest of the afternoon re-hanging the curtains and cleaning the cottage from top to bottom. Cobwebs that had been in the beams for what seemed like centuries stuck like candyfloss to her hair and the sheepskin duster she was using. Dust particles danced around the house in the beams of bright sunshine that in the last half hour had

201

been shining across the Cotswold countryside, casting its golden rays across the late spring landscape. Megan felt, as she cleansed the cottage of the smoke and grime, that she was somehow moving forwards. She was climbing out of a time that had too much despair and gloominess in it, into a brighter and more satisfying period of her life. She knew she had a little way to go and that the transition would still have its pitfalls, but finally, there was some light at the end of the long and dark tunnel.

By seven o'clock that evening she was exhausted, but felt satisfied and uplifted about what she had achieved. She went to the fridge and opened a bottle of white wine; pouring herself a glass, she took it out into the garden. Placing a cushion on the damp seat, she sat at the small table and chairs on the patio at the back of the house. She could see swans on the river, regally gliding on the dark waters; swifts dipped and rose, as their name suggested, catching their supper and singing their sweet, high melody; the wind moved the long branches of the weeping willows, their young, yellow-green leaves touching the water like fingers being cooled in a stream on a warm summer's day. Megan took a deep breath and sighed, a contented sigh. Her gran would be happy to see that she was relaxing and enjoying the place she loved most in the world. She must have known that, given time, Megan would be happy here, just as she had been.

Her mobile vibrated – a message.

> *I hope you're getting on ok.*
> *We've had the go ahead from Mrs Smythe!*
> *See you there at 9.30 in the morning.*
> *What time's dinner tomorrow eve?*
> *Fin*

She replied:

> **Great news! Cottage sparkling,**
> *you won't recognise it.*
> *Dinner's at 7.30. x*

Shit! She blushed realising that she'd sent it with a kiss at the end, would he notice? Oh well, wasn't much she could do about it now!

> *Great. I'll bring wine.*

No kiss. Her heart sank a little. Was she really beginning to have strong feelings for him, or was it that she was lonely? She could not, and would not, start another love affair right now – things were looking up for her, she did not want to complicate her life any further. It would be much better if they remained colleagues, or friends at the very most.

Megan showered, removing all the grime and cobwebs from her hair. Afterwards she felt refreshed and wondered if the house also felt the same, as she had given it a good spring clean. She had done some surface cleaning since moving in, but she hadn't cleaned the depths: the corners, behind the cupboards, beneath the sofas as she had today. Megan gave Bartie his dinner and cooked herself poached eggs on toast before sinking into the sofa to watch the T.V.

Awakening the next morning cramped and stiff, she found herself still on the sofa, the T.V. amusing itself and Bartie licking her toes that hung off the end of the cushions. She giggled, then winced as the pain in her neck shot across her shoulders. She glanced at the clock on the sideboard and as her eyes focussed on the time of eight-thirty, she sprang into action – she was going to be late if she didn't hurry!

She boiled the kettle, grabbed a slice of bread and stuck it into the toaster and let Bartie out of the back door. He charged off round the garden, barking madly at the birds and welcoming the new day. Megan raced upstairs muddle-headed, and washed quickly before putting on her clothes and racing back downstairs. She spread some butter on her toast and grabbed her thermos cup from the cupboard, filled it with coffee, sweet and strong, then ran out of the house and stomped quickly towards the town and Mrs Smythe's house; Bartie leading the way along the river bank. Ahead of her, she saw Fin's barge, she knew he would have left ages ago and was probably hiding a few yards from the Smythe's driveway waiting for nine-thirty to come so he could go and discover what was buried beneath the surface of Batsborne Manor's gardens.

Megan couldn't believe how heavily she'd slept; there were no dreams, no awakenings in the night from strange noises or happenings – things were really getting better. Perhaps the strange happenings were linked to her grief and now she was beginning to feel she could progress in her life again, things were settling down. It was as if she'd had a slight mania attached to her for a while...crazy but true. However, with a new home and new job, she had something to focus on and feel positive about, to let go of the negativity.

When she arrived at Batsborne Manor, she made her way round the side of the large mansion and into the rear garden, where she found the team discussing what and where they were going to dig. Mrs Smythe had her arm around Fin's back and she saw an elderly man eyeing them up with a dark look upon his face – Mr Smythe...Megan wasn't sure if he was displeased with his wife's arm being around another man, or the fact that the archaeologists were about to dig up his well-manicured lawn.

"Morning," said Megan, as she stood beside Mrs Smythe.

"Hi," replied Fin.

"Good morning, dear," said Mrs Smythe.

Fin continued to address the team of his wishes on where to start digging a first trench; it was to be close to where the loom weights had been found. By lunchtime there was an excited buzz about the place, with Jinny dishing out cups of tea and cake under the watchful eye of Mrs Smythe.

In the afternoon, Fin was working in a trench with Megan, when he suddenly stopped scraping and looked up at her excitedly. "I think we may be onto something here..."

"What is it?"

"Look closely."

Megan looked at the ground by his feet...she couldn't really make anything out except a darkness to the soil that didn't match the rest of the trench, so looked up at him with a frown.

"It's a post hole. This is where a structure, possibly a hut, would have been!"

"You mean this...this could be where the settlement, the village, might have been?"

"Yes."

Megan felt her heart do a leap inside her chest, Fin's excitement was contagious.

"We mustn't jump to conclusions too quickly, but we need to establish if there are any others."

Just then Oscar called over to Fin from a trench not far away. Fin and Megan walked over to him. He was smiling excitedly too. "I think I have just discovered a fire pit...the central fire that would have been in the middle of a Saxon hut!"

Fin stepped carefully down into the trench and crouched down beside Oscar. "You're right, that's exactly what that is."

"Have you found something exciting?" asked Mrs Smythe, appearing at the edge of the trench next to Megan.

Megan climbed up out of the trench. "Yes, we have found a post hole and a fire pit...it's looking promising," said Megan, smiling at the excitement in the old lady's face.

"That's marvellous!" she screeched, hugging Megan tightly and making her laugh.

"We need to dig a few more trenches if that's ok?" said Fin.

"Oh, that's fine..."

"What about Mr Smythe?"

"Oh don't worry about that old bugger, he's not done away with me yet, you just leave him to me! This is too good an opportunity to miss."

Fin and Megan laughed, as she scurried away across her lawn towards the house.

"She's bonkers!" said Megan.

"How wonderful that she came to see us though – just think, if she hadn't, we might never have known where the village was."

"So you really do think it was here?"

"I do." Fin said and smiled a smile that lit up his bright blue eyes even more.

Later that evening, when Megan had been home for a while and was still on a high after the amazing discovery that day, she decided she would cook an Indian curry; nothing too spicy but a flavoursome and authentic recipe she had found on the internet after deciding that there wasn't anything suitable in her gran's recipe books. It was a recipe where she wouldn't have to spend much time in the kitchen, so before she showered she took the marinated meat from the fridge and added the sauce she'd made earlier, before placing it in a warm oven for it to cook slowly, ensuring that the lamb would be as tender as possible. She laid the table for two, but was indecisive about whether or not to put a candle on the table or to leave it bare. Eventually she placed a small glass candlestick between the two place settings, and put a small vase of spring garden flowers in the middle of the table, which she'd picked from the garden.

After her shower, she suddenly realised that she hadn't really thought about what to wear and it was already 7.15pm – what if he was early? She swept through her wardrobe of clothes and decided on a simple grey linen dress – it was a bit creased but she decided it would have to do, since she didn't have time to iron it.

Bartie started barking from downstairs, no time for makeup! She quickly sprayed a little perfume onto her neck and hurried downstairs to find Bartie jumping at the front door like a dog possessed.

Megan took a deep breath and opened the door. Bartie shot out and passed Fin, making Fin laugh and move quickly out of the dog's way.

205

Fin smiled at Megan and handed her a bottle of champagne, then he leant forward and kissed her on the cheek. "A 'welcome home' gift," he said.

"Thanks," she replied, taking the bottle of champagne from him. "I'll pop it in the fridge."

Fin followed her into the kitchen. "It doesn't smell of smoke at all, just something delicious."

"Lamb curry," she replied opening the fridge. "What can I get you to drink?" she asked. "Bubbles, red or white wine, or beer?"

"I'd love a beer, thirsty work all this digging!"

"Not that you do much of the back-breaking digging..." she teased.

"No I don't, but it's a lovely evening, I could do with a nice cold beer to refresh me after a long week."

Megan handed him a beer and poured herself a glass of champagne – she wanted to celebrate moving back home. "Shall we go in the garden? Dinner will be about thirty minutes."

He nodded and followed her out through the back door into the garden, which was full of evening sunshine and long shadows. "Beautiful garden," he said.

"My gran was a very keen gardener; in later years she had to have help, but she was always tending the flowers. I think she would be very disappointed in me not keeping up the good work. I think I might have to get someone in, I don't know very much about gardening."

"Me neither, I have a couple of vegetable boxes on top of the barge as you know, but I'm only an amateur myself."

They chatted easily and Megan felt herself relax more and more with the champagne. After a while, from the kitchen, a timer marked that the curry was ready. Megan went indoors to attend it; Fin left her to it, as if knowing she would prefer not to be watched whilst preparing their dinner.

When everything was ready she went to find Fin. He was wandering around the garden looking at the river with ducks and swans floating past, beer in his hand, looking very relaxed and handsome.

"Dinner's ready," she called out, approaching him.

Fin turned and smiled. "Great, I'm really hungry."

They walked together back to the house. "I saw that traveller guy just now...walking amongst the trees opposite...does he often come this way? He does seem to pop up quite a bit don't you think?"

Megan felt her heart sink; she didn't really know how to respond. "I may have seen him a couple of times..." She certainly didn't want

206

to talk about Kai. Fin seemed to have a real dislike for him, although she didn't know why. Besides, why *was* he walking over there amongst the trees; had it been him that had been staring at the house in the past all along? She felt a shiver run through her.

They sat at the table and ate slowly, chatting away about the dig and their exciting week. When they had finished the curry, Fin stopped her mid-sentence. "Sorry, I meant to say...I've got your brooch here." He felt in his pocket, pulled out a box, and handed it to her.

Megan put down her glass and took hold of the box. Inside was the brooch, it had been cleaned and looked amazing – nothing like the brooch Bartie had dug up in the garden. "Wow, they've done a fantastic job!"

"It's beautiful, isn't it? A piece of art."

She nodded, then felt a strange sensation creep through her as she thought about her gran's diary and what she had said about the brooch – what if it *was* cursed? Did she really want it here in the house again; her gran clearly hadn't!

She realised that Fin was talking to her. "Sorry? Say that again."

He smiled. "I was just saying, I don't know if you're interested...but there is a vacancy coming up at the university...I know you wanted some time out of the academic side of things, but we have somebody in the faculty who's moving to America for work and we'll be looking for a replacement in September. It's quite a few months away."

Megan's heart leapt – what an opportunity! However, Fin was right, did she really want to go back to academia again, or was she happy just being out in the field at the moment? She wasn't sure she was ready for that yet. She had felt so rejected after her redundancy; taking it personally even though she knew that she had been a valued member of the team – what if it happened again? Could she work with David as her boss and Fin in the same faculty? She got on with both really well, but was that because she knew this was a short term position, no ties?

Fin must have gauged her mental struggle. "It's all right, you don't have to tell me now – you can think about it. If you're not ready, that's fine, it's just David and I think you would be perfect for the position! I'll understand if it's not what you want right now."

"I will think about it, thank you for telling me," she said.

Fin changed the subject. "That curry was delicious; the meat was so tender, thank you." He had cleared his plate clean.

"It's just my way of saying thank you for helping me out after the fire. I have a small gift for you too." She walked over to the side and picked up a bottle-shaped, gift-wrapped present and handed it to him.

He took it from her with a frown and opened it slowly as if he didn't get gifts very often and wanted to savour the moment. He took out the aged whisky and let out a whistle. "We must be paying you too much…" he laughed. "Thank you. How did you know it was my favourite?"

"I noticed you had a shot each evening before you went to bed…so I was hoping that it was a favourite." She laughed, suddenly feeling shy.

He blushed as though it was a guilty secret he had been trying to hide.

Megan stood up and cleared away the dishes. She walked to the fridge and got out her home-made lemon tart, a recipe of her gran's that was always a favourite at dinner parties in the past; she put it onto the table and cut them each a generous slice.

"Wow, you're really an excellent cook!" said Fin, through his first mouthful of lemon tart.

After dinner, they returned with more drinks to the garden. The sun was setting and there was a beautiful red-pink-orange sky with purple clouds on the horizon; the colours were reflected in the river and the evening took on a slightly timeless impression.

"I can see why you wanted to keep the cottage," said Fin, lounging back into the bench that overlooked the river's edge.

"I would never sell it," replied Megan. "Unless I was forced to, but I would fight with every ounce of myself to keep hold of it."

There was a moment of silence, not uncomfortable.

"Have you always lived on narrow boats?" she asked.

He shook his head. "No, I grew up in a house in Oxford, my parents are still there. However, I love the outdoors, the freedom that river living gives me…during the holidays I can just up sticks and move my home to anywhere I fancy. I love Britain and although I've taken the barge abroad a few times, this is where my heart is…the waterways of England mainly…rather too traditional perhaps, but that's who I am. My mother says that she rues the day when she read me endless stories of *Wind in the Willows*, she's certain that's what made me the adult I am!" He laughed.

Megan smiled. "My gran used to read me Enid Blyton books all the time – I wonder what that says about me?"

"You're probably quite an adventurer or somebody who believes in magic, fairies and the like…or perhaps a bit of both?"

They both laughed together this time, and Megan felt Fin's eyes linger a little longer on hers than usual; she felt her body temperature rise and hoped that the heat didn't show in her cheeks.

It was midnight when he rose to leave, reluctantly heaving himself out of the armchair in the sitting room where they had withdrawn after the temperature dropped quite quickly once the sun had set.

"I'll see you on Monday," he said. "Best of luck with the cottage; take your time to change things…it's hard to move on after somebody you care for dies."

It occurred to Megan that perhaps he knew this from personal experience; he had been very perceptive of her needs after the fire, and he knew how recently her gran had passed away.

"I shall have to go back to my empty barge now, I think I'd got quite used to the company, maybe I'll have to get myself a dog…" He patted Bartie on the head and leant over, kissing Megan on the cheek. "Thanks for a lovely evening."

She smiled and he was gone.

Walking back into the lounge, she retrieved the brooch, in its box, from the coffee table and climbed slowly up the stairs; Bartie charging past her in an attempt to beat her to the most comfortable position on the bed. She walked into her room, the moon was full and its silvery light caressed the room. Placing the box which held the brooch onto the bedside cupboard, she went to the bathroom before returning and finally putting her head on the pillow.

She lay for a while, her head a little muzzy from the wine, and thought back over the evening. Realising, with surprise, how much she would miss his company of an evening; she had got used to him over the past few days – his smiling, friendly face; his easy, but intelligent chatter. Fin was a really nice man, he was very observant about things and perceptive to her feelings. She wondered again at her thoughts earlier, had he lost somebody close to him? Is that why he was so intuitive to her needs right now?

Her thoughts turned again to the brooch and how her gran had thought it brought bad luck. If it was the same one, and it did seem too much of a coincidence not to be, perhaps she really should just give it to a museum. She certainly didn't need any more bad luck at the moment.

The woman's face was familiar somehow…her blonde locks loose around her anxious face; her green eyes held fear, but with that fear a determination was prominent.

209

"You must not let her have it...please...she must never be able to take it away...it is the only thing that holds the truth, my truth...I must have it, I need..."

Bartie growled.

Megan slowly opened her eyes...her heart leapt into her mouth as she watched a dark shadow slide away from the bed and disappear into the blackness of the room: the silver moonlight had now dispersed but there was enough light from the landing light to see it slip into a gloomier part of the room. The shadow had been of average height, but that was all she could ascertain.

The next instant Bartie shot off the bed and stood growling, hackles raised, at the bedroom door which stood open. Megan flicked on the bedside lamp and sat straight up, her heart thumping in her chest; she looked round to see if her mobile phone was nearby, damn she must have left it downstairs...slowly she got out of bed, noticing the lumps of earth on the floor – Bartie was standing still, his tail between his legs, snarling and baring his teeth at whatever it was behind the door.

My God, there was actually something there...

"Ok, boy, it's all right," Megan said her voice hoarse.

Walking slowly, step by step, towards the door, Megan could feel the fear rising inside her...she took a deep breath and quickly kicked the door...it swung into the room revealing what was hidden behind.

A rat.

She shrieked, ran back to the bed and quickly jumped onto it.

The rat looked at her with its watery black eyes; it was twitching, with either fear or aggression, she couldn't tell. Bartie didn't pounce, but backed away, still snarling as the rat darted forward and disappeared downstairs, the dog in hot pursuit. Adrenalin drove Megan down the stairs where she found the rat in the hall, Bartie now barking frantically. She went to the front door in the vain hope that if she opened it the rat would make a run for its freedom – she didn't care if Bartie killed it outside, but she didn't want it in here for another moment. Opening the door, the rat squealed loudly as it ran past her and out of the door, Bartie following. She slammed the door shut and leant against it. Her breath came in short, sharp gasps; her heart raced in her chest and her pulse hammered in her temples too.

It took a few minutes for her heart to steady, consequently she found herself shaking. Bartie woofed to come in and she turned on the outside light to make sure he didn't have the rat in his mouth. It had gone. There was no sign of blood on Bartie's jaws so she had to assume that it had got away. She must contact pest control in the morning; there was no way she wanted to share the cottage with rats.

Megan sighed deeply and went to the kitchen, where she flicked on the kettle and sat at the table, trying to steady her nerves. She looked round the kitchen: remnants of last night's dinner still cluttered the work surfaces and table; she might as well tackle that, she thought, as she was now wide awake. Megan stood again, still shaking slightly and got to work, trying to shake off the feelings of terror that hung around her like a threatening storm cloud. Bartie sat by the Aga, now calm as if nothing had happened.

As she cleaned, her thoughts returned to her dream...she remembered where she had seen the woman before – at the kitchen window; as she remembered that, she didn't dare look up at the pane of glass before her. What was it that she didn't want somebody to have? She'd said that she mustn't let her have it...have what? The brooch? Was the brooch linked to this woman in her dreams, and who she had seen in real life in the fields around the cottage? But what of the rat? What was that all about...she thought back to the shadow she had seen slipping behind the door of her bedroom, the shadow had been far too big to be that of a rat, the shadow had looked human...female. For some reason, Megan was certain that this female was not the same as the woman in her dream, this woman felt far more sinister.

She climbed the stairs, wearily and with trepidation. Bartie pushed his way past her and immediately went to check behind the door of her bedroom where the rat had been. Finding nothing there, he jumped up onto the bed and slumped down in a curled up heap, sighing loudly. Megan's lamp was still on and it spread a low, golden glow about the room, making it feel warm and welcoming. Megan walked up to the bed and glanced at the rug at the bedside...there was still mud: damp, dark, heavy with clay...had it been a rat all along that had brought lumps of mud indoors? Megan tried to convince herself that it was, it had been a rat all along that had been 'breaking in' and leaving lumps of earth behind – but how *could* it be? The lumps of soil had been far too large to be brought in on the small feet of some rodent.

Megan turned and looked at the box which stowed the brooch. Slowly picking it up, she unclasped the lid and lifted it out. She turned the piece of jewellery over in her hands and wondered at its purpose. Her gran had wondered if the brooch, if it was the same one, had been cursed – did she, Megan, believe that things, inanimate objects, could hold some energy; powerful, negative energy? She had certainly heard of talismans, used for protection or for manipulation of others through the use of magic, but this was the 21st century…did that make it impossible…or was it an ancient belief, that could still hold some kind of power throughout the generations – slipping through time like a lost soul?

She shivered.

Something strange was definitely going on – Sasha had suggested counselling…perhaps she would give her friend, Katy, a call tomorrow – see what she had to suggest, as she was a fully qualified 'head doctor' as Megan often called her. With a new resolve in place, however tenacious, she felt her nerves settle and she put her head on her pillow: within moments she was asleep.

Outside, a cold breeze stirred the branches of the weeping willows, sending whispers upon the wind, whispers that were only meant to be heard by a certain few…but the wind carried those whispers across the landscape to where a traveller lay sleeping; it crept in through the cracks of the wooden caravan and caressed his sleeping form – as he heard the words spoken to him, his lips curved into a smile, as if he'd understood and agreed to what those whispers were asking him to do…

Chapter Seventeen

Lindi collected some nuts and berries from the woodland that surrounded the caves; they were running low on food and needed to replenish their supplies if they were to stay here for a few more days. They mustn't stay too much longer in case Wilheard's men were to search the area. She was not naïve enough to think that Wilheard wouldn't seek another seer to help in the search for his treasonous brother. She had buried her ties with the king and his people, but with Wulfric she knew she had a future...a future with power and happiness and perhaps even heirs...she placed her hand on her belly and smiled. Wulfric was coming round to her plan even though she knew to start with he had been against it, but the more he thought about it and listened to her ideas, the more determined he became. He had nothing to lose now that his brother wanted him for treason.

Strolling next to the river, which wound its way through the rocky valley towards the sea to the south-west, Lindi caught a glimpse of a shadow in the water. She turned, stunned and stared carefully into the moving silver waters; sunlight glistening and casting coloured sparks on the rocks and grass around her. There it was again, the shadow.

Mildryth.

What was she doing? Lindi looked closely at Mildryth's form as it walked through the countryside, a horse and a man, not Wilheard, at her side; she had belongings with her – she was searching for them! So, the little queen thought she would follow them, did she? She began to laugh at the ridiculousness of Mildryth's actions, but slowly her smile began to fade...Lindi swallowed. What if Mildryth told Wulfric of the child? Would he assume that the child was his? This couldn't happen...she, Lindi, was carrying the future heir – if Wulfric knew that Mildryth was carrying his child, Lindi feared he would cast her aside; kill his brother and then take over as king! Then, then he could marry Mildryth...

What could she do? She frantically searched her thoughts for a solution and started, for the first time, to feel a panic rise inside her chest. She hadn't for a moment thought that Mildryth would be strong enough, or stupid enough to follow them – what was she planning to do? She had clearly underestimated Mildryth. Had Wilheard been told the truth? Was Mildryth now in search of Wulfric and his protection? By the gods, she couldn't allow her to find them. She hoped that Mildryth still wore the brooch – if she didn't, then there would be no hope of controlling her...

***

"I think you should rest, my lady," said the horseman. "You are looking pale. We can camp here tonight, and I will watch over you."

Mildryth looked gratefully at the horseman, Piers; she wouldn't have stopped if he hadn't suggested it. He had been her horseman since she was a child and although he was reluctant to go with her, he had seen her anxiety and trusted her to know that what she was doing was the right thing, however dangerous. He would rather go with her as her protector than let her go alone.

Mildryth was driven by desperation to find the two that had betrayed her. To try to set things straight with Wilheard, to have him forgive her in front of the gods, was the only thing her heart desired. Out of choice she would never have lain with Wulfric; she loved her king, her Wilheard...Lindi's use of magic appalled and sickened her, and the fact that Wulfric had accepted that help, even after the events of his own birth, meant that she felt betrayed by the two people she had known all her life as her *friends, her family*. Tears started in her eyes and she sat down on a fallen tree, suddenly aware of how weary she felt. She took some water from the flask Piers held out to her. He watched her closely. "I will build us a fire," he said. "Rest."

She watched as he collected wood and sticks from beneath the trees that surrounded the clearing, thinking back to when she had been just a child and he had taught her to ride a horse. He couldn't have been much more than a child himself at the time because he was still young now and strong – a good protector as well as a horseman; someone to be trusted.

Once the fire had been lit and the meat they had taken from home, cooked above it, Mildryth ate hungrily and drank the wine Piers offered. As the light bled out of the sky, leaving strong reds and pinks to the west, the air turned colder. Mildryth huddled closer to the fire and watched the flames dance skywards, the dark smoke snaking its way towards the stars; the moonlight blanketing everything in silver, making it look like everything had a fine dusting of frost upon it. Mildryth shivered and snuggled deeper into the wool blankets, glad that she'd thought to bring them. As she drifted between wakefulness and sleep, a face appeared in the fire...it was not a face she recognised. It was of a young woman with a look of anxiety in her eyes, but Mildryth sensed that this stranger was a friend, not a foe. The soft features of the dark haired woman vanished and were replaced by the features of Lindi. Her face was now amongst the flames, stronger, more malevolent, and her ice-like eyes laughed at her from wherever she was…Mildryth knew, instinctively that she was close by and wondered if she knew she was coming…

***

"Gone…gone? Where has she gone?" Wilheard raved at Ayken, his blue eyes glinting with rage.

"She cannot be found, Sire," replied Ayken calmly, but with fear in his eyes. "I've had men out searching since you woke and discovered she was not beside you."

"I slept so heavily…do you think I was drugged? I *have* to find her; she is carrying my child, the heir to this kingdom…"

"I am sure she will come home…perhaps she needed some time alone to think…she has often done that in the past, you know your queen – she does take herself off, especially to see her mother's grave…"

Ayken saw the hope light up in Wilheard's eyes, but he shook his head quickly. "We searched the burial site first thing this morning, she wasn't there."

With horror Ayken could see the king's eyes fill with tears and he ushered all the other aides from the chamber. He filled a horn full of wine and handed it to Wilheard, his eyes now cast at the wooden floor. Wilheard swiped the horn from Ayken's hand, blood red wine spilling over the floor, soaking into the skins and blankets of the bed where he and Mildryth had lain together, limbs and bodies as one. A sob escaped his throat and he sank onto a wooden bench, where he put his head in his hands and wept. Where was she? Had she run away – why? Or had someone taken her…his fears lay with the latter theory and his heart thumped faster and harder as he thought about why and who could have taken her – there was only one, possibly two people, who dared…

Akyen stood watching the king, his heart heavy with grief, for although he was their servant, to him they were his family. He had been in their service since he was six years old, his father and mother had also served Aelle. He had always thought that the family would survive; they were strong, unconquerable it seemed for many decades, but recent events had that certainty teetering on the edge of new possibilities. Darkness, like a cancerous growth increasing in strength and fortitude, was now threatening the peace which had endured for a long time.

***

Megan awoke to the sound of the distant church bells tolling from the town across the fields. Sunlight was shining through the flowery curtains at the window, she must have slept in – she glanced at her clock, 9.45. She stretched and groaned as Bartie trod on her, saying his good morning. Sitting up, she glanced at the floor by the bed; the earth was still there, sending a shiver of fear down her back as the events of the previous evening came flooding back. *Pest control,* top of the list. However, it was Sunday, so not much chance of contacting anyone today.

Downstairs in the kitchen, she smiled to herself as she saw all the clear surfaces and clean crockery on the draining board by the sink – at least one good thing had come out of last night. Bartie woofed by the back door and she opened it to let him out. Walking to the table where her laptop was, she flicked it on – she could at least search for a pest control company and get somebody lined up for tomorrow.

Sipping her coffee, she watched Bartie in the garden. She wondered who she could talk to about the events of last night and her growing fears about the brooch...Sasha would have been her first choice, but she was still in Italy. Katy, her counsellor friend would be more than happy to help, but she really did feel rather awkward about it – what if she really was going a bit crazy? Her rational mind refused to believe this, but how many people with mental health problems admitted or actually *knew* they were ill? She couldn't talk to her mum, she would just scoff in her face...that only really left Fin. She had broached the subject with him before about the strange happenings...he had taken her seriously. He had also insisted that she talk to the police, something else she felt reluctant to do. Window locks were the other thing she needed, pest control and window locks; not that rats came in through windows...but burglars could. She would take Bartie for a walk and then go to a DIY store to buy the locks too – that would give her something to do today, keeping her mind from wandering further.

Her mobile indicated a message. It was from Fin:

> *Thanks for a lovely dinner last night.*
> *I had a really nice time. Excellent cooking.*

She replied:

> *You're welcome – great to have you over.*
> *Thanks again for letting me stay while*
> *the cottage was out of use – enjoy the whisky.*

She waited but no reply came.

Stuffing her thickly clad feet into her boots, she pulled on her gran's wax coat and called to Bartie as she walked round the side of the house. He came charging towards her from the back of the house and followed her down the track towards the bridge. He flew past her at top speed, eager to get ahead of her. The wind was cool, but the sun was warm and she enjoyed the feeling of it upon her face. It seemed that Bartie had chosen his route for the morning and she followed him along the riverside…ahead she could see Fin's boat and she wondered if he was home. She could see some smoke coming from the chimney, and as she got closer, could see that the curtains were all pulled back, but the doors and windows were closed – he was out. She couldn't help wondering where he'd gone, he hadn't mentioned that he was going anywhere to her last night – but then why should he? He may have gone for a run, or to see friends.

She felt her heart sink a little but continued along the river, watching a cluster of ducks being fed by a young family, all smiling together and laughing as the little girl threw a whole slice of bread at a swan; accidently hitting it in the head.

As she and Bartie were walking back down the track towards the cottage, having gone full circle on their walk, Megan saw Kai and Angus coming towards them. As he got nearer, he smiled at her and called her name.

"Hi," she said, giving Angus a fuss and trying to hide her reluctance at speaking to him.

"Morning," he said, his grey eyes sparkling and friendly this time. "What are yer up to?"

"Not much, taking it easy with some DIY," she smiled at him, wondering why he seemed to be more friendly than usual.

"Anything I can help yer with?" he asked. "I'm quite handy."

Surprised, Megan shook her head. "No, thank you, quite a simple task really and I've got some sorting out to do too, gran's stuff."

"Sure," he said, nodding and holding her gaze for a moment too long, making her feel uncomfortable. "Just let me know if there is anything I can do to help, with the fire and things I expect you've lots to do…yer know where I am."

"Thank you."

"Come on, Angus," he called, then he stopped and turned back to face Megan. "By the way, me band's playing at the pub a week on Friday, come along if yer can. Might not be yer cuppa tea, it'll be good folk music! Something to do around here for a Friday night, there's not always much, is there?"

217

As he laughed, his eyes met hers again and held them – in that instant, Megan felt a strong, if reluctant attraction to him. Thanking him again, but making no promises, she walked away, feeling very confused and unsettled about her inexplicable mixed feelings towards him. He was a bit of an odd one...not usually that friendly and clearly the 'property' of Bridget, or so Bridget thought. Best steer clear of that one, even if she did feel that reluctant attraction...

Later that day, Megan had successfully fitted the window locks and was sitting at the kitchen table with a toasted sandwich and her gran's diary. She carefully flicked back to the date where her gran had written about the brooch and how she was going to bury it again. Lying on the table in an open box, the brooch was beautifully cleaned and preserved, and looked harmless enough. Did the Saxons believe in and use magic? She wasn't certain, but she did know somebody who would know – should she give him a call?

She picked up her mobile phone and found Fin's name in her contacts...his phone went straight to his voicemail. Sighing, she decided she would just have to deal with this issue herself. She was an intelligent, independent woman, therefore did not need somebody else to make this decision about the brooch for her. Her gran had believed it had brought her bad luck, she trusted her judgement on nearly everything in her life. But, was this her being irrational, just as she herself had been feeling recently, or was there more to it than that? Her heart was telling her to get rid of it, but her more rational side was telling her to look into it in more detail before making a rash decision. Come on, Megan, she scolded herself...you can deal with this and you must...

She flicked on her laptop and put in a search for Anglo-Saxon beliefs about talismans. Whilst she researched the endless pages of information on the internet and flicked through a reference book that Fin had lent her, she finally concluded that the Anglo-Saxons did believe and often used talismans. Most were used for protection, but there were some theories that suggested that if they could be used for protection, then they could be used for more evil purposes too. She looked at the brooch on the table in front of her and wondered what purpose it could have had. If it had been cursed with evil powers, then what was its purpose – if not protection, then what about manipulation in order to harm somebody? You didn't have to look back at ancient history to know that some people wanted to cause harm to others, due to breakdowns in relationships: parents who had let their children down; jealousy of siblings; broken love affairs – all these cause pain, even in the 21st century, and sometimes brought about feelings of revenge.

Revenge.

Although the sky outside was now getting darker, Megan's thoughts were becoming clearer. If this brooch was somehow connected to an ancient grudge or act of revenge...then maybe that was why it seemed so important.

The phone rang and made her jump. She didn't recognise the number, hoped it wasn't Tom, but could see the caller was from London. "Hello?"

"Is that Megan?" asked an unfamiliar voice at the end of the phone.

"Yes..."

"My name is Gerald. I am a friend of your mother's..."

Immediately Megan knew something was wrong. "What's happened?"

"Your mother is in hospital, Megan, I'm sorry, but they think she's had a stroke. She's stable but not well, can you come?"

"Of course...I'll be there as soon as I can."

Gerald gave her the details of the hospital and said he would stay with her mother until she got there.

Megan's heart was in her mouth. Not her mother too, not now, please! She couldn't take another loss. She ran upstairs and threw some items of clothing into a suitcase, at the same time phoning Mrs Clark to explain the situation and to see if she could drop Bartie off at her house for a couple of days.

Lugging the suitcase down the stairs, and trying hard to ignore Bartie's sorrowful face, she went into the kitchen to check the sandwich toaster was switched off. The brooch glinted at her, reflecting the kitchen light that she had just turned on, what should she do with it for now? Take it with her, or hide it in a cupboard – there was no time to make a final decision on it now – her mother....

She grabbed the brooch and put it on top of the kitchen dresser, out of sight, then called to Bartie to get in the car. She got her handbag, dragged her case outside, and then turned the key in the lock to secure the cottage.

As she drove away from the cottage, down the rutted lane, she didn't know that two pairs of eyes were watching and wondering where she was going and when she would return...at that moment in time she had no idea herself, she had to get to London, and prayed it wouldn't be too late!

***

Lindi sat next to the fire, searching the flames for a clue as to where Mildryth was…she couldn't be wearing the brooch now for it was much harder to see her whereabouts, to track her movements. The talisman had proved very useful and had enabled Lindi to manipulate Mildryth much more easily; keep her and her thoughts where she wanted them. She took out her runes and spread them about, hoping they might be able to help her now. Suddenly, her thoughts were interrupted by heavy footsteps outside the cave; a shadow fell across the entrance – Wulfric. He had a deer flung across his shoulders, and looked very pleased with himself.

"I caught us some food," he said, flinging the carcass down on the ground. "Come here woman…" He grabbed hold of Lindi and held her hard against him, she could feel his hardness beneath the furs and she pushed hard against him, enjoying the knowledge that it was she that drove him to this desire…

Later, after she had helped him cook the deer over the fire, the sweet scent of the flesh making them hungry, she watched as Wulfric tore the flesh of the animal with his teeth. He was a strong and powerful man, he would make a good king; she would make a great queen. She was not naïve enough to think that Wulfric loved her, but if she could keep him happy long enough…

Wulfric was watching her carefully as she ate. "What is it?" she asked.

"You, Lindi, when I come to think about it, you were always quiet when we were children. Although you're a few years older than me, I could tell something ran deep within you – now I realise what that was…"

"What, what runs deep within me?"

He smiled. "Ambition…"

"What's wrong with a woman being ambitious?" she snapped.

"It can take you far, but it can also get you killed…or me," he shuddered.

"It doesn't seem to have concerned you thus far," she sneered. "I would say that you had ambition too. After all, you know I killed your father…"

"Don't talk about that!"

"Why not? When I suggested it, you agreed it needed to be done."

"I never gave…"

"You never needed to, now there is only one more person in your way, before you can become king…"

Wulfric looked doubtful. "My brother is the rightful king, however much I hate that...do you really believe that Mercia will attack if I say so? There has been peace for decades now..."

"Yes, but they have a new king too...a different generation, perhaps he could be coerced into thinking that one large kingdom would be better than two – who knows where it could lead!"

"Probably death...yours and mine."

Lindi smiled at him, purposely letting her cloak slip from her shoulder to reveal her naked breast. "Not necessarily, I think if we're careful..."

"Enough!" he shouted, shaking his head and getting to his feet. "Get some sleep."

Startled at his sudden anger, she rearranged her clothing quickly and sat up straight. She must be careful; there was a fine line, she realised, between being able to seduce him and making him feel vulnerable.

Lindi watched him leave the cave, his anger tangible within the constraints of the cavern. Lying down, she pulled the furs about her – where was he going? Was he becoming more aware of her power and knew he had to distance himself from her? She didn't want that, couldn't bear it now, not now that she had tasted his desire. It was necessary to take things more slowly, she was going too fast...but then she didn't know how long they'd got...time could be running out – especially if Wilheard's men or Mildryth were to discover them.

Pulling the dagger from beneath her layers of clothing and bringing it closer towards where her head lay, she watched its glinting blade reflect the flames of orange that danced around the walls of the cave. She knew she had to stay vigilant and patient; most of all patient although she felt nothing of the kind. This was the opportunity she had been waiting for her whole life; the opportunity to earn the respect of the people who she felt had always looked down on her...she loved Wulfric, yes, and she wanted his body, but she wanted the power more, the power of being a queen – she'd show Mildryth how to be a proper queen, one that would rule with a dominance that would be the envy of all women...and men.

***

Gifre stood amongst the trees to the north of the king's hall, clutching his still-warm kill from that morning. His hunting partner pointed out a group of armed men marching around the village, clearly demanding information about something from the villagers. There was a desperate air amongst them which unnerved Gifre – something was wrong...

221

As they walked down out of the trees and towards the centre of the village, they were approached immediately. The guards' faces were full of concern and their eyes fearful.

"Halt, Gifre, Acwel – have you been hunting since dawn?" demanded Aart, who was clearly in charge.

Gifre nodded. "What's happened?"

"The queen has gone missing; did you see anybody about this morning in the village or the forest? Or even the queen herself?"

Gifre felt the shock go through him, but he shook his head, "Not a soul, do they think she has been taken?"

Aart looked weary. "They don't know, she has just disappeared...wasn't in her bed this morning when the king awoke!"

"Have they checked down near her mother's burial – I have seen her there on occasions," suggested Gifre.

Aart told the men where they had searched and that there had been no sign of her. "The king thinks he was drugged – he slept too heavily for it to be a natural slumber. He was the last to see her and now he blames himself. We must find her!" Aart's frustration was clear and he ordered his men to continue their questioning and searching of the village and the surrounding countryside.

Gifre walked with Acwel to the store where they would hang the dead animals ready to be cooked later. He made his excuses and walked back to his hut, knowing his wife and children would be busy with the sheep out in the pasture and at the weaving loom. He took a large jug of wine from the shelf and drank a few mouthfuls, his heart beating fast in his chest. What was he supposed to do? He knew he should tell his king, but surely then the king would ask why he hadn't said anything before, and would probably feed him to the wolves in the forests as he'd previously feared.

He sat in the darkness, listening to the sounds from the village outside: men and women talking in urgent voices, children shrieking, oblivious to the crisis unfolding around them. The sunlight streamed through the doorway and Gifre watched as the particles of dust danced around him, as erratic as his thoughts and fears...he had to make a decision about what to do, and soon – didn't his king have a right to know what his so-called innocent queen had been up to with his brother? How dare she lay with the bastard brother...the heir she was carrying could also be illegitimate – would the people really want that? They would never accept Wulfric as their king, so why would they want a bastard's child as their future heir? No, he had a duty to follow...

The sun disappeared behind some dark clouds and although the dancing specks of dust could no longer be seen, Gifre knew they were still there, just as the truth was concealed from the king, hidden but not forgotten – Gifre now knew he had no choice. If he didn't tell Wilheard then the gods would punish him, and he felt that Wilheard's punishment, although it meant almost certain death, it would not be as bad as what the gods would do to him if he didn't tell the truth of what he knew.

***

Megan looked at the small figure of her mother lying with her eyes closed amongst the white sheets and blankets of the hospital bed. She went straight over to her and gently kissed her on the top of the head, afraid of knocking any of the wires that were attached to her. The room was lit by a small lamp and smelled of disinfectant.

"I'm here, Mum," she said softly, as if it would be better now that she was there. How could it be really, though? She had no medical knowledge...no idea or control over how ill her mother really was.

There was no response.

Tears that she had managed to keep hold of, on the two and a half hour drive to London, suddenly overflowed and ran down her cheeks. She looked up as a white handkerchief was offered to her and met the green eyes of an elderly man. He smiled kindly, his eyes full of concern.

"I'm Gerald," he said.

"I'm Megan," she replied wiping her tears onto the soft cotton and sniffing loudly. "How is she?"

"Like I said over the phone, she is stable but it *was* a stroke and they won't know anymore until she regains consciousness."

Megan gazed at the man. She remembered her mother mentioning this man last time they spoke. She wondered how close they were, how long they had been seeing each other. Gerald seemed a bit different to the other men her mother usually had tagging along – he seemed warm and friendly, quite shy in fact. Perhaps it was the circumstances.

"When did it happen?"

"We were at home...er...your mother's...having dinner together. She declined the wine I offered at the beginning of the meal..."

"That's unlike her..." Megan smiled.

Gerald gave a little laugh. "She ate about half her dinner and then her speech went slurry like she *had* been drinking. I am...was, that is, I was a doctor before I retired...I knew immediately what was going on and called an ambulance."

"Thank you for taking care of her."

"Would you like me to go?"

Megan wasn't sure she wanted to be alone. "You're welcome to stay too if you want to." She could see that he was genuinely concerned about her mother and that he cared a great deal too.

The two of them sat in silence, Gerald giving Megan the space to sit close to her mother and hold her hand. After a while, Gerald disappeared and returned with a cup of hot chocolate for Megan. The smell immediately reminded her of her gran and how she'd always made her hot chocolate when she was sad or unwell. Tears sprang to her eyes again. Suddenly, she thought of Fin – she must phone him...tell him she wouldn't be at work in the morning. "I have a phone call to make," she told Gerald.

He nodded and took her place next to her mother, holding onto her hand, his head bent.

Out in the corridor, Megan dialled Fin's number. It was one o'clock, she hoped it would go to answer phone then he would pick the message up in the morning. His sleepy voice made her wish she'd waited until morning to call.

"Megan, are you all right?" he asked.

"I'm in London, I'm at the hospital with my mother – she's had a stroke."

"Oh."

"I won't be at work in the morning," she replied, again close to tears.

"No, no of course not," he replied.

There was a woman's voice in the background.

Shocked, Megan tried to finish the conversation, "I'll call..."

"I hope she'll be ok," interrupted Fin, more alert now. "Let me know if there's anything I can do...Bartie, anything..."

The woman's voice again, quiet, insistent.

"Thank you. I will call you when I know more." She hung up – her heart was thumping in her chest. Who was the woman with him...he had never mentioned anyone, had been so kind...perhaps that was it, he was just a kind person; he had been kind to her as he would be to anyone else.

Her sorrowful feelings were interrupted by a doctor appearing from the room where her mother lay. She hadn't noticed anyone go in, having walked down the corridor away from her mother's room and around a corner. "Miss...."

She swept aside her thoughts of Fin and focused on the doctor.

"Your mum's just woken up...you can see her, but keep it brief."

Megan flew into the room where her mother's eyes were still closed. Gerald wasn't there.

"Mum?" she said, gently.

Her mother moaned and slowly opened her eyes, one was definitely droopy, in fact, the whole left side of her face had dropped quite noticeably. "Meggie," she said, in a hoarse whisper and tried to smile, but her eyes closed again and she lost consciousness, or fell asleep, Megan was not sure which.

She glanced at the doctor who had followed her in. "She recognised me...does that mean she'll be ok?"

The doctor looked her in the eye. "It's too early to tell just yet, but it's a good sign. I think you should go and get some sleep..."

"Can't I stay?"

"I think you need some sleep, she's stable, but also needs to rest. We can call you if there is any change."

Megan nodded and took her mother's hand in hers. She stroked the roped hand and felt its papery thinness. She realised, not for the first time, that her mother was ageing too, that one day she too would be gone, just like her gran. A sob caught in her throat and she wept, not able to hold back the wave of emotion that threatened to drag her to her knees. She sat on the chair next to the bed, weeping onto her mother's hand, not caring that she couldn't be strong in this situation. She realised how much she loved her mother, even though they had never been that close, and the smile her mother had given her when she woke, only for an instant, reassured Megan that she loved her too.

"Come on, Megan. I'll drive you to your mother's, you can sleep there," said Gerald.

A little while later, Megan crawled into the spare bed at her mother's house and although she felt she would not be able to sleep, it consumed her immediately. Unfortunately, her sleep was fitful and her dreams were troubled: her mother not responding when she spoke to her; Fin in the arms of a woman, a blonde woman who turned and sneered at her, her eyes those of Bridget's...

Chapter Eighteen

Gifre took a long swig from the horn of wine and prayed to the gods for forgiveness – he should have told Wilheard right at the start of all this; should have told him that his woman had betrayed him with his brother *before* they were joined together as man and wife. He took a deep breath and stepped, slightly awkwardly, out of his hut into the rain. The rain had started not long since and the air was thick with the smoke from peoples' fires; it hung around the villagers' huts like a blanket of mist concealing what was really there.

Trudging up to the hall, with its large buck antlers hung over a heavily carved doorway, Gifre pleaded entrance to see the king. One of the guards disappeared inside for what seemed like ages, making Gifre's stomach tie itself in knots; the wine churned within his gut and made him feel like he would vomit.

The guard reappeared and beckoned to Gifre to follow. He felt light-headed and hoped he wouldn't bring up the wine he'd drunk, all over the wooden floorboards of the hall, the king's seat. Gifre noticed the sweat on Wilheard's face, even though the day was cool and the fire low in the hall. Wilheard turned and faced Gifre, his eyes full of anger...and fear.

"Do you have news of Mildryth?" he asked, hopefully.

Gifre swallowed and glanced around him then at the floor. "Might I have a private word, Sire?"

Wilheard glanced round the room, there were five guards and Ayken. With a nod of his head in the direction of the guards he dismissed them, but told Ayken to stay. The aides left the hall, muttering amongst themselves.

Wilheard waited until the men had left, then he rounded on Gifre. "What is it man...what do you know? Can you tell me where my wife is...you couldn't tell me where my brother was, even though you were his closest aide, so how do I know I can trust what you say?" His voice got louder and louder as he spoke and he got closer and closer to Gifre, his hand on his sword handle that lay in its sheath, but could be drawn in an instant.

Gifre fell to his knees. "Sire, what I am about to tell you, I should have told you before now and I ask for the gods' forgiveness and yours..."

"Out with it!" cried Wilheard.

"Your wife Mildryth, I believe, has gone off to find your brother."

"Liar – why would she do that?"

"I saw them, my Lord, laying together in the spring, not long before your joining with her...I believe that the child she carries is Wulfric's and that she has gone to him...betraying you, Sire..."

Gifre felt the blow to his head and then the heat of the fire close to his face – Wilheard had him by the throat and held his cheek to the hot embers of the fire. "You lie!" he cried. "Mildryth would never do such a thing..."

"I swear by Woden that it is the truth...I saw them with my own eyes."

Another blow to the head and Wilheard screeched in his ear; "You lie, swine, tell me you lie!"

"It is the truth."

"Never, *never* would Mildryth do that, she is a sweet and innocent woman; I have known her my *whole* life, I would have known if there was something going on..." Wilheard stopped...he remembered that he *did* know that Wulfric was in love with Mildryth, except he never thought that it was requited, not for a moment; perhaps he had been wrong? Perhaps he had been taken for a fool by them both? He felt the rage boil within him, he glanced at Ayken looking for reassurance, but Ayken was silent, he stared at Wilheard and shrugged.

Infuriated, the anger in him boiling over, Wilheard grabbed his sword and plunged it deep into Gifre's stomach. He didn't notice the surprise on Gifre's face or the shock on Ayken's as he howled his anguish into the smoke-filled room, before sinking to his knees from the force of his immeasurable grief.

Wilheard bawled like a young child and Ayken placed a hand upon his shoulder; he tried to lift Wilheard to his carved wooden throne but Wilheard threw him off. The old man muttered an apology and retreated to the far side of the room, not really knowing what to do.

After a while, Wilheard's sobs subsided slightly and he got himself into the throne where he sat with his head in his hands, shaking his head and making his long, blonde hair fall about his handsome face.

"I'm such a fool..."

Ayken knelt at Wilheard's feet. "Then she had us all fooled, Wilheard...I can't believe it is true..."

"Why would he tell us lies? We both know that Wulfric has always been in love with Mildryth...I never thought..." A sob caught in his throat. "My heir, we do not know that it is mine, how do we know Gifre didn't tell the whole village?" He glanced at Gifre's lifeless form. "Get rid of the body."

Ayken went to the door and called to the guards. As they entered they looked first at the body and then at Wilheard, their faces full of questions and concern.

"Remove the body," Wilheard ordered, not looking at his men.

Wilheard watched as the men carried the body out of the hall, then looked at Ayken. "I am sorry for that..."

"What are you going to do, Wilheard?"

Wilheard shook his head. "I will have my men search this land until they find them both; I will not stop until they are both dead!"

"But what if Gifre was wrong about them?"

"I don't see why he would lie, he must be telling the truth – why risk his life in order to tell me something that wasn't true? He must have known that if he told me, I would have him killed."

"I have to confess that I did see them walking together a couple of times, but I never thought anything was going on between them. You have all known each other since you were children...and how does Lindi come in to all this? She has disappeared too..."

"Maybe she knew...perhaps she fled as she couldn't or wouldn't hide the truth anymore. She also held a special place in her heart for Wulfric. Maybe her jealousy drove her away from us."

Ayken shook his head.

Wilheard felt the anger and pain rise within him again...they had all been friends their whole lives, how could this be happening now...just when he thought he had everything he wanted: the throne; the woman he loved; his people who loved him; loyal servants.

"Saddle the horses; gather my most trusted aides and we will go after them...I will not rest until I know the truth!" Wilheard flung himself from the chair and stomped across the hall towards his bed chamber, where he pulled on his battle clothing – something he had only ever worn for practice of an invasion in this time of peace. However, that peace was shattered and the time to fight had come; the battle his father had always spoken about was not the battle that he now faced. This was a battle of a more bitter kind.

***

The next morning Megan was disorientated when she first awoke, was she on the barge, in the cottage...no, her mother's house, of course...Oh, God, her mother. She slipped out of bed and checked her phone...no calls, just a message from Sasha saying she was returning that day and could they meet for a drink later. Megan decided she would reply to Sasha later. Now she must shower and get to the hospital...no news was good news, right?

229

Gerald arrived just as she was grabbing some toast for breakfast. He knocked on the door and Megan wondered where he had slept last night, did he have his own place or did he mostly stay with her mother – she didn't know...hadn't snooped around looking for razors or spare toothbrushes – she realised she didn't mind either way, if it made her mother happy. Gerald seemed like a nice man.

He drove them to the hospital and let Megan go on ahead at a pace in her eagerness to see her mother again. When she got to her room, her mother was sitting up in bed supported by many pillows. Her eyes were closed though – was she asleep?

Her mother opened her eyes slowly as she kissed her on the top of the head. "Morning, Mum," she whispered.

"Meg," she said. Her mother's mouth curled at one side as if she was trying to smile, but the other side still hung lifelessly.

Megan felt her heart break and tears spring to her eyes.

"How are you feeling, Mum?"

"Awful...but better now you're here..."

Thank God her mother knew who she was and was speaking coherently, that must be a good sign, no brain damage...

"Where's...em...em...goodness...*Gerald*. I, I couldn't remember his name for a moment." The look of terror on her mother's face made her realise that she couldn't take for granted that there was no damage at all.

"He's coming; he's gone to fetch some coffee."

"That's just like Gerald...isn't he lovely? Don't you think so, Megan?"

Megan nodded. Her mother clearly was very fond of this man, this man that Megan knew barely anything about. She had thought it was another of her mother's 'boyfriends' who had always seemed to tag along when her mother felt like it; clearly this one was different. And now, there he was, walking towards her mother with a bunch of flowers and a look of such undisputable love that Megan felt she should step aside and give them some space.

"Darling, Eleanor, you're awake," he said, placing the coffees and flowers on the cupboard by the bed and holding her close to him, trying to avoid the wires that were connected to her body.

"Yes, but feeling awful..."

"I'm sure...we won't stay long, we'll let you rest."

Gerald sorted the flowers into a vase and Megan sat on the side of her mother's bed, holding her hand.

"You gave us quite a scare," she admitted.

"I found it all rather frightening myself," she said, her eyes giving away just how terrifying she was finding it. "The doctor will be here shortly to give me some more information about what happened."

Megan felt the sudden urge to cuddle her mother, she didn't do it very often, her mother was not the cuddly type, but as she held her mother in her arms she realised that her mother's response was very different to normal; she held onto her far longer than she would normally do and she felt her mother tremble. Her mother was human after all, it was a tough exterior that hid a much humbler and emotional person; Megan realised, for the first time (and was shocked at herself for this), that her mother perhaps had been much more upset and affected by her father's death all those years ago than she'd realised. The string of men she'd had in tow since then was probably her way of looking for company, love – she had never been able to find anyone to fill his shoes...until now perhaps...

They stayed for about another half an hour, then Eleanor looked tired and started to fall asleep; Megan told her they would come back later.

This time Megan drove her own car from the hospital to her mother's house and searched the cupboards for a tin of soup that she could heat for her lunch, she found that she was now ravenous and felt a little chilled. Putting the soup onto the hob to heat through, she heard her phone alert a text message. Her bag was on the table and she rooted through it, pulling out the phone a few moments later. It was from Fin.

Good Morning. I hope your mum is ok?
Don't feel you have to rush back to work,
we are managing ok x

A kiss, he had put a kiss. A mistake, or was it guilt at not telling her about his girlfriend? She had to assume it was a girlfriend he'd had with him last night on the barge. However, he hadn't made any move towards her in that sense either...had just been kind and often perceptive to her needs, he was probably just a really nice person...and what the hell was she thinking like this for anyway? She wasn't ready for another relationship, but it didn't stop her feeling a slight sense of sadness that he wasn't interested in her in that way, or that he was not actually available.

Stirring her soup with one hand and replying to his text with the other, she wrote:

> *Should have more info later today.*
> *Mum seems better than she could*
> *have been in the circumstances.*
> *Speak later. X*

She didn't want to seem petty.

> *Ok, speak later.*

No kiss! She sighed. She didn't have the emotional strength to get agitated and discarded the phone to her pocket and served up her soup. Taking it through to her mother's beautifully designed Georgian style sitting-room she turned on the TV to watch the one o'clock news.

Having finished her soup, she sank down into the sofa, placing her mobile on the coffee table, and let the daytime women's chat show wash over her. She felt tired and emotionally drained, her thoughts were all over the place and she wondered again whether Sasha had been right about her getting some counselling. She had been through a lot of grief and upheaval in a short space of time and now her mother's stroke...life did seem to feel particularly cruel at the moment; she couldn't help wondering what she might have done in a previous life to deserve such bad luck. For now at least, her mother was still with her and had been given more time. The voices of the women on the TV dropped into background noise and she fell asleep, warm and comfortable on her mother's sofa.

Her heart was pounding painfully in her chest, she could feel the beat of it in her temples as she raced alongside the torrential waters of the deep, dark river. The soft, leather-worked shoes on her feet slipped in the mud and her long skirts thwarted her escape. The persecutor was close, she couldn't see his face but she could feel the horse's hooves vibrating through the ground very close by. The vibrations continued...her mind was confused...the feelings of terror and immense sadness filled, not just her whole being, but her soul too... the galloping hooves were so close, so close...

Megan sprang into sitting position, her head spinning; the horse's hooves from her dream continued seemingly inside her mother's sitting-room...no, not horse's hooves, she realised as her consciousness began to clear...her mobile. It was her mobile vibrating.

Sasha: the voice of reason.

Megan grabbed her phone and through her bleary eyes tried to hit the green answer button.

"Sasha," she breathed, relieved.

"Megan, are you ok? You sound...sleepy."

Megan laughed, but even to herself it sounded a little nervous.

"Megan, what's going on? I went to the house earlier as I hadn't been able to get hold of you. Your back door had been wrenched open...."

"What!"

"You were nowhere to be seen, no Bartie, no answering my calls...when I went round the back, the door had been forced and there was mud everywhere..."

"Shit. Are you still at the house?"

"Yes, I've called the police, didn't know what else to do...Megan, where *are* you?"

"London."

"London?"

"Yes." Megan explained.

"Christ, Megan. I am so sorry – what can I do to help?"

"Get a locksmith to fix the door?" she laughed wearily. She couldn't believe that somebody had broken into the house, especially in these circumstances; it was almost as if they had been watching the house – seen her leave! Perhaps they had...

"It's strange, Megan, but it looks like nothing has been taken...your TV is fine, and the computer is still on the table."

The brooch! Should she ask Sasha to check if it was still on top of the dresser, or would that be just putting her in danger too?

"Have strange things still been happening while I've been away?" asked Sasha.

"A few little things..."

"Like? Oh, the police have arrived...I'll go and speak to them...don't worry about anything, Megan; you look after your mum and I'll look after everything here. I'll call you later."

Megan stared at the phone in her hand. So at least she knew she wasn't going mad...if other people were seeing the strange things she was seeing, then they *had* to be real, whatever the explanation turned out to be. Who had been at the house again? It had to be the same person each time and she was almost certain now that they were looking for the brooch. As soon as she got back to Gloucestershire, she would ask Fin where she could take it; she no longer wanted it

233

anywhere near her home. Her gran, as always, had been right – it was definitely cursed.

Driving back to the hospital later that afternoon, Megan thought back to her dream. It had felt real, just as strange dreams sometimes do; like it was part of your own reality. But she knew it must have been associated with a film or a book she had read, because although the river had felt familiar, a little like the Thames, the clothes she had been wearing and the fact that she was being chased by a man on a horse with a sword in his hands, reinforced the fact that it certainly was not part of her own reality! However, strange as it seemed, she was suddenly reminded of the blonde woman who appeared to her now and then; a blonde woman in search of something...a brooch, maybe?

***

Mildryth awoke as the sun was climbing above the trees, she must have slept longer than she'd expected. Piers was stoking the fire and looked over at her as she sat up.

"You must have been tired," he said, handing her a piece of bread.

She yawned, nodded and took the bread, taking a bite. She noticed a rabbit hanging from a nearby branch.

"Supper," said Piers. "I thought I should make the most of the time you were sleeping..."

"You left me alone?"

"I was only over there at the edge of the trees, the rabbit just wandered past...easiest meal I've ever caught."

She smiled and took another bite of the bread.

"I'm going to fetch water, it's not far...shout if you need me and I will return immediately."

"Thank you, Piers...I..."

"It's all right, you don't have to explain. I've known you since you were a child Mildryth and I trust you – you need my help, I'm here to give it, no questions asked. I know it must be important, I'm glad you felt you could ask me." He smiled, then walked through the trees to the nearby river.

Sitting by the fire chewing on her bread, Mildryth heard a bird screech in the trees and it flew off deeper into the forest. Was there somebody there? Should she scream for Piers to return? A moment later, a large hare appeared before her in the clearing. He stared directly at her, his hazel brown eyes boring into hers, then suddenly he ran away, large legs and feet speeding past then disappearing into the trees. Had Eostre sent her a sign? Would everything be alright? She stroked her stomach and smiled...perhaps it was the goddess's way of telling her that her child would be well; Wilheard would forgive her.

The morning felt surreal, as if she were in some type of dream, but she felt refreshed from her sleep and eager to move on and find Wulfric and Lindi – surely their friendship all these years stood for something...if they would tell Wilheard the truth, with her promise that she would insist they were unharmed – it would clear her name, her honour and that of her child. Maybe then Wilheard would be able to forgive her. But what if she couldn't find them? The thought was too painful to bear. She had to find them, deep down she knew she was on the right path, but what if Lindi could see her coming, be one step ahead of her, perhaps she would never find them? She had to try.

Piers returned. "I can see you're eager to get going."

"Yes, I'm sure we're on the right track, I hope to catch up with them today."

"You're certain they are together?"

"Almost."

"You have your dagger?"

She nodded, feeling inside her cloak for the hard metal object that might just save her life, if necessary.

"Good. I have my sword too," said Piers, moving his cloak aside and showing her the scabbard. "Your father had this made for me, when I was sixteen, to replace the one he gave me as a child when I became your horseman – I think he would have me killed if he knew I was helping you."

"I think they all probably know that you've come with me by now...they would have noticed you missing too."

"Of course."

"You're not afraid?"

"No. When I became your horseman I took an oath to protect you from whatever threats you faced."

"You are a dutiful man, Piers," she said.

He dipped his head towards her and smiled again. Kicking the ash into the fire to put it out, he then helped her onto her horse.

"Which way?" he asked.

Mildryth pointed towards the west where she knew there were caves. If she was correct, they would be there about sunset that day. Her hopes were pinned on meeting them...they had to help her...it was her last chance of happiness with Wilheard; her very last chance.

Chapter Nineteen

Megan arrived at the hospital to find her mother laughing and smiling, albeit a little lopsidedly, with Gerald. Her eyes had regained some of their mischievous sparkle and Megan gave a long sigh of relief. Clearly the next few days were critical, but with the medication and hospital keeping a close eye on her, she knew she was in very good hands.

"Meggie, I have some very exciting news..."

"Should you be getting excited in your condition?" said Megan, suddenly full of concern again.

Her mother held out her hand to her and looked at her expectantly. Megan walked towards her, took her hands, and gave her an awkward hug. Something wasn't quite right...had her mother's hand or arm been affected by the stroke? Her mother giggled.

"What is it?" asked Megan, pulling away from her mother's awkward embrace.

"Look," said her mother, holding her hand up again.

This time Megan didn't miss the glinting diamond on her mother's hand. "Gerald's asked me to marry him."

Megan stared at her mother, then at Gerald, who looked away from her eyes, embarrassed. Megan took a moment or two to realise what was going on, then she smiled and hugged her mother hard. "That's marvellous news!" she gasped, with a sudden realisation that she really was pleased...it was out of the blue, but it had made her mother look more alive than she had in years, not just the past few days, so it had to be good.

"Congratulations," she said to Gerald, kissing him on both cheeks. "I hope you know what you're letting yourself in for?"

Gerald laughed. "I certainly do," he said, smiling at Eleanor, who slapped him playfully on the arm. He stretched down and pulled a glass bottle out of a shopping bag. "I thought we should raise a glass."

"I don't think that's a good idea with Mum's condition," scolded Megan, suddenly feeling protective.

Gerald smiled as he pulled out some champagne flutes from another bag. "It's all right, I got sparkling grape juice...just for now," he added, as both women's faces fell in disappointment.

They raised their glasses to Eleanor's future as Mrs 'Gerald' and Megan watched as her mother glanced lovingly at Gerald, then with what Megan suddenly realised was gratefulness in her direction – she had obviously wanted Megan's approval, perhaps had always wanted it...

It was ten o'clock when Megan sat with a real glass of wine on her mother's sofa to watch the BBC news. Whilst watching the headlines, she realised that her mobile was still switched off from being at the hospital. She wasn't sure if the stories were true about them messing with hospital equipment, but she wasn't going to take any chances where her mother was concerned. For the first time in so many years, they were close again, and sadly she realised that it had taken her mother's near death to make her realise her mother was only human after all.

Turning on the mobile she noticed she had some missed calls and some voicemail messages.

She listened to her messages. The first one was from Sasha:

"Hi, it's me. I've spoken to the police and told them everything I know. I explained that your mother was ill and that you were in London. They said that when you come back they'll speak to you, but for now they'll write up what's happened although they found it odd that there was nothing missing. Oh and I remembered later, after I'd spoken to you, that when I was walking to your house I passed that woman, the traveller-turned-pub landlady, coming away from your cottage...I don't want to cast aspersions, but seemed quite odd and she seemed to be acting a little shifty, especially when she saw me...I didn't tell the police, not yet...thought I ought to speak to you first. Anyway, give me a call when you get this, whatever time. Bye.

Bridget? Why had she been near the house, or had she been over the fields to see Kai? Were they getting back together again? Oh who cares, she had far too many other more important things to be sorting out. Like her next message, which she knew would be from Fin, having seen her list of missed calls.

Hello Megan. It's Fin, I've been calling you all day, and I can't get hold of you. I hope your mother is getting better? I'm not chasing you to come back to work, but I bumped into Sasha and she told me about the break-in – another one! I'm glad she contacted the police and reported it...I think you need to be careful when you come back. When you get this message, call me and we'll have a chat...I've something to tell you.

Was he going to tell her about the woman she'd heard with him last night, she wondered? Did she want to know? She ought to call Sasha and Fin but she found herself dissolving into tears, great big sobs of pent-up emotion from the past twenty-four hours, and knew

238

she would call neither of them tonight. When her tears had subsided enough, she made herself a steaming mug of hot chocolate and decided to text them both instead.

Megan had just sent her text through to Sasha, when there was a knock at the door. Who could possibly be knocking on her mother's door at this late hour, unless it was Gerald...She walked out into the hall and turned on the outside light so that she could use the security peep hole to see who was at the door. Her heart skipped a beat.

Fin.

Slowly, she opened the door, still in shock at seeing him standing outside her mother's front door.

He smiled at her, sheepishly. "I decided to come and see if you were all right...neither Sasha or I had heard from you all day, I wondered...is your mum..."

"She's getting married."

Fin stared at her, aghast.

Megan stepped aside to let Fin inside; he followed her into the lounge.

She *seems* ok, a little bit of a wonky smile and slightly slurred speech at times...she was lucky. Her boyfriend has just proposed to her though, he clearly thought he was going to lose her and has decided to pop the question while he can...it has made her happier than I've ever seen her."

"That's great, but how are *you*?" He placed a hand gently on her upper arm.

"Falling apart, it seems," she smiled through the tears in her eyes, trying to stay strong, but with her emotions in turmoil.

"You've had a lot going on recently, but you're a strong woman."

"I don't feel very strong right now," she admitted but stood tall, not wanting to let the tears come again. "Would you like some wine, I have an open bottle?"

"Just a small one, I have to drive."

"Fin, it's almost eleven, surely you wouldn't drive back to Gloucestershire tonight?"

He nodded as she passed him his wine, sinking down into the sofa looking tired.

"How did you find my mum's address?"

"Sasha, she said she'd had to give it to the police. I asked her not to let you know I was coming, I knew you'd try to stop me."

"You were right."

"I'm guessing that Sasha has been keeping you in the loop about the break-in?"

Sighing deeply, Megan sat down at the opposite end of the sofa, trying to hold her glass steady and not spill the red wine onto her mother's cream sofa.

"She has. I'm glad she was there to deal with it, otherwise I would have had to come back to sort that out too."

"She's a good friend."

"Considering we've only known each other such a short time, we seem to get on really well. She's so uncomplicated and a real laugh too – unlike me, who seems to be in constant turmoil at the moment." She looked up at Fin and saw he was watching her closely. "Sorry, I really shouldn't be offloading all my woes on to you."

"Why not?"

"Well...because..." Megan stopped. She wasn't sure why not. Instead she tried to steer the conversation away from herself. "In your message, you said you had something to tell me..."

He seemed unprepared for her statement, but clearly knew what she was talking about. Leaning forward, he placed his wine glass on the coffee table in front of them and looked at his hands in his lap; they were strong and he had thick, blonde hairs on his lower arms. She imagined what it would feel like to have his arms wrapped around her, but tried hard to turn her thoughts away from the ridiculous notion.

Megan could see that he felt uncomfortable, was distressed in some way about what he was going to tell her. *Was* he married? Was it his wife whose voice she'd heard on the phone last night? Suddenly, she knew she didn't really want to know...however he was already talking to her, telling her...

"...so, I really do think we need to do something about it."

"Sorry, Fin, I'm tired...about what, we need to do something about what? I thought you were going to tell me that you're married..."

"*Married?* What has that got to do with the brooch?"

Megan blushed...he was talking about the brooch...how stupid of her, what was she thinking – but wait, there had been a woman's voice.

Realisation crossed Fin's face and he smiled. "Ah...last night...yes, you did hear a woman's voice. That woman is my sister, Clare. She came for dinner and stayed, we don't see each other much these days and we always get drunk together and stay up far too late chatting and reminiscing. She's visiting the UK from Canada, where she now lives. She came over and said she'd love to have a couple of days with me at the dig, that's why I said don't rush back, I have an extra pair of hands, but only temporarily."

"Oh." Megan really didn't know what to say.

Fin smiled at her, his eyes watching her carefully again and glistening in the lamp light, mischievously. "Would it matter to you if I was married?"

Shaking her head, too embarrassed to speak, she looked at his face, warm, open, friendly and felt a kind of peace pass over her. Not understanding the emotion, and disliking the embarrassment, she directed the conversation back to the brooch. Fin had been talking about the brooch after all.

"You were talking about the brooch, Fin?"

His smile faded. "Yes. I know it sounds rather odd, but I've been giving your break-ins some thought. Have you told anyone about the brooch you found in your garden?"

"No, only you and perhaps, Sasha, I really can't remember if I told her or not. I have spoken to her about the strange goings-on in the house and the woman who seems to appear now and then."

"If somebody overheard you talking about it, then maybe they know it's at the cottage and is trying to steal it. It is worth a great deal of money."

"Wait a minute...Sasha said she saw Bridget, the barmaid from the pub, near the cottage when she discovered the break-in...perhaps she overheard us talking about it?"

"How many times has somebody broken in?" Fin asked.

"I've lost count exactly, but I know when somebody has been there because there's always lots of mud on the floor."

"So, it wasn't Bartie after all...they have been in my boat too...whilst I was sleeping!" Fin visibly shuddered. "How on earth did they know that it was on my boat at the time?"

"An optimistic guess?"

"Where is the brooch now?"

"Hidden. Only I know where it is and I'm not going to tell anyone until I've checked it's still there...I'm sure whoever went into the house wouldn't have found it where I've hidden it.

"This is much more serious than I first thought. As soon as you are able to, you must come home and speak to the police – tell them everything, and I mean everything...but your mum comes first, I understand that."

Megan nodded. "What I find most strange is that the brooch seems to be what set off this series of events...Bartie dug up the brooch, and from then on I've seen the blonde woman on different occasions searching for something...perhaps that's it...she's searching for the brooch, but..." Megan frowned, her heart skipping in her chest. "The woman I have seen is not Bridget...she is much slighter and although they are both blonde, the woman I have seen has much longer hair, almost to her waist *and* she wears strange clothes."

"What sort of clothes?"

"A long tunic, I thought at first she was some kind of hippy."

Fin's eyes shot a look at her that she couldn't read.

"What is it?"

"I – I'm not sure...I had a sudden thought, but no, that's ridiculous."

"Tell me."

Fin laughed and his face softened again. "It's getting late, I ought to go."

Fin had clearly decided he wasn't going to share his 'ridiculous' idea with her and she was too tired to push him. "It's gone eleven thirty, you can sleep here, if you wish, in the spare room there's plenty of them."

Fin looked as if he was about to protest, but then he glanced at his watch and shook his head. "If you're sure that's ok?"

"Of course, make up for some of the time that I spent sleeping on your boat." Megan rose and nodded to Fin to follow. She showed him where the bathroom was and the room he could sleep in.

"I'll see you in the morning," she said lightly.

"Sure. I hope you sleep well." He bent and gave her a kiss on the cheek, taking her by surprise and making her nearly lose her balance. "I hope you didn't mind me coming?"

She smiled at him, her stomach doing a flip. "No, not at all, in fact I'm glad you came."

He returned a smile and she walked out of the room to her own. Climbing into bed she realised how exhausted she was. Why exactly had Fin come? Did he really want to see that she was all right, or was he more interested in the brooch than she had first thought?

***

It was the echoing cry of the bird of prey that circled above their heads that made them stop and stare above them. Some way ahead there were small plumes of smoke coming from the entrance of a cave in the rocks; somebody was there, or had been. Mildryth hoped that they were still there; she had recognised the landscape and area of the south-west as a place where she had stayed during a hunting trip a few years ago. She remembered poignantly that she, Lindi, Wilheard and Wulfric had crept away from the hunting party camp fire and explored the caves, which were vast and deep. It had been the first time that Wilheard had kissed her and the dawning of the realisation of

Wulfric's desire for her too. Wulfric had seen the kiss and had stormed off, his face full of pain, rage and jealousy. She wondered now if Lindi had noticed it too, had she carried this resentment with her for all these years, she wondered now. That would explain some of her most recent actions; she was jealous of Mildryth, envious that she had the affections of both the brothers. However, did Lindi not realise that she had never encouraged Wulfric, had always been open about her affection and attraction for Wilheard? Did that not count for anything?

Ahead of her, Piers stopped and held up his hand.

Mildryth stood still and listened but could hear nothing, see nothing. The bird of prey cried its eerie call and went on its way. They continued slowly through the valley. At the bottom of the path which led to the caves above, Piers stopped again. He whispered in to her ear, "Stay here. I will go and see if there is anyone there."

"I'm coming with you," she insisted.

He shook his head. "It could be very dangerous."

"With Lindi's powers, she probably knows we're approaching anyway."

"All the more reason to be cautious."

Piers walked on ahead. They had left the horse tied to a tree some way back in the woods, knowing that if it made a noise, it would warn anyone in the local vicinity of their arrival. Taking the pathway, he strode easily up the steep embankment towards the mouth of the cave, his hand at the ready to draw his sword in an instant.

Mildryth watched him as he cautiously, but confidently approached the cave entrance, then disappeared. After a few moments, when he didn't reappear she started to fear something had happened to him. Why had she involved him? She should have just come alone, but he had insisted on helping. It was his duty to protect her, but even knowing all this, she felt guilty and afraid. He too had a young wife and two small children, if something happened to him...

"Mildryth, come up, all is clear, there is nobody here," called Piers from the top of the narrow pathway.

Relief flooded through her that he was all right, but disappointment too that nobody was there. Mildryth walked towards Piers apprehensively; Lindi must have seen them coming and moved on.

Inside the cave there was a low, smoky fire burning, but no belongings indicating that whoever was there had moved on quickly, kicking some ash onto the fire in their haste to hide their use of the cave.

"What would you like to do? Go home?" asked Piers.

Mildryth felt a fear grow inside her. "No, I must keep searching, Piers. Go back to your family if you wish, but I *must* continue."

"I'm not going back without you – if you wish to continue searching, then I will be at your side."

Mildryth smiled and walked out of the cave into the bright sunshine. It took a few moments for her eyes to adjust to the light and in the distance she heard the horse whinnying – was somebody still close by?

Piers looked at her with concern and they quickly and carefully made their way back down the narrow, rocky path towards the woods where they had hidden the horse. Walking through the trees they noticed the whinnying had stopped, so had the birdsong. The forest was silent around them; unnervingly so.

As they stepped out into the clearing, they saw the horse had gone, its tether cut through and hanging loosely from the tree branch where they had tied him. Piers looked at Mildryth with a frown on his face. A cold shiver ran down Mildryth's spine as she looked around the trees that swayed and creaked gently in the breeze; their branches like arms waving in some kind of ritualistic dance. She realised a second too late that a figure, dark, fast and with sword in hand, leapt from the dense undergrowth and sliced his sword with a sickening ease through every layer of Piers' skin to his heart. Piers slumped face down to the ground, dead.

Mildryth gave a cry and ran to his side. Tears of anger, grief and guilt rolled down her face. "What have you *done*? Why did you kill him?" she screamed at Wulfric.

Wulfric's eyes met hers; his steel-grey glare full of mixed emotions. "I thought he was one of Wilheard's men..."

"Wulfric, you have just killed an innocent man, what are you *doing*?" She stood now and faced him. "Are you going to kill me too?"

Wulfric shook his head.

Mildryth took a deep breath and felt relief flood through her as he lowered his sword, then dropped it to the ground. He looked around him. "Are there others?"

Mildryth shook her head, the tears still rolling down her cheeks. "Why are you here?"

"I have come to ask you to tell Wilheard the truth. He must know the truth of the magic potion, must know that I did not lie with you because I was in love with you. I love Wilheard, Wulfric, I always have..."

"I know, but I wanted you for myself, I have loved you for as many years as my brother has...I knew that it was unrequited, but I

244

had to have you...he had everything...I had nothing..." he took a step towards her, she flinched.

"You had the love of your father and brother and a sisterly kind of love from me. Lindi loves you, you *must* know that. Isn't all that enough for one man, Wulfric?"

"I do know that she loves me and she is a beautiful woman, but she is not you, Mildryth. She does not have your kind and gentle ways; she is a vindictive woman and has an ambition that will get her killed...and probably me too."

"Have you seen her?"

He nodded.

"Where is she now?"

"I believe she has moved the horse, she will return soon, I'm sure."

"Wulfric, I beg you, will you and Lindi tell Wilheard the truth, *please?* If he knows the truth, he might be able to forgive me."

Wulfric's eyes grew soft for an instant, nevertheless, he shook his head and his face hardened. "I cannot tell him the truth, not now, not ever."

Mildryth felt her stomach lurch.

"Wilheard has had everything all his life. Our father treated me with contempt and him with love..."

"That's not true..."

"It is. He has the love of our people; the love of our father and your love too."

"I have never led you to believe anything different, Wulfric. Yes, I have always loved you as a brother, I have always admired you as such, but you betrayed your brother, our kingdom and you have betrayed me..."

"Betrayed *you...*"

"In the worst possible way, you used magic to try to possess me; well I'm not yours to possess...the love I give you as a sister should have been enough!"

He was silent for a few moments then his face hardened. "You enjoyed it though, didn't you? That was so evident in the way you screamed..."

Mildryth felt a surge of excitement tinged with fear as she recalled the small amount of what she did remember. Wulfric's arms around her, his caresses...it had been good, great, passionate...but, but it was not real, not as it was with Wilheard. His love and passion were not a selfish love and passion, but a gentle and giving kind of love; with Wulfric it had been the magic potion that had coerced her into his arms."

"I will never be yours, Wulfric and I *cannot believe* that you would stoop so low as to use magic to persuade me into your arms...especially after what happened with your own mother and father."

Wulfric moved so suddenly, she was unprepared for his strong grip around her throat. He squeezed hard and stared into her eyes, his face close to hers; his breathing was more erratic. "I could take you now; see how much you enjoy it again *without* the magic..."

Mildryth coughed and tried hard to remove his hands. "What...would be...the point?" She choked out.

Wulfric growled and threw her to the ground. She started to sob, big gulps ripping through her already painful throat. "Wulfric, *please, please* tell Wilheard the truth, you have nothing left to lose."

"I still have everything...if I can't take you from Wilheard, then I will take his kingdom..."

"No, Wulfric, do not even try, if you kill your brother....wait, wait...you killed your father didn't you? You killed Aelle, your own father!"

Shaking his head, Wulfric looked furious. "It was not me that killed my father, it was Lindi, she poisoned him...she told me...she has a plan, she wants to usurp you and become queen, she wants me to become king and until now I have relented, but now, now...I will succumb to her...as you no longer want me..."

"I never did!" Mildryth felt the panic rise in her chest. If Lindi was capable of killing Aelle; of using magic on her dearest childhood friend, then she was capable of killing Wilheard! She had to warn him, but how?

"I have to go back to Wilheard, see if he will forgive me, if he will believe my word..."

Wulfric started to laugh, a bitter, sinister laugh. "Go back to Wilheard, you daft whore...he will not have you back...you had your chance to be my queen, dear Mildryth..." He grabbed her by the arm and lifted her to standing. "You and I could have ruled the kingdom together, we still could..." He roughly grabbed her close to him and kissed her hard on the lips, she could not get free he was so strong...his kiss was not gentle or passionate this time, but angry and threatening.

"I am with child..." She looked him directly in the eye.

"Am I supposed to believe the child is mine?"

"It could be...for its sake, please help me..."

Wulfric stared into her eyes, the grey of them hard steel. "It is not mine." With that, he threw her to the ground again and walked away, not looking back.

***

Approaching the clearing where she had left Wulfric, Lindi stopped dead in her tracks. Ahead of her she could see her man kissing the woman he loved...and in that instant, all her dreams and ambitions of them ruling together splintered like a freshly felled tree, leaving her reeling and determined that she would have her revenge; not just on Mildryth, but on Wulfric too. Her chance would come, and she knew it was coming soon.

Chapter Twenty

*The two faces stared down at her: both fair – one woman, blonde with
an unforgiving glare and one man with sky-blue eyes. She was
trapped; there was no escape, no escape from their anger, their
hatred. Kneeling, begging, she looked at them each in turn. The ice-
blue of the blonde woman's stare held something like satisfaction, but
it was the bright sky-blue eyes that held the worst for her...betrayal,
rage...hatred, nothing like the love that was once there...she knew now
she was in trouble, nobody was going to save her.*

*"Please..." she begged the blue-eyed man, but instead of
forgiveness, there was only the glint of a blade...*

"Megan..." she felt hands on her upper arms, familiar, warm.
Opening her eyes, she stared, stared into sky-blue eyes, she retreated
from Fin, trembling; felt ice-cold, but knew she was perspiring.

"What is it?" asked Fin, his face full of concern, his eyes gentle,
searching hers.

"A dream," said Megan. "Only a dream, but so realistic...God, it
was just like I was there."

"Do you want to tell me about it?" he asked.

Feeling the terror easing ever so slightly, she sat up in bed. Those
people, they seemed familiar, yet not people she knew...the blonde –
was it Bridget from the pub? What had she been doing in her dream?
Or was it the blonde woman that she had seen around the cottage and
fields back home?

"I'll make you some tea," said Fin, disappearing from the room.

She looked around the room of her mother's house. It felt odd
being here, she felt she should be back home, in gran's cottage...if her
mother was ok in the morning, she would return to the cottage, go
back to work...she needed some normality, but she also needed to deal
with the burglary and the brooch; her decision had been made, finally.

A few moments later, Fin reappeared with a steaming mug of
tea. "Feeling any better?"

She shrugged.

Fin sat down on the edge of the bed and handed her the tea. She
took it from him and was startled to see her hands were shaking. He
gently placed his hand over hers on the mug and eased it from her
hands, placing it on the bedside table. He kept one of her hands in his.
It was warm and felt comforting.

"Sorry I disturbed your sleep, Fin."

"No worries, I just heard you shouting and wondered what the hell was going on...I hope you didn't mind me waking you, but you sounded so distressed, you actually screamed."

"It was weird, there were all these people, two of them, we were by a river...I don't know who the people were, although they did seem familiar and they appeared to know me – to hate me!"

"You're under a lot of stress, dreams can affect people badly at times...I'm sure it will fade, most dreams do."

"I need to go home..."

"It's two in the morning." He gently caressed her hand with his fingers, and she felt a frisson of electricity run through her.

Megan managed a small smile. "In the morning...I'm going to go to the hospital to see how Mum is. If she's all right, I'll go home from there. I need to get back to work..."

"There's no rush."

"No, but I need to focus on something good...and normal."

He laughed, brought her hand to his mouth and kissed it softly. Holding on to it for a moment longer, he gently placed it back on the bed and rose to leave. He looked into her eyes and smiled, and her heart flipped inside her chest. Watching his retreating back, she shook her head. She was so tired that the look could have meant everything, or nothing at all.

***

Wilheard and his soldiers rode south-west. Other groups of men had been sent in other directions of the kingdom; his determination to find his brother and his queen apparent to all involved. Word among the community was that his brother, Wulfric, had betrayed him, he was to be found and brought before the king, as was the queen – both alive. The king's seer, Godric, who had replaced Lindi when she had disappeared, had said that they were most likely to be in the lands where the sun set every night; that if Wilheard searched the forests and caves of that area, then his treasonous family would be found and brought to justice.

Wilheard was riding in front, with two of his most trusted aides either side of him, a few more mounted men were behind; there were ten in all, plus the seer. They had ridden for two days, were close to those who had betrayed them (or so Godric has assured them), and were exhausted. They decided to set up camp for the night. Wilheard was restless, but knew his men must sleep, although it was unlikely that he would.

250

The men slept soundly, all except the seer, Wilheard and his chief soldier, Aart. Amongst the trees in the woods, the seer sat close to the fire chanting and staring, searching the flames for clues as to which direction they should take in the morning; where the caves in which they hid were. Aart sat with Wilheard in silence, also watching the flames of the fire dance their way towards the darkening sky. The night was cold but clear and the stars shone brightly above them.

Wilheard wondered to himself again how he could not have seen the betrayal of his closest family before now. His hurt had turned into a fury he had not thought himself possible of feeling. He had trusted and loved Mildryth his whole life and despite what Wulfric thought, he had loved his brother too. Now his father was gone, murdered; his brother had betrayed his trust and position and Mildryth had broken his heart and betrayed him. He sighed heavily and accepted the wine Aart offered him.

"You must try to sleep, Sire," Aart said, quietly.

"I cannot."

"You will need your wits about you at dawn and your strength."

Wilheard nodded, knowing Aart was right, but his head was spinning with thoughts and images, most of which he wished he could not see. All of a sudden, in the light of the fire, Wilheard saw a dark shadow move out from among the trees. The three men were on their feet in seconds, swords drawn and with their shouts the others arose, instantly alert.

"Who goes there?" asked Wilheard.

The figure stood as still as a statue in the light of the fire, the flames projecting their orange glow upon the simple garbs in which it was dressed.

"I'm unarmed." A female voice, familiar.

Aart was upon her in a moment, his arm around her chest, to secure her.

"There's no need..." Lindi said.

"What are you doing here?" demanded Wilheard. "Where's my brother and my wife?"

"So you know they are together then?" A smirk crossed Lindi's face.

"I have been informed of their betrayal, yes."

"So it's true?" asked Aart, loosening his grip from behind and swinging her around to face him.

Lindi looked from Aart to Wilheard. "They lie together as we speak."

Wilheard let out a cry of anguish that echoed around the hills.

"Where are they?" asked Aart.

"I won't tell you, not yet. First you must listen to what I have to say."

"Why should I trust you?" spat Wilheard. "I've always known you've loved Wulfric, how do I know you're telling the truth?"

"I did love Wulfric once, but he loves your wife and she him, and because I am the only one who has not betrayed you..."

"Don't trust her..." warned Aart.

"Wulfric and Mildryth lay together even before you were married, Wilheard. I tried my best to persuade her to do the right thing and leave him alone, but she wouldn't, she wasn't satisfied in only having you, she wanted both brothers and knew that she could have both. I am only telling you this because I fear what will happen next...I think they may be planning to kill you and take the throne for themselves."

Swinging his sword, Wilheard struck it into a nearby tree, where it stuck fast. "Traitors!"

"When Wulfric disappeared I thought I would try to find him, and see if I could make him see that what he was doing was wrong, treasonous...we've all known each other since we were children...I couldn't bear to see all our friendships, our family being torn apart."

"You didn't foresee any of this?" Wilheard's question was a sneer.

Lindi shook her head and held his gaze. "I can't always see everything. I used everything I had to try to track him down, then today I finally found him, but he was not alone...I found them together, kissing amongst the trees."

Wilheard let out another cry of anguish. "You must take me to them; I *will* have my revenge!"

"I need your assurance that my place amongst our people is safe, Wilheard. When you see them, I don't know what they will say...they may deny it, might embellish the truth. They are devious and ambitious. Beware."

"I can't let you go," said Wilheard.

"You won't kill me. You need me alive to show you where they are hiding."

"I may yet. I have Godric, who has led us this far."

"Let me go and I give you my word on Woden that I will return at first light."

"No, you stay here tonight. Aart, tie her up."

Lindi shrugged and held out her wrists towards Aart.

"I'll never trust anyone again," seethed Wilheard.

Lindi sat down near the fire, her hands and feet tied so she could not escape. Wilheard left two men on watch and ordered Aart to sleep.

As his eyes grew heavy and he drifted between wakefulness and sleep, Mildryth's face appeared before him, it was so real and so close, the look in her eyes so tender, that he felt if he reached out he would be able to touch it...but he would never caress her face again, never hold her close, never join his body as one with hers again. The rage subsided, and in its place was only heartache and pain.

***

The sun shone brightly through the white curtains and cast a rectangle of light onto the duck-egg blue walls of the spare bedroom. Megan glanced at the clock. It was ten o'clock. Sitting up, she felt a slight panic rise in her chest...she never slept that late! She listened for sounds coming from other parts of the house, but there was nothing; she could just hear the birds singing from the trees in the garden.

Walking out onto the landing she noticed the other spare bedroom door was wide open, the bed was made, Fin was gone. She felt a sudden loneliness so deep, it took her by surprise.

In the kitchen she found a note:

> *Thanks for letting me stay, really appreciate it.*
> *Heading back now, but there's no rush for you,*
> *take your time and check your mum first.*
> *Stay if needed.*
> *Fin*

Megan smiled, remembering how kind he'd been the night before, but his sudden appearance at her mother's house had unnerved her slightly. Could he really be that nice? Her more cynical side played with her thoughts...was it possible he wanted the brooch for himself after all? Surely not! He'd had his chance to take it...hadn't he?

A little later she walked through the corridors of the hospital towards her mother's ward. Eleanor was sitting up against her pillows and smiled brightly – still a little lopsided – as Megan approached. To Megan's relief she really did look much better, she no longer looked as pale as death; her cheeks were more colourful and her eyes brighter.

"Good morning, Meg."

"Hi, Mum," said Megan, bending and kissing her on the cheek. "You're looking so much better."

"I feel so much better too."

Megan sat down in the chair next to the bed. "No Gerald this morning?"

Eleanor shook her head. "He's off making arrangements."

Megan frowned. "Not..."

"Yes, wedding arrangements. We've decided not to put it off...we're going to see if we can arrange it for a month's time."

"Aren't you rushing things a bit?"

"Isn't that a question a mother should ask her daughter, not the other way round?" she laughed.

Megan smiled. "Yes, if everything was as it was supposed to be in the fairy tales, I guess you would be asking me...not that I have any intention of getting married."

"Not ever?" asked her mum. "What about that chap who phoned me, Tim, wasn't it?"

"Tom, and no, we're not together."

"You will meet the right person one day, Meg. In the meantime, Gerald and I have decided that we have no reason to wait, so we're going ahead as soon as we can."

"I'm so pleased for you, Mum."

"You are?" She sounded surprised, her eyes filled with tears.

"Of course, it's lovely to see you so happy, even in these awful circumstances. Gerald seems so nice too and obviously makes you happy."

Her mother seemed embarrassed. "Yes, he does. He's the first man in a long, long time that I can really relate to and trust," she admitted.

"I am glad, Mum."

"I think they're going to let me go home today or tomorrow."

"That's great news, but promise me you'll take it easy, Mum. Do you want me to stay on for a few days?"

"No, darling, you have your own life and Gerald has promised to look after me...if you don't mind?"

"Of course not, I really should get back to work. I could come back at the weekend if you'd like me to?"

"Thank you, sweetheart."

Driving fast down the M4, Megan was eager to get back home, she wanted to check on the brooch, to make sure it hadn't been stolen after the most recent break-in. More than that, she didn't really want to be away from work too much, or rather, Fin. Megan could feel her body responding to her thoughts of him and how his kiss had felt on her hand in the early hours of the morning. She knew that she was falling for him, but she couldn't help that slight nagging doubt about what his interest in her was, exactly. He looked at her in a way she knew was not just friendship, but she had been duped by men before, one in particular and she now found it hard to believe anyone was genuine. What if he was just after the brooch? It seemed a little unlikely because he had been kind and perceptive before he even knew about it. He had let her stay on his barge and he'd had the brooch cleaned and preserved. If he had wanted to steal it, that would have been his opportunity. Who else knew about it? It was, after all, both beautiful and valuable.

Images from her dream during the night seeped into her thoughts, the terror, the sorrow she had felt. The expressions on each of the stranger's faces were locked in her mind, none of them had been happy with her...especially one: sky-blue eyes, so similar to Fin's - yet so different – full of anger and hatred, not kindness and warmth. That one seemed to be more important than the others, it felt as if it was him that she had to satisfy, to make *him* believe she was innocent of something, but what – what was she supposed to have done that warranted such a venomous stare...and what of the blade...would he have killed her if Fin hadn't woken her at the moment he did? She shuddered. Picturing the face of the woman in her dream, she did look very much like Bridget, or was she now projecting her own daytime memories into her dreams? If it was Bridget, why was she looking so satisfied, as if she had got one over on her?

The blast of a horn brought her to her senses, she realised almost too late that she had drifted into the next lane and cut up another vehicle.

I must concentrate, she scolded herself. As soon as I get home I'll call Sasha, see if she can make sense of any of this crazy stuff that's going on. Sasha was always level-headed and made sense of things where Megan couldn't always do so.

Having picked Bartie up from Mrs Clark's, Megan drove down the lane towards the cottage. It stood golden in the early afternoon sun. The budding leaves of the weeping willows were a bright yellow-green, giving the scene the impression of a beautiful, water-colour painting. The brown water of the river meandered past the cottage on its way to Oxford, lapping at the banks due to the previous day's heavy rainfall.

Bartie jumped out of the boot of the car and ran into the garden, barking his delight at being home again. Megan felt a slight shiver of fear as she approached the house. What would she find this time? What if there was someone there now? She walked slowly towards the door, thankful of Bartie's presence...he would have been barking like mad if there was someone there.

Unlocking the door and cautiously entering the hallway, Megan discovered that nothing had been disturbed. Taking off her boots and coat she immediately went to the kitchen where she'd hidden the brooch on top of the dresser. Retrieving the brooch and turning it over in her hand she felt a sense of relief wash over her. It was still there...thank goodness.

Her mobile rang, making her jump. She quickly put the brooch back on top of the dresser and fished her phone out of her pocket.

Sasha.

"Hi, how are you?"

"More to the point how are *you*?" Sasha replied, her voice full of concern.

"I'm ok. Mum's on the mend and she's getting married!"

"*Married?* I thought she'd had a stroke?"

"She has, but thankfully it wasn't too severe and now she has decided to get married."

"That's great..."

"It is. Sasha, I'm back home, are you working today?"

"I am, but I can come over if you need me to. Michelle can keep an eye on things here."

"Yes, please, if you wouldn't mind. I need a person with a rational mind."

"I'm not sure if I'll be able to find one of those before I get there!"

Megan laughed. "See you in a bit."

"I'll bring lunch and some milk. You're probably out if you've been away."

Megan hadn't even thought about provisions, thank goodness Sasha was so thoughtful.

Before Sasha arrived, Megan walked through the house to check that nothing else was missing. In her bedroom, the little drawer to the dressing table had the key in it, had she left it like that? She looked in the drawer: her gran's diary was still there and walking to the cupboard she checked the other diary was still there too.

Sasha and Jess arrived with not just milk, but hot sausage rolls from the bakery and a good bottle of wine. "I thought we might need these."

They sat in the garden in the sunshine. The day was cool but the sun was warm on the sheltered patio near to the house. They ate their sausage rolls and Sasha poured the wine for them both.

"I'm pleased your Mum is all right, but I'm awfully worried about you," said Sasha.

Megan smiled. "I'm a bit worried about me too, if I'm honest."

"I think that you have had a lot going on recently and that can take its toll on even the most sane people."

Megan felt the tears well up in her eyes. She didn't want to cry, she wanted to talk things through, to try to make sense of what was going on.

"Did Fin come and find you?" Sasha asked, with a smile on her face. "He really is smitten, you know."

Megan felt a kind of relief to hear it from someone else, to have her own thoughts affirmed. "He did come, he's so lovely, but I'm afraid to trust him."

"Really? He seems like one of the most trustworthy guys I've met, really genuine..."

"That's what worries me, what if it's just a front?"

"You're not quite ready for another relationship yet, are you; not a serious one?"

Megan shook her head. "I don't want to encourage him in case I fall apart, I don't want it to be a disastrous fling, or a relationship that is haunted by my past baggage. If it's going to happen, I want it to be good, really good and I don't want to ruin it."

"That's understandable, have you tried to explain that to him?"

"No. I think he's pretty perceptive, he knows about Gran and the strange goings on, but he doesn't know about Tom."

"Perhaps he feels that you need time."

"Then why come all the way to London?"

"To show you that he cares, but is in no rush..."

Megan hesitated, "Or...is he after the brooch?"

"The brooch?"

Megan went on to explain in further detail about the brooch.

"What?"

Megan told Sasha of her fears, but she shook her head.

"I don't think that's the case at all."

"Perhaps not, I would like to think that he is genuine. I'm just struggling, with everything it seems."

"You'll get there, it's just a transition period." She smiled gently at Megan. "But what do you think is going on here though, with another break-in?"

"I've come to the conclusion that someone is after the brooch, even if it isn't Fin. It is extremely valuable."

"What's the brooch like?" Sasha asked, pouring more wine into their glasses.

Megan retrieved the brooch from the kitchen dresser then returned to Sasha, uncovered it and placed it on the table.

257

"Wow. That's beautiful, despite the corrosion. Did you find it at the dig?"

"No, here in the garden – Bartie dug it up."

"What a coincidence, him finding it and now you working on a Saxon dig, not far away. But what has that got to do with the break in?"

"Well, you know how you saw Bridget coming away from the cottage the day of the break-in? I wondered if she was trying to find it...she might have overheard Fin and I talking about it in the pub."

"Sounds quite likely...but we can't just accuse her."

"I know, but I'm also confused because although Bridget is obviously involved somehow, I still don't know who the blonde woman is that keeps appearing...what if she's after the brooch too?"

"Have you figured out who this woman is yet?" asked Sasha.

Megan sighed deeply. "I don't know, but I do think that they are all linked somehow. Remember the diaries?"

"Yes?"

"Don't you see? My gran was going through a difficult time, a love affair and she had sightings of this blonde woman and the hare too – just like me."

"And?"

"Well, perhaps the blonde woman is searching for the brooch for whatever reason and gran couldn't or wouldn't help her, so she has waited until now to see if I am able to help her," replied Megan.

"I agree, I think the brooch is the key, perhaps she does need it for something...however there is still Bridget..."

"Why would *she* want it?"

"Because it's valuable..."

"It is, yes...oh God, this all sounds rather far-fetched."

"Come on, you know that not all things can be explained by science...take your work for example, there's so much left for interpretation."

A realisation dawned on Megan. "Sasha...shit," she paused. "This sounds crazy, but what if uncovering the graves of the Anglo-Saxons has released a spirit of one of the women...the blonde is dressed in long robes, perhaps they are Saxon...perhaps she's a Saxon ghost!"

Sasha was silent for moment. "But why is she haunting you?"

"I have no idea, perhaps she sees me as someone that can help her...if she needs the brooch then perhaps I should give it to her."

"No. She might need the brooch for something bad..."

Megan laughed nervously, "I can't believe we're having such a discussion."

"No, it isn't your everyday conversation is it? What are you going to do?"

"To be honest, I really don't know. If this Saxon woman is a ghost and she does want the brooch for some reason, then who am I to withhold it from her? Perhaps it belonged to her in the first place?"

"It might have."

"I've thought about giving it to the museum and then she wouldn't get it, neither would Bridget."

"You don't think that the Saxon woman and Bridget could be connected in some way?" asked Sasha, frowning.

"In what way?"

"Well, some people believe that the spirits of the past can possess people in the here and now..."

"What, you mean that the Saxon woman is getting Bridget to act on her behalf? No, that really is a little far-fetched!"

"Perhaps the ghost is trying to make Bridget get it for her, because she's unable to physically collect it herself..."

"Or perhaps Bridget is trying to get it for herself and the Saxon woman is trying to stop her...why would she do that?"

"I think I've drunk too much wine, this is all sounding ridiculous now."

"What other explanation is there?"

Megan shook her head. "I really don't know."

"I'm sorry, Megan, I forget that others don't see things in the same way I do. My belief in the fact that our ancestors are a large part of who we are makes me see things in a very different way. If the Saxon woman is a ghost and she needs that brooch for something, the fact that Bridget is involved at all makes me think that there must be a connection."

Megan sighed. "Well, when and if you can work it out, let me know. Wait a minute...my dream the other night...in fact my dreams recently have been about people I don't really know, except the other night Bridget was in it! There was me, a man and Bridget – although I'm not sure I was me, if that makes any sense. I could see and feel everything that was going on around me, but thinking about it now, I'm not sure it was me...and the man...oh, this is so strange and bewildering."

"Come on, let's go for a walk and clear our heads a bit...I'm causing you more anxiety and that's not what I meant to do." Sasha called to the dogs and stood up.

"Yes, let's change the subject...what are you up to Friday night?"

"Nothing, although Brad has his exhibition starting Saturday morning, so I might need to help him."

259

"Kai's band is playing at the pub...do you fancy going? Could be good..."

"Sure, why not."

Megan followed her and the two spaniels through the garden, across the bridge and out into the open fields by the river. Megan didn't notice as she wandered across the fields that the woman they had been talking about was watching them from the garden, where she had been listening all the time to their conversation.

***

The woman who watched and listened sighed heavily. Her hope was fading...it couldn't happen again...she had to get through to Megan, she was her last chance. With the disturbances of the graves and the discovery of the village which had been hidden throughout the centuries, this was her final chance for the truth to be known. Otherwise, she would be forced to wander in despair for eternity.

***

Mildryth lay awake watching the flames of the fire slowly die down to a red glow, the ropes cutting into her skin around her wrists and ankles. She couldn't sleep, she was too afraid of what Wulfric would do to her...too upset at what Wilheard would think of her. The sky had darkened and night had fallen, Lindi had not returned. This didn't seem to concern Wulfric, he had said she would come back when she was ready, she was clearly up to something but whatever it was, he believed it was necessary.

Mildryth wondered what Wilheard had thought about her disappearance. Was he worried she had been taken, or that she had left him? She had always been so loyal to him, she loved him more than anything, but had betrayed him in the worst possible way. I need to escape, I need to get back home, she thought to herself. I must tell Wilheard everything But even as she thought of that conversation, of admitting to having had sex with Wulfric – even though magic had been used – she was unable to gauge whether Wilheard would believe her, or worse, if he would forgive her. She felt the tears upon her cheeks and Hope faded like a puff of smoke that lingers a moment and then is gone; dispersed into the abyss of time.

***

Fin smiled as Megan approached him. He was standing in a trench at the back of Batsborne Manor. "Well, this is a surprise. I'm guessing your mum is feeling much better?"

Megan nodded. "She's coming out of hospital today and Gerald is going to look after her."

"That's great." Fin climbed out of the trench in which he and Bella had been stood. Bella gave Megan an insincere smile, Megan didn't acknowledge her.

"How are things going?"

"Well, this is definitely the centre of the Saxon village. There are post holes for some smaller structures, but this one here seems to be the main hall, where Bella is standing."

"Wow, I've missed loads."

"Yes. Also, we've found more precious stones, loom weights, pottery shards...this is a very important site; I believe we might be uncovering one of the most important Anglo-Saxon sites in England."

Megan watched Fin's animated face as he showed his excitement at his discoveries. "That's amazing. As important as Sutton Hoo?"

"Possibly," he replied. "Anyway, when did you get back?"

"Yesterday, early afternoon. Sasha and I spent some time together. I really needed a friend to talk to. I thought about coming back to work, but you did say I should take my time."

"Of course, my sister was here yesterday helping out, but she's gone to see my parents today in Oxford. She's back off to Canada on Friday so I have to take her to the airport. Will you be all right to oversee things here then, unless you're needed elsewhere?"

"Certainly, I'm just sorry I've let you down the past few weeks, not exactly the best employee, what with the fire and my mum..."

He smiled kindly at her and lowered his voice. "Megan, all of those things are out of your control...don't be so hard on yourself." He stroked her upper arm with his hand quickly, gently.

"When will you be back on Friday? It's just that there's a band playing Friday night in the Red Lion, Sasha and I were thinking of going. I wondered if you'd like to join us all?"

"I don't think I'll make it I'm afraid, my sister's flight is quite late and I've promised her dinner before she goes."

Megan felt her heart sink, but she smiled. "No worries."

"If I get back in time, I might pop in for quick pint if the pub's still open."

"I think it's quite likely they'll have a lock-in, they quite often do on a Friday night!"

"Great."

David arrived. "Fin, Megan," he said looking at both in turn. "I've got some good news and thought I would come and share it with you. Time for a coffee break? Ah, Megan, sorry to hear about your mum, but glad that she's on the mend."

Fin nodded and winked at Megan. "We've been working hard for hours..."

The three of them walked the short distance into the High Street and found a bakery and coffee shop that had recently opened. Entering the warm, not overly crowded shop they found themselves a table and sat down. A young waitress took their order and went away to have it prepared.

"What's the good news?" asked Megan.

"The university have agreed to give us more funding for this project. They understand the importance of this site and are giving us some more money so that we can complete the archaeological dig and move the project towards completion. Furthermore, the museum in Cirencester is keen to give us space too, to have a Saxon exhibition."

"That's fantastic news," cried Fin.

"Brilliant," said Megan.

"Hopefully this will persuade you to take the position I mentioned from September," grinned Fin, winking.

"Absolutely, I would be a fool not to," replied Megan, her heart lifting.

"Let's drink to that," said David, raising his coffee cup and chinking it against first Megan's, then Fin's. "Here's to a great team."

"Cheers!"

That night Megan poured a glass of wine and sat, next to the cold stove, now too damaged to use after the fire, with her thoughts. She had spoken to her mother and discovered she was home and comfortable; happy that Gerald was with her. Feeling satisfied that her mother was in good hands, she turned her thoughts to the brooch again. She *had* to do something. Either give it to the museum or bury it back beneath the earth in the garden where Bartie had found it, where it could do no harm.

Later, going into the kitchen, she took the brooch from its hiding place and carried it upstairs to her bedroom. She needed to know it was safe, so she placed it upon the dresser with a frown; she snuggled down into her duvet and waited for sleep to come.

The two women glared at each other, green eyes determined: ice-blue eyes venomous. Ahead of them something glinted in the grass among the fingers of light between the trees. Something precious... all

at once they raced towards it, nearer and nearer...hands outstretched,
grabbing, grasping...

"It should be mine!"

"You gave it to me...it is my only proof, Wilheard will know it is
cursed!

"He will never know..." laughed the ice-blue eyes.

"Never is a very long time..."

A low growl from Bartie awoke Megan with a start.

Sitting up she saw the same dark female shadow as before,
then...a rat!

Suddenly, Bartie was off and chasing it down the stairs. Megan
followed then opened the door and let them both out into the night.
Shutting the door, a noise from upstairs startled her – a voice?
Quickly, quietly she ascended the stairs: the familiar odour of damp;
ice cold air.

Returning to her room she was surprised, although fearful, to see
the figure of the blonde woman standing next to the bed. Megan
couldn't move, or speak – was she still dreaming? She watched as the
woman walked to the dresser and picked up the brooch. The woman
didn't look like a ghost, the figure was tangible, not like she had
expected. Holding the brooch against her chest, the woman smiled at
Megan, then vanished.

Trembling slightly, Megan moved towards the dressing table.
There was no sign of the woman now and the brooch had gone, just
the empty box sat on the dressing table. She wondered now if she
would ever see the woman again, why she needed the brooch, for what
purpose? What if the brooch was needed for something evil after all?
Megan hoped she'd done the right thing...and her instinct told her that
she had.

***

At last the knot loosened and Mildryth managed to wriggle her hands
free of the ropes that bound her. Wulfric's snores could be heard a
short distance off in the darkness. Mildryth fumbled with trembling
hands with the knots which imprisoned her ankles, until finally, they
too, came undone.

With her heart in her mouth, she moved silently towards the
entrance to the cave as quickly as she could. What if Lindi chose this
moment to come back? What if she was watching the cave in case an
attempt at escape was made? Stealthily, Mildryth stepped out into the
open air, the chill of the night clasping her in its cold breath. Running

quickly and quietly through the woods, away from the cave and her captives, praying to the gods she would get far enough away. She jumped as an owl screeched nearby.

For two days she followed the river westwards; she knew if she returned to Wilheard now he would not forgive her, knew it was too soon and he would not believe it was only through magic that she had coupled with his brother; she had betrayed him...that is how he would see it and she couldn't blame him for that.

If Wulfric and Lindi were searching for her, she didn't know – she would keep going west; get to her sister; Sunniva would know what to do.

***

At dawn, Wulfric awoke to find Lindi leaning over him.

"Where is she you fool?" she spat.

"She's *gone*?" Wulfric sat up and stared at the discarded rope on the floor of the cave; the fire now dead.

"Wilheard and his men are outside this cave, waiting for me to bring you both out..."

Wulfric was on his feet in seconds. "*You* brought them here?"

"They captured me...the only way I could get back to you was if I brought them too."

"Bitch!" he cried, striking her hard across the face, knocking her off balance.

"Wait!" she cried, holding up her hands. "There's another way out..."

"Show me."

Lindi scrambled to her feet and towards the back of the cave which led to a tangle of tunnels and their escape.

***

Outside the cave, Wilheard ordered his men to go in after Lindi, she was taking too long. A moment later he knew he had been duped.

***

By the time Mildryth reached her sister's village, she was exhausted and hungry; she staggered through the gates and collapsed on the ground.

A few hours later she awoke. As she opened her eyes she saw what she thought, for a moment, were the eyes of her mother.

264

"Mother?" she said, her sight not yet fully focussed.

"No, dear Mildryth, it is I, Sunniva."

Mildryth smiled at the familiar form, then lost consciousness again.

There was darkness surrounding the hut in which she lay; next time she awoke, lamps were burning nearby and again her sister was at her side.

"Sunniva."

Her sister smiled and took her hand. "Mildryth, you had us all scared...what are you doing here?"

"H-have you sent for Wilheard?"

Sunniva shook her head. "Instinct told me to wait...I knew there had to be a reason that you came here, alone."

"Oh Sunniva, I am in such terrible trouble, I don't think that Wilheard will believe me when I tell him the truth!"

"Tell me what's happened."

***

Meanwhile in the lands of Mercia, Wulfric was grunting around the hut like a wild boar.

"What is it?" Lindi asked him, irritably.

"I've tried to convince them a night attack would be best...but I can tell they are reluctant."

"Why?"

"I fear their allegiance is stronger than we first thought."

"They'll come round..."

"I think it may be dangerous for us to be here now. We leave tonight."

"What?"

"These people of Mercia are too loyal to Wilheard." He spat on the floor before taking another huge gulp of wine.

"But we've come so far..."

"Yes. But I think they will hand us over if we don't leave tonight – they want peace too."

"But the runes said..."

"I don't care what your bloody runes say...you've been wrong in past...we leave – now!"

265

Chapter Twenty-One

The moons came and went. Mildryth's belly swelled and she could feel her child move inside; this brought her happiness, but sorrow too.

Sunniva had kept her promise and looked after her well, despite her own husband's reservations. Some of Wilheard's men came in search of her; but disguised as a cousin of her brother-in-law, nobody knew that Mildryth was not who she pretended to be.

Mildryth lived among her sister's family, biding her time and planning what she must do when the child came. She would not let go of that last glimmer of hope that eventually Wilheard would forgive her...he would realise she was innocent in all of this, but she could not risk the life of her unborn child. Once the child was born, she would look for Wulfric once more and ask him to tell his brother the truth. If he would not and if Lindi would not, then there was only one other way...revenge.

One morning as the sun's golden rays peeped through the gaps in the hut's wooden walls, Mildryth felt her stomach tighten and a pain rip through her in waves.

A few hours later a baby boy was handed to her, wrapped in the fur of a wolf, blood still sticky in his hair; his face wrinkled but beautiful to his mother. As Mildryth held her son in her arms, not knowing who his father was for sure, she knew what she had to do.

***

Weeks went by. Mildryth was besotted by her baby boy, but was saddened at the circumstances she found herself, and him, in. She had always had high hopes for the child, to be part of a happy family as hers had been. Then, early one morning while Mildryth was nursing her infant, she looked up as Sunniva entered the hut. Her son was latched onto her breast and drank hungrily, innocent to his mother's distressed thoughts.

"I have news," said Sunniva, taking her sister's hand and looking into her eyes.

"You know where they are?"

Sunniva nodded. "Are you sure you want to know, you want to do this?"

Mildryth looked down at her son's face; tears sprang into her eyes, but she knew she had to face them; face Wilheard too – tell him her side of the story, if he'd listen. "Yes, I must."

The following morning, Mildryth kissed her son on his soft head, inhaling the sweet smell of him into her soul; then she handed him to Sunniva.

"Take care of him. If I never return no-one must ever know he survived...whose son he really is," she said tears falling down her cheeks.

"I will treat him as my own, but I believe all will be well," said Sunniva, embracing her sister with her free arm and cradling the infant with the other.

After gathering some belongings together, Mildryth got onto her horse and rode away, without looking back to where her sister stood cradling her son – the son she may never see again.

***

Simultaneously, as if the gods were playing a game, Wilheard was told of the whereabouts of Wulfric and Lindi.

"Finally!" he cried. "I will have my vengeance. Saddle my horse, gather my men."

Months had passed by, his pain and rage alternately driving his search for the three childhood friends and family who had betrayed him so badly. He found himself hoping that he would find Mildryth alive, but then, that he would find her dead, so he wouldn't then have to kill her himself. He would gladly kill the other two; with his bare hands if necessary.

***

Mildryth had refused the horseman. She did not want another man to die for her sake, like Piers. She had provisions, a horse and her dagger. She rode north for three days before she came to the edge of the forest where she had been told they were hiding out.

Entering the forest, she understood why they had chosen this hiding place. Its dense foliage and eerie atmosphere, which was damp and misty even on a sunny day, would deter most people from entering such a place. Even the gods might decide against it, instead allowing dark spirits to rule the sinister, mossy habitat.

Mildryth tied the horse to a tree near the small river and stepped quietly through the trees. No birds sang. She crept carefully, trying to avoid any foliage that might break, snap beneath her feet and send out a warning to anyone in the vicinity. After walking a fair distance into the woods, she suddenly found a dagger at her throat...

***

Some hours later, Mildryth was following Lindi through the forest. The sunlight filtered through the broadleaved trees, but Mildryth felt no warmth from its rays. There was no birdsong from the treetops and occasionally a tree creaked eerily, moved by a gentle wind.

"Where are you taking me?"

"Not far to go now."

Mildryth sighed, she was tired and now more afraid. She couldn't believe she had been captured so easily, especially as she had been so careful. They hadn't walked much further when ahead of her she could see a clearing in the woods; Wulfric was there, building a fire.

Lindi called out to him and he stood up. The look of shock on his face at seeing Lindi's prisoner was soon replaced by one of rage.

"Where the hell did she come from?" he yelled. "How did she find us?"

"I found her wandering in the woods."

He walked towards Mildryth and she wondered if he would strike her. Now she was with them, she realised how futile her journey had been; they would never tell Wilheard the truth. She felt her resolve leave her and wondered at her own stupidity – she shouldn't have come; should have stayed on with Sunniva and brought up her son, alone. She felt her heart tear open inside her chest at the thought of never seeing her child again.

Wulfric spat in her face; the warm saliva ran down her cheek and she shuddered, feeling like she would vomit.

"I see I still disgust you."

"You didn't used to, Wulfric, only since you betrayed me do I despise you – before that you were my friend, my brother...you should have left Wilheard and I alone to be happy, but you were never satisfied. Now you have the woman you deserve."

He struck her, a blow to the side of her head which sent her reeling.

He looked at her slim figure. "Where's the child?" he asked.

Mildryth looked him straight in the eye. "The boy died."

"You killed my son?"

"We don't know that it was your child...you denied its existence before...sound familiar?" The bitterness overcame her.

He struck her again.

***

269

Mildryth sat close to the fire, but despite the warmth she shivered. Encumbered with the ropes, which bound her legs, she was eating bread and drinking water slowly, each mouthful difficult to swallow from the bruising she had to her jaw where Wulfric had struck her. Wulfric and Lindi had tied up her ankles and then disappeared off into the trees, leaving her alone with her pain. They seemed to be gone for ages...she hadn't heard any movement or voices for some time now and was becoming anxious. Were they just going to leave her here to die, at the mercy of the wolves that lived and hunted within this very forest? Surely they wouldn't have fed her if that were the case.

"Hello?" she called, but only her echo replied, that and the leaves whispering above her.

She shivered even more and threw the remainder of her uneaten bread away, feeling sick. Nearby there was a sharp looking rock...if only she could cut the rope that bound her feet together, she might just be able to escape before they returned. They had tied the ropes tightly after her previous escape. Shuffling along the ground she managed to reach the rock. She rubbed it hard against the rope; it would take an awfully long time to cut through, but she didn't have anything else to do.

Mildryth's heart began to race as the rope frayed further and further as she cut and cut as hard as she could...the rope was almost through, perhaps with some real force, she would be able to break the final threads and escape! All of a sudden, she heard a noise. Small branches underfoot could be heard snapping as somebody approached. She quickly threw the rock and covered the frayed rope beneath her long skirts and cloak; her hands were still tightly bound. Out of the trees approaching her was the figure of a man on horseback, a man with a sword at his side.

Wilheard!

She squinted, was it really him, or was he just a vision? Standing and pulling at the frayed ropes at her legs, they gave way and she kicked them free from her feet then started to run towards her husband, tears in her eyes. Gaining on him she realised he wasn't smiling, didn't seem pleased to see her, in fact the look on his face was of pure, unadulterated hatred...she slowed. Was this some kind of awful nightmare where nothing made sense, yet it all felt so real?

"Wilheard?" she called.

"You traitor!" he roared and pulled his sword, raising it above his head.

In an instant Mildryth turned and ran – the tight ropes had numbed her feet and she stumbled; the sound of the horses' hooves

270

were gaining on her. She kept on running, sprinting as fast as she could away from him. Her mind was confused and all she kept thinking of was why? *Why?* He must know, somebody must have told him what had happened. But where were Lindi and Wulfric now?

Suddenly, she came out of the trees. Below her was the deep, dark river. She stumbled down the slope and started to run along the bank, her long garments impeding her progress; her leather shoes slipping in the damp grass and mud – her breath was burning in her chest, her heart thudding...she couldn't run anymore.

She stopped, turned. "Wilheard wait, please..." she begged.

The pain and anger were evident in Wilheard's face, which was still as handsome but drawn and pale. "I can't believe that you have lain with my brother before *we* were married! You whore," he bellowed. "Where have you been all this time? With him, still with him..."

"Wilheard, I can explain..."

"No need," said Lindi, emerging on horseback from the trees behind Wilheard. "I already have."

"No, Lindi, Wilheard, please you have to listen to *me*..."

Wilheard climbed down from his horse, sword still in hand. Lindi smiled - a look of deep satisfaction in her ice-blue eyes.

Mildryth sank to her knees, her husband and childhood friend stared down at her. There was no sympathy, no love remaining in Wilheard's sky-blue eyes; they just held betrayal, rage and worse still...loathing.

"Please..." she begged Wilheard, but it was as if he hadn't heard her. He brought the blade down upon her, cutting through every layer of her flesh, piercing her heart...and in that moment, before Death came, Mildryth knew Wilheard would *always* believe her guilty of a crime she didn't commit...

***

Wilheard's cry of anguish echoed round the forest and in the distance a wolf's howl replied, long, deep, guttural. Wilheard sank to his knees, and tears streamed down his face and on to the sword which now lay at his feet, covered in his wife's blood.

A sound came from behind him and swiftly Wilheard saw Wulfric appear. He tried to jump to his feet and grab his sword, but Wulfric was too quick and knocked him back to the ground. Wulfric pinned Wilheard to the floor. The brothers glared at each other, the coldness of the blue and the grey eyes locked with hatred.

"You killed her!" There were tears in Wulfric's eyes.

271

"She betrayed me, she is a traitor and so are you!"

Wilheard pushed with all his might, unbalancing Wulfric, who fell backwards, giving Wilheard the chance to spring to his feet and grab his sword. Swinging it high, he brought it down onto Wulfric's shoulder; Wulfric howled with pain and came back at Wilheard, but he dodged and Wulfric missed.

"You killed our father too..." cried Wilheard.

Wulfric pointed at Lindi. "Not I, but her...she administered the poison..."

"At your command, I dare say..." He took his eyes off his brother for an instant and looked directly at Lindi, who stood watching them with a look of amusement on her face. A small doubt entered Wilheard's mind.

"It's true...she wants to be queen!"

The two men danced around each other, swords clashing and impacting off the other. Wulfric gouged a chunk of skin from Wilheard's arm, which made him falter and lose his balance.

"You've always wanted to be king!" Wilheard regained his balance and raised his sword again, this time swinging it in from the side towards his brother's ribs.

He struck.

Wulfric bellowed with pain and rage then sank to his knees. "I *will* be king, when you are dead and buried..."

"I suppose you are going to be the one to do that?"

Wulfric laughed, despite his obvious pain. "Lindi is not the only one who wants it all...I wanted your throne, your kingdom and *your wife*...and I'm taking them one by one."

"You bastard!" Wilheard grabbed Wulfric by the throat, squeezed as hard as he could.

Wulfric saw his chance and brought his sword from below and up into Wilheard's stomach.

Wilheard felt it enter and knew immediately what it meant...he stared into his brother's wolf-like eyes. "We could have shared the kingdom, brother. I was willing...to forgive you your jealousy of that...b-but..." The pain was now unbearable, the warm blood seeping out of him. "I could never...f-forgive you or Mildryth for betraying my trust...she was the love...of my life..."

A look of satisfaction passed over Wulfric's face. "*She* didn't betray you, *brother,* I used magic and now you'll go to your death knowing that you killed your beautiful...*innocent*...wife!"

Wilheard's blood froze. Wulfric laughed and with it Wilheard, with the last bit of strength he had left, pushed the dagger, he'd hidden in his robes, into his brother's chest.

272

As he saw the life leaving his brother's eyes and felt his own spirit begin to leave him, Wilheard murmured his final oath. "Mildryth, I'm sorry; I will search for you in the next life; you must know that I forgive you, even if that takes an eternity for me to achieve, I owe it to you, my precious one..."

As his spirit left his human form on the floor of the dark, damp forest, Wilheard looked down upon the scene that lay beneath him: Mildryth's body lay still and limp, her beautiful golden hair now sticky, streaked with blood; Wulfric's gory form slumped forward onto his knees; but just as disturbing as those things were, he saw Lindi raise her hands above her head, throw her head back and laugh.

***

Aart watched miserably as the four soldiers set the pyre alight. The flames quickly took hold of the wood which supported the body of their king; the funeral of the second king they had seen murdered within a year. The villagers watched as the smoke rose towards the sky and drifted away from them across the valley – like his spirit leaving them and going on to the next life.

Aart's thoughts turned to the guilt he felt in not being able to save Wilheard, his king, his friend. He'd watched, horrified and helpless, as the two brothers had fought with hatred and rage before finally slaughtering each other. He had sunk to his knees in grief at the scene that lay before him. His friends...his family...all dead; all dead except for one. The one that then laughed: a cold, bitter and resentful cackle. Aart had sprung to his feet at once and held a dagger to Lindi's throat.

"I should kill you," he said bitterly, pressing the dagger deeper into the skin on her throat.

"You can't do that," she sneered. "I am carrying an heir."

"What do you mean, whore?"

"I carry Wulfric's child, the next in line to the throne – there is nobody that can touch me. If you kill me, the gods will punish you."

Aart felt his blood freeze. She was right – if he killed her the gods would punish him severely. A moment later, he had felt the warmth of her blood ooze through his fingers...it was worth the punishment!

As Aart and the other soldiers rode through the village towards the Great Hall, the villagers came out of their huts to greet the wretched sight that met their eyes. In turn they all fell to their knees as they were told that their king and queen were dead, murdered. The third body, their slaughterer, was being dragged along the ground

273

behind one of the horses; its limbs lifeless with blood and sludge – dark hair matted with grime. Howls of grief and anger rose up among the community, shouts for justice and a sense of doom came down upon them. The fourth body, the unspoken one, was left to rot amongst the trees of the dark forest.

Their queen had been buried, at her father's request, at dawn the same day. Situated in a grave within the village's burial ground, but as the law dictated, away from where Wilheard's cremation pot would be; she had deserted him, no more than that was known. As the coffin that held her body was lowered into her grave, her father and sister arranged her belongings around her; things they believed she might need for the next life. They had made sure she was dressed as a queen should be, in fine clothes and jewels. Sunniva had pinned the bronze, square-headed brooch that held her cloak in place, thinking that it must have been a gift from Wilheard and therefore was precious to her. She had discovered it in a pot near the king and queen's bed in their chambers, probably for safe-keeping, Sunniva had thought.

Mildryth's family were alone at the graveside, and after they had lowered her coffin into the earth, they covered it with rocks, all the while praying to the gods to welcome her into the next world. The rising sun tinted the sky with her red blood.

Sunniva stood next to her father, hot tears running down her cheeks. The child in her arms gave a desperate cry; Sunniva embraced him more closely and said a silent prayer of her own.

Now, as Wilheard's body became one with the fire, the sky began to darken and the villagers dispersed back towards the Great Hall where a feast was being held in honour of their king.

Aart stayed, alone by the dying fire, hot tears running down his face, and he asked for the gods to forgive him. A chill breeze whipped across the valley from the river. There was just one more body to deal with.

It was time to feed the wolves.

***

Sasha and Megan, with their dogs at heel, entered the pub. The crowd were lively, it was rammed full of locals and others that had come from further afield; already the music was in full swing. Kai caught Megan's eye as she walked past the band and he smiled and winked. A tingle of excitement ran through her...he was attractive, but it would never be a good match; they were worlds apart. She knew deep down it was just a sexual attraction, lustful, passionate, but no real sincere feelings of love. Those feelings seemed reserved just for Fin; there the feelings were more legitimate, the lust and passion were there too, but there was a sense of something much stronger, much deeper - more sustainable.

"Not very subtle, is he?" Sasha laughed. "You'd be a lot better off with Fin."

Megan laughed. "I know, but like I said earlier, I'm really not ready yet." Even as she said it, part of her wanted to dive head first into his arms and his life, but she knew deep down that wasn't the best idea. She had to be patient, and if it was meant to be, it would be.

"Did you say Fin is going to come along later?" asked Sasha.

"He's hoping to, he's taking his sister back to Heathrow, where they're going to have dinner before she flies back to Canada. What about Brad?"

"He's going to pick me up about eleven; he was going to come along but we've got an early start tomorrow, his Venice photography exhibition is starting at ten at the Arts Centre and he wants to make sure it's perfectly set up. We have to be there at seven."

"That *is* early for a Saturday."

"Yes, but I think it will be worth it. There are some amazing photos...I think he's going to be very successful."

"His work *is* amazing."

Sasha beamed with pride, but her smile faded as she looked up and into the eyes of Bridget, who was standing just to the side of their table.

"Another bottle?" she asked.

Bartie growled quietly from beneath the table.

"No, not at the moment, thank you," replied Sasha.

Bridget's gaze moved to Megan. "Good to be back? I think Kai's pleased you're here, he hasn't stopped staring at you all evening."

Megan was dumbfounded, she just didn't know when to stop that woman...it was none of her business!

"We'll come to the bar if we need another drink," said Sasha in a dismissive tone.

Bridget turned and left them, and headed back to the bar, but not before blowing a kiss to Kai in front of everyone. He looked uncomfortable and a few laughs rose above the loud conversations that were going on in the bar. Kai caught Megan's eye again, but she looked quickly down at her drink.

"I can't believe the nerve of that woman..." said Sasha.

"It's okay, she's just trying to get a reaction and seems to be succeeding..."

"She'll get a reaction from me too, if she continues. She is really jealous of you, isn't she?"

"Jealous?"

"Sure, that's the only explanation I can think of to explain her behaviour...she hates the idea that Kai fancies you and is no longer interested in her."

"I really don't know. I thought perhaps she was odd with me because of Kai, but it might be because of the brooch, perhaps she did want it after all."

"I'm going to ask her about it..." said Sasha, starting to stand.

Megan grabbed her arm. "No, don't, you'll only let on that we're suspicious of her..."

"I'm worried what she'll do to get the brooch though." Sasha sat back down. "Be careful of her, Megan. I have a strange feeling about her."

"Me too, but it's all right, Sasha. The brooch has gone," she sighed.

"Gone?"

Megan nodded. "The woman took it..."

Sasha looked confused.

"She came in the night, there were two women...both Saxon I'm sure; the blonde one, the one who I keep seeing – she's taken the brooch. The other woman disappeared, seemed to change into a rat and then Bartie chased her away!"

"So you're saying they *are* ghosts and that they have been searching for the brooch for some reason..." The colour had faded from Sasha's face.

"I haven't seen either of them since."

"So why is Bridget still being so cold with you?"

"I suppose it could be because she knew about the brooch too and doesn't know that it has gone, so is still hoping she'll get it...although perhaps it is to do with Kai and nothing to do with the brooch at all." She sighed heavily, felt emotionally drained.

"Well it could be – after all the man she's in love with is clearly infatuated by you!"

Megan frowned. "He won't be for long, not when he realises how boring I am."

"Rubbish."

The two women laughed. At that moment, both of their mobiles went off simultaneously.

"Weird!" said Megan.

"Mine's from Brad, he says he'll be here in half an hour."

"Fin says he'll be here in about 45 minutes."

"Excellent timing," said Sasha. "Time for one more drink then."

The music had stopped playing and the band were all at the bar, raising their glasses to another successful gig. Megan went to the ladies' toilets, and on her return she found Kai talking to Sasha with two glasses of wine in his hands.

"For you ladies," he said. "I hope yer enjoyin' the music this evening."

"Yes, it's great," replied Megan, truthfully.

"Glad yer having fun, enjoy the wine, they're on me."

"Thanks."

Sasha winked at Megan. "He's not even hiding the fact he's keen."

"I know, it's quite embarrassing. When I first met him, he was really distant, but now he's really rather over-friendly!"

"Just enjoy the fact you're upsetting Bridget! Look at her face...she's positively glowering."

Megan glanced up and saw the venom in her eyes. Perhaps she did have something to worry about after all.

Half an hour passed and Brad arrived, looking rather dishevelled and stressed. He smiled at Megan and was polite, but she could tell he was eager to get going.

"Are you sure you'll be all right if I go?" asked Sasha.

"I'll be fine. Fin said he'll be here soon. You go and get some sleep before your early start! Fin will see me home. I'll see you both tomorrow at the exhibition."

Megan watched as Brad and Sasha left the pub arm in arm, then sat back to enjoy the music. She tried hard to ignore the blatant look of interest on Kai's face. She knew when Fin arrived it would piss Kai off. Kai had mentioned that his band were playing to her before and she now wondered if he had taken her presence there as some kind of hidden message that she was keen to be near him, oh God, she hoped not. She wished Fin would hurry up. He was now 15 minutes later than he had said, where was he?

Another half hour passed, it was midnight and the band were now singing their final songs...if he didn't turn up, she would have to walk home on her own. She didn't relish the idea of that, either. Had he stood her up, or was he hurt? Had there been an accident? Why did she feel insecure all of a sudden – she really couldn't decide if she thought he was genuine or not, she wished that her past baggage would stop interfering and spoiling her present opportunities. She would be really upset if he had stood her up, but why would he tell her he'd be there and then not turn up...there really were only two reasons she could think of, and she didn't like either of them...

277

Finally, she decided to call his mobile. It went straight to voicemail. How frustrating.

"Something wrong?" asked Kai, as he approached her with another glass of wine. "Yer look worried."

"Oh, em, hi, no nothing wrong..."

"Here's another wine for yer."

"I'm not sure I should..."

"Go on, one more won't hurt yer, just stay in bed a bit longer in the morning." He laughed and his grey eyes sparkled mischievously, holding her gaze. She glanced away.

Although she tried hard to fight it, her body responded to his flirting, but she was determined to play it down. However, Fin *had* just stood her up, perhaps she could...just for a night of fun; that would be so out of character for her though, she'd only ever had a single one-night stand before when she was in her early twenties and although it had been a good night, she had been disappointed when 'Mike' didn't call her; had felt hurt and rejected, even though he'd said he wasn't looking for a relationship. She didn't think it would be any different now – although she wasn't looking for a relationship, she knew she would feel all wrong about it in the morning.

Her head swam from the wine and she began to wish she was home now, snuggled up in bed, but Kai was animatedly speaking to her. As the hurt of Fin's possible rejection sank deeper within her, she started to force herself to enjoy the company that she did have. She found that Kai with a few beers inside him was really funny, and he told her many stories of his travels around and how he often managed to upset quite a few people without even trying very hard.

Her mobile indicated a text message...Fin:

> *Really sorry, Megan, the car broke down in a spot with no signal, fixed now and on the way home although still an hour away. I hope you're ok and got home all right. Phone me when you're home, I want to know you're safe. x*

Broken down, no signal? She cursed herself as the nagging doubts filtered through the alcohol. Her head was spinning and she noticed that Kai's face was emerging in and out of focus.

"I need to go home, I am *so* tired," she stated, standing up.

"I'll walk yer," suggested Kai, standing too.

"There's no need, thank you."

"I'm going most of the way anyway..."

278

Realising that Bartie was pulling hard on his lead, she didn't really have any choice; it would be better having some company than walking alone back to the cottage – what if the ghost of the other woman was there again, not the one that took the brooch, but the other, the more sinister one? Perhaps she should let Kai walk her home after all, or perhaps, he would only walk as far as his caravan.

Kai pulled on his coat and called to Angus who trotted before all of them and waited by the door. As she was leaving the pub, with Bartie at her heel and the door swinging closed behind them, she heard a woman laugh...it must have been Bridget, but it was a low sinister laugh that sent a chill straight through her...a laugh she'd heard before a long, long time ago.

They took the dark road which led them to the ancient bridge, the Thames Path and home. The route would take them past Kai's caravan first, which, on one hand, filled Megan with a sense of relief that she wouldn't have to invite Kai in, but fear on the other in case there *was* anyone at the cottage who shouldn't be there. And what of the man who watched the house from the trees opposite? She'd still not worked out who that was.

Megan tried to steer the conversation away from herself. "Bridget is still in love with you, you know," she said realising that the drink had loosened her thoughts and her tongue.

"Hmm...I know. We did 'ave a good thing goin' at one time, but it was never true love, not on my part anyway."

"How long were you together?"

"About five years, but we knew each other before that."

"She is rather possessive of you." Megan stated, letting Bartie off the lead to follow Angus along the riverbank. The Thames slithering like a silver snake through the fields surrounding them; a vixen screeched in the distance.

"You've noticed then?"

"You can't miss it."

"What about yer archaeologist boyfriend then, where's 'e tonight?"

"His car broke down, he's on his way back, but he's not my boyfriend. I don't have one at the moment."

"He's *not* yer boyfriend?"

"No. We're colleagues."

"That's a surprise, I've seen you two togevver, and 'e's besotted!"

Megan laughed inwardly, remembering Sasha's comment about Kai being 'besotted' with her. *Boy, aren't I popular, now I don't want to be?*

Megan found that her mind was becoming more fuddled, the drink was affecting her badly; she must be tired. Her thoughts were becoming slightly peculiar, strange images kept popping into her mind. There seemed to be others around her and Kai...she knew that they weren't really there, but were in her subconscious. She was aware of Kai speaking to her, but she could also hear other voices now, urgent...persistent...then faces...the faces from her dream. Her thoughts were like smoke, intangible but sinister.

Suddenly, they were standing by Kai's van, and a sense of fear shivered through her. "I need to get home, Kai. I'm not feeling too good...I need to sleep," she heard herself say, but it felt like the words were coming from somebody else's mouth. Megan stared up at Kai, his face mostly in shadow in the darkness that surrounded them, his grey, wolf-like eyes glinting silver like the river in the moonlight. She felt a flicker of fear course through her veins. Her instincts were screaming danger at her.

"Come on, let me help yer..." Kai held onto her arm and led her up the steps to the small space inside. It smelt of wood smoke and something else...marijuana? There was a red glow inside the wood-burning stove, which cast strange shadows around the inside of the caravan and made her feel as if she were in a cave.

Again, the strange voices became urgent whispers in her head...one particularly stronger than the others. "*Run, you must run...don't let him close...Wilheard must know the truth...it's my only chance...*"

"Kai, who else is here?"

"Nobody's 'ere, Megan, just you and me. He pushed her gently down onto the bed and sat beside her."

Another voice, male...more distant this time, not Kai's. "You betrayed me!"

A woman's laugh, sinister, cold.

Megan was suddenly aware of Kai's hands upon her body, his lips pushing hard against hers – she tried to sit up, but it seemed her body would not react to the signals her brain was trying to give her...

"Kai, no, that's not what I want!" she cried, but she could see a faraway look in his eyes that turned the small trickle of fear she'd felt previously into a torrent of terror!

"*It's all right, Mildryth...I've got you...I've got you...at last.*"

A woman's scream.

The distant cry of a vixen.

"*Wulfric, no...no, not again!*"

Chapter Twenty-Two

Having phoned and been unable to get hold of Megan, Fin phoned Sasha.

"I've not seen her since I left her at the pub. I thought you were going to pick her up!"

"I broke down."

"I'm going to phone the police," said Sasha.

"You're probably right with all the recent events!" said Fin. "I'm not far away now, I'll go straight there."

Fin looked at the clock on his dashboard. It was just past one o'clock, it really was too late to call in on Megan, but he hadn't heard from her...she was probably mad at him. He didn't blame her, it did sound like a pathetic excuse for not turning up or calling, but it really was legitimate and he needed her to know that. He was confused about the car, it had been fine – must have just been one of those things, but today of all days! Fin had fallen for Megan hard when he first met her, but he'd heard from David that she'd recently split from a long-term relationship, so decided it was best not to try to get involved. However, the more time he spent with her, the more he knew that they would be so good together. She was understandably cautious; but he had a feeling that she did feel something for him too, had seen it in her eyes.

He swung the car into the lane that led to the cottage. It was dark and his headlights caught the fluttering insects and the odd rabbit that darted across the mud track. As the cottage came into sight, he noticed that the hall light was on. His heart thudded in his chest as he drove over the little bridge and onto the driveway. He braked suddenly as ahead of him, standing stock still, was a large hare; it stood on its huge hind legs and stared and stared at him...he revved the engine slightly, but it didn't move. Fin watched incredulously as the hare stayed still whilst he opened the car door. He got out. A vixen cried in the distance.

The hare shot off.

It ran in the direction from which he'd come, probably scared of the vixen. He walked across the drive, his shoes crunching on the gravel as he moved towards the front door. He knocked loudly, but was startled to find that the door was ajar and there were muddy foot prints, not clumps this time, all through the hallway.

He entered.

"Megan," he shouted loudly. "Megan, are you here?" The silence enveloped him, she clearly wasn't, but if she wasn't here, where was

281

she? He felt a shiver run through him, although the air around him was thick and stifling. Everything was still, too still. Oppressive.

A noise upstairs startled him. Taking the walking stick from by the front door, he walked slowly and steadily up the stairs. He turned the corner, near to the top of the stairs and froze as an enormous black rat darted past him and down the stairs. He shouted and followed it. The rat scurried across the stone floor towards the front door, which he had left open, and squealed as it went out into the dark, as if a large cat might be after it.

He returned upstairs to check the bedrooms and ensure Megan was not sleeping in her bed. She wasn't.

Returning down the stairs, he tried her mobile once again: straight to voicemail. As he glanced out of the front door which was still ajar, he spotted the hare again in glow of the halogen lamp...It vanished, but in its place stood a woman ...Megan? No, this woman had long, golden hair. He shuddered as he watched her beckon him to follow her; at least that seemed to be what she wanted...she hoisted up her long skirts and ran in the same direction the hare had run. Was this the woman Megan had been talking about?

Another noise beside him made his heart race even faster; things were happening so fast that his mind couldn't comprehend what was happening. "Bartie!" he cried and ruffled the dog's coat, so pleased to see him. "Where's Megan?"

Bartie stared at him with his deep, brown eyes, confusion and concern written all over them. There was definitely something wrong...Why the hell had his car broken down? He'd never had a car break down on him before, ever, and now it seemed that because of it, Megan was in danger.

Why had he not told Megan that he loved her when he'd had the chance at her mother's house? Why had he been so cautious...*Please don't let it be too late! I want her to know how I feel about her.*

"Bartie, do *you* know where she is?" Bartie barked at him and ran off down the drive towards the bridge, the same direction that the woman had gone.

Fin raced after him, what if she had fallen on her way home and was hurt, unable to walk home? He quickened his pace. Bartie had run on ahead and was nowhere to be seen now. Fin was about to give up hope when he saw the woman again, she was standing ahead of him, her outline clear in the light of the full moon, at the bend in the road. One way led to the town, the other to more fields and a bridle path. She again beckoned him to follow. He felt like he was in some kind of nightmare and nothing was making sense, he was just riding the wave of the dream as if he had no control over anything. He stumbled along the unmade track, deep ruts where the tractors ploughed their way through to the arable fields made it difficult to pick up much speed.

Fin called to Bartie, but he didn't appear. Getting his mobile out of his pocket he touched the screen on Megan's name...this time the phone rang on and on.

The moon went behind a cloud and it took a few moments for his eyes to adjust to the pitch black around him. He felt a cold shiver run down his spine. He had to find Megan, he just had to. Walking on further, he heard an owl screech and Bartie barked up ahead...good he was still there, but where was the woman, *who* was the woman – the same as Mildryth had seen? The moon appeared again, casting its silver light over the Cotswold countryside. A couple of fields away he could see the mercury river, gliding its way through the countryside as it had done for thousands of years. In the light he could see the woman; in fact there seemed to be two, both blonde, one more substantial, seemingly unaware of each other. They both stood looking into the hedge and as he turned the corner he realised that they were both looking at a traveller caravan...

A jolt hit Fin in the chest, so hard that he felt like he had been physically struck, but there was nobody close to him.

So, was Megan with Kai, then?

He realised that if she was, then it was his own fault...he had stood her up, so she had decided to get her revenge and go with Kai? The pain he felt was surprisingly hard. He stood in the shadows of the trees, unsure what to do next. Should he go and confront her, or leave them to it? But who were the two women and why were they both watching the caravan – something was not right. He walked a few paces forward, staying in the dark shadows of the trees and hedges. One of the women he did recognise, Bridget – what was she up to? A cold breeze ran through him, although the evening was rather mild, but this was no ordinary breeze, and on it he heard the voice of a man... *"I must tell her...I must find her...I must tell her I forgive her, before it's too late again..."* Fin looked behind him, there was nobody there, but he was suddenly aware of a strong presence beside him.

Bridget was standing on the steps outside the caravan door, listening, waiting. As Fin approached slowly, he was horrified to discover that she was holding a knife in her hand. Bartie raced up the steps and growled at her; she kicked him hard, once in the head. From the force he was thrown down the steps, whimpering as he hit the ground hard, then lying still on the floor.

Fin's breath caught in his throat.

"Help me..." the same male voice continued on the breeze.

"Who are you?" Fin asked.

Nothing but the wind.

Why had Megan not heard Bartie's growls? What was she doing in there? Did he really want to know? Was she asleep or was she in Kai's arms? Fin's mind whirled with the possibilities. He moved along the track a little further towards the caravan. Smoke could be seen coming out of the chimney, Bridget still stood, waiting, but waiting for what? A twig snapped loudly beneath his foot, Bridget's head swung in his direction; she stared into the darkness. Fin stood stock still.

Suddenly, Bridget grabbed at the door of the caravan and flung it open; there was a man's shout and the caravan rocked violently from the struggle within. Fin sped into action and ran down the track towards the caravan. He stood in the doorway trying to gauge what was happening. Bridget and Kai were facing one another – the knife raised in one hand, Kai had hold of her wrist; Megan lay on the bed, partially unclothed, but seemingly asleep – how could she sleep through this, unless she was unconscious...

Suddenly a strange, still cold seemed to envelop them. Fin felt like he was watching everything through a distorted lens...time seemed to stand still for a moment or two, then:

"I'm going to kill you, you bastard!" shouted Bridget, brandishing the knife.

"Yer crazy bitch, yer know it's over between us, has been for years!"

"But I thought there was hope, hope until *she* turned up," she screamed, swinging the knife in Megan's direction.

Kai lunged at her and caught her by the arm, shouting in an unfamiliar voice: "*I am not going to let you kill her...not this time...nobody is going to kill her, Lindi, she is going to be mine!*"

Uncannily Bridget's voice seemed to change too, "*Wulfric, she will never be yours, never has been, never will be...*"

Fin felt himself move forward into the small, dark room. He looked at Megan's lifeless form on the bed and wondered if she was still alive...what had Kai done to her? He somehow knew deep down that it wasn't Megan at fault here, even though she was half undressed...something sinister and dark had happened here this evening and he shuddered at the thoughts that entered his head.

Suddenly, there was a knife at his throat.

"Hello, brother!" said Kai, who stood in front of him. Bridget was still the one with the knife.

"Wulfric..." Fin heard himself say, and knew at once where he was and who he was.

The two stared at each other through the light amongst the trees: wolf-grey eyes challenging sky-blue.

"We meet again..."

"So it seems..."

"Let's end this now," said Wilheard. "I swore that I would find you..." Behind him, Bridget sniggered.

"I will beat you again..." said Wulfric.

"Not this time," stated Wilheard. "I have grown in strength and I am forewarned this time."

Wulfric laughed. "Yes, but I still have Mildryth..."

Fin shook his head. "No, you don't, you have had to use magic again, to lure her into your trap. Just because it's the 21st century doesn't mean it's any different, only different drugs are used...I know this now and I can forgive her; united we will always be stronger!"

"She's not very strong at the moment though, is she?" Bridget laughed, looking Fin in the eyes.

"You'd be surprised," said Megan, lunging heavily from the bed and hitting Bridget over the head with a hard, metal pan. Bridget collapsed onto the floor.

Instantly, Fin threw a punch at Kai, breaking his nose, and he too fell to the floor, clutching his face, with blood pouring out between his fingers.

"Come on, we have to get you out of here!" cried Fin, helping Megan.

Fin helped her down the steps of the caravan and out into the fresh air. The night was cooler. Fin held her closely against his chest as she sobbed.

At that moment, blue lights appeared on the track and Sasha and Brad could be seen running towards them, shouting. Help had arrived.

***

Through the mists of her subconscious Megan felt strong arms around her and felt a sense of peace.

A voice whispered in her ear, "I love you. *I'm sorry. I am sorry I didn't listen.*"

Bright blue eyes looked down into hers; eyes of a person who was very dear to her, the pain and hatred gone, in its place just love...love...and forgiveness.

***

On waking, Megan felt the after-effects of the alcohol and drugs that Kai had plied her with the previous night. Her head thumped and her heart raced in her chest; she felt sick and her head was fuzzy.

By the bed were some flowers and a card from Sasha:

"I'm so sorry I left you to go home alone!" xx

Hardly Sasha's fault.

Megan tried to remember back to the night before; Kai had drugged her, that was obvious and he'd had awful intentions for her too. Worse still was the fact that Bridget had intended to kill them both while they slept.

Noticing the orange-red glow from the sky outside, Megan walked over to her bedroom window, where the sun's glare made her squint. Bartie was sniffing around the garden, his tail wagging as fast as it could. She opened the window, felt the warmth of the sun on her face and called to him. He looked up at her, his ears forward, the mad spaniel look in his eyes; he returned to his sniffing.

Glancing out across the river, which ran golden-orange through the fields of green; she marvelled at the sight. She truly was lucky to live in such a glorious place, *thanks, gran.* She smiled to herself and was about to turn back to the bed, her head beginning to spin, when she caught a glimpse of something from the corner of her eye on the far bank of the river, beneath the weeping willows...a hare. It stared still as a statue, straight at her and then bounded across the open field...free. Moments later, she saw the silhouette of a couple embracing each other, disappearing into the low lying mist which hung above the valley floor.

***

As Megan walked into the sitting-room, Fin glanced over to her and smiled; his blue eyes glistened as he stood and approached her, quickly taking her in his arms and holding her tightly against him.

"I thought I'd lost you," he murmured into her ear.

She held him tighter, not wanting the moment to end; she felt the unification as naturally as if he had always been hers...would always be hers. "I wasn't sure..."

"I didn't want to rush things, knew you were aching with the pain of the loss of a man and your gran – had I spoken sooner, perhaps none of this would have happened. There was a moment though that I doubted you wanted me, the traveller...he...he..."

"He may have wanted me, Fin, but I didn't want him...only you, only ever you."

286

Megan glanced up into his sky-blue eyes and felt herself become a part of him as he brought his mouth down onto hers.

***

The following day, Sasha and Brad arrived, Sasha waving a newspaper at Megan as soon as she got out of the car. Embracing her, Megan could feel Sasha's heart racing in her chest.

"What have you got there?" asked Fin.

"The local paper is full of the news..."

"What does it say?" asked Megan, suddenly fearful that her name and the events of the other night might be common knowledge by now.

Sasha read: "Two local residents were arrested on Friday night following an incident in which another female resident was kidnapped and held prisoner in a caravan. The two have been kept in custody until further investigations can be carried out. It is thought that the two were involved in a conspiracy to steal artefacts from the local archaeological dig and were planning to kidnap one of the team working on the dig in order to hold her to ransom!"

"Wow, they certainly know how to embellish the truth!" cried Fin.

"Perhaps it's best that the public do believe that story. I don't think they would believe what really happened," replied Megan.

"I'm having a lot of trouble believing it myself," said Sasha. "Even though *I* know it is true."

"Yes, not quite as much as I did," said Fin, not competitively. "I still can't fathom exactly who the other people were..."

Megan looked at them all in turn. "I know now that the voices in my head were real...I believe that we unearthed more than artefacts when we opened up those graves..."

Brad looked incredulously at her. "You mean you set some of the Saxon spirits free?"

She nodded, feeling her cheeks go red. "It sounds ridiculous, but when I put together everything that has happened recently, I know that is exactly what happened."

"What about the brooch? What are you going to do about that?" asked Fin.

Megan and Sasha exchanged a glance.

"The Saxon woman already has it...I think she needed it to ensure that an ancient grudge was put right...when I was drugged, I could hear her talking to me, through me in fact."

287

"So that's what was happening...I thought I was hearing and seeing things!" interrupted Fin.

Megan held his gaze. "You were..." she replied.

***

The autumn sunshine had shone through the red, gold and brown leaves as Megan and Fin drove towards Cirencester. They arrived at the museum together, both full of anticipation for the success of the museum's Anglo-Saxon exhibition. They were surprised by how many members of the Press were lined up outside. The Anglo-Saxon exhibition was opening in an hour and Fin had been practising his opening speech each hour for the past 12 hours; Megan had insisted that they had lunch and that he left his speech alone until he finally delivered it at two o'clock.

Megan was excited and proud of the work that had gone into the discovery of the Anglo-Saxon community. Nobody had envisaged that such an important and rare discovery was hidden beneath the town and surrounding countryside of the modern-day community that now stood on the banks of the river Thames. Many would never know the true events of what had gone on when the graves of those Saxons were unearthed.

Fin delivered his speech to the flashes of the photographers and the public. Some of his old colleagues, and historians from around the country and from abroad, came to the ceremony to hear about the exciting and important discovery in a small Cotswold town.

As Megan listened to Fin's speech, she watched as people listened intently, their faces full of awe at what he was able to tell them. She was proud of his work and exhilarated by his enthusiasm. Megan was reminded of her gran by an elderly lady who stood close to her, and she wondered what her gran would have made of all the recent events. Without a doubt, Megan knew her gran would be excited by the discoveries, but horrified to know that her granddaughter had been in real danger. Gran would have approved of Fin too. Finally, she felt she was where she belonged...home...in the Roundhouse cottage with Fin at her side.

That evening, just as Megan and Fin were leaving the opening ceremony, her mobile rang: it was Sue from the lab at the university. They had been doing some DNA testing on the body of the Saxon 'princess'. David and the team had decided to test a few, select, local residents to see if their DNA matched that of the Saxon 'princess' and a couple of others, whose graves had been discovered. A recent study at Oxford University had suggested that some Britons hadn't moved far out of their tribal areas since Anglo-Saxon times, therefore suggesting that some of the local people in the town might be descendants from the Anglo-Saxons that lived there over 1,500 years ago.

"Hi Sue," Megan said, raising her eyebrows at Fin. She was surprised to be hearing from her at this time of the day, they had usually gone home by now. "What have you got for us, any of the local residents related to our 'Princess'?"

Sue's voice came in excited waves over the phone. "Megan, you're never going to believe this...you know how you gave some of your DNA for helping with the students studying the DNA testing for the Saxon dig... and that your ancestors were quite local?"

"Yes..."

"Your DNA shows that *you* are a direct descendant of the princess!"

Megan felt a chill of excitement run through her. "A *direct* descendent?"

"Yes."

"Wow, thanks, Sue."

Megan hung up and turned to Fin who was looking at her with a look of astonishment on his face. "So, the woman who was asking for your help was, in fact, an ancestor of yours..."

Megan nodded slowly. "I can't quite believe it...what a strange coincidence!"

Fin smiled. "I don't think there is much of a coincidence in this case."

Megan frowned. "What do you mean?"

"I'm not really sure...only that some might call it Fate."

Megan grinned. "And some might call me insane..."

"Not everyone knows the full story about what happened to you."

"No, and I'll never know the full story of what happened to her either...I just hope that whatever I did to help has actually made a difference..."

"I'm sure it has," said Fin taking her in his arms and holding her close.

Feeling his arms around her and thinking back to the couple she had seen from the cottage window, vanishing into the early morning mist a few months ago, she believed that she had. From across time, whatever that really was, her family had reached out for her and she had been there for them; just as Fin was here for her now, and she knew as he kissed her, he always would be.

Epilogue

I now know that nobody will ever really know my true story, what happened to me; it is in the past and the past remains what it is...history.

As I watch her walking arm in arm with the man she loves, along the banks of the same river that I did all those centuries ago, I can smile and feel content. Now, that I know she is safe from harm and that Wilheard has truly forgiven me, things are as they should be. I can finally rest and we can both move forward in our own times.

Acknowledgements

There are so many people who have helped me along the way to completing this novel, far too many to name individually. However, my first acknowledgement has to be to the woman whose grave it was that inspired me to write this fictional Anglo-Saxon and present day tale. On this note, I would like to thank the Corinium museum in Cirencester, especially Emma Stuart, for her help in research.

Next, I would like to thank Emma Wilkinson, who helped me edit the book and stayed up very late in order to help me meet those deadlines. Also, Trevor Hart for his photography skills in getting the front cover just right.

The cover design of the square-headed brooch was illustrated by Sarah Elizabeth Butler: a talented young lady and an inspirational illustrator. www.sebutler.co.uk

In fond memory of John Brackenbury, who helped me build a belief in myself that I could write, 'marvellously duckling' and for endless encouragement over the years – he is sadly missed.

I would like to thank my wider family (especially my siblings) who have always encouraged my dream to write. Thank you to my husband, Paul, who spends hours endlessly listening to my ideas and reading my work to give constructive criticism and praise; Isolda, my daughter, who is an inspiration in my daily life and makes every waking moment a joy – however early! Thank you to my Mum for introducing me to books at a very young age, which led to a passion for reading and writing throughout my life; and my sister, Kay, for singing to me and telling me bedtime stories when it was too dark to read!

Also, I am very fortunate to have some amazing friends. I would like to thank you all for your encouragement over the years, including the book club ladies.   There are two friends I would like to thank individually: Vanessa Smith, my best friend who I've known nearly my whole life; and Rachel Bayless, both whose support has been invaluable.

Finally, I would like to thank you, my readers!

Sandra grew up in the Kent countryside. She read English and American Literature at the University of Kent, Canterbury and went on to teach English for many years. With a lifetime passion for reading and writing, Sandra decided to write her debut novel, *Shades of Time*, after having had some success with short stories and historical articles.

Happily married, she has lived for the past ten years in the Cotswolds with her husband, Paul, daughter, Isolda, a mad spaniel and two cats.

More of her work can be found on her Website:
www.sandradenniswrites.wix.com/sandra-dennis

You can follow her on twitter @sdenniswrites